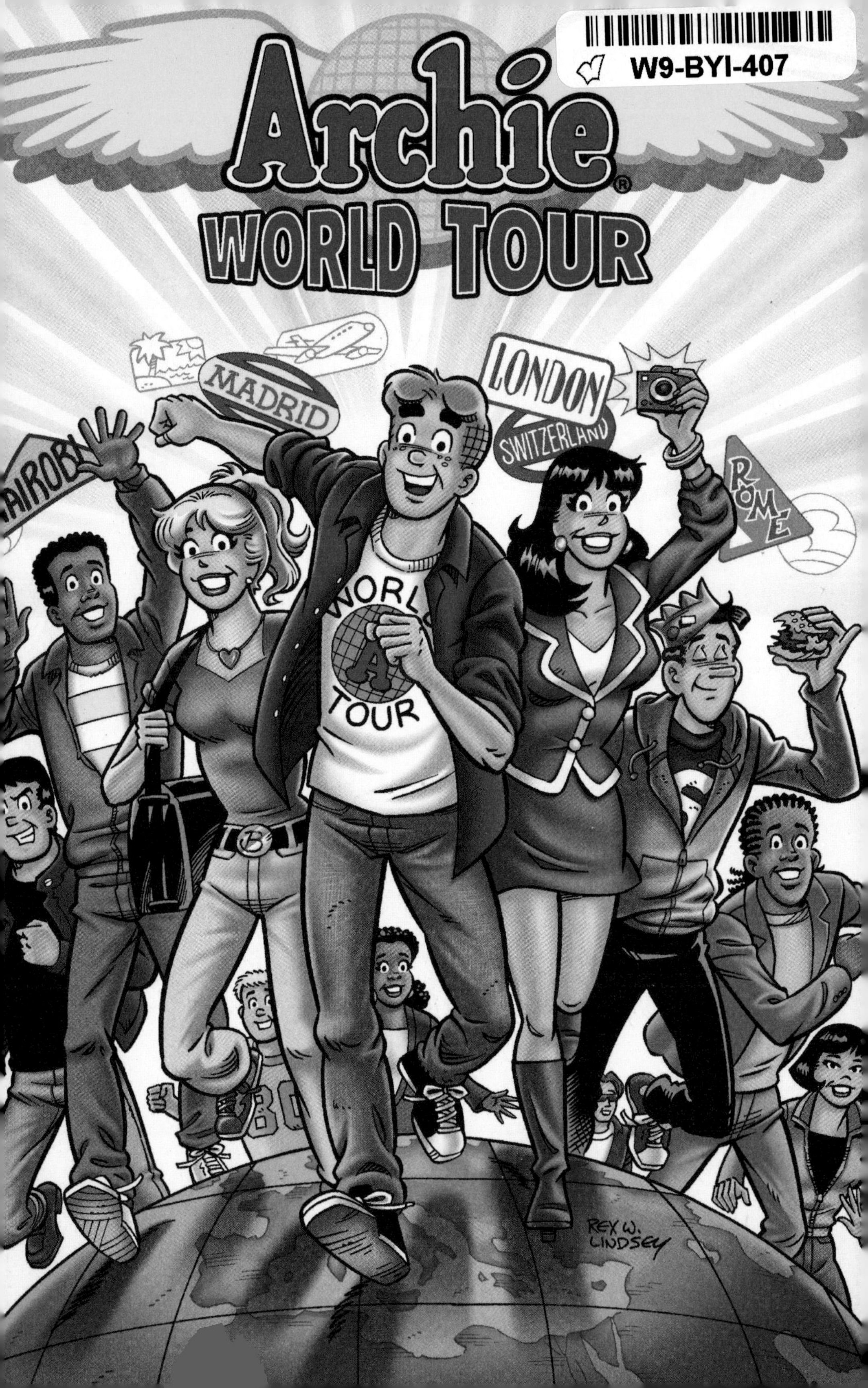
Archie®
WORLD TOUR
MADRID
LONDON
SWITZERLAND
ROME
NAIROBI
WORLD TOUR
REX W. LINDSEY

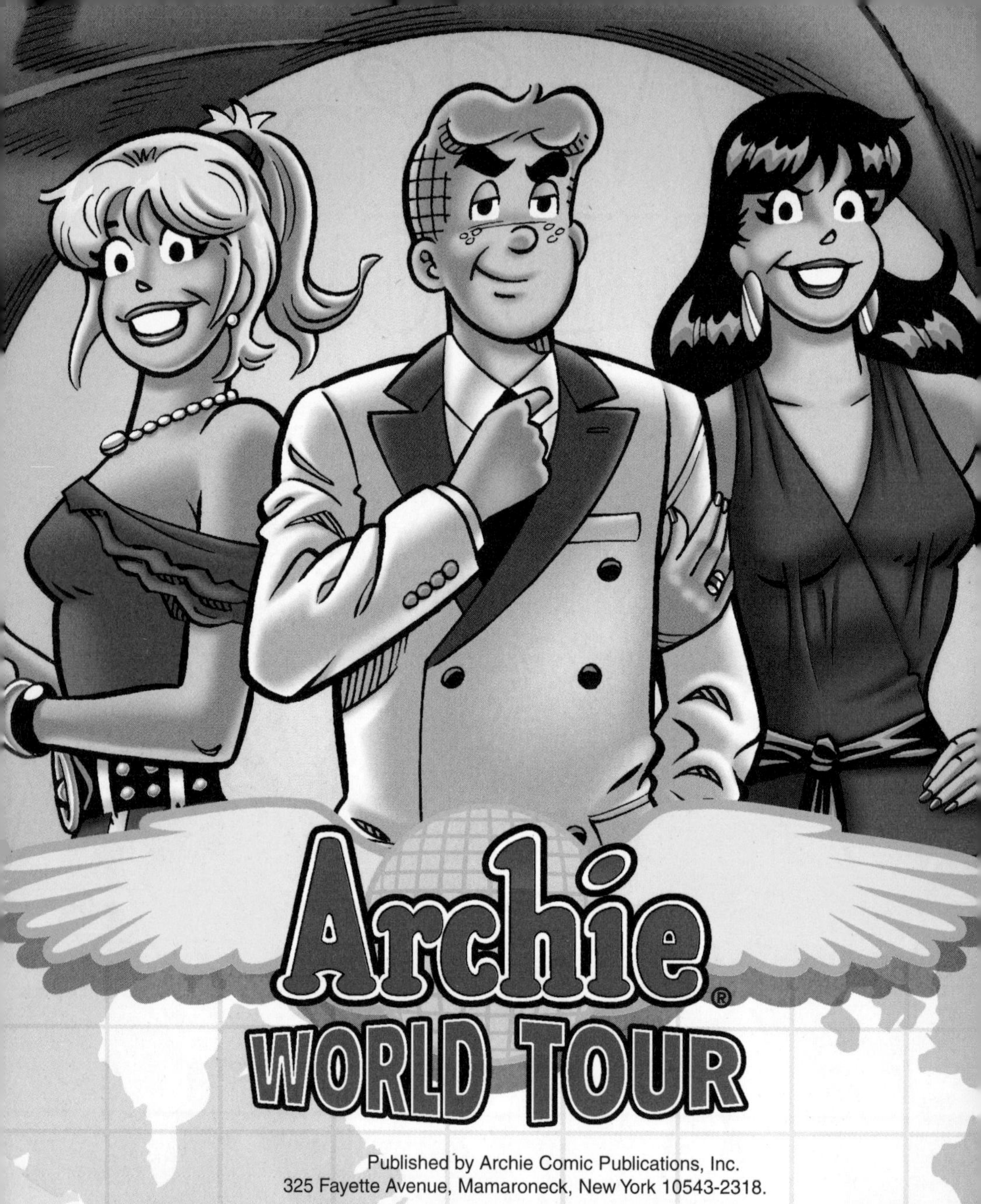
Archie®
WORLD TOUR

Published by Archie Comic Publications, Inc.
325 Fayette Avenue, Mamaroneck, New York 10543-2318.

Ellie Kim

ArchieComics.com

ISBN: 978-1-879794-73-3

10 9 8 7 6 5 4 3 2 1
Printed in U.S.A.

Archie® WORLD TOUR

WRITTEN BY
ALEX SIMMONS

PENCILED BY
REX LINDSEY

INKED BY
JIM AMASH &
AL NICKERSON

LETTERED BY
TERESA DAVIDSON
PATRICK OWSLEY
& PHIL FELIX

COLORED BY
GLENN WHITMORE
& STEPHANIE VOZZO

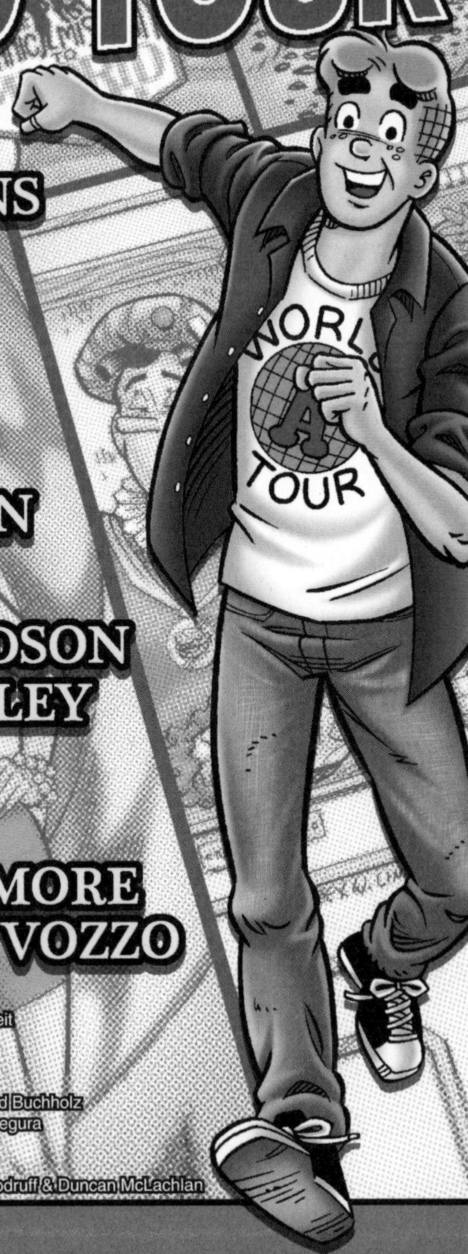
WORLD
A
TOUR

Co-CEO: Jon Goldwater, Co-CEO: Nancy Silberkleit
President: Mike Pellerito
Co-President/Editor-In-Chief: Victor Gorelick
Director of Circulation: Bill Horan
Executive Director of Publishing/Operations: Harold Buchholz
Executive Director of Publicity & Marketing: Alex Segura
Project Coordinator: Joe Morciglio
Production Manager: Stephen Oswald
Production: Carlos Antunes, James Duffy, Pat Woodruff & Duncan McLachlan

London

Location: London, England
Continent: Europe
Population: 7,600,000
Size: 607 square miles
Spoken Languages:
British English, Welsh, French,
Gaelic and Hindi to name a few.

Welcome to London, the capital of England!

The Romans founded the city nearly 2000 years ago. Back then, the city was called Londinium. Since then, London has been the home of famous people like the playwright William Shakespeare, the author Charles Dickens and the scientist Charles Babbage. Today, London is a major cultural and economic center.

London is a diverse city, with over 300 languages spoken within its borders. London is famous for its grand architecture and iconic scenery, of which Buckingham Palace, Westminster Abbey, London Bridge and Big Ben are some of the most famous.

While in London, Archie, Betty, Veronica, Reggie, Jughead and the rest of the Riverdale High students are greeted by Timothy Britt who acts as the class tour guide and cultural expert. The Gang is also introduced to an all-new system of currency. In England, they use pounds, shillings and half pennies instead of dollars and cents!

With so much going on and so much to see, it's hard to imagine visiting London without missing something. The first stop for the Gang really helpes out with that.

Even though it resembles a giant Ferris wheel, the famous "London Eye" offers a spectacular view of over 50 of London's famous landmarks. Some of those include Cleopatra's Needle on the Victoria Embankment (which is a genuine Egyptian obelisk in the City of Westminster near the Golden Jubilee Bridges that closely resembles the Washington Monument in Washington, DC) and the Dome of St. Paul's Cathedral (which is a very large Catholic church that features extensive catacombs, was consecrated on September 29, 1792 and was the first Catholic church built in England after the English Reformation).

Some other sites that the group visits but that are not expressly mentioned are Buckingham Palace, home of the Queen of England and the rest of the Royal Family; the Sherlock Holmes Museum, which offers a tour of the home of fictitious super sleuth Sherlock Holmes who was created by Scottish author Sir Arthur Conan Doyle; Trafalgar Square; London Bridge; Waterloo station, the world-famous Harrod's department store; Windsor Castle and the British Museum.

Archie® WORLD TOUR

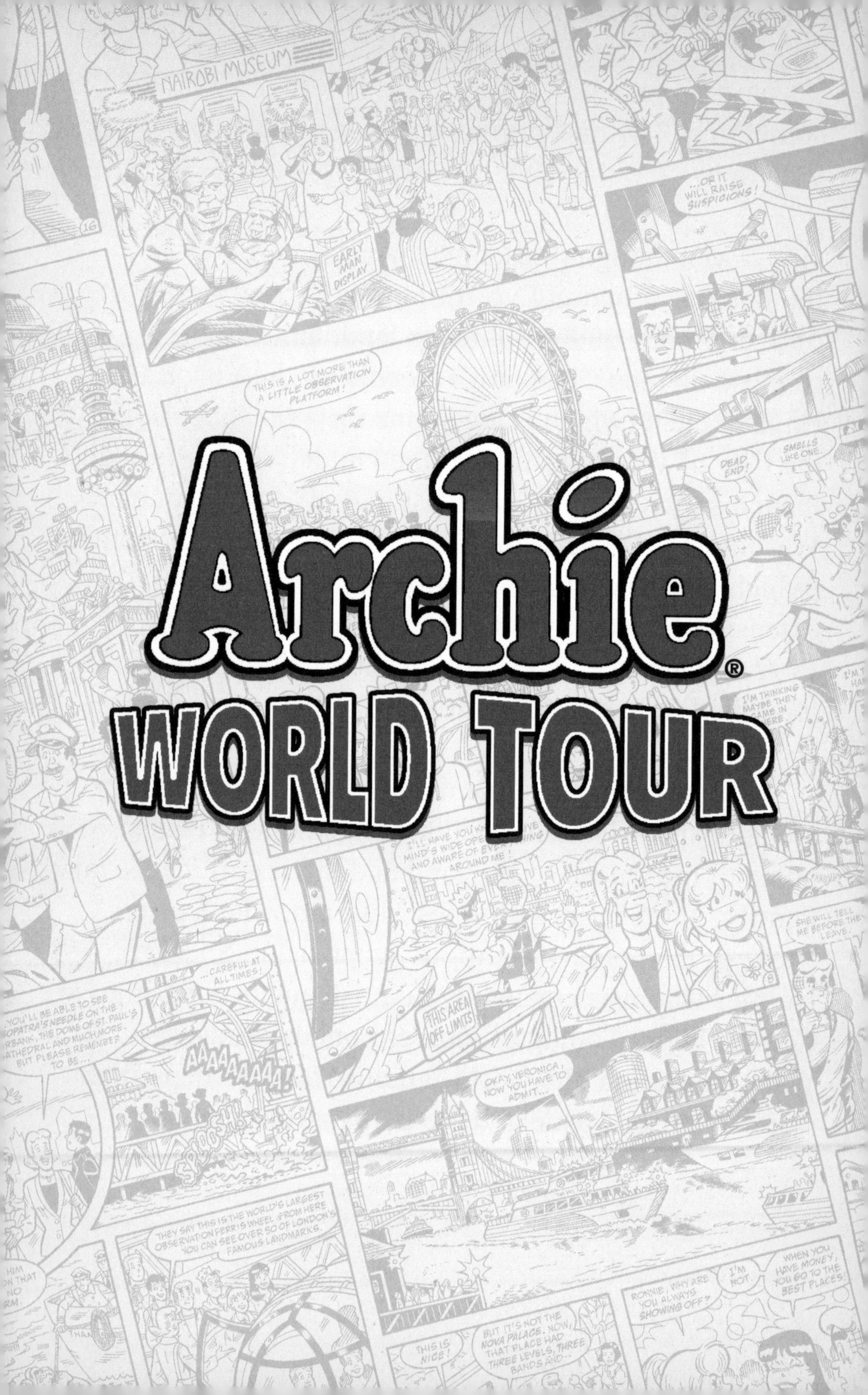

CHAPTER 1: LONDON

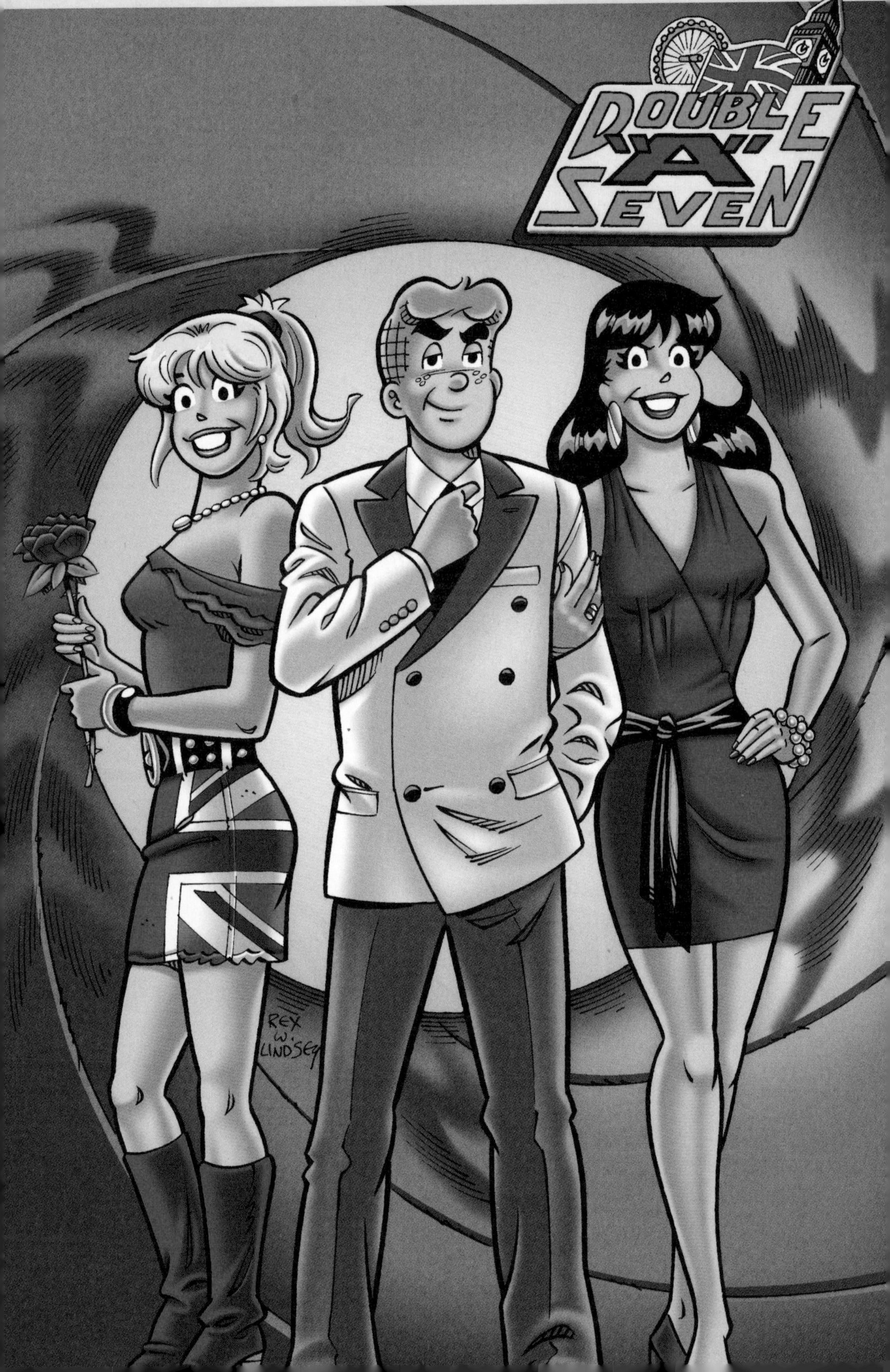
DOUBLE "A" SEVEN
REX W. LINDSEY

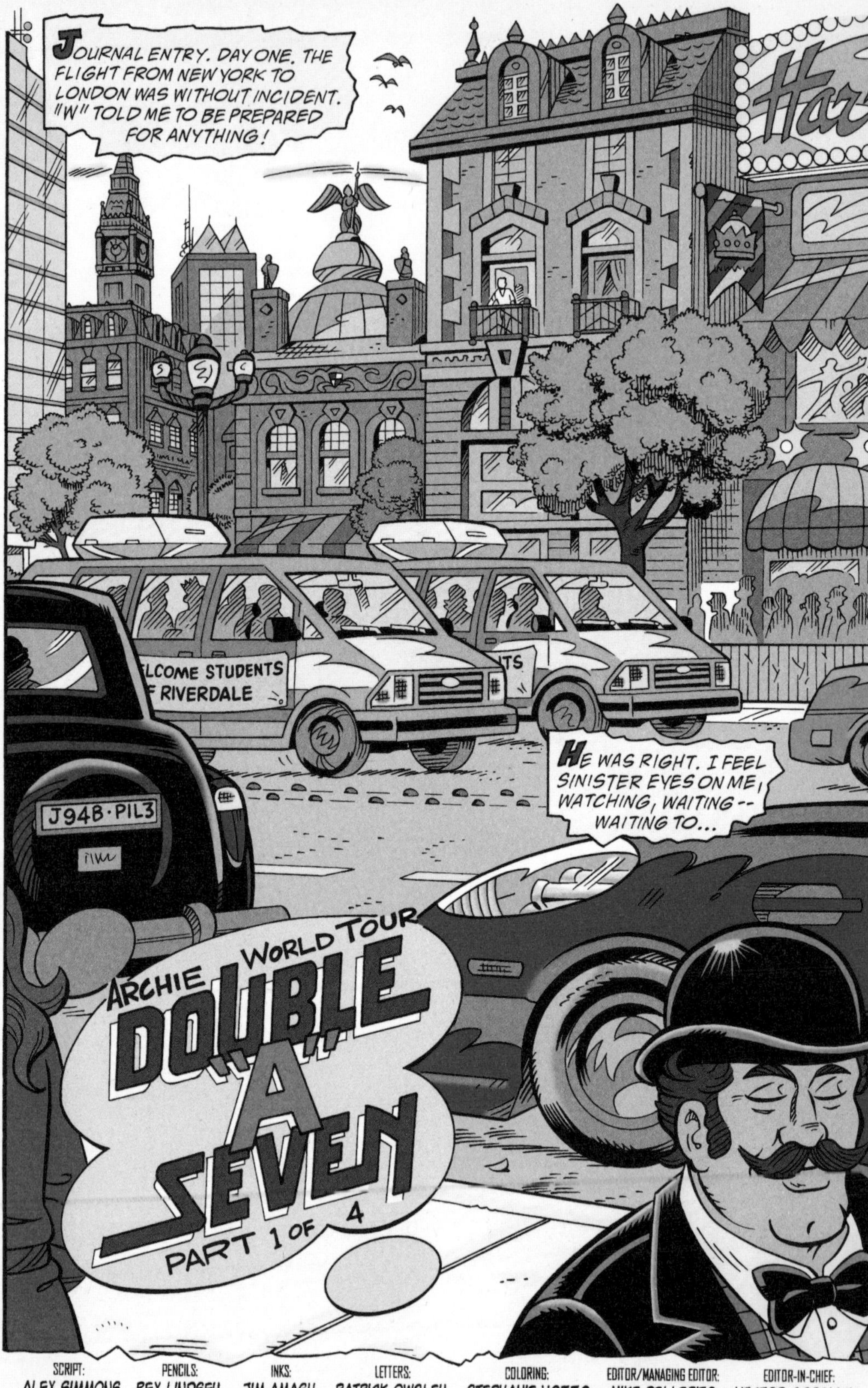
JOURNAL ENTRY. DAY ONE. THE FLIGHT FROM NEW YORK TO LONDON WAS WITHOUT INCIDENT. "W" TOLD ME TO BE PREPARED FOR ANYTHING!
ELCOME STUDENTS F RIVERDALE
J94B·PIL3
HE WAS RIGHT. I FEEL SINISTER EYES ON ME, WATCHING, WAITING -- WAITING TO...
ARCHIE WORLD TOUR
DOUBLE "A" SEVEN
PART 1 OF 4

SCRIPT: ALEX SIMMONS PENCILS: REX LINDSEY INKS: JIM AMASH LETTERS: PATRICK OWSLEY COLORING: STEPHANIE VOZZO EDITOR/MANAGING EDITOR: MIKE PELLERITO EDITOR-IN-CHIEF: VICTOR GORELICK

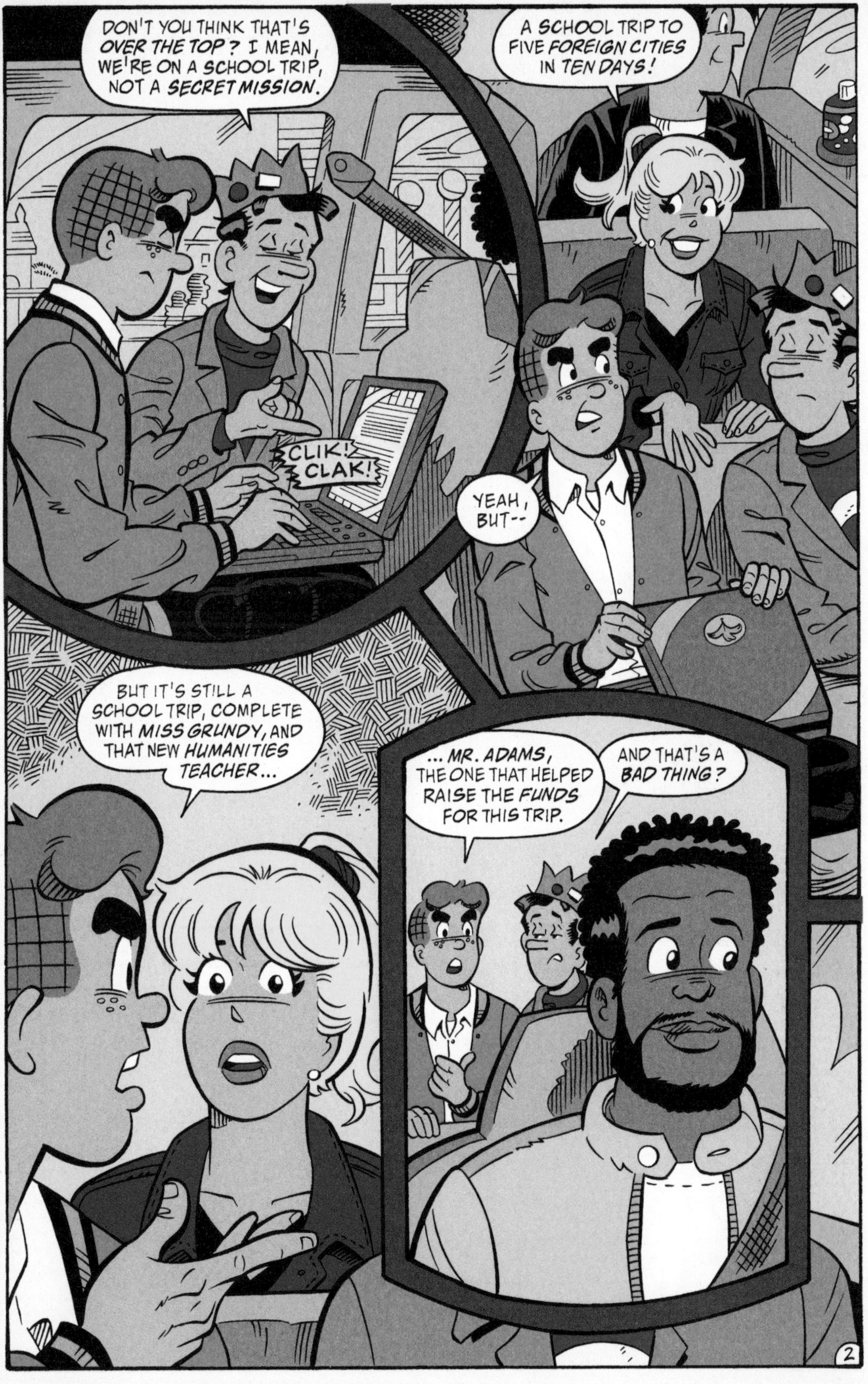
DON'T YOU THINK THAT'S OVER THE TOP? I MEAN, WE'RE ON A SCHOOL TRIP, NOT A SECRET MISSION.
CLIK! CLAK!
A SCHOOL TRIP TO FIVE FOREIGN CITIES IN TEN DAYS!
YEAH, BUT--
BUT IT'S STILL A SCHOOL TRIP, COMPLETE WITH MISS GRUNDY, AND THAT NEW HUMANITIES TEACHER...
... MR. ADAMS, THE ONE THAT HELPED RAISE THE FUNDS FOR THIS TRIP.
AND THAT'S A BAD THING?
2

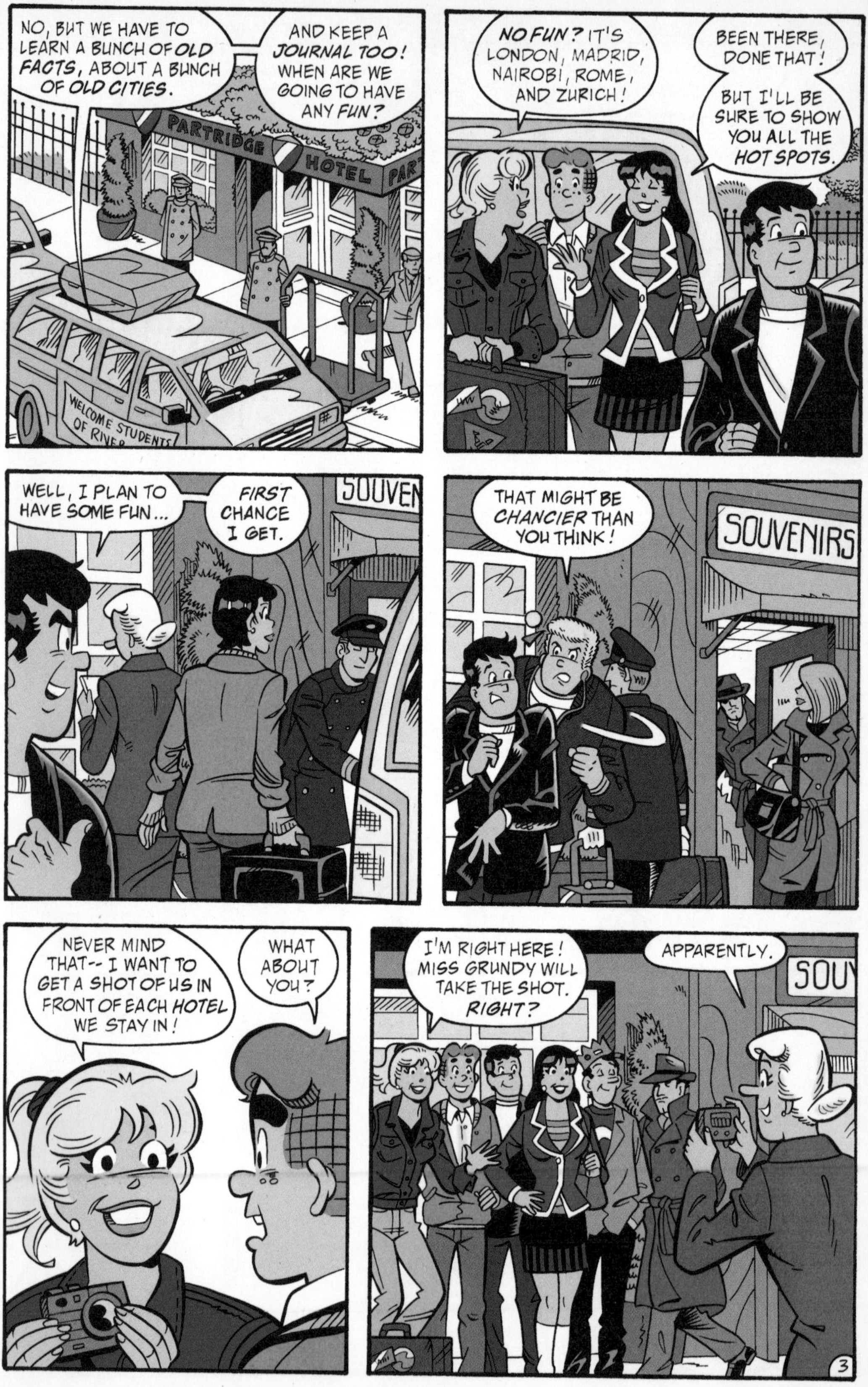
NO, BUT WE HAVE TO LEARN A BUNCH OF OLD FACTS, ABOUT A BUNCH OF OLD CITIES.
AND KEEP A JOURNAL TOO! WHEN ARE WE GOING TO HAVE ANY FUN?
PARTRIDGE HOTEL
WELCOME STUDENTS OF RIVER
NO FUN? IT'S LONDON, MADRID, NAIROBI, ROME, AND ZURICH!
BEEN THERE, DONE THAT!
BUT I'LL BE SURE TO SHOW YOU ALL THE HOT SPOTS.
WELL, I PLAN TO HAVE SOME FUN...
FIRST CHANCE I GET.
THAT MIGHT BE CHANCIER THAN YOU THINK!
SOUVENIRS
NEVER MIND THAT-- I WANT TO GET A SHOT OF US IN FRONT OF EACH HOTEL WE STAY IN!
WHAT ABOUT YOU?
I'M RIGHT HERE! MISS GRUNDY WILL TAKE THE SHOT. RIGHT?
APPARENTLY.

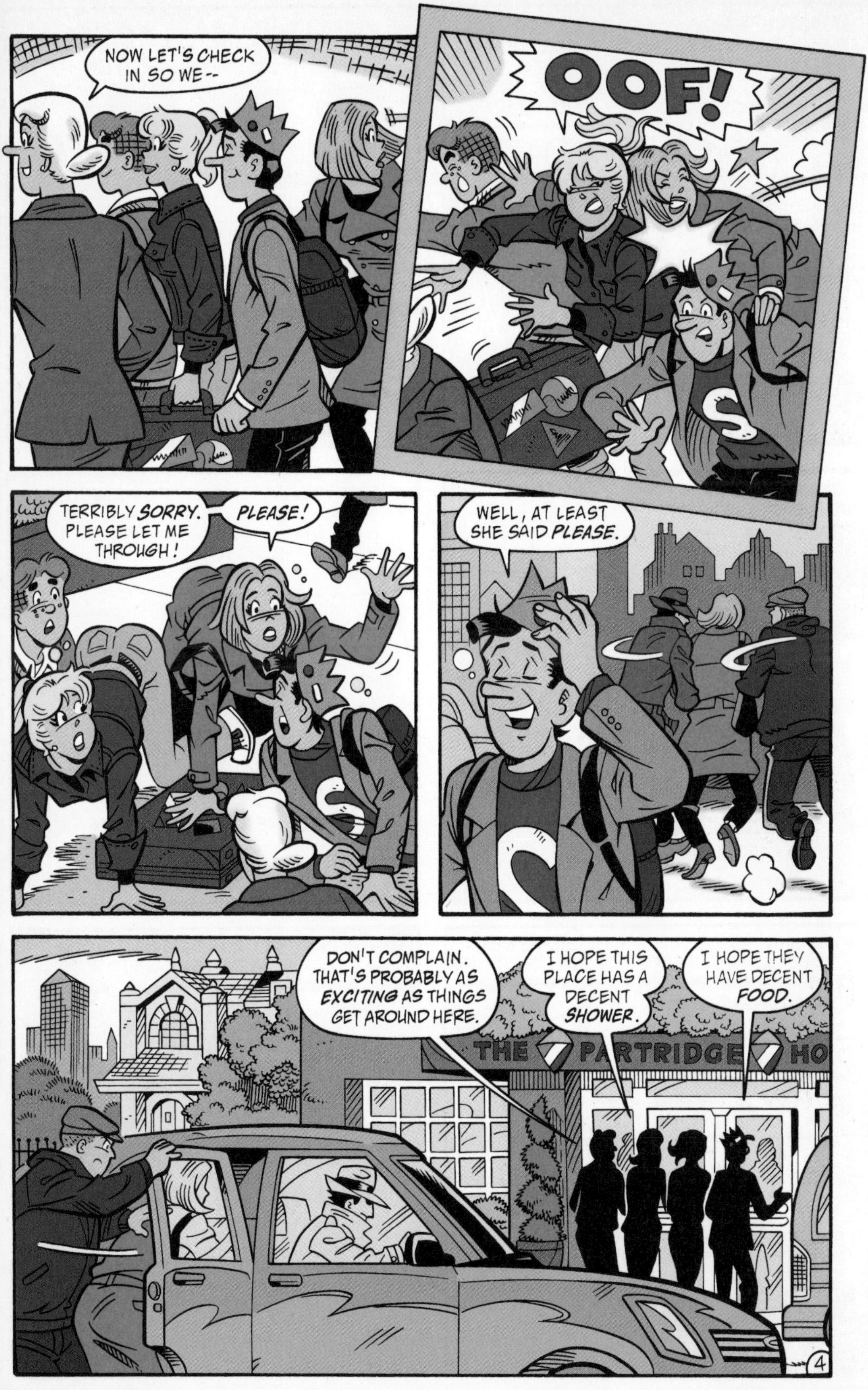
NOW LET'S CHECK IN SO WE--
OOF!
TERRIBLY SORRY. PLEASE LET ME THROUGH!
PLEASE!
WELL, AT LEAST SHE SAID PLEASE.
DON'T COMPLAIN. THAT'S PROBABLY AS EXCITING AS THINGS GET AROUND HERE.
I HOPE THIS PLACE HAS A DECENT SHOWER.
I HOPE THEY HAVE DECENT FOOD.
THE PARTRIDGE HO

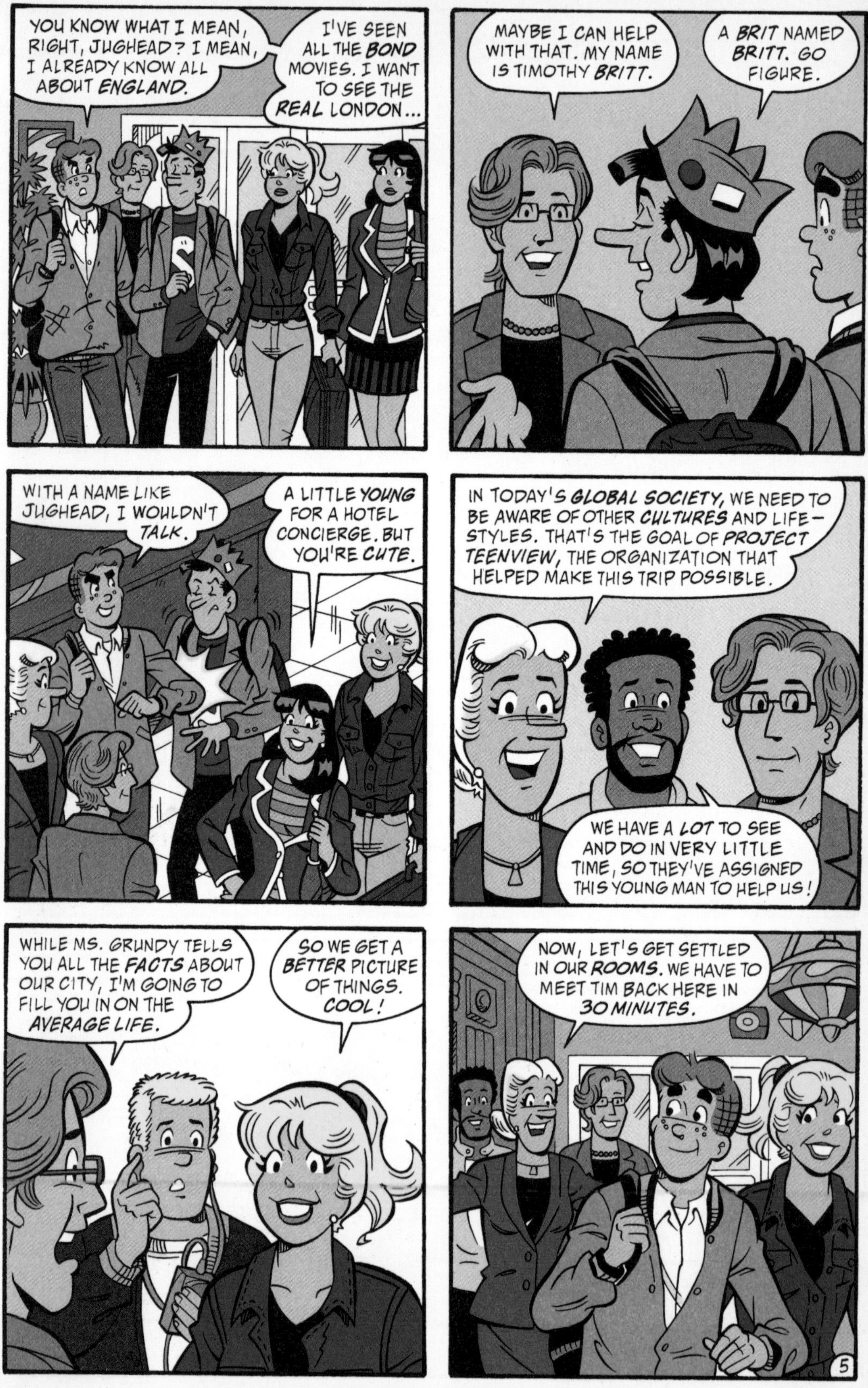
YOU KNOW WHAT I MEAN, RIGHT, JUGHEAD? I MEAN, I ALREADY KNOW ALL ABOUT ENGLAND.
I'VE SEEN ALL THE BOND MOVIES. I WANT TO SEE THE REAL LONDON...
MAYBE I CAN HELP WITH THAT. MY NAME IS TIMOTHY BRITT.
A BRIT NAMED BRITT. GO FIGURE.
WITH A NAME LIKE JUGHEAD, I WOULDN'T TALK.
A LITTLE YOUNG FOR A HOTEL CONCIERGE. BUT YOU'RE CUTE.
IN TODAY'S GLOBAL SOCIETY, WE NEED TO BE AWARE OF OTHER CULTURES AND LIFE-STYLES. THAT'S THE GOAL OF PROJECT TEENVIEW, THE ORGANIZATION THAT HELPED MAKE THIS TRIP POSSIBLE.
WE HAVE A LOT TO SEE AND DO IN VERY LITTLE TIME, SO THEY'VE ASSIGNED THIS YOUNG MAN TO HELP US!
WHILE MS. GRUNDY TELLS YOU ALL THE FACTS ABOUT OUR CITY, I'M GOING TO FILL YOU IN ON THE AVERAGE LIFE.
SO WE GET A BETTER PICTURE OF THINGS. COOL!
NOW, LET'S GET SETTLED IN OUR ROOMS. WE HAVE TO MEET TIM BACK HERE IN 30 MINUTES.

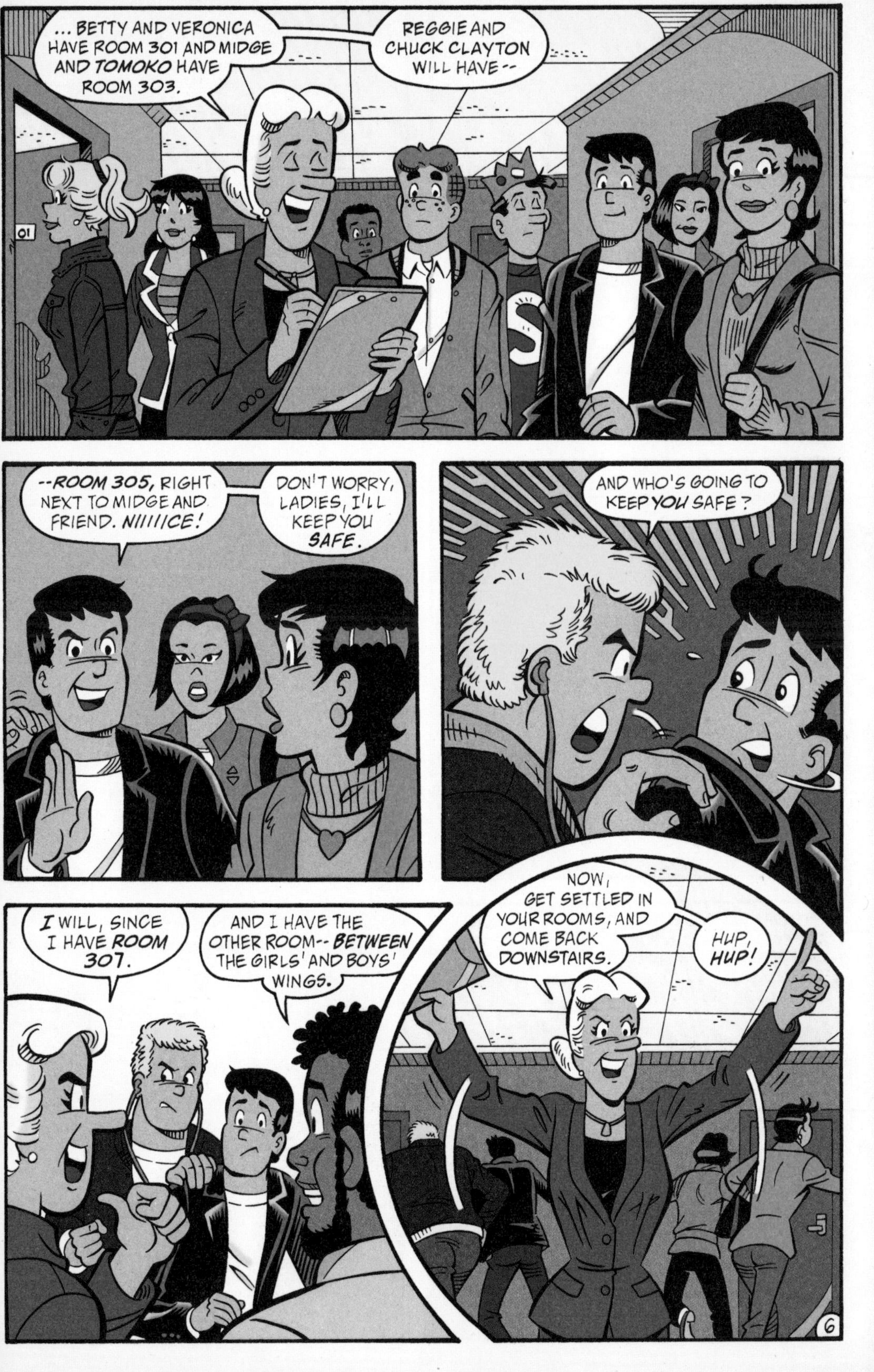

... BETTY AND VERONICA HAVE ROOM 301 AND MIDGE AND TOMOKO HAVE ROOM 303.
REGGIE AND CHUCK CLAYTON WILL HAVE --
01
--ROOM 305, RIGHT NEXT TO MIDGE AND FRIEND. NIIIIICE!
DON'T WORRY, LADIES, I'LL KEEP YOU SAFE.
AND WHO'S GOING TO KEEP YOU SAFE?
I WILL, SINCE I HAVE ROOM 307.
AND I HAVE THE OTHER ROOM-- BETWEEN THE GIRLS' AND BOYS' WINGS.
NOW, GET SETTLED IN YOUR ROOMS, AND COME BACK DOWNSTAIRS.
HUP, HUP!

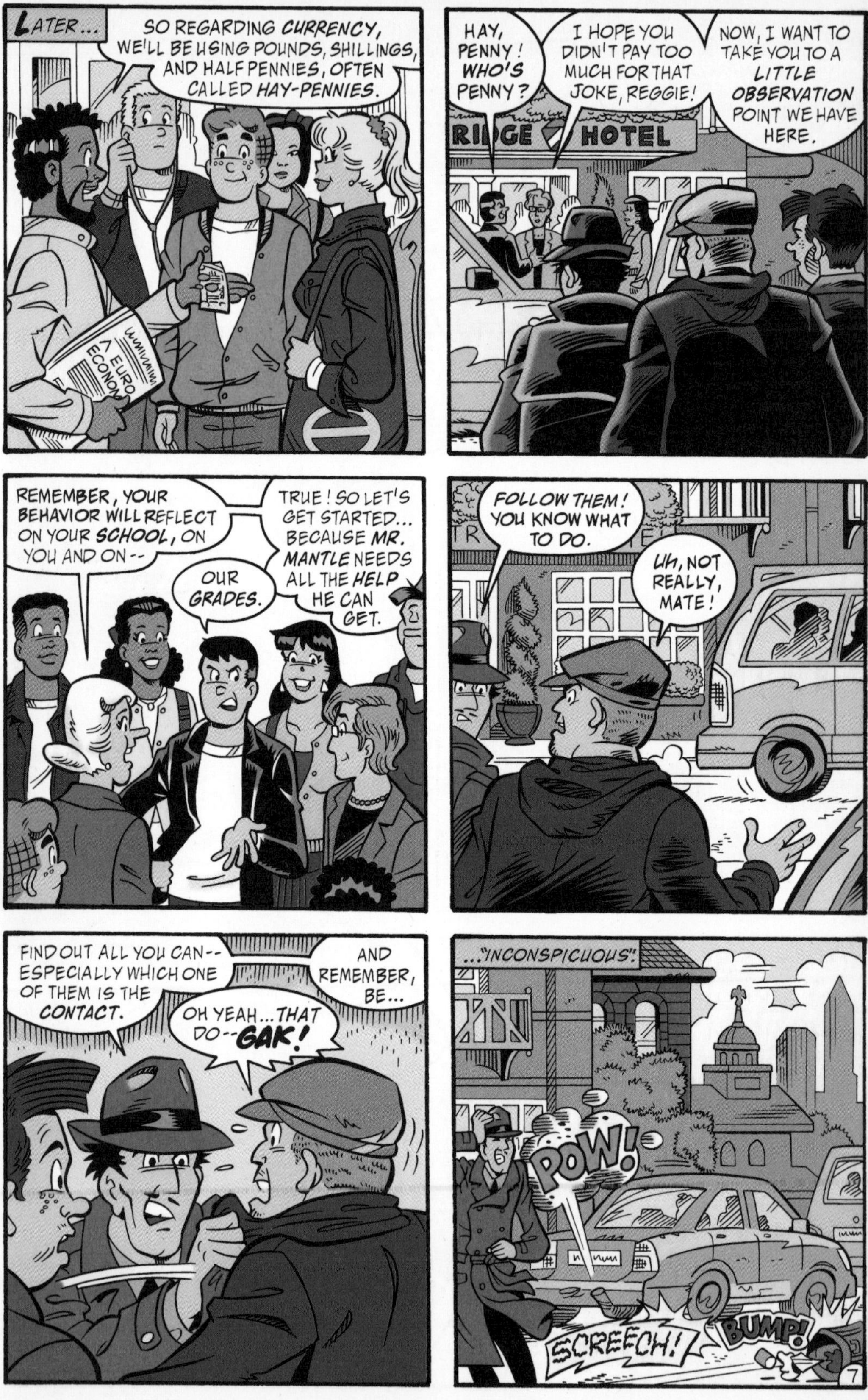
LATER...
SO REGARDING CURRENCY, WE'LL BE USING POUNDS, SHILLINGS, AND HALF PENNIES, OFTEN CALLED HAY-PENNIES.
EURO ECONOM
HAY, PENNY! WHO'S PENNY?
I HOPE YOU DIDN'T PAY TOO MUCH FOR THAT JOKE, REGGIE!
NOW, I WANT TO TAKE YOU TO A LITTLE OBSERVATION POINT WE HAVE HERE.
RIDGE HOTEL
REMEMBER, YOUR BEHAVIOR WILL REFLECT ON YOUR SCHOOL, ON YOU AND ON--
OUR GRADES.
TRUE! SO LET'S GET STARTED... BECAUSE MR. MANTLE NEEDS ALL THE HELP HE CAN GET.
FOLLOW THEM! YOU KNOW WHAT TO DO.
UH, NOT REALLY, MATE!
FIND OUT ALL YOU CAN-- ESPECIALLY WHICH ONE OF THEM IS THE CONTACT.
AND REMEMBER, BE...
OH YEAH... THAT DO--GAK!
..."INCONSPICUOUS".
POW!
SCREECH!
BUMP!

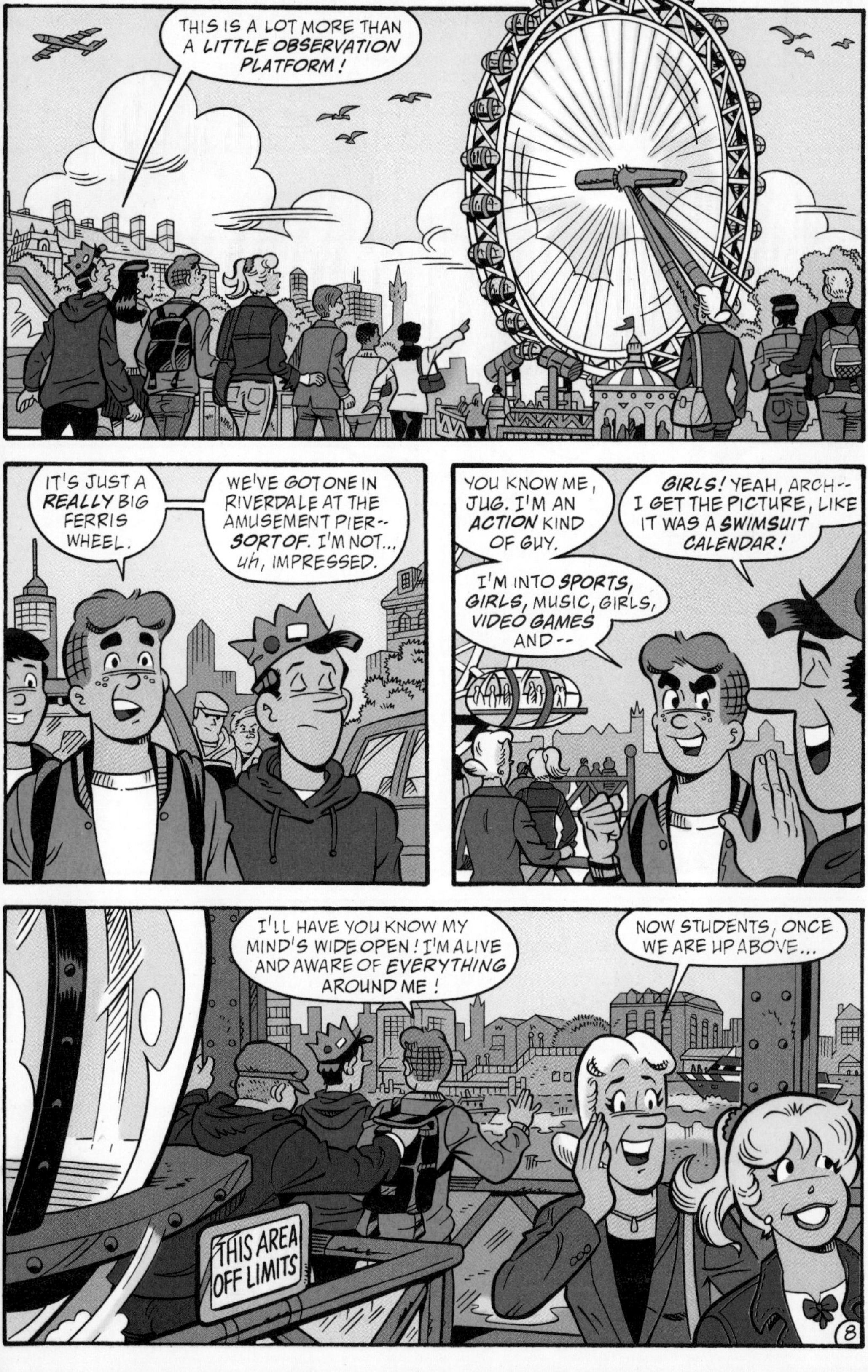
THIS IS A LOT MORE THAN A LITTLE OBSERVATION PLATFORM!
IT'S JUST A REALLY BIG FERRIS WHEEL.
WE'VE GOT ONE IN RIVERDALE AT THE AMUSEMENT PIER-- SORT OF. I'M NOT... uh, IMPRESSED.
YOU KNOW ME, JUG. I'M AN ACTION KIND OF GUY.
I'M INTO SPORTS, GIRLS, MUSIC, GIRLS, VIDEO GAMES AND--
GIRLS! YEAH, ARCH-- I GET THE PICTURE, LIKE IT WAS A SWIMSUIT CALENDAR!
I'LL HAVE YOU KNOW MY MIND'S WIDE OPEN! I'M ALIVE AND AWARE OF EVERYTHING AROUND ME!
NOW STUDENTS, ONCE WE ARE UP ABOVE...
THIS AREA OFF LIMITS
8

SNAG!

...YOU'LL BE ABLE TO SEE *CLEOPATRA'S NEEDLE* ON THE RIVERBANK, THE DOME OF ST. PAUL'S CATHEDRAL AND MUCH MORE. BUT PLEASE REMEMBER TO BE...

...CAREFUL AT ALL TIMES!

AAAAAAAAA!

SPLOOSH!

THIS AREA OFF LIMITS

I GIVE HIM A *2.5* ON THAT ONE. NO *FORM.*

THEY SAY THIS IS THE WORLD'S LARGEST OBSERVATION FERRIS WHEEL. FROM HERE YOU CAN SEE OVER 50 OF LONDON'S FAMOUS LANDMARKS.

WOW!

DITTO, ARCHIEKINS.

WE'VE GOT NOTHING LIKE *THIS* AT THE AMUSEMENT PIER.

I'LL WAGER YOU HAVE NOTHING LIKE OUR NEXT STOP EITHER.

9

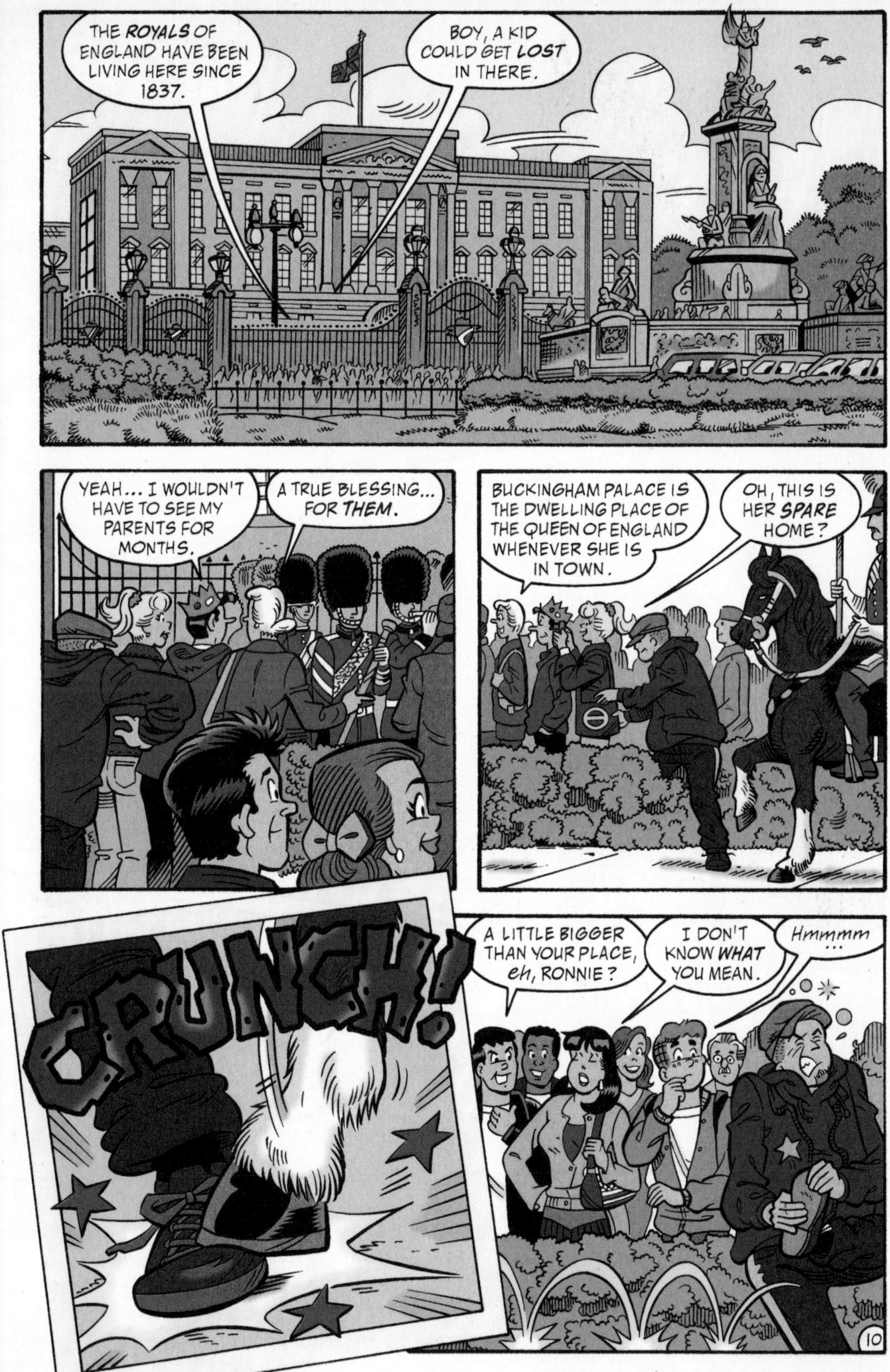
THE ROYALS OF ENGLAND HAVE BEEN LIVING HERE SINCE 1837.
BOY, A KID COULD GET LOST IN THERE.
YEAH... I WOULDN'T HAVE TO SEE MY PARENTS FOR MONTHS.
A TRUE BLESSING... FOR THEM.
BUCKINGHAM PALACE IS THE DWELLING PLACE OF THE QUEEN OF ENGLAND WHENEVER SHE IS IN TOWN.
OH, THIS IS HER SPARE HOME?
CRUNCH!
A LITTLE BIGGER THAN YOUR PLACE, eh, RONNIE?
I DON'T KNOW WHAT YOU MEAN.
Hmmmm...
10

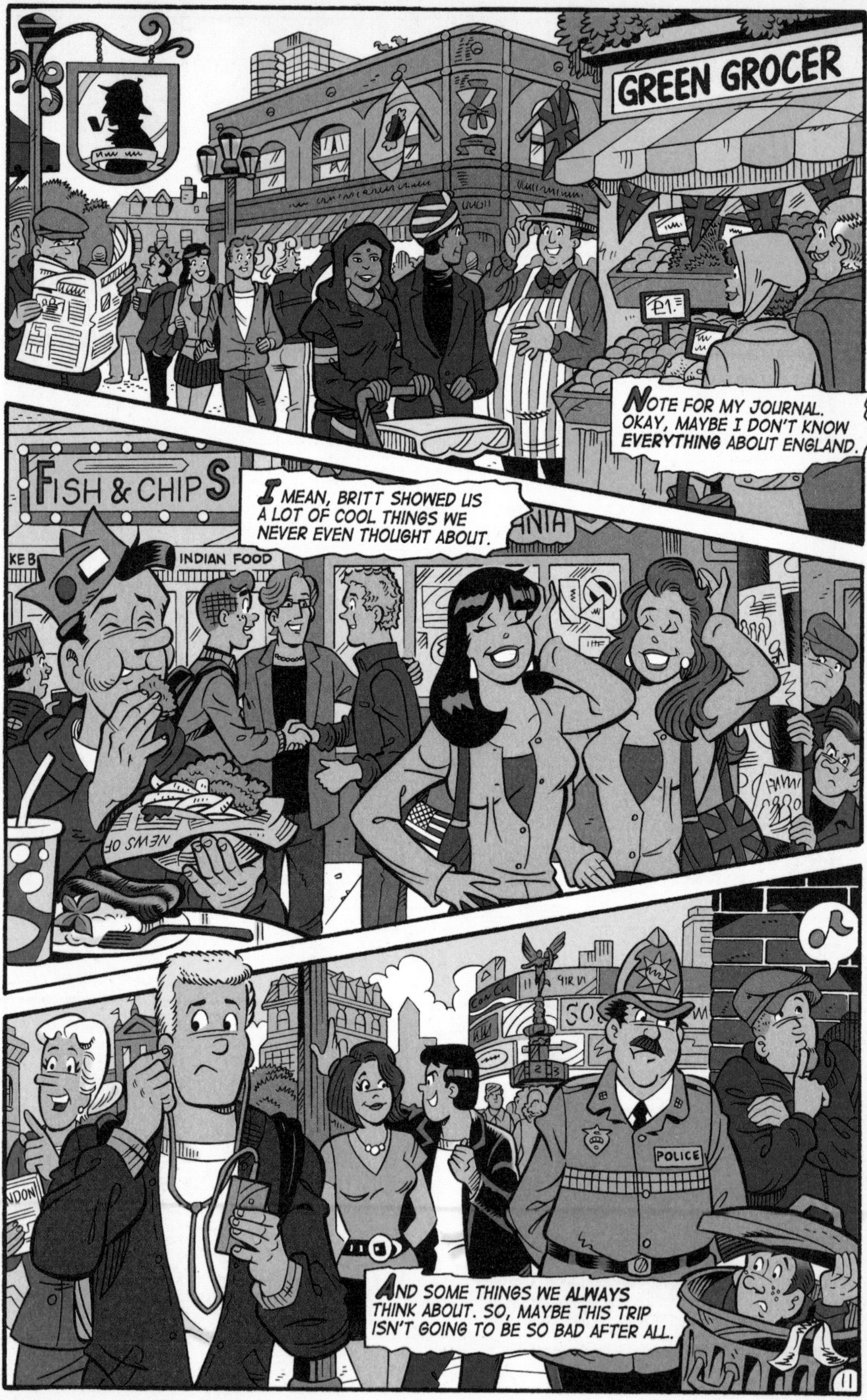
GREEN GROCER
NOTE FOR MY JOURNAL. OKAY, MAYBE I DON'T KNOW EVERYTHING ABOUT ENGLAND.
FISH & CHIPS
I MEAN, BRITT SHOWED US A LOT OF COOL THINGS WE NEVER EVEN THOUGHT ABOUT.
INDIAN FOOD
NEWS OF
POLICE
AND SOME THINGS WE ALWAYS THINK ABOUT. SO, MAYBE THIS TRIP ISN'T GOING TO BE SO BAD AFTER ALL.

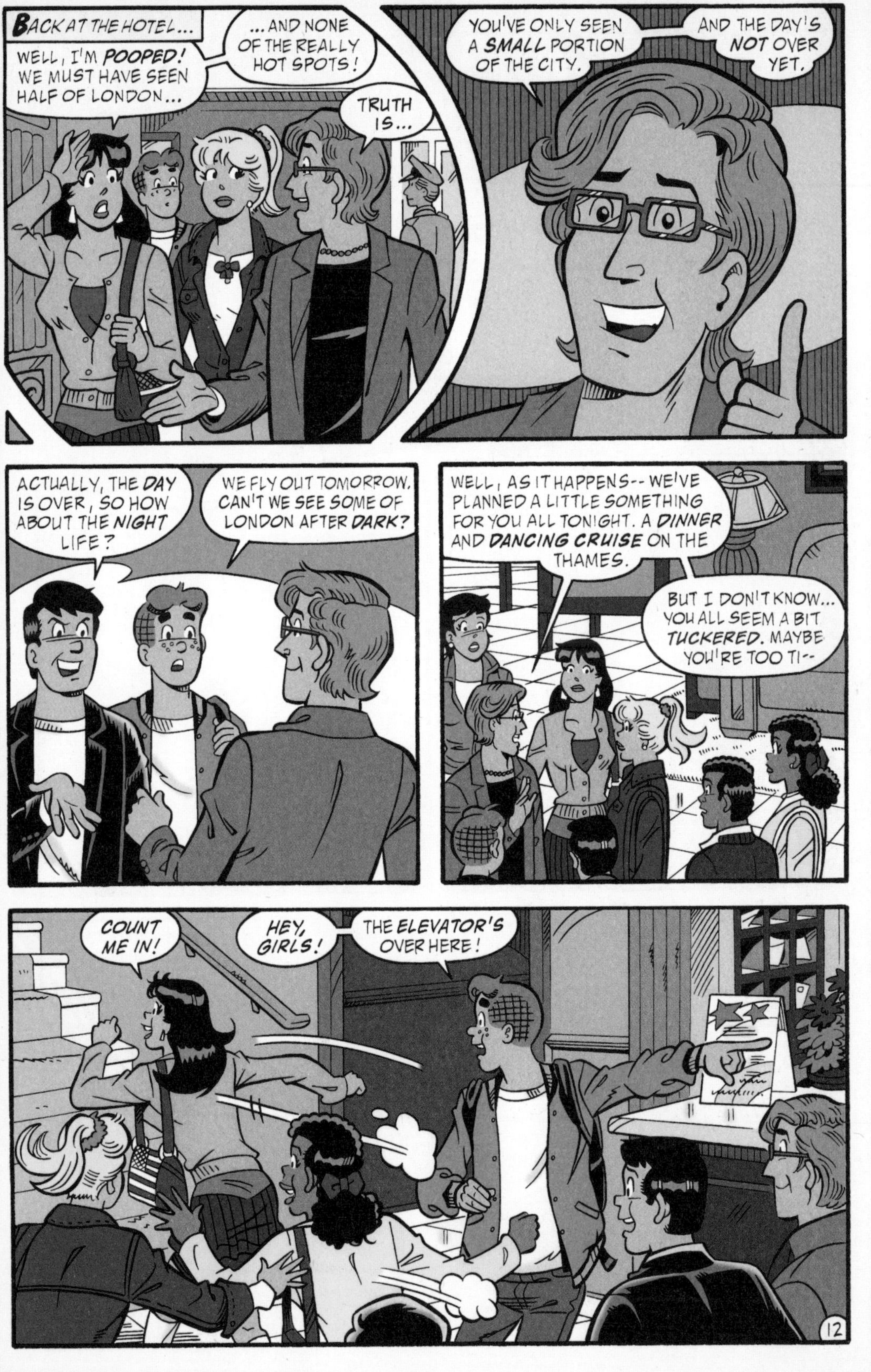
BACK AT THE HOTEL...
WELL, I'M POOPED! WE MUST HAVE SEEN HALF OF LONDON...
...AND NONE OF THE REALLY HOT SPOTS!
TRUTH IS...
YOU'VE ONLY SEEN A SMALL PORTION OF THE CITY.
AND THE DAY'S NOT OVER YET.
ACTUALLY, THE DAY IS OVER, SO HOW ABOUT THE NIGHT LIFE?
WE FLY OUT TOMORROW. CAN'T WE SEE SOME OF LONDON AFTER DARK?
WELL, AS IT HAPPENS-- WE'VE PLANNED A LITTLE SOMETHING FOR YOU ALL TONIGHT. A DINNER AND DANCING CRUISE ON THE THAMES.
BUT I DON'T KNOW... YOU ALL SEEM A BIT TUCKERED. MAYBE YOU'RE TOO TI--
COUNT ME IN!
HEY, GIRLS!
THE ELEVATOR'S OVER HERE!

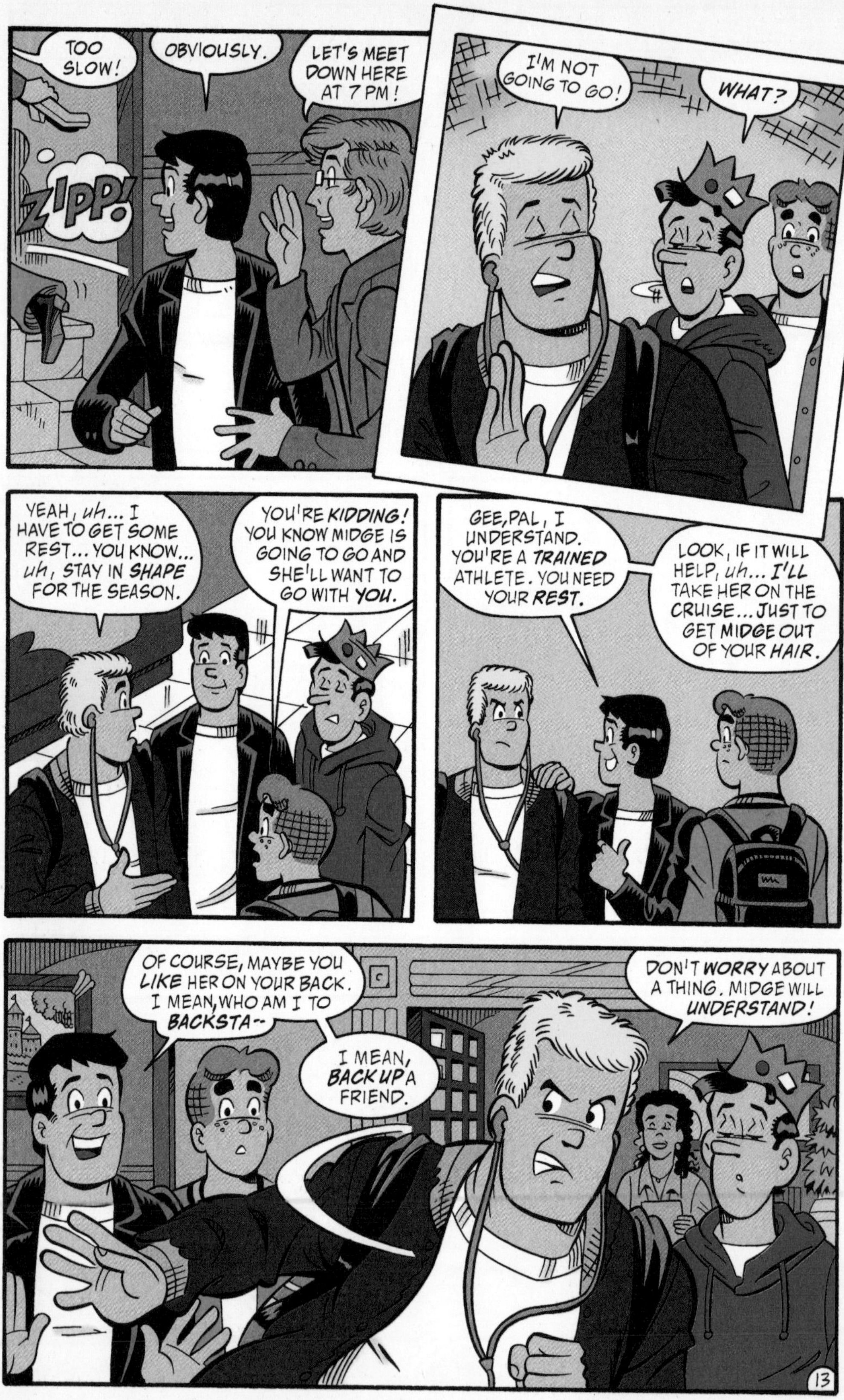
TOO SLOW!
OBVIOUSLY.
LET'S MEET DOWN HERE AT 7 PM!
ZIPP!
I'M NOT GOING TO GO!
WHAT?
YEAH, uh... I HAVE TO GET SOME REST... YOU KNOW... uh, STAY IN SHAPE FOR THE SEASON.
YOU'RE KIDDING! YOU KNOW MIDGE IS GOING TO GO AND SHE'LL WANT TO GO WITH YOU.
GEE, PAL, I UNDERSTAND. YOU'RE A TRAINED ATHLETE. YOU NEED YOUR REST.
LOOK, IF IT WILL HELP, uh... I'LL TAKE HER ON THE CRUISE... JUST TO GET MIDGE OUT OF YOUR HAIR.
OF COURSE, MAYBE YOU LIKE HER ON YOUR BACK. I MEAN, WHO AM I TO BACKSTA--
I MEAN, BACK UP A FRIEND.
DON'T WORRY ABOUT A THING. MIDGE WILL UNDERSTAND!

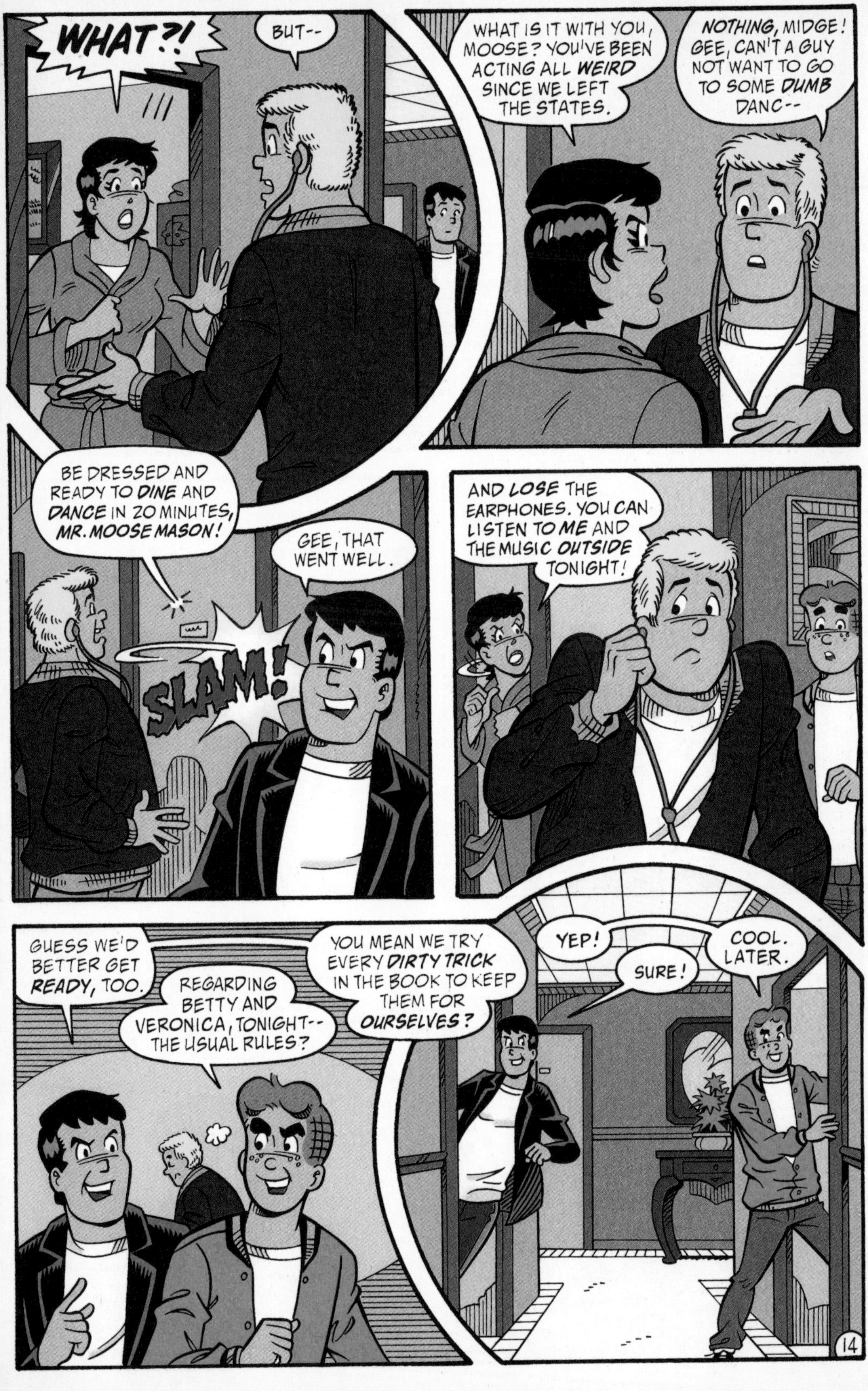
WHAT?!
BUT--
WHAT IS IT WITH YOU, MOOSE? YOU'VE BEEN ACTING ALL WEIRD SINCE WE LEFT THE STATES.
NOTHING, MIDGE! GEE, CAN'T A GUY NOT WANT TO GO TO SOME DUMB DANC--
BE DRESSED AND READY TO DINE AND DANCE IN 20 MINUTES, MR. MOOSE MASON!
SLAM!
GEE, THAT WENT WELL.
AND LOSE THE EARPHONES. YOU CAN LISTEN TO ME AND THE MUSIC OUTSIDE TONIGHT!
GUESS WE'D BETTER GET READY, TOO.
REGARDING BETTY AND VERONICA, TONIGHT-- THE USUAL RULES?
YOU MEAN WE TRY EVERY DIRTY TRICK IN THE BOOK TO KEEP THEM FOR OURSELVES?
YEP!
SURE!
COOL. LATER.

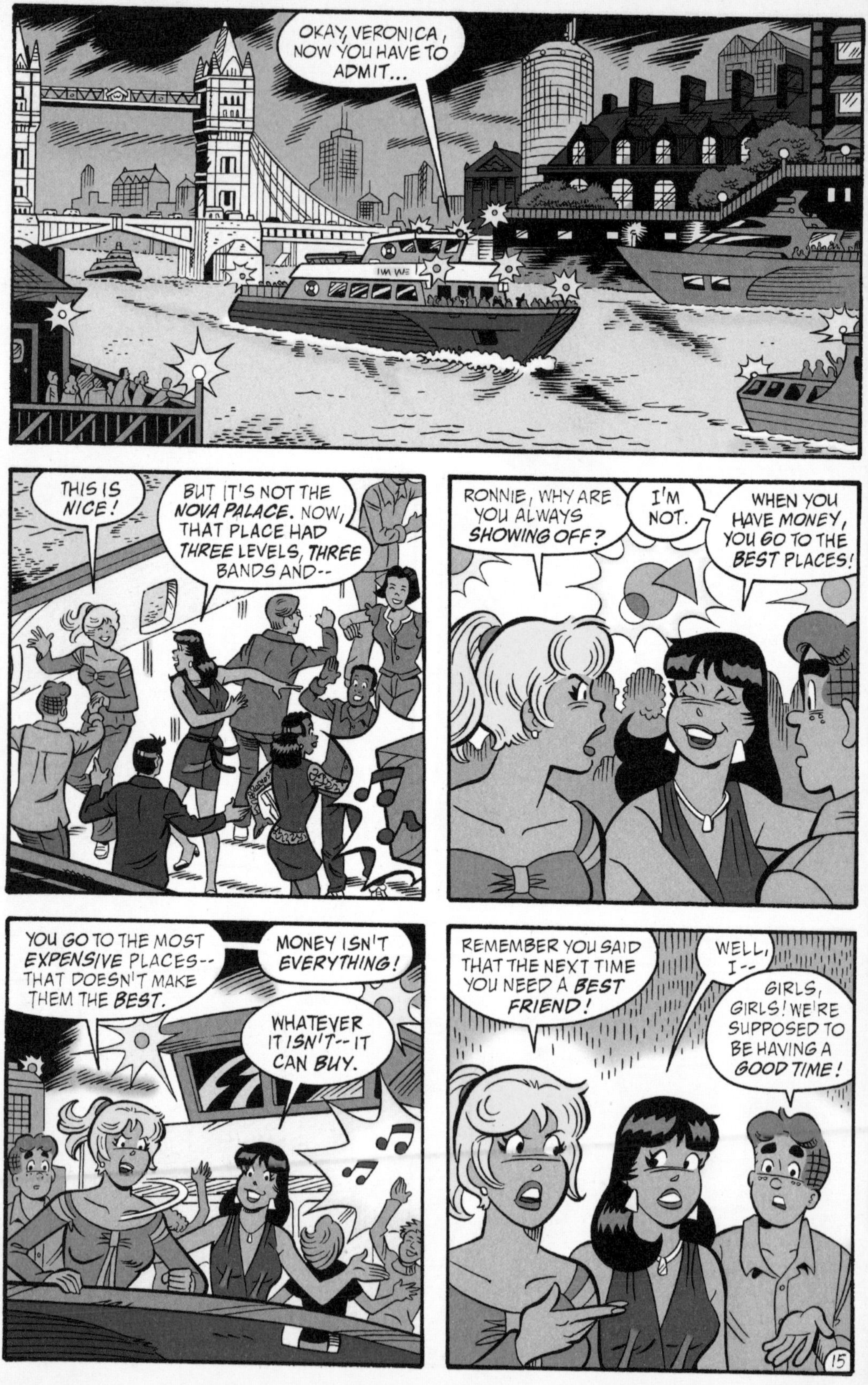
OKAY, VERONICA, NOW YOU HAVE TO ADMIT...
THIS IS NICE!
BUT IT'S NOT THE NOVA PALACE. NOW, THAT PLACE HAD THREE LEVELS, THREE BANDS AND--
RONNIE, WHY ARE YOU ALWAYS SHOWING OFF?
I'M NOT.
WHEN YOU HAVE MONEY, YOU GO TO THE BEST PLACES!
YOU GO TO THE MOST EXPENSIVE PLACES-- THAT DOESN'T MAKE THEM THE BEST.
MONEY ISN'T EVERYTHING!
WHATEVER IT ISN'T-- IT CAN BUY.
REMEMBER YOU SAID THAT THE NEXT TIME YOU NEED A BEST FRIEND!
WELL, I--
GIRLS, GIRLS! WE'RE SUPPOSED TO BE HAVING A GOOD TIME!
15

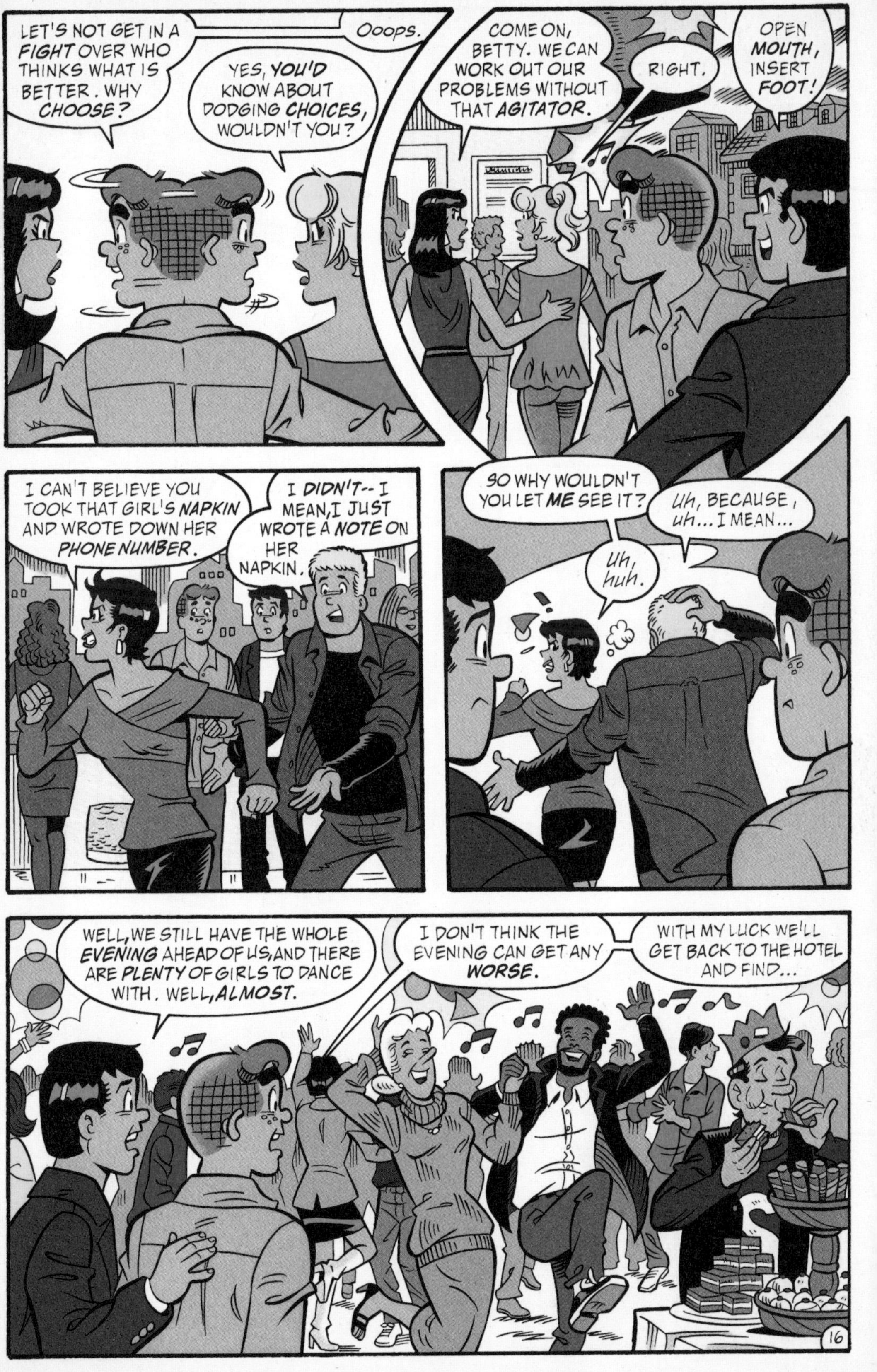

LET'S NOT GET IN A FIGHT OVER WHO THINKS WHAT IS BETTER. WHY CHOOSE?
YES, YOU'D KNOW ABOUT DODGING CHOICES, WOULDN'T YOU?
Ooops.
COME ON, BETTY. WE CAN WORK OUT OUR PROBLEMS WITHOUT THAT AGITATOR.
RIGHT.
OPEN MOUTH, INSERT FOOT!
I CAN'T BELIEVE YOU TOOK THAT GIRL'S NAPKIN AND WROTE DOWN HER PHONE NUMBER.
I DIDN'T-- I MEAN, I JUST WROTE A NOTE ON HER NAPKIN.
SO WHY WOULDN'T YOU LET ME SEE IT?
Uh, BECAUSE, uh... I MEAN...
Uh, huh.
WELL, WE STILL HAVE THE WHOLE EVENING AHEAD OF US, AND THERE ARE PLENTY OF GIRLS TO DANCE WITH. WELL, ALMOST.
I DON'T THINK THE EVENING CAN GET ANY WORSE.
WITH MY LUCK WE'LL GET BACK TO THE HOTEL AND FIND...
16

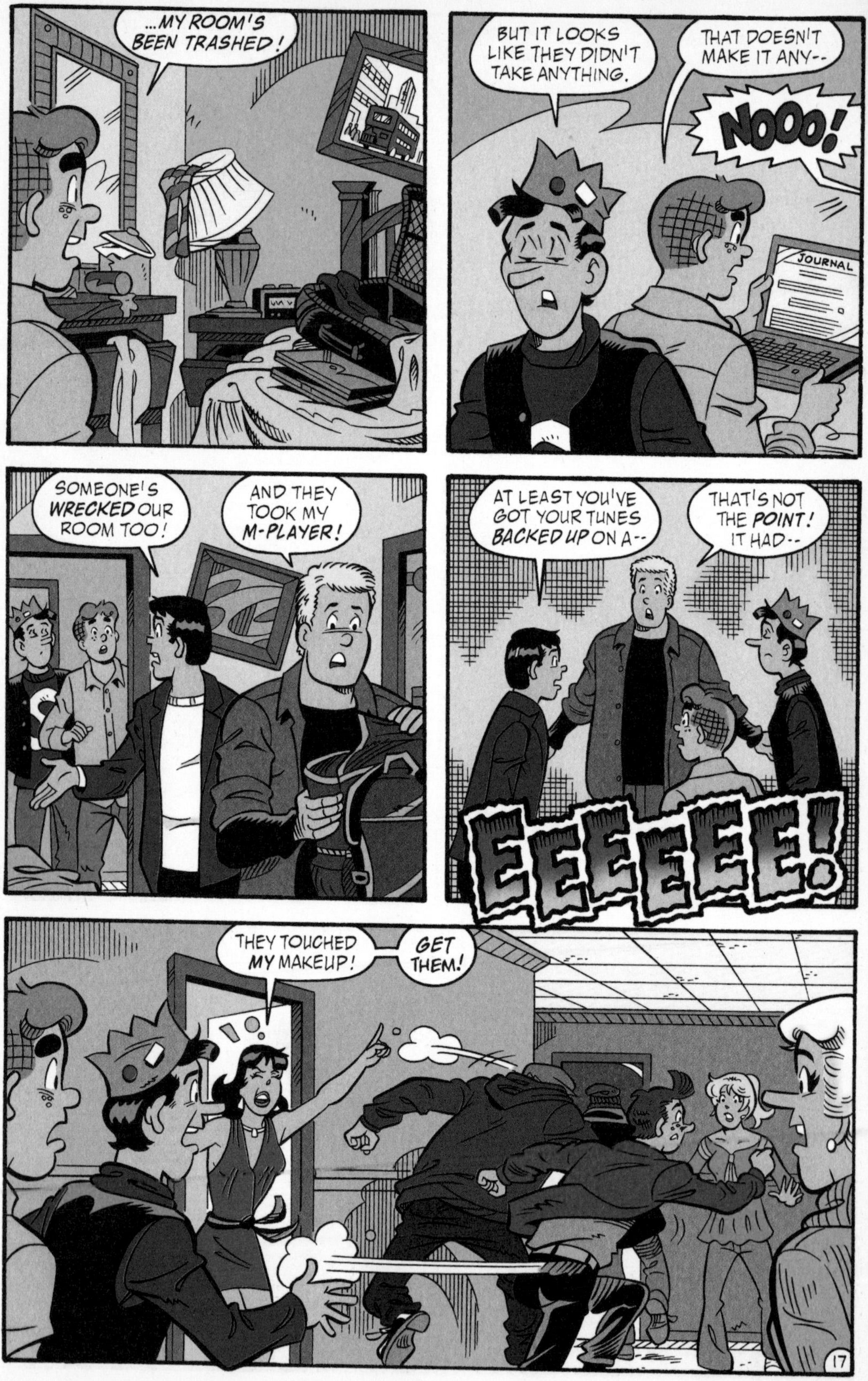
...MY ROOM'S BEEN TRASHED!
BUT IT LOOKS LIKE THEY DIDN'T TAKE ANYTHING.
THAT DOESN'T MAKE IT ANY--
NOOO!
JOURNAL
SOMEONE'S WRECKED OUR ROOM TOO!
AND THEY TOOK MY M-PLAYER!
AT LEAST YOU'VE GOT YOUR TUNES BACKED UP ON A--
THAT'S NOT THE POINT! IT HAD--
EEEEEE!
THEY TOUCHED MY MAKEUP!
GET THEM!

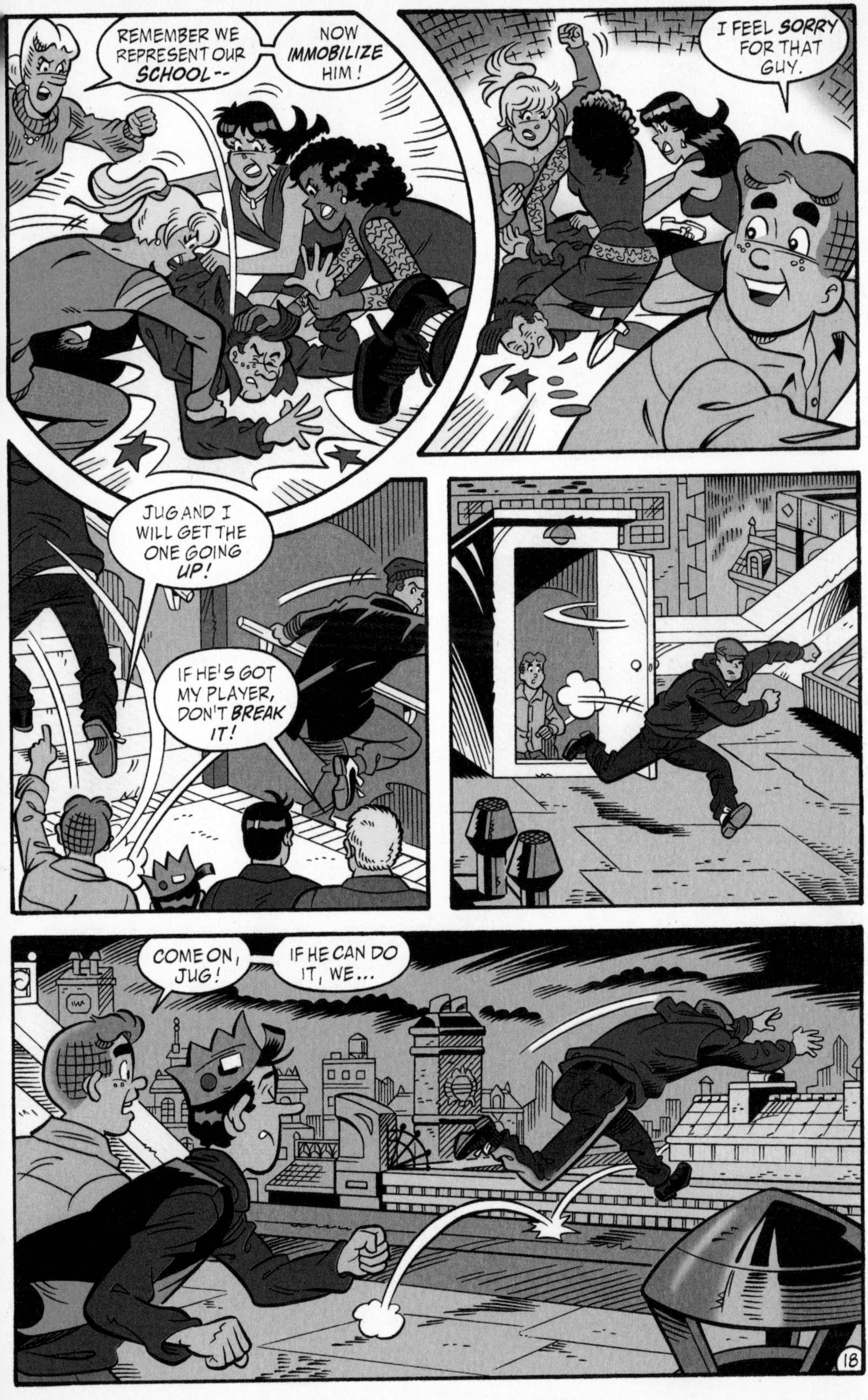
REMEMBER WE REPRESENT OUR SCHOOL--
NOW IMMOBILIZE HIM!
I FEEL SORRY FOR THAT GUY.
JUG AND I WILL GET THE ONE GOING UP!
IF HE'S GOT MY PLAYER, DON'T BREAK IT!
COME ON, JUG!
IF HE CAN DO IT, WE...
18

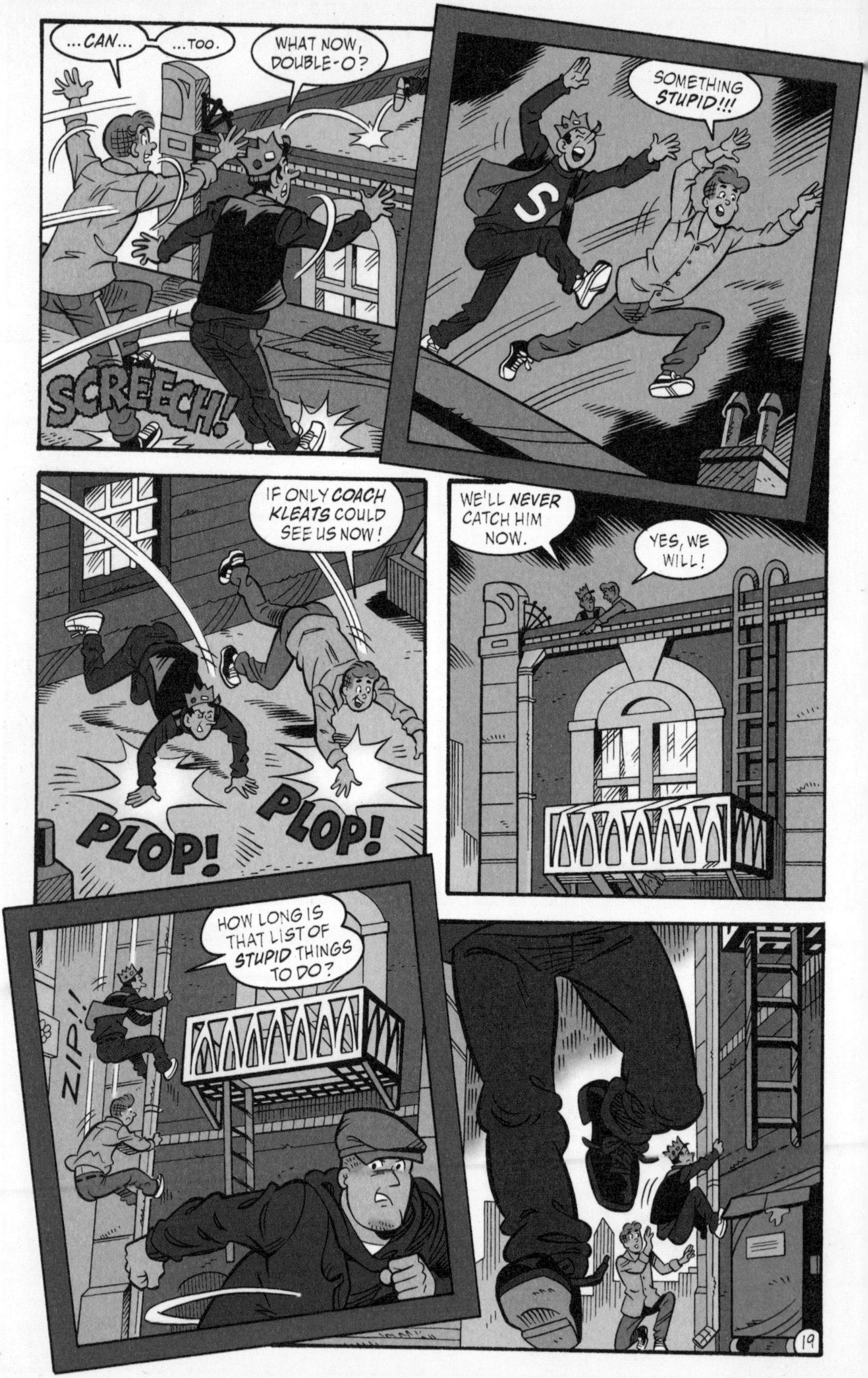

...CAN...
...TOO.
WHAT NOW, DOUBLE-O?
SCREECH!
SOMETHING STUPID!!!
IF ONLY COACH KLEATS COULD SEE US NOW!
PLOP!
PLOP!
WE'LL NEVER CATCH HIM NOW.
YES, WE WILL!
HOW LONG IS THAT LIST OF STUPID THINGS TO DO?
ZIP!!

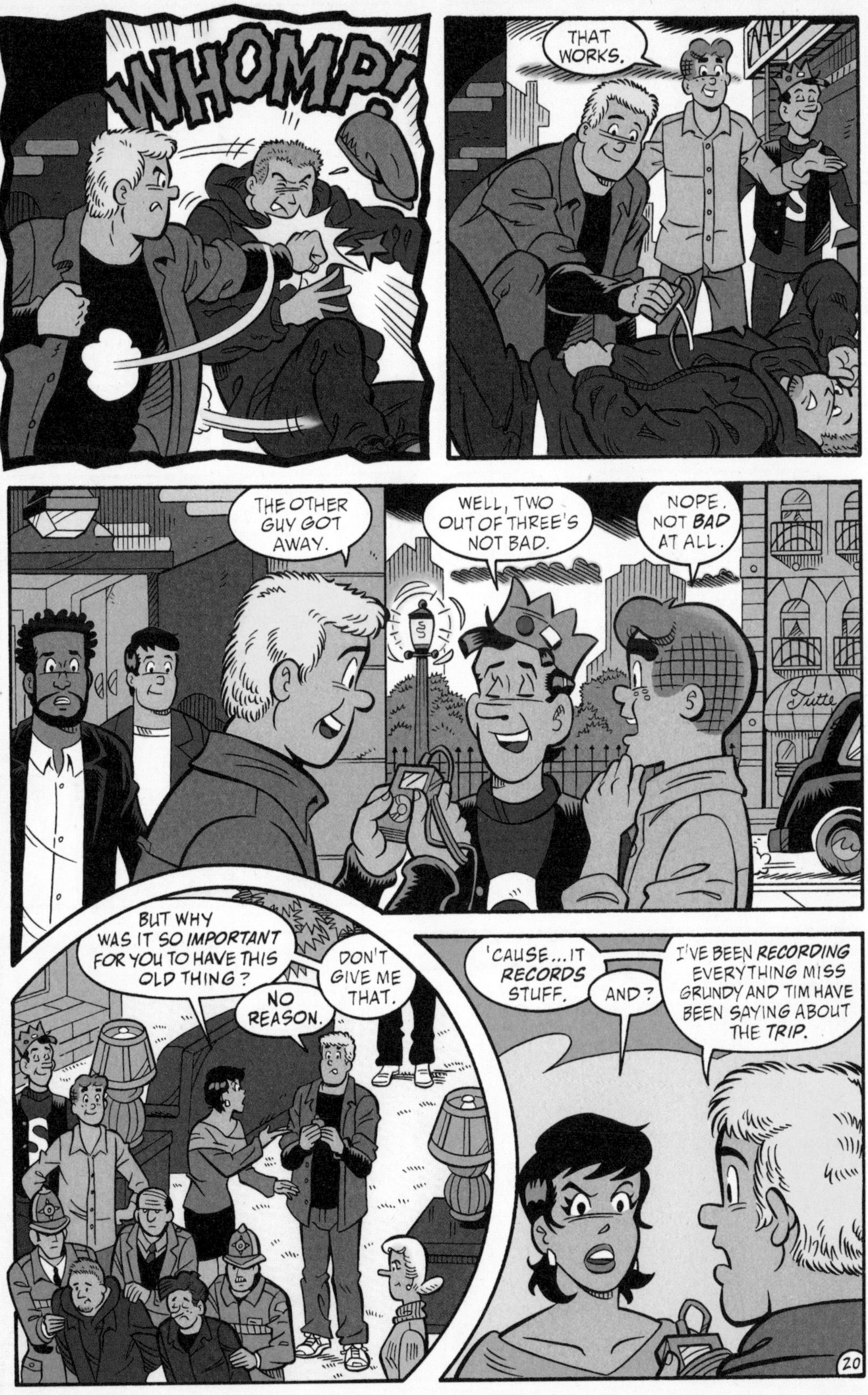

WHOMP!
THAT WORKS.
THE OTHER GUY GOT AWAY.
WELL, TWO OUT OF THREE'S NOT BAD.
NOPE. NOT BAD AT ALL.
BUT WHY WAS IT SO IMPORTANT FOR YOU TO HAVE THIS OLD THING?
NO REASON.
DON'T GIVE ME THAT.
'CAUSE... IT RECORDS STUFF.
AND?
I'VE BEEN RECORDING EVERYTHING MISS GRUNDY AND TIM HAVE BEEN SAYING ABOUT THE TRIP.

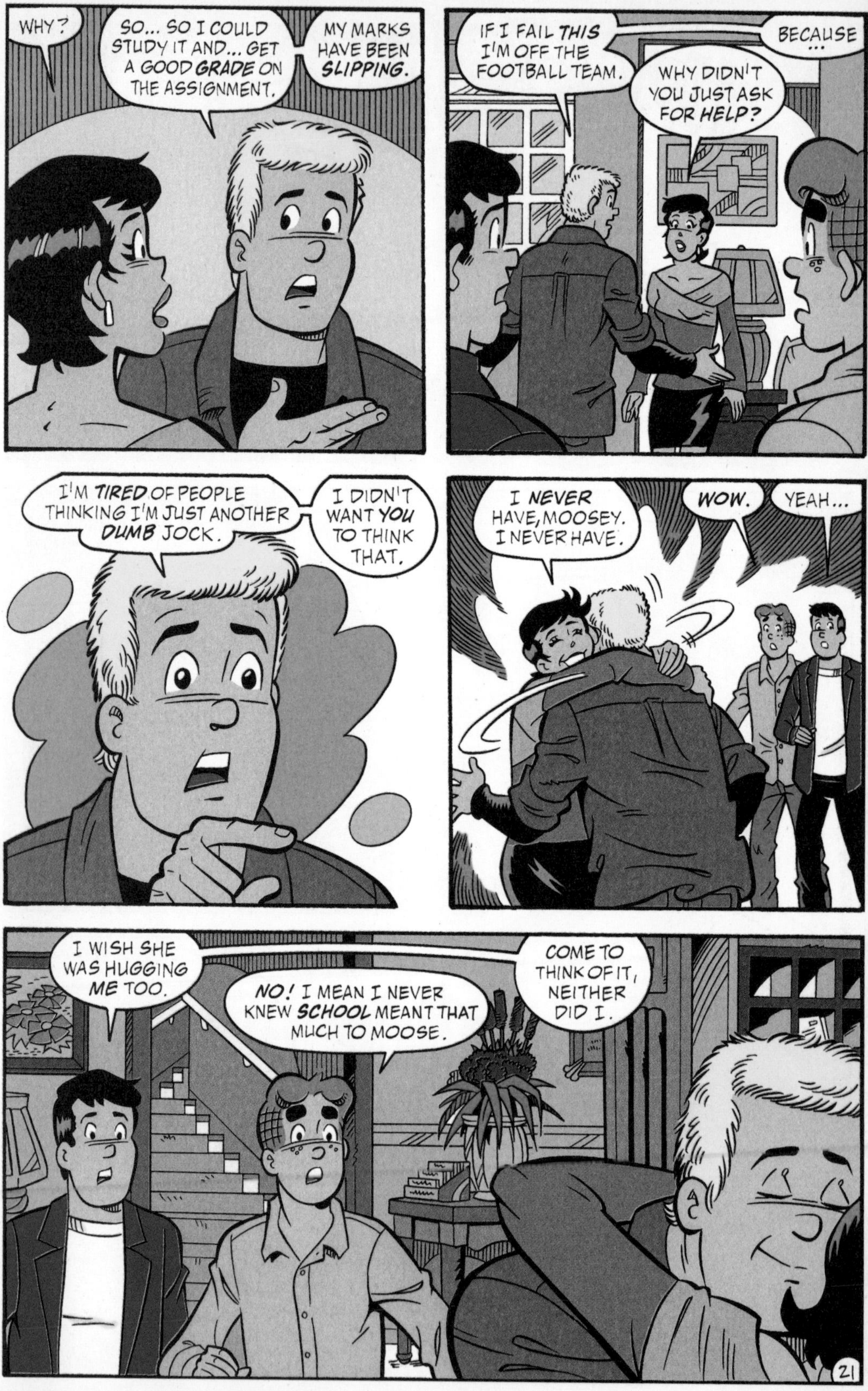
WHY?
SO... SO I COULD STUDY IT AND... GET A GOOD GRADE ON THE ASSIGNMENT.
MY MARKS HAVE BEEN SLIPPING.
IF I FAIL THIS I'M OFF THE FOOTBALL TEAM.
BECAUSE ...
WHY DIDN'T YOU JUST ASK FOR HELP?
I'M TIRED OF PEOPLE THINKING I'M JUST ANOTHER DUMB JOCK.
I DIDN'T WANT YOU TO THINK THAT.
I NEVER HAVE, MOOSEY. I NEVER HAVE.
WOW.
YEAH...
I WISH SHE WAS HUGGING ME TOO.
NO! I MEAN I NEVER KNEW SCHOOL MEANT THAT MUCH TO MOOSE.
COME TO THINK OF IT, NEITHER DID I.
21

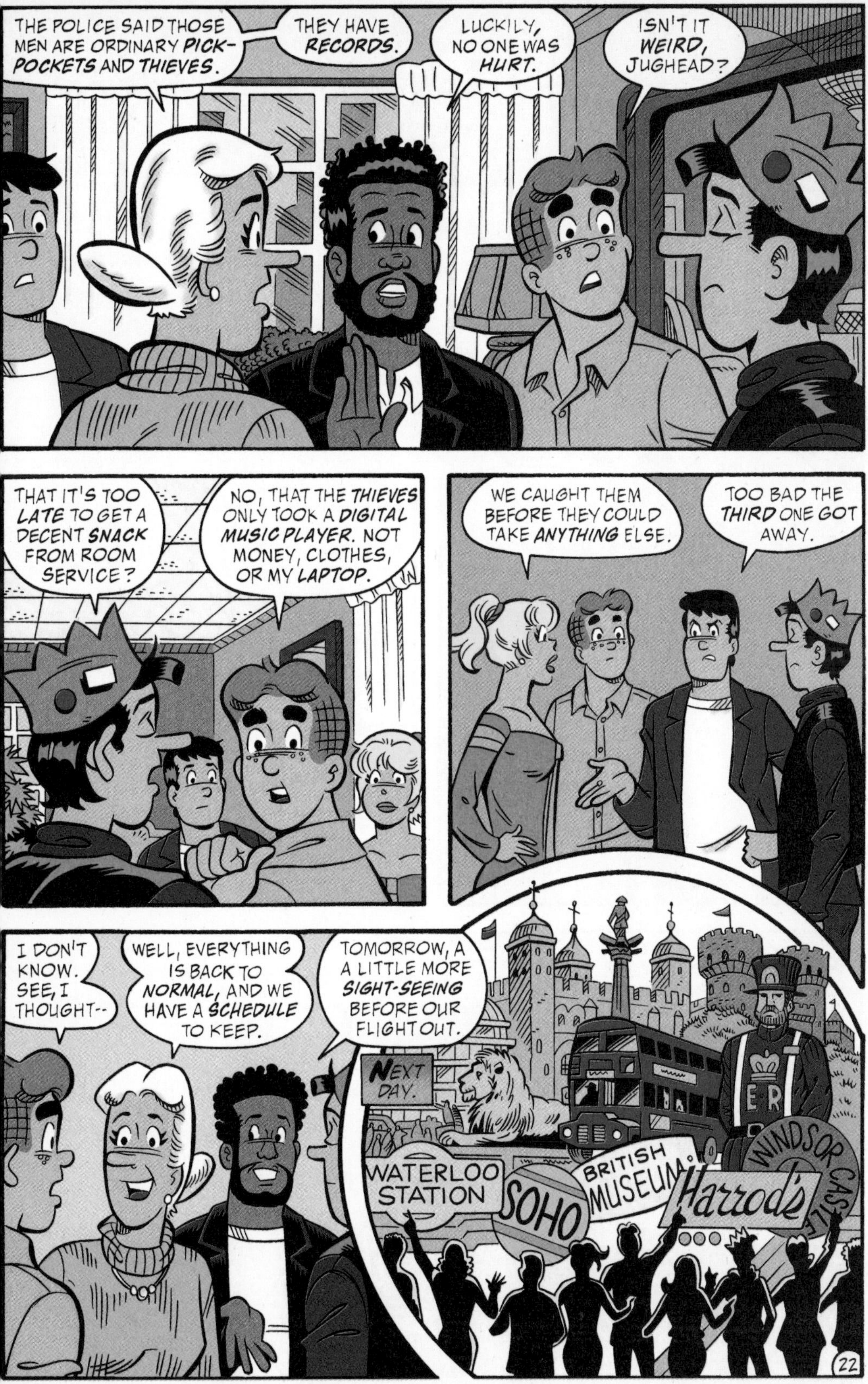
THE POLICE SAID THOSE MEN ARE ORDINARY PICK-POCKETS AND THIEVES.
THEY HAVE RECORDS.
LUCKILY, NO ONE WAS HURT.
ISN'T IT WEIRD, JUGHEAD?
THAT IT'S TOO LATE TO GET A DECENT SNACK FROM ROOM SERVICE?
NO, THAT THE THIEVES ONLY TOOK A DIGITAL MUSIC PLAYER. NOT MONEY, CLOTHES, OR MY LAPTOP.
WE CAUGHT THEM BEFORE THEY COULD TAKE ANYTHING ELSE.
TOO BAD THE THIRD ONE GOT AWAY.
I DON'T KNOW. SEE, I THOUGHT--
WELL, EVERYTHING IS BACK TO NORMAL, AND WE HAVE A SCHEDULE TO KEEP.
TOMORROW, A LITTLE MORE SIGHT-SEEING BEFORE OUR FLIGHT OUT.
NEXT DAY.
WATERLOO STATION
SOHO
BRITISH MUSEUM
Harrod's
WINDSOR CASTLE
E R

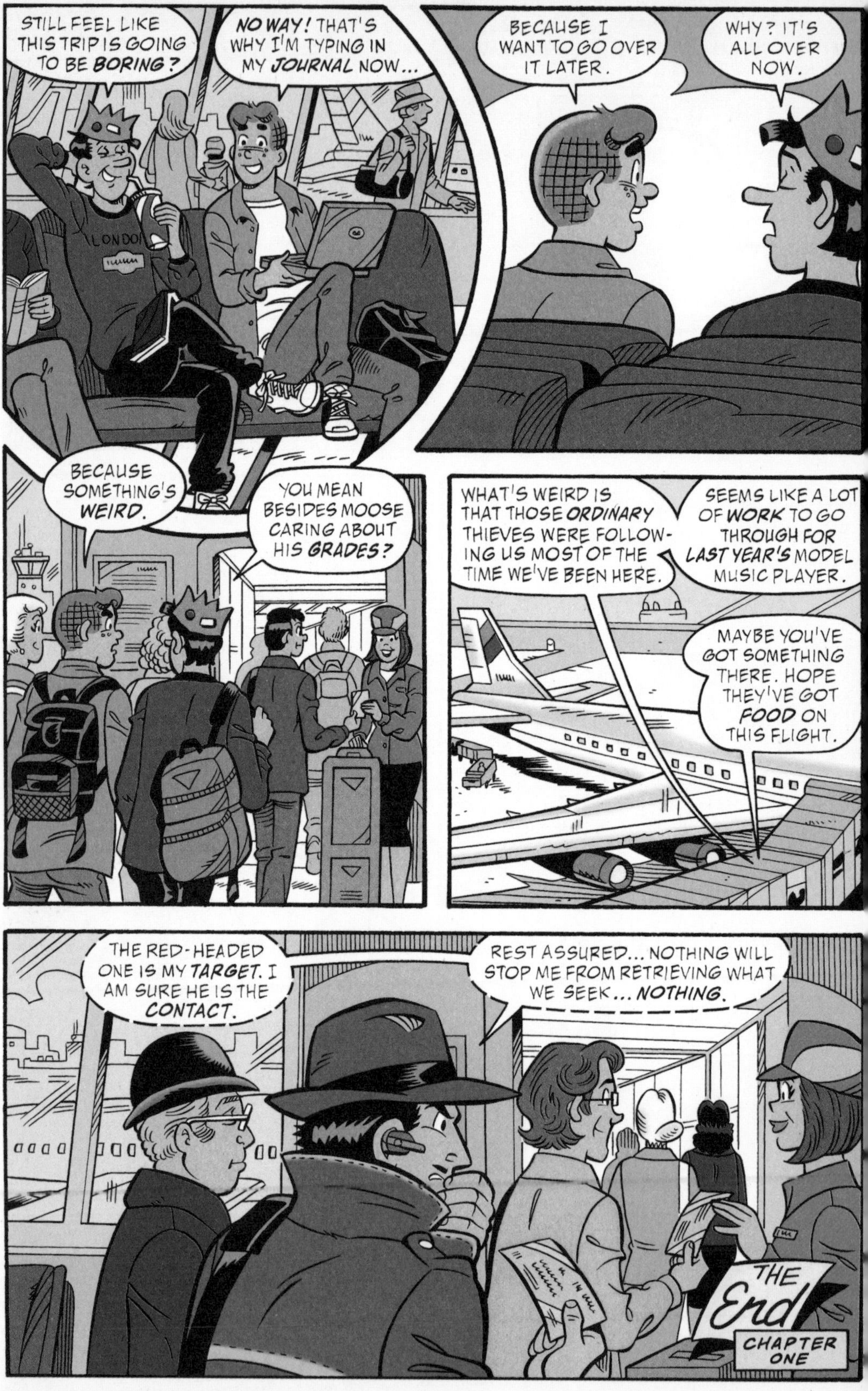
STILL FEEL LIKE THIS TRIP IS GOING TO BE BORING?
NO WAY! THAT'S WHY I'M TYPING IN MY JOURNAL NOW...
LONDON
BECAUSE I WANT TO GO OVER IT LATER.
WHY? IT'S ALL OVER NOW.
BECAUSE SOMETHING'S WEIRD.
YOU MEAN BESIDES MOOSE CARING ABOUT HIS GRADES?
WHAT'S WEIRD IS THAT THOSE ORDINARY THIEVES WERE FOLLOW-ING US MOST OF THE TIME WE'VE BEEN HERE.
SEEMS LIKE A LOT OF WORK TO GO THROUGH FOR LAST YEAR'S MODEL MUSIC PLAYER.
MAYBE YOU'VE GOT SOMETHING THERE. HOPE THEY'VE GOT FOOD ON THIS FLIGHT.
THE RED-HEADED ONE IS MY TARGET. I AM SURE HE IS THE CONTACT.
REST ASSURED... NOTHING WILL STOP ME FROM RETRIEVING WHAT WE SEEK... NOTHING.
THE End CHAPTER ONE

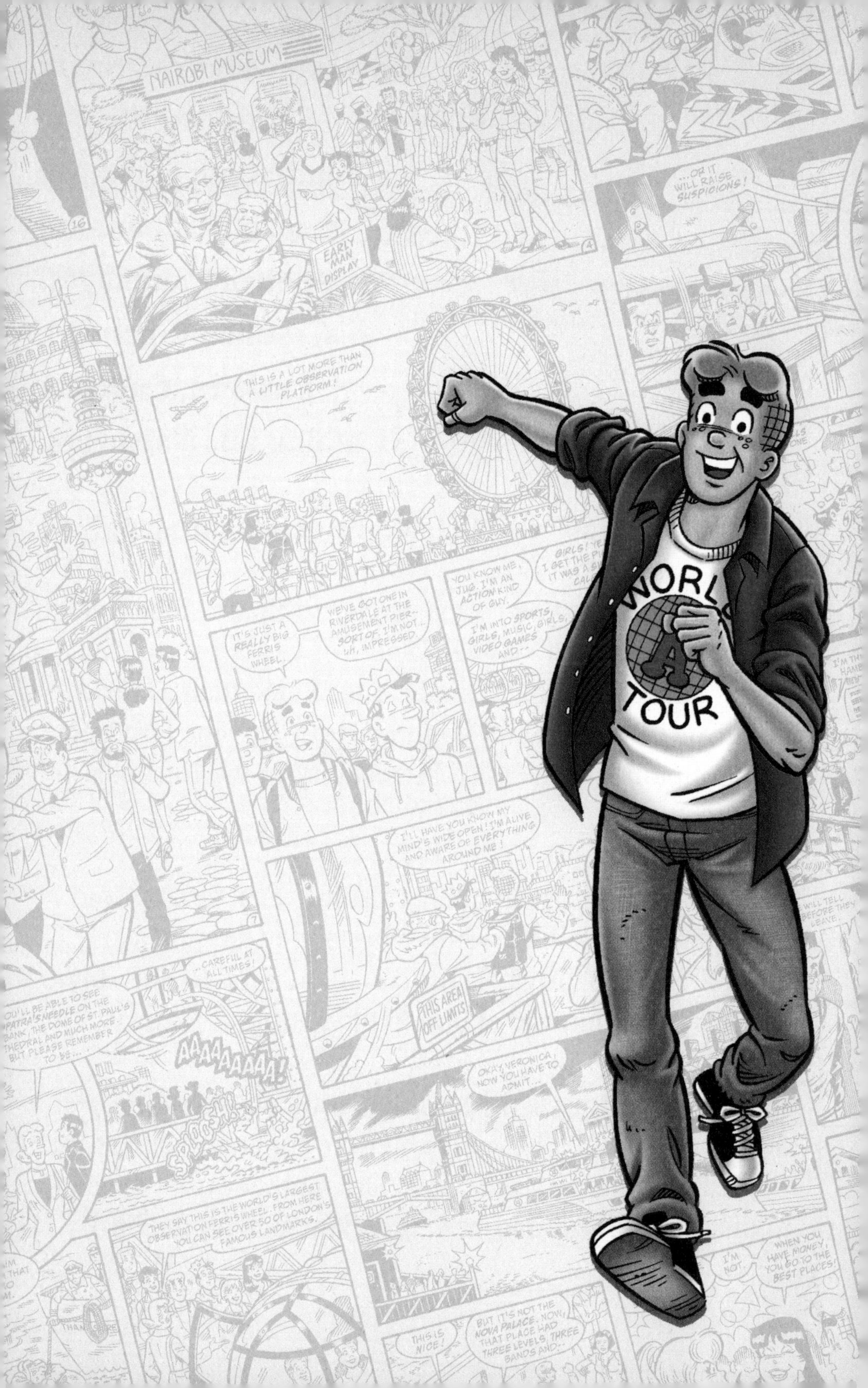
NAIROBI MUSEUM
EARLY MAN DISPLAY
...OR IT WILL RAISE SUSPICIONS!
THIS IS A LOT MORE THAN A LITTLE OBSERVATION PLATFORM!
IT'S JUST A REALLY BIG FERRIS WHEEL.
WE'VE GOT ONE IN RIVERDALE AT THE AMUSEMENT PIER-- SORT OF. I'M NOT... UH, IMPRESSED.
YOU KNOW ME, JUG. I'M AN ACTION KIND OF GUY.
I'M INTO SPORTS, GIRLS, MUSIC, GIRLS, VIDEO GAMES AND--
WORLD TOUR
I'LL HAVE YOU KNOW MY MIND'S WIDE OPEN! I'M ALIVE AND AWARE OF EVERYTHING AROUND ME!
...CAREFUL AT ALL TIMES!
THIS AREA OFF LIMITS
OKAY, VERONICA, NOW YOU HAVE TO ADMIT...
THEY SAY THIS IS THE WORLD'S LARGEST OBSERVATION FERRIS WHEEL. FROM HERE YOU CAN SEE OVER 50 OF LONDON'S FAMOUS LANDMARKS.
I'M NOT.
WHEN YOU HAVE MONEY, YOU GO TO THE BEST PLACES!
THIS IS NICE!
BUT IT'S NOT THE NOVA PALACE. NOW, THAT PLACE HAD THREE LEVELS, THREE BANDS AND...

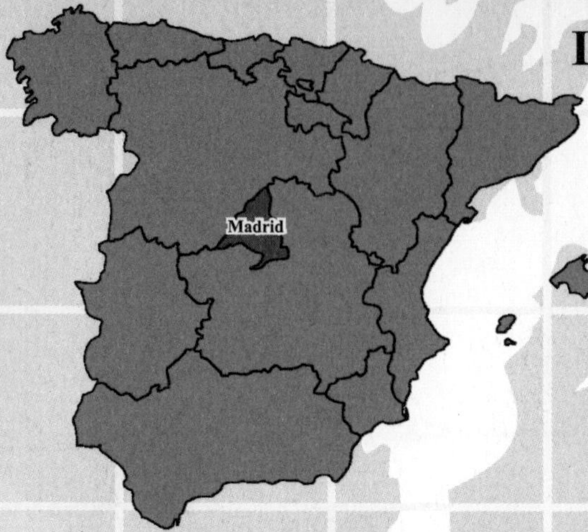
Madrid

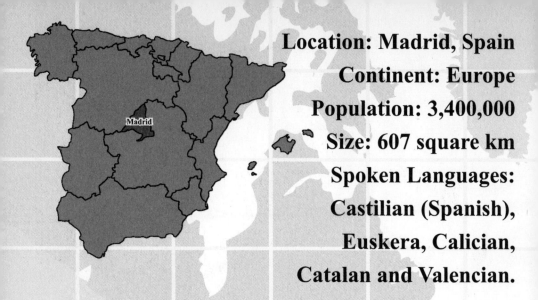

Location: Madrid, Spain
Continent: Europe
Population: 3,400,000
Size: 607 square km
Spoken Languages: Castilian (Spanish), Euskera, Calician, Catalan and Valencian.

"Bienvenido" to Madrid, the capital of Spain!

Madrid has been a major city in Spain since the 9th century. Back then, Muhammad I of Córdoba ordered a small palace to be built on the site. Since then Madrid has grown by leaps and bounds. Now, it is the largest city in Spain and the third largest city in the Europen Union.

Madrid has been home to some very famous and important people like writer Miguel de Cervantes and artist Francisco Goya. Madrid is also home to one of the world's most unusual sports, bullfighting.

Bullfighting is a very interesting and very dangerous sport. The bullfighter or "matador" enters thc ring carrying only a red cape. The matador uses the cape to distract the bull and basically dances with the bull.

While in Madrid, Archie and Jughead get to show off some of their own matador skills. However, unlike true matadors who rely on their own speed and physical prowess, Archie uses a moped to avoid the bulls! In addition to battling bulls, Archie and the Gang visit several sites and immerse themselves in new experiences.

One of the first sites is the Fountain of Cibeles. Designed by Ventura Rodríguez, the Fountain of Cibeles, named after Cybele (or Ceres), the Roman goddess of nature, is seen as one of Madrid's most important symbols. Some other sites that the group visits but are not expressly mentioned are:

• The statue "El Oso y El Madroño," sometimes translated as the "Bear and the Strawberry Tree." The Madroño tree is not native to Madrid and it is not a strawberry tree. The berries of the Madroño tree are red like strawberries, however they are not very sweet and are best eaten when made into a jam.

• The "Puerta de Europa" towers, translated as the "Gate of Europe." They are twin office buildings in Madrid, towering to a height of 374 ft with 26 floors. They were designed by American architects Philip Johnson and John Burgee and completed construction in 1996.

Archie® WORLD TOUR

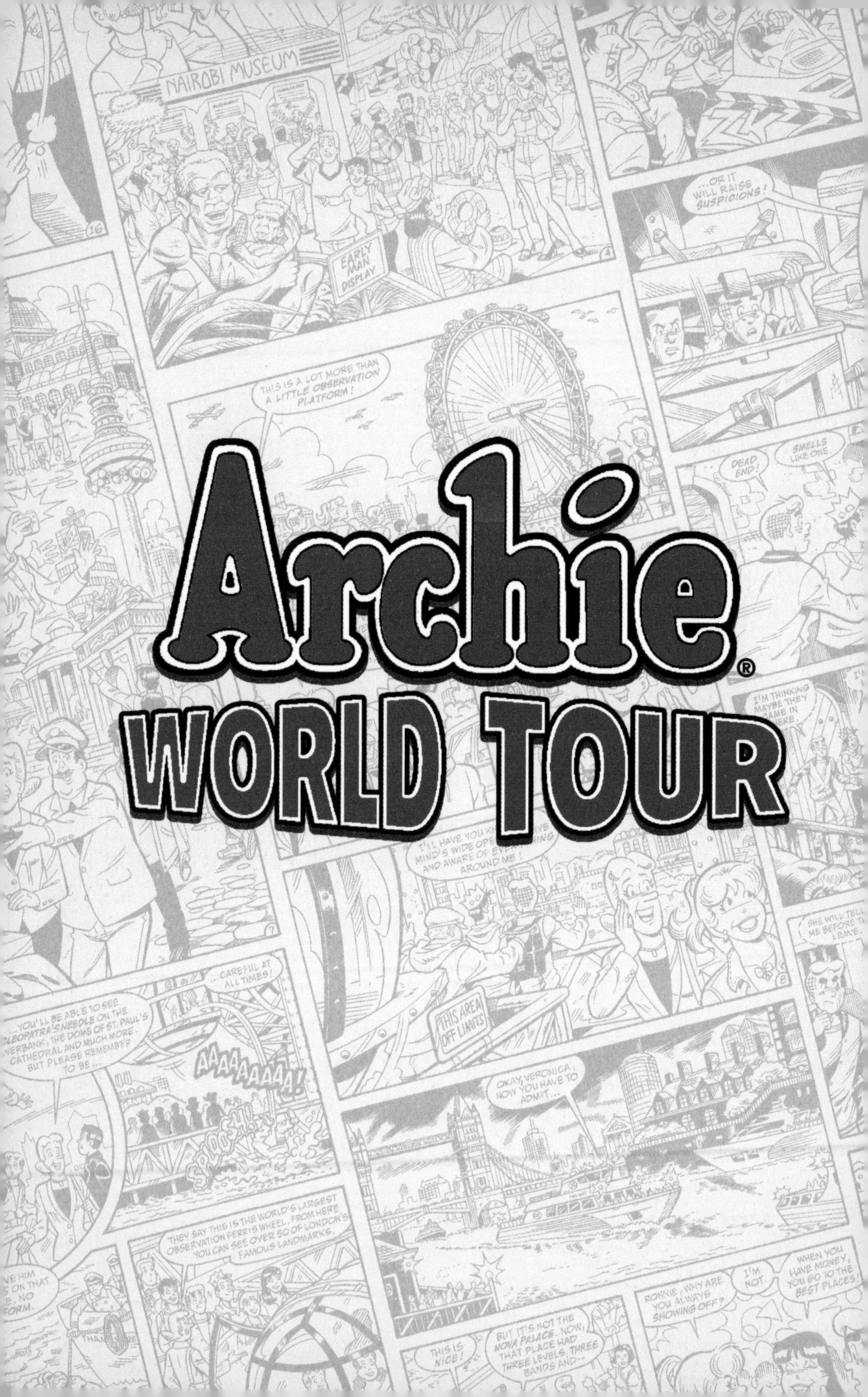

CHAPTER 2: MADRID

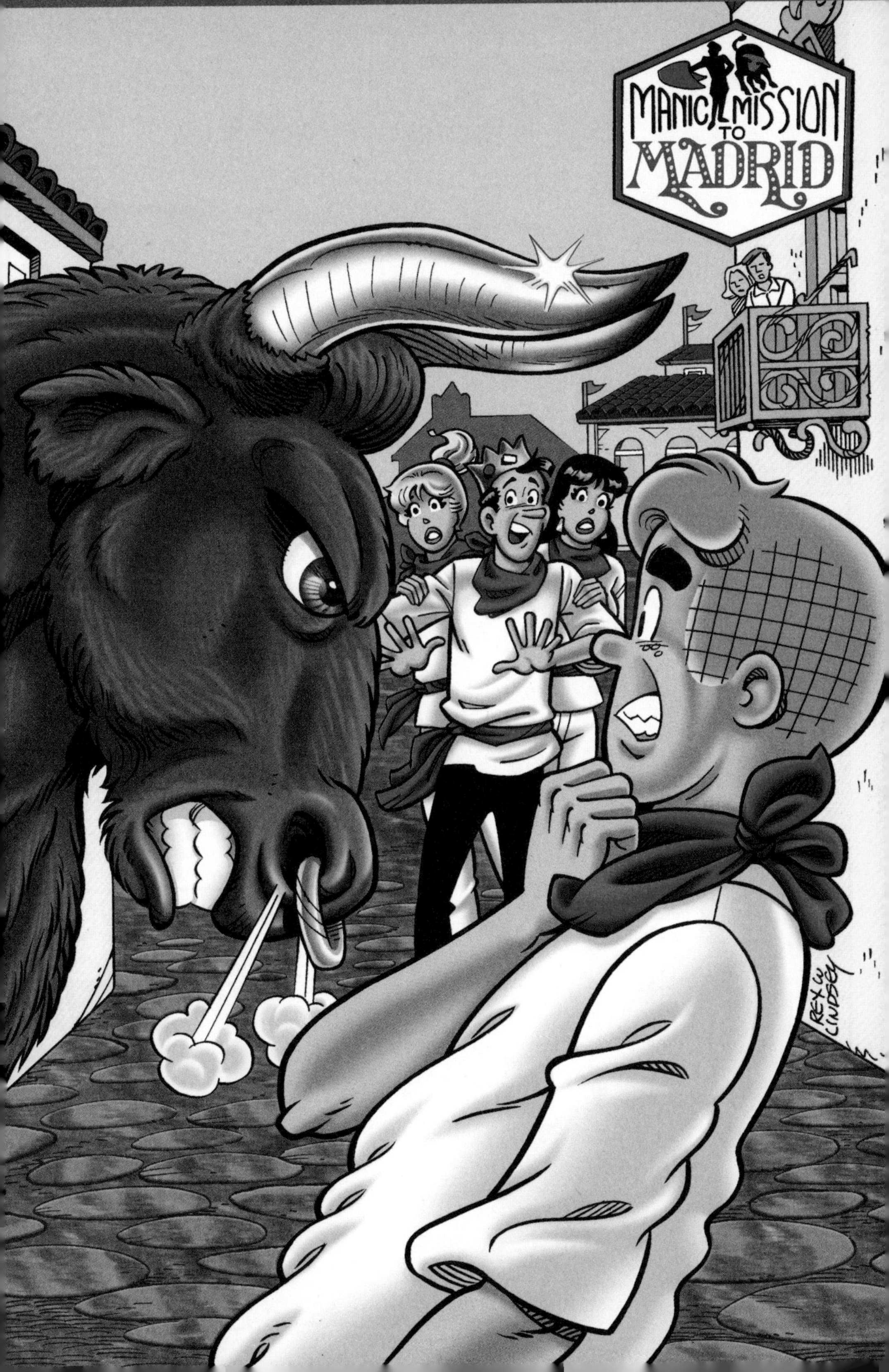
MANIC MISSION TO MADRID
REX W LINDSEY

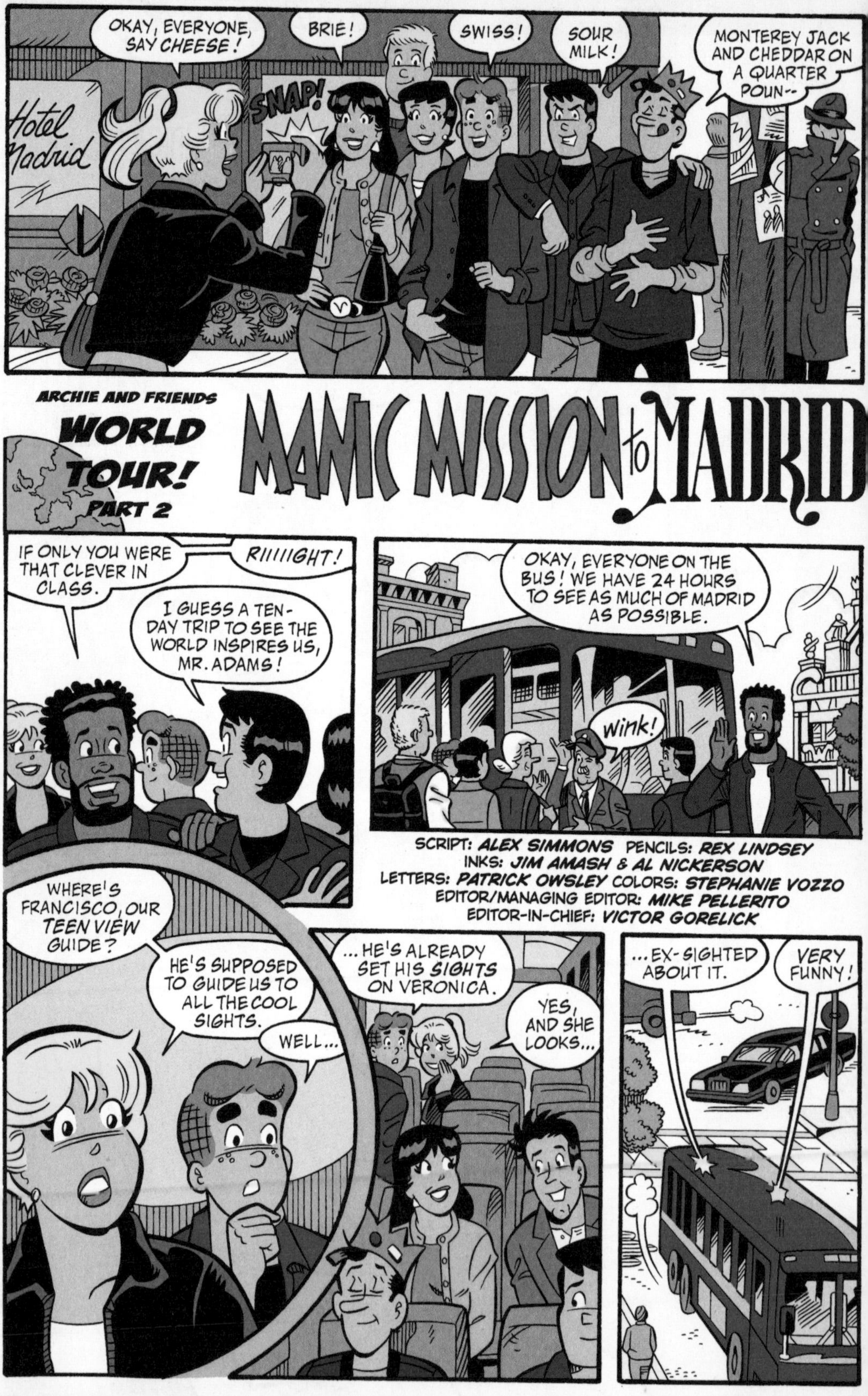
OKAY, EVERYONE, SAY CHEESE!
BRIE!
SWISS!
SOUR MILK!
MONTEREY JACK AND CHEDDAR ON A QUARTER POUN--
SNAP!
Hotel Madrid
ARCHIE AND FRIENDS
WORLD TOUR!
PART 2
MANIC MISSION to MADRID
IF ONLY YOU WERE THAT CLEVER IN CLASS.
RIIIIIGHT!
I GUESS A TEN-DAY TRIP TO SEE THE WORLD INSPIRES US, MR. ADAMS!
OKAY, EVERYONE ON THE BUS! WE HAVE 24 HOURS TO SEE AS MUCH OF MADRID AS POSSIBLE.
Wink!
SCRIPT: ALEX SIMMONS PENCILS: REX LINDSEY
INKS: JIM AMASH & AL NICKERSON
LETTERS: PATRICK OWSLEY COLORS: STEPHANIE VOZZO
EDITOR/MANAGING EDITOR: MIKE PELLERITO
EDITOR-IN-CHIEF: VICTOR GORELICK
WHERE'S FRANCISCO, OUR TEEN VIEW GUIDE?
HE'S SUPPOSED TO GUIDE US TO ALL THE COOL SIGHTS.
WELL...
...HE'S ALREADY SET HIS SIGHTS ON VERONICA.
YES, AND SHE LOOKS...
...EX-SIGHTED ABOUT IT.
VERY FUNNY!

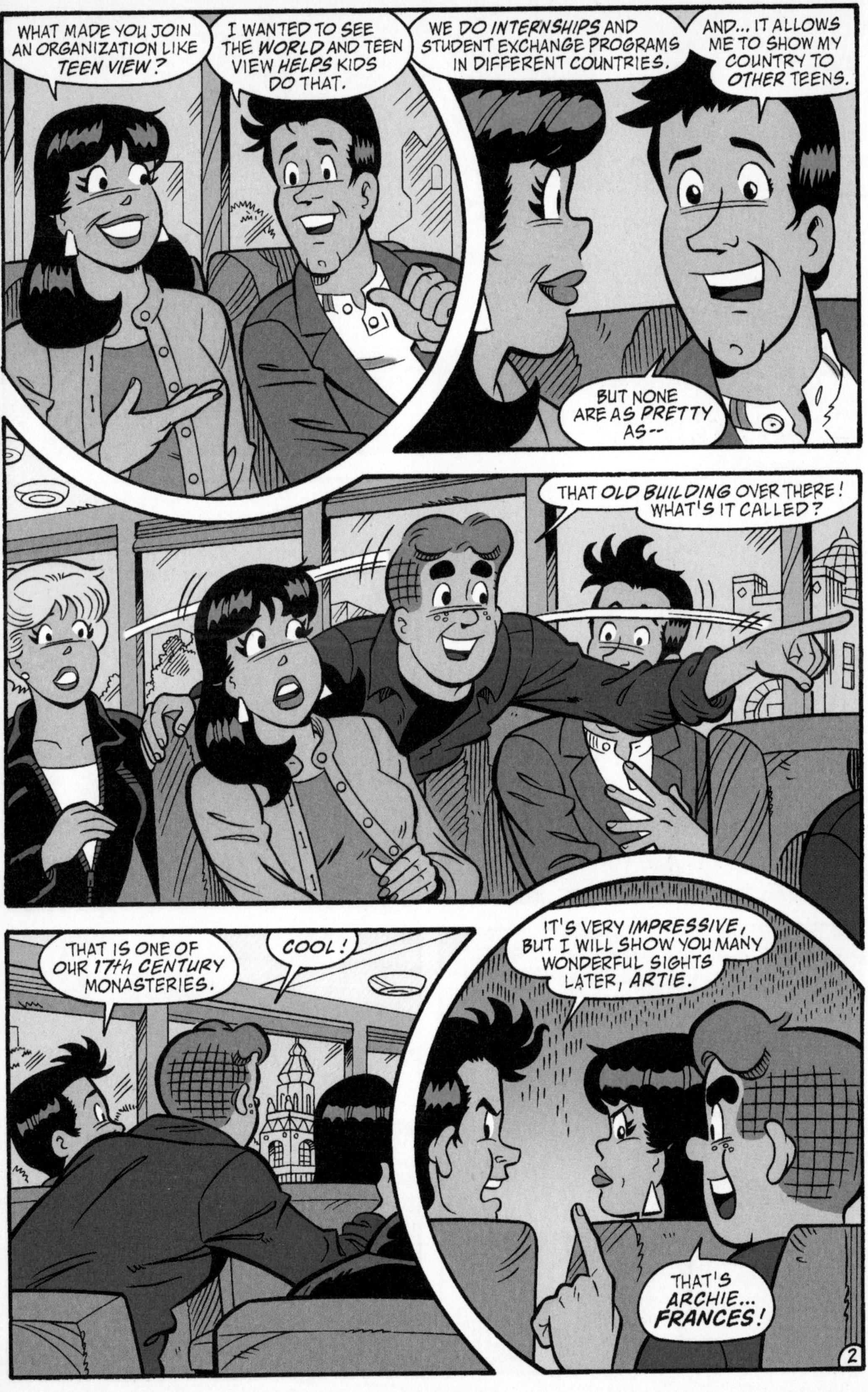
WHAT MADE YOU JOIN AN ORGANIZATION LIKE TEEN VIEW?
I WANTED TO SEE THE WORLD AND TEEN VIEW HELPS KIDS DO THAT.
WE DO INTERNSHIPS AND STUDENT EXCHANGE PROGRAMS IN DIFFERENT COUNTRIES.
AND... IT ALLOWS ME TO SHOW MY COUNTRY TO OTHER TEENS.
BUT NONE ARE AS PRETTY AS--
THAT OLD BUILDING OVER THERE! WHAT'S IT CALLED?
THAT IS ONE OF OUR 17th CENTURY MONASTERIES.
COOL!
IT'S VERY IMPRESSIVE, BUT I WILL SHOW YOU MANY WONDERFUL SIGHTS LATER, ARTIE.
THAT'S ARCHIE... FRANCES!
2

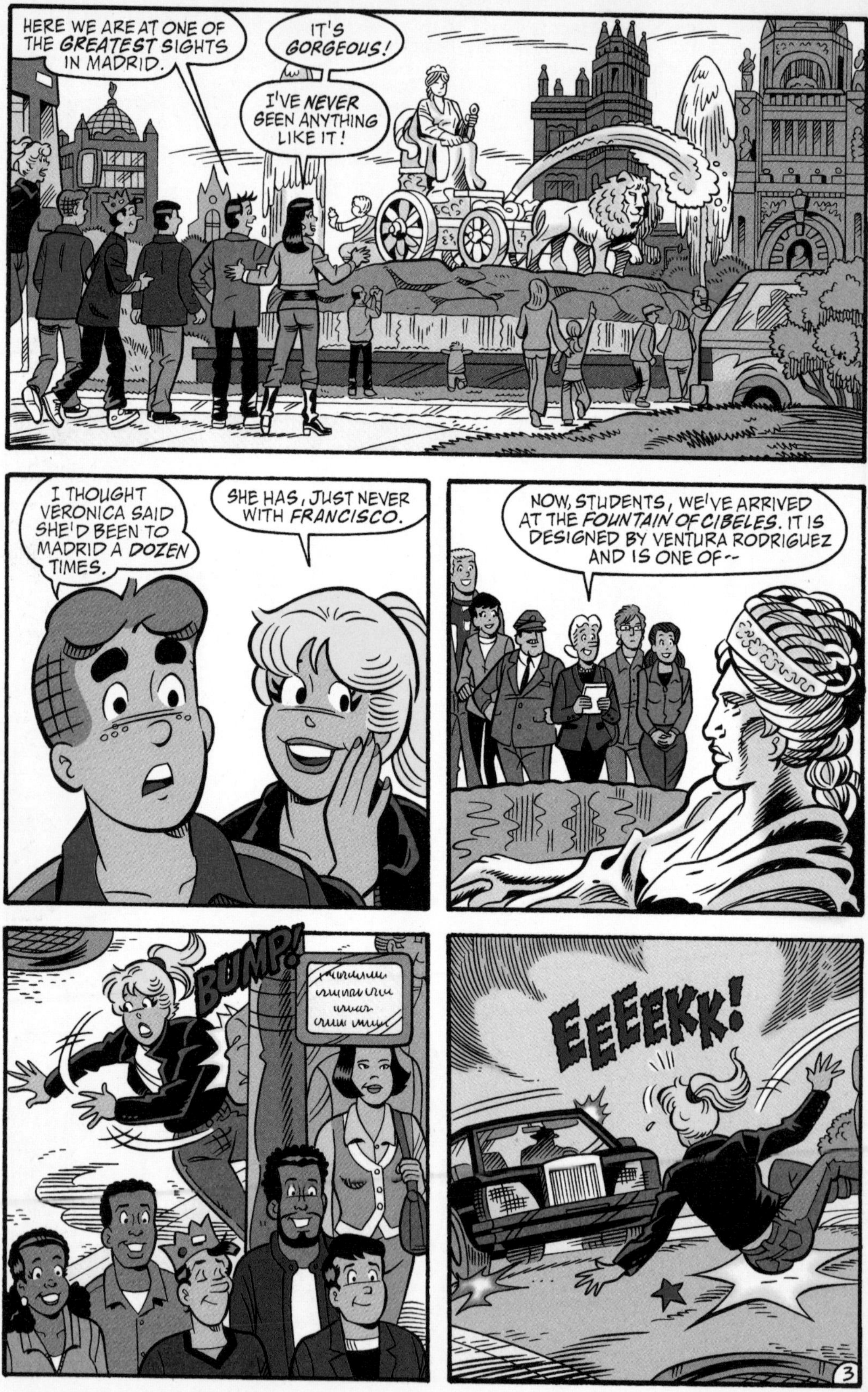
HERE WE ARE AT ONE OF THE GREATEST SIGHTS IN MADRID.
IT'S GORGEOUS!
I'VE NEVER SEEN ANYTHING LIKE IT!
I THOUGHT VERONICA SAID SHE'D BEEN TO MADRID A DOZEN TIMES.
SHE HAS, JUST NEVER WITH FRANCISCO.
NOW, STUDENTS, WE'VE ARRIVED AT THE FOUNTAIN OF CIBELES. IT IS DESIGNED BY VENTURA RODRIGUEZ AND IS ONE OF--
BUMP!
EEEEKK!
3

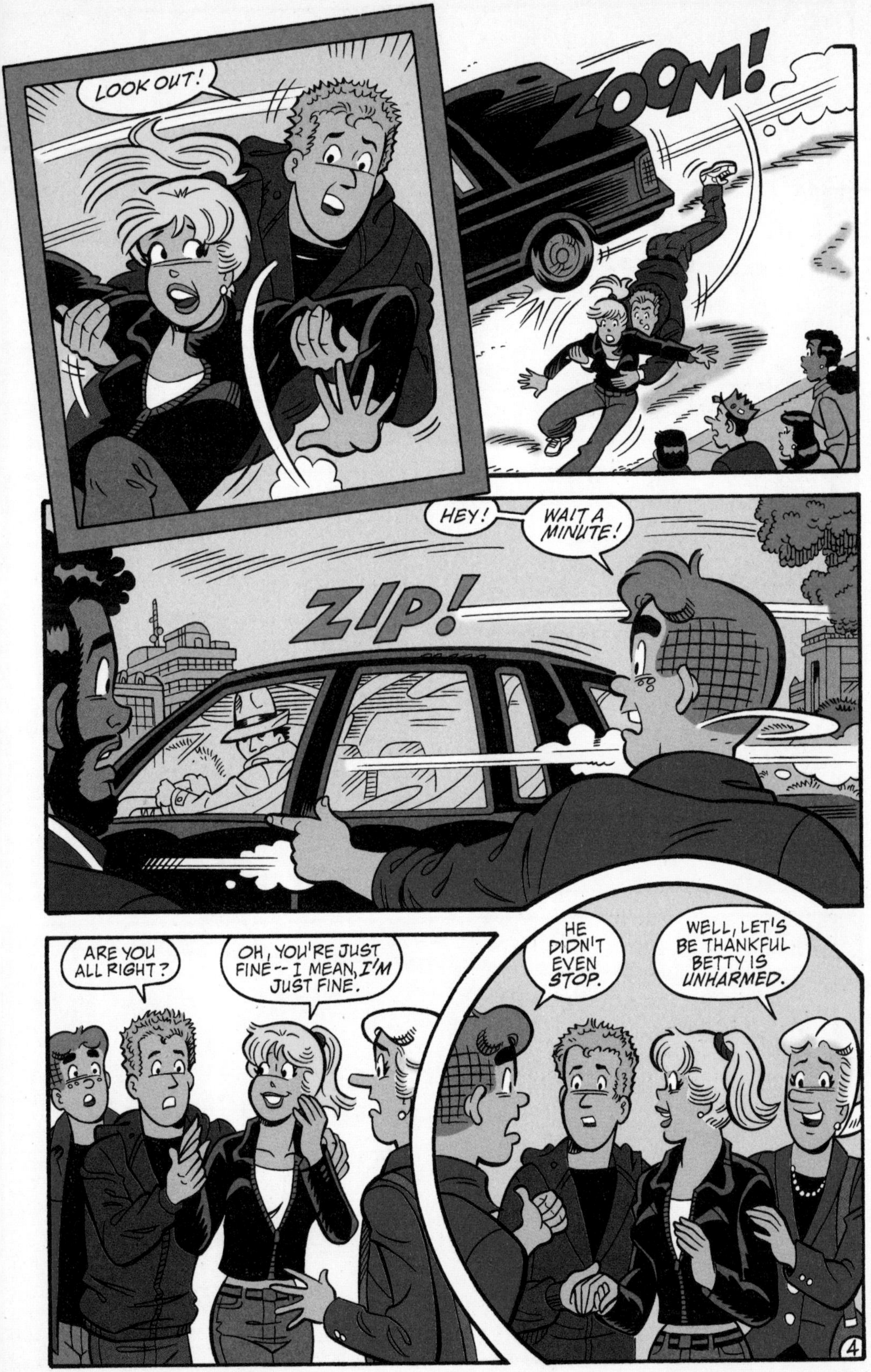
LOOK OUT!
ZOOM!
HEY!
WAIT A MINUTE!
ZIP!
ARE YOU ALL RIGHT?
OH, YOU'RE JUST FINE -- I MEAN, I'M JUST FINE.
HE DIDN'T EVEN STOP.
WELL, LET'S BE THANKFUL BETTY IS UNHARMED.

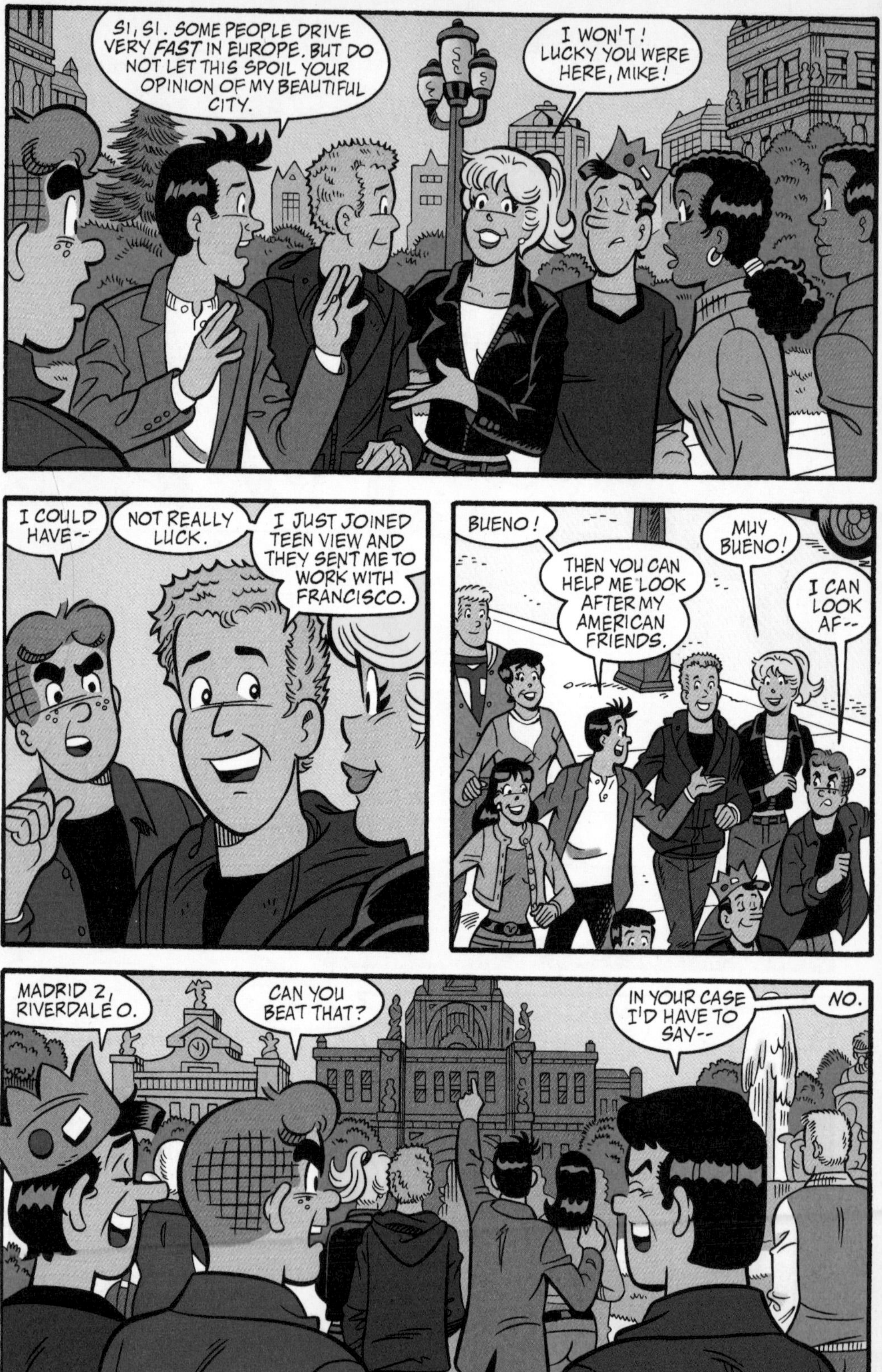
SI, SI. SOME PEOPLE DRIVE VERY FAST IN EUROPE. BUT DO NOT LET THIS SPOIL YOUR OPINION OF MY BEAUTIFUL CITY.
I WON'T! LUCKY YOU WERE HERE, MIKE!
I COULD HAVE--
NOT REALLY LUCK.
I JUST JOINED TEEN VIEW AND THEY SENT ME TO WORK WITH FRANCISCO.
BUENO!
THEN YOU CAN HELP ME LOOK AFTER MY AMERICAN FRIENDS.
MUY BUENO!
I CAN LOOK AF--
MADRID 2, RIVERDALE 0.
CAN YOU BEAT THAT?
IN YOUR CASE I'D HAVE TO SAY--
NO.
5

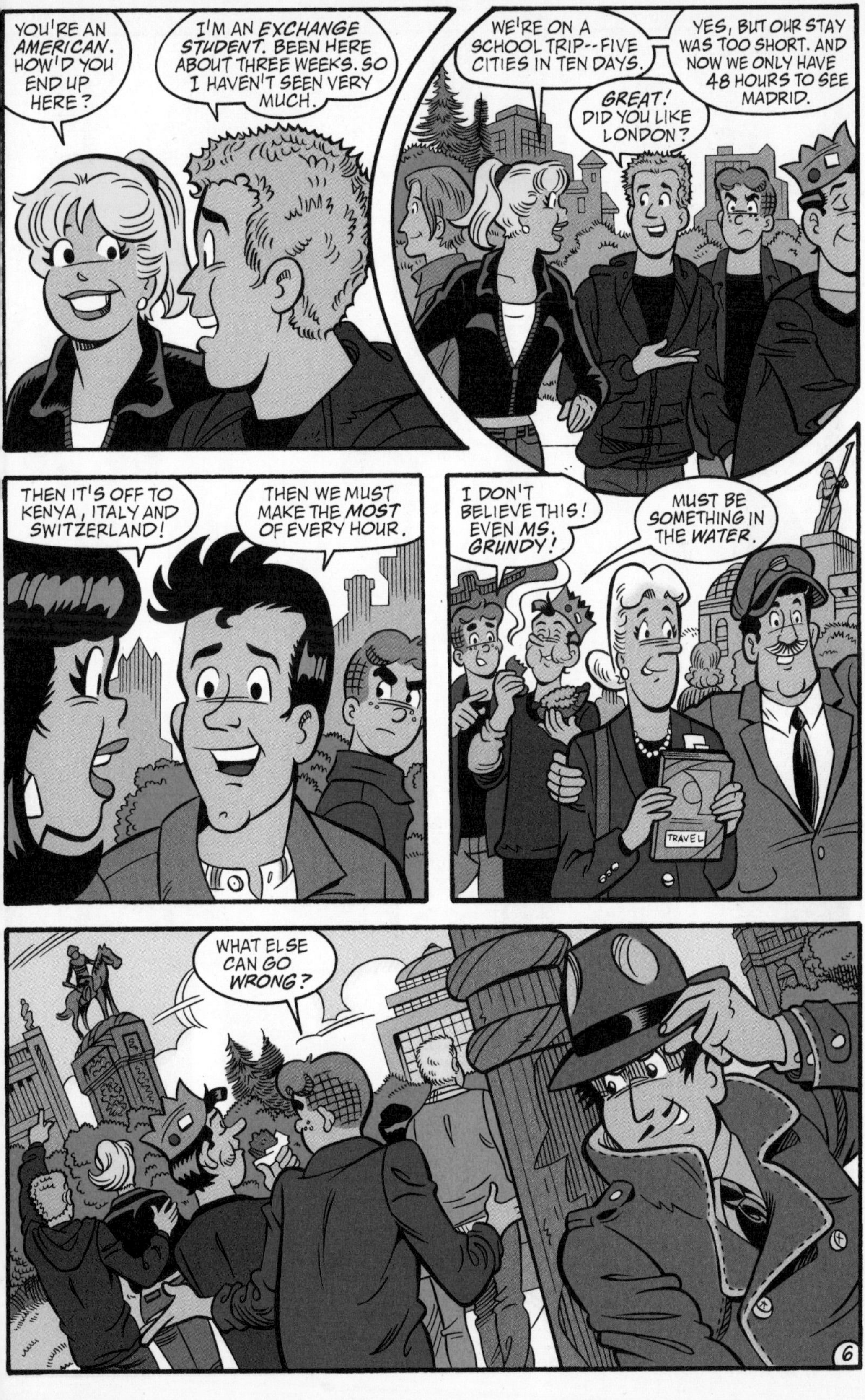
YOU'RE AN AMERICAN. HOW'D YOU END UP HERE?
I'M AN EXCHANGE STUDENT. BEEN HERE ABOUT THREE WEEKS. SO I HAVEN'T SEEN VERY MUCH.
WE'RE ON A SCHOOL TRIP--FIVE CITIES IN TEN DAYS.
YES, BUT OUR STAY WAS TOO SHORT. AND NOW WE ONLY HAVE 48 HOURS TO SEE MADRID.
GREAT! DID YOU LIKE LONDON?
THEN IT'S OFF TO KENYA, ITALY AND SWITZERLAND!
THEN WE MUST MAKE THE MOST OF EVERY HOUR.
I DON'T BELIEVE THIS! EVEN MS. GRUNDY!
MUST BE SOMETHING IN THE WATER.
TRAVEL
WHAT ELSE CAN GO WRONG?
6

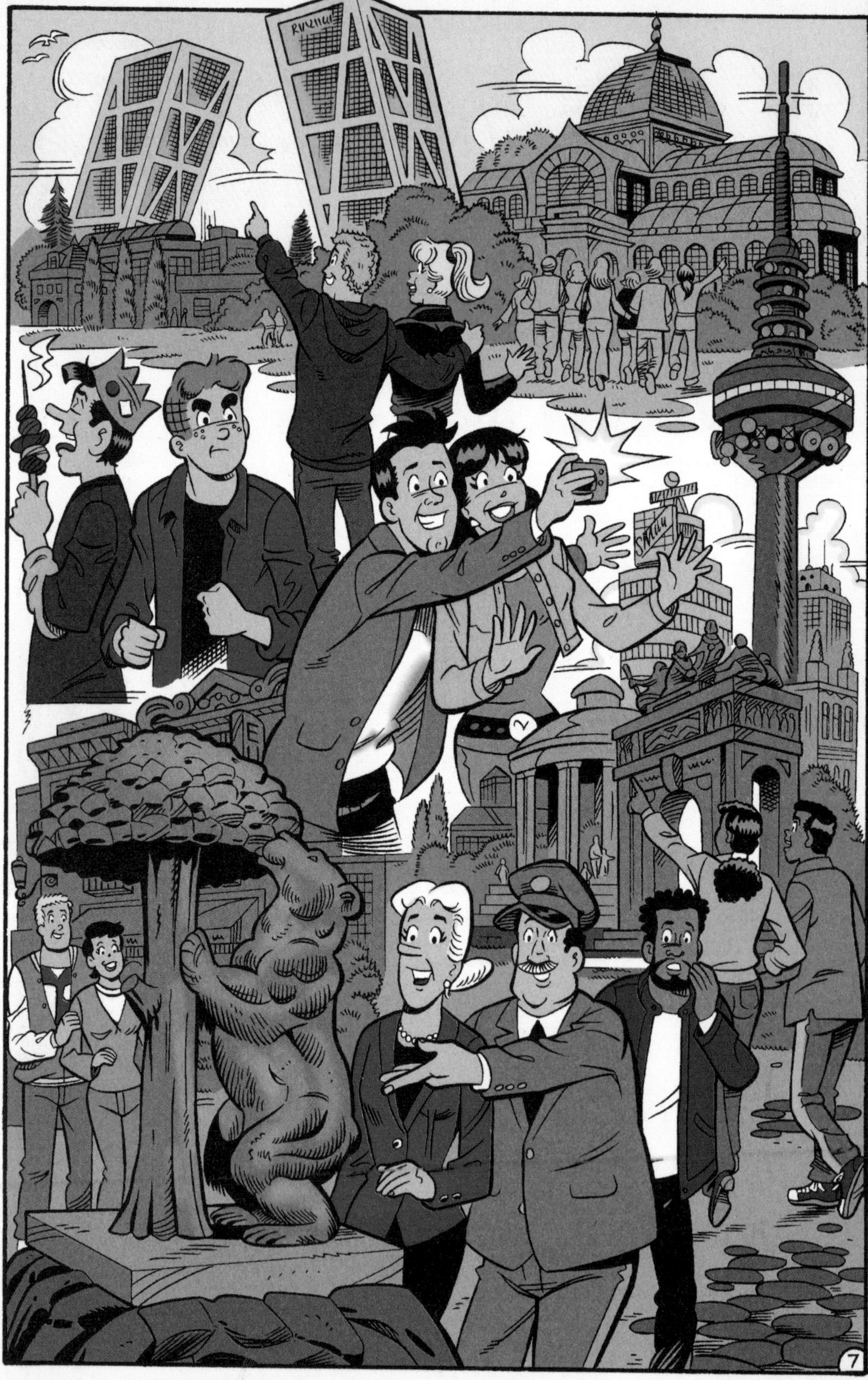

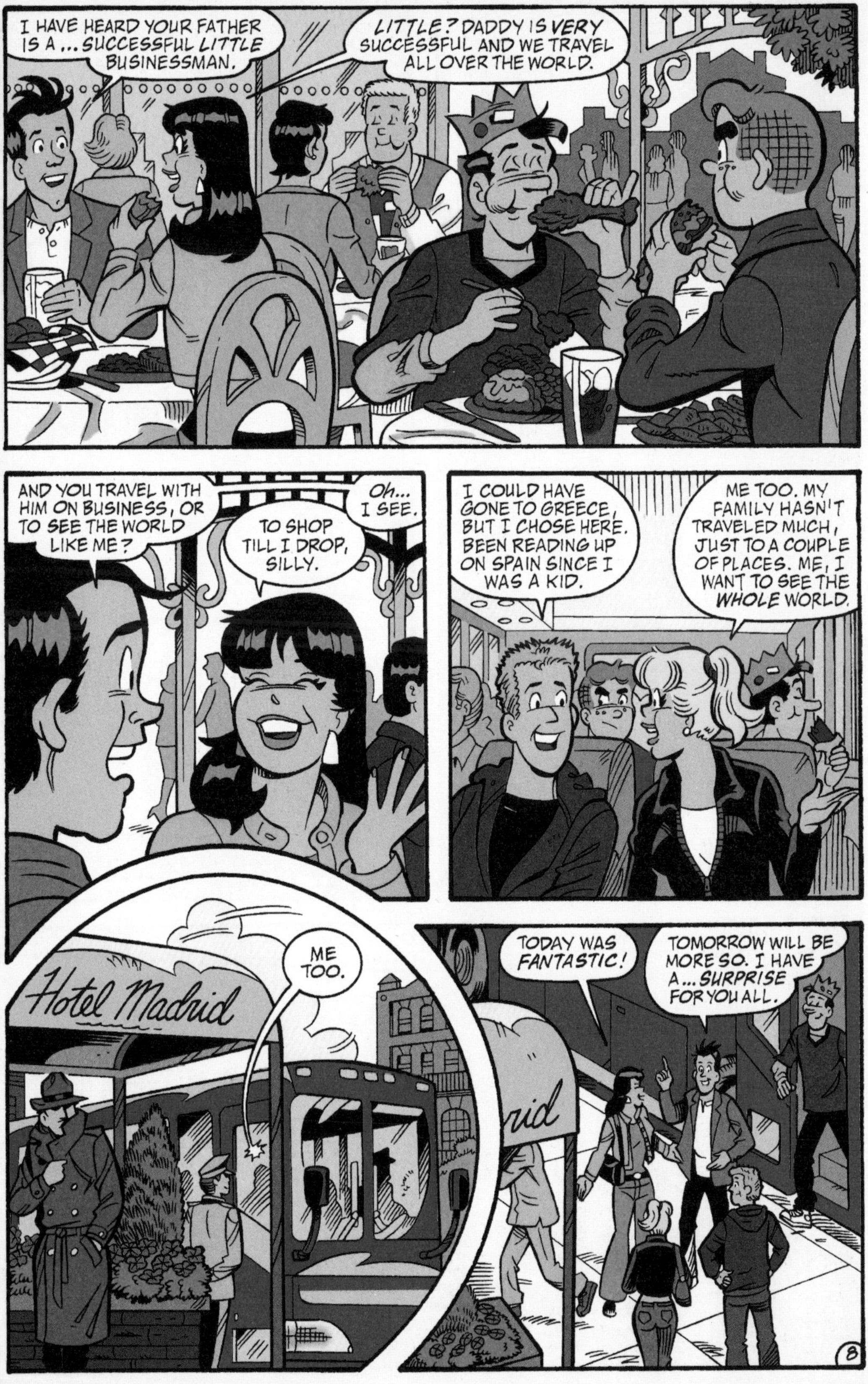
I HAVE HEARD YOUR FATHER IS A ... SUCCESSFUL LITTLE BUSINESSMAN.
LITTLE? DADDY IS VERY SUCCESSFUL AND WE TRAVEL ALL OVER THE WORLD.
AND YOU TRAVEL WITH HIM ON BUSINESS, OR TO SEE THE WORLD LIKE ME?
TO SHOP TILL I DROP, SILLY.
Oh... I SEE.
I COULD HAVE GONE TO GREECE, BUT I CHOSE HERE. BEEN READING UP ON SPAIN SINCE I WAS A KID.
ME TOO. MY FAMILY HASN'T TRAVELED MUCH, JUST TO A COUPLE OF PLACES. ME, I WANT TO SEE THE WHOLE WORLD.
Hotel Madrid
ME TOO.
TODAY WAS FANTASTIC!
TOMORROW WILL BE MORE SO. I HAVE A... SURPRISE FOR YOU ALL.
8

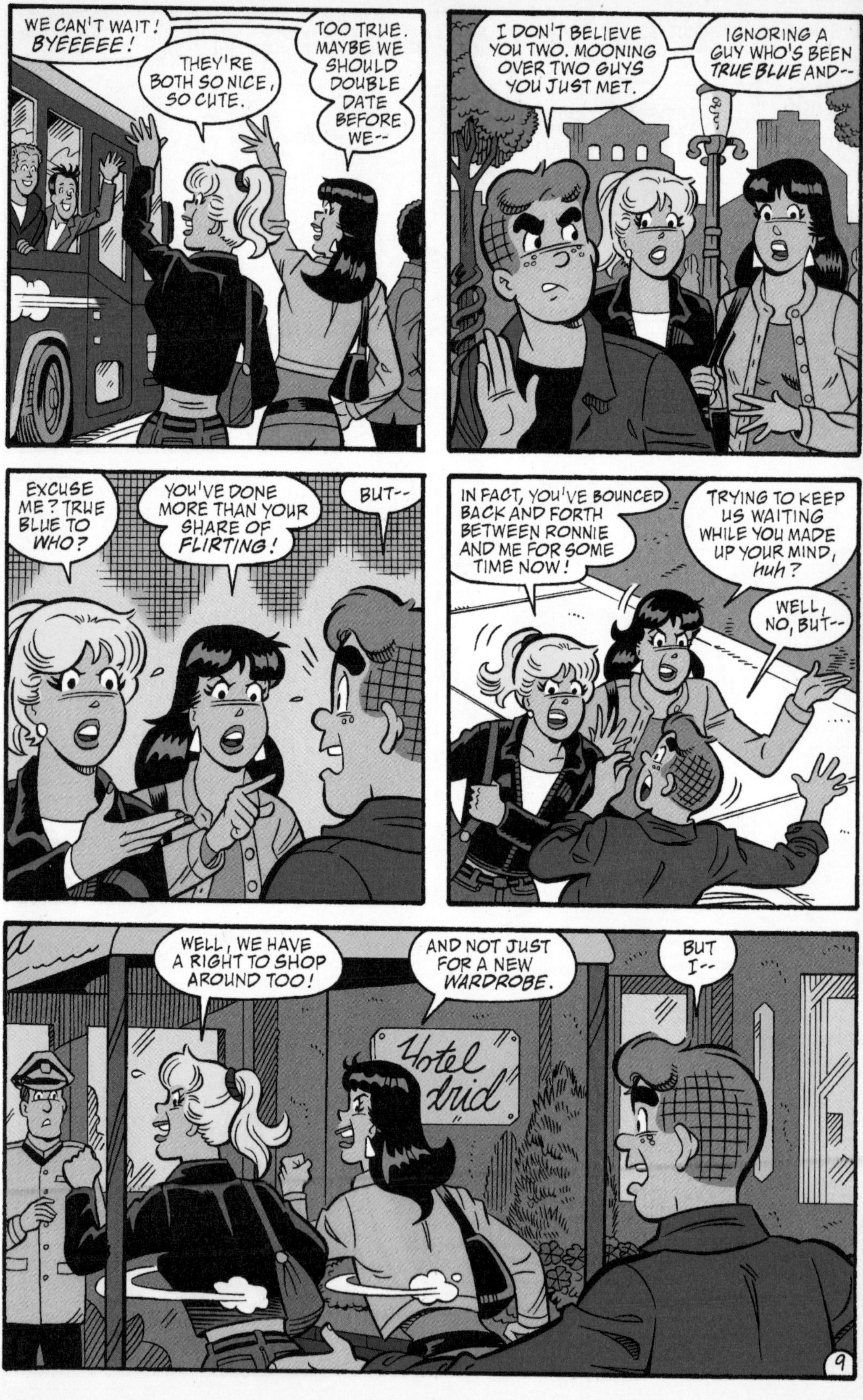
WE CAN'T WAIT! BYEEEEE!
THEY'RE BOTH SO NICE, SO CUTE.
TOO TRUE. MAYBE WE SHOULD DOUBLE DATE BEFORE WE--
I DON'T BELIEVE YOU TWO. MOONING OVER TWO GUYS YOU JUST MET.
IGNORING A GUY WHO'S BEEN TRUE BLUE AND--
EXCUSE ME? TRUE BLUE TO WHO?
YOU'VE DONE MORE THAN YOUR SHARE OF FLIRTING!
BUT--
IN FACT, YOU'VE BOUNCED BACK AND FORTH BETWEEN RONNIE AND ME FOR SOME TIME NOW!
TRYING TO KEEP US WAITING WHILE YOU MADE UP YOUR MIND, huh?
WELL, NO, BUT--
WELL, WE HAVE A RIGHT TO SHOP AROUND TOO!
AND NOT JUST FOR A NEW WARDROBE.
BUT I--
Hotel
drid
9

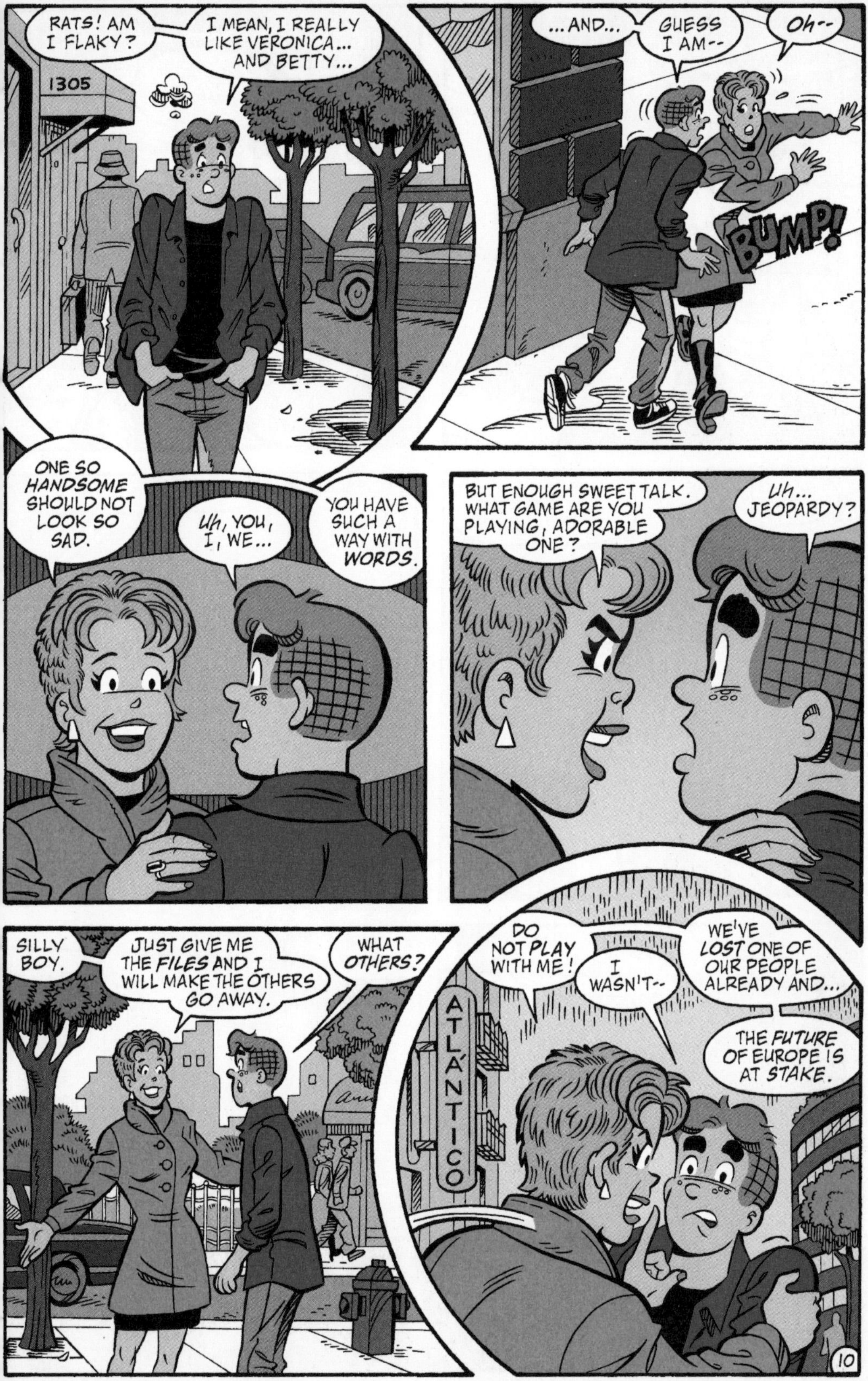
RATS! AM I FLAKY?
I MEAN, I REALLY LIKE VERONICA... AND BETTY...
1305
...AND...
GUESS I AM--
Oh--
BUMP!
ONE SO HANDSOME SHOULD NOT LOOK SO SAD.
Uh, YOU, I, WE...
YOU HAVE SUCH A WAY WITH WORDS.
BUT ENOUGH SWEET TALK. WHAT GAME ARE YOU PLAYING, ADORABLE ONE?
Uh... JEOPARDY?
SILLY BOY.
JUST GIVE ME THE FILES AND I WILL MAKE THE OTHERS GO AWAY.
WHAT OTHERS?
DO NOT PLAY WITH ME!
I WASN'T--
WE'VE LOST ONE OF OUR PEOPLE ALREADY AND...
THE FUTURE OF EUROPE IS AT STAKE.
ATLÁNTICO

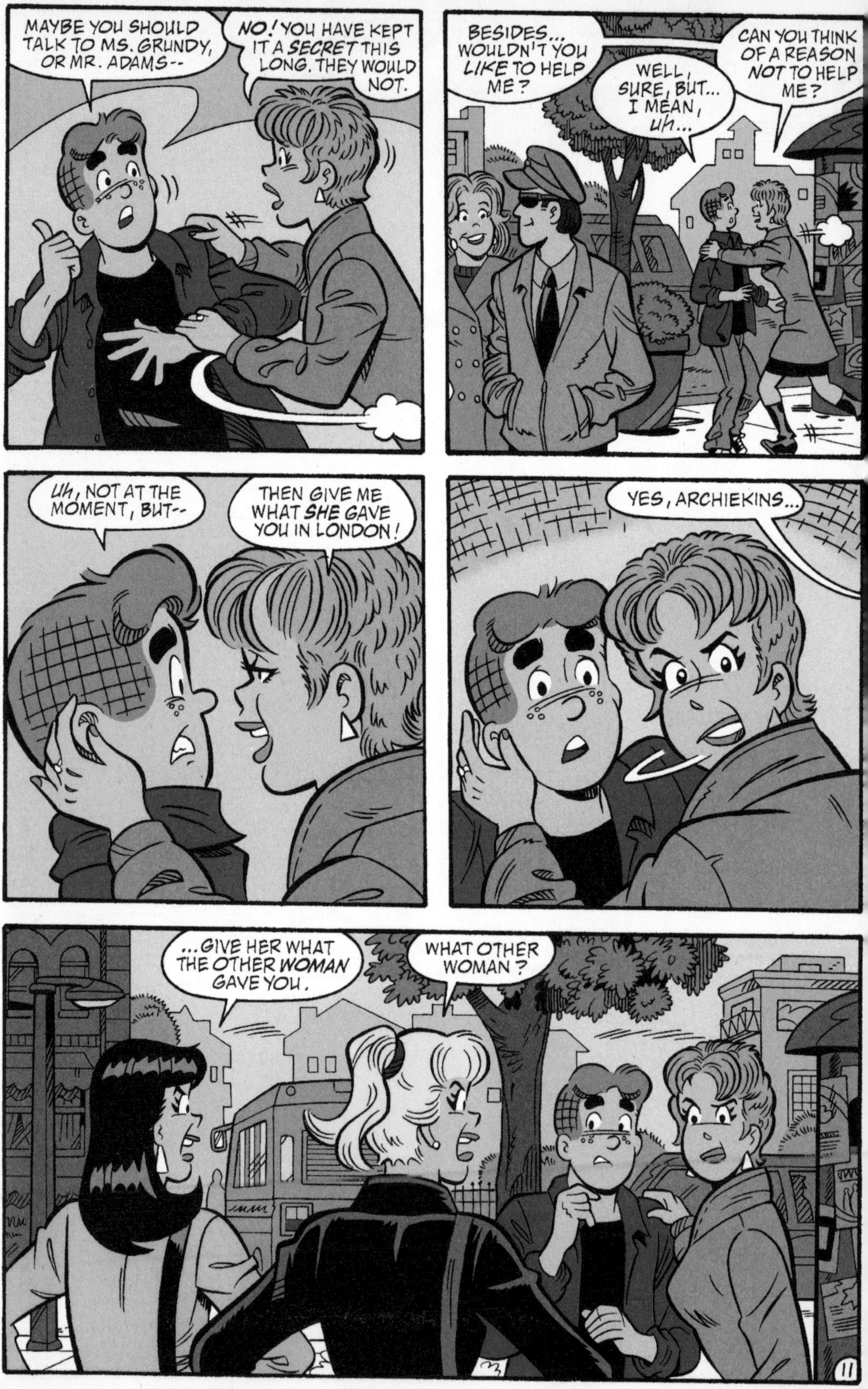

MAYBE YOU SHOULD TALK TO MS. GRUNDY, OR MR. ADAMS--
NO! YOU HAVE KEPT IT A SECRET THIS LONG. THEY WOULD NOT.
BESIDES... WOULDN'T YOU LIKE TO HELP ME?
WELL, SURE, BUT... I MEAN, UH...
CAN YOU THINK OF A REASON NOT TO HELP ME?
UH, NOT AT THE MOMENT, BUT--
THEN GIVE ME WHAT SHE GAVE YOU IN LONDON!
YES, ARCHIEKINS...
...GIVE HER WHAT THE OTHER WOMAN GAVE YOU.
WHAT OTHER WOMAN?

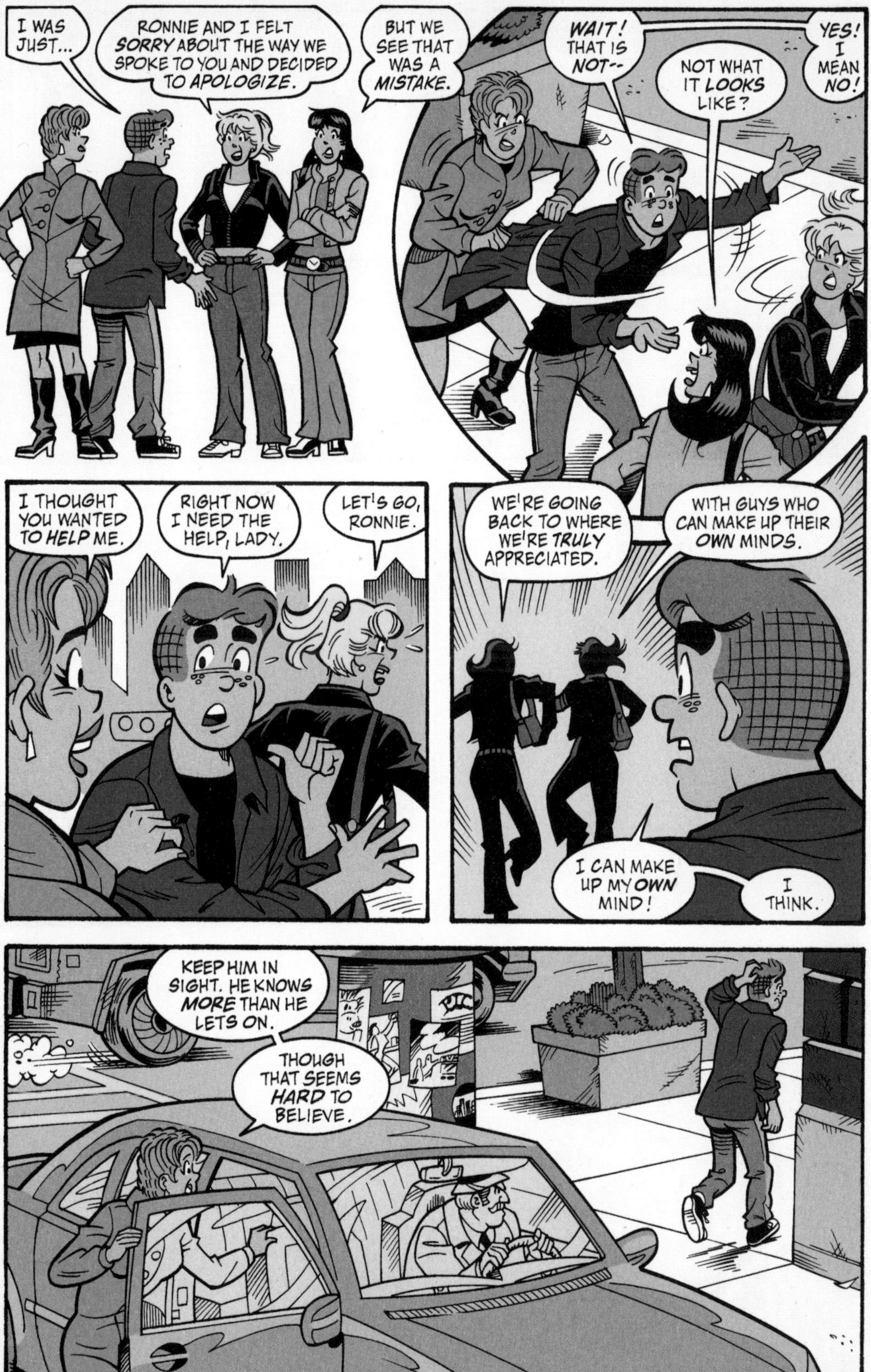
I WAS JUST...
RONNIE AND I FELT SORRY ABOUT THE WAY WE SPOKE TO YOU AND DECIDED TO APOLOGIZE.
BUT WE SEE THAT WAS A MISTAKE.
WAIT! THAT IS NOT--
NOT WHAT IT LOOKS LIKE?
YES! I MEAN NO!
I THOUGHT YOU WANTED TO HELP ME.
RIGHT NOW I NEED THE HELP, LADY.
LET'S GO, RONNIE.
WE'RE GOING BACK TO WHERE WE'RE TRULY APPRECIATED.
WITH GUYS WHO CAN MAKE UP THEIR OWN MINDS.
I CAN MAKE UP MY OWN MIND!
I THINK.
KEEP HIM IN SIGHT. HE KNOWS MORE THAN HE LETS ON.
THOUGH THAT SEEMS HARD TO BELIEVE.
12

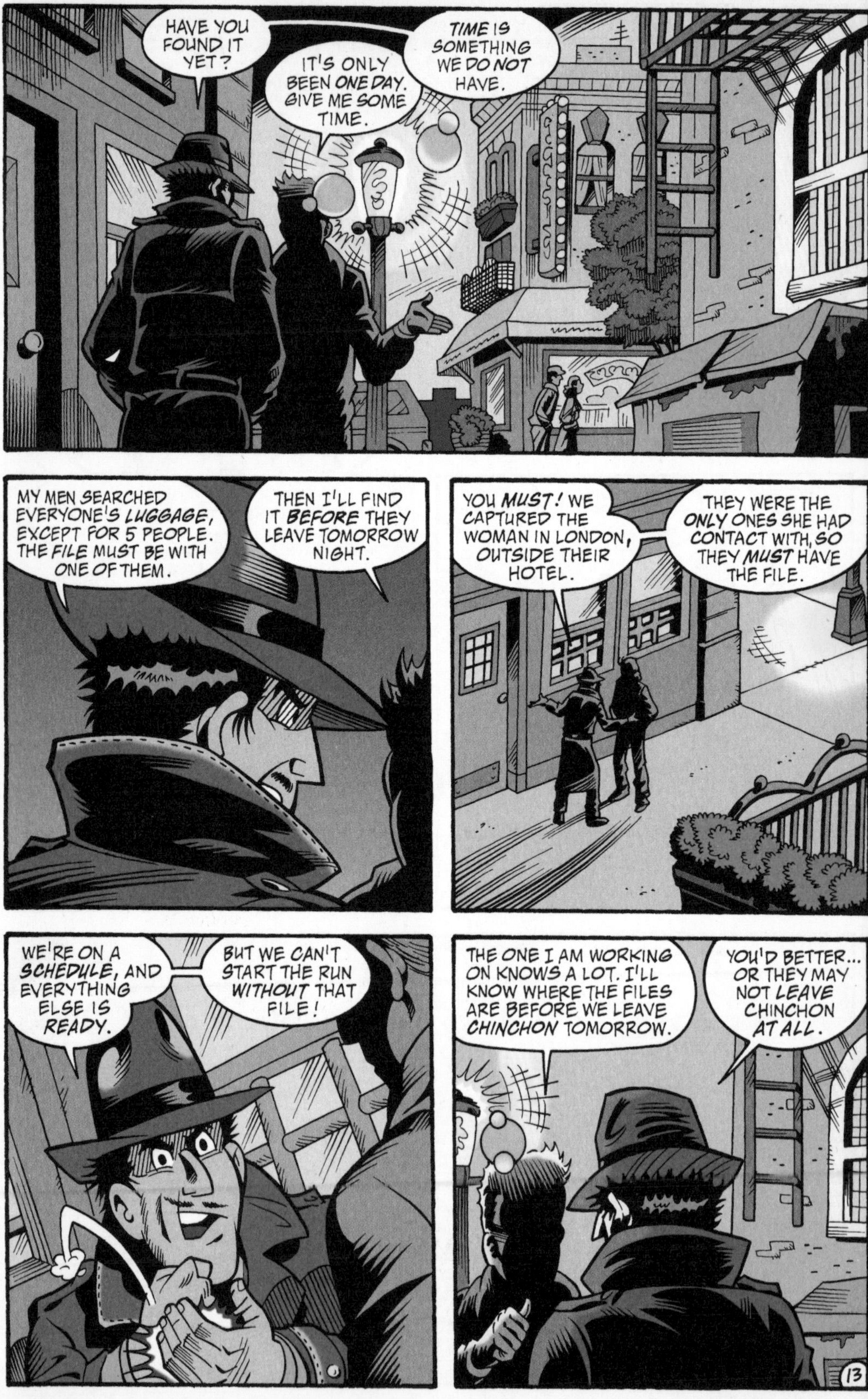
HAVE YOU FOUND IT YET?
IT'S ONLY BEEN ONE DAY. GIVE ME SOME TIME.
TIME IS SOMETHING WE DO NOT HAVE.
MY MEN SEARCHED EVERYONE'S LUGGAGE, EXCEPT FOR 5 PEOPLE. THE FILE MUST BE WITH ONE OF THEM.
THEN I'LL FIND IT BEFORE THEY LEAVE TOMORROW NIGHT.
YOU MUST! WE CAPTURED THE WOMAN IN LONDON, OUTSIDE THEIR HOTEL.
THEY WERE THE ONLY ONES SHE HAD CONTACT WITH, SO THEY MUST HAVE THE FILE.
WE'RE ON A SCHEDULE, AND EVERYTHING ELSE IS READY.
BUT WE CAN'T START THE RUN WITHOUT THAT FILE!
THE ONE I AM WORKING ON KNOWS A LOT. I'LL KNOW WHERE THE FILES ARE BEFORE WE LEAVE CHINCHON TOMORROW.
YOU'D BETTER... OR THEY MAY NOT LEAVE CHINCHON AT ALL.

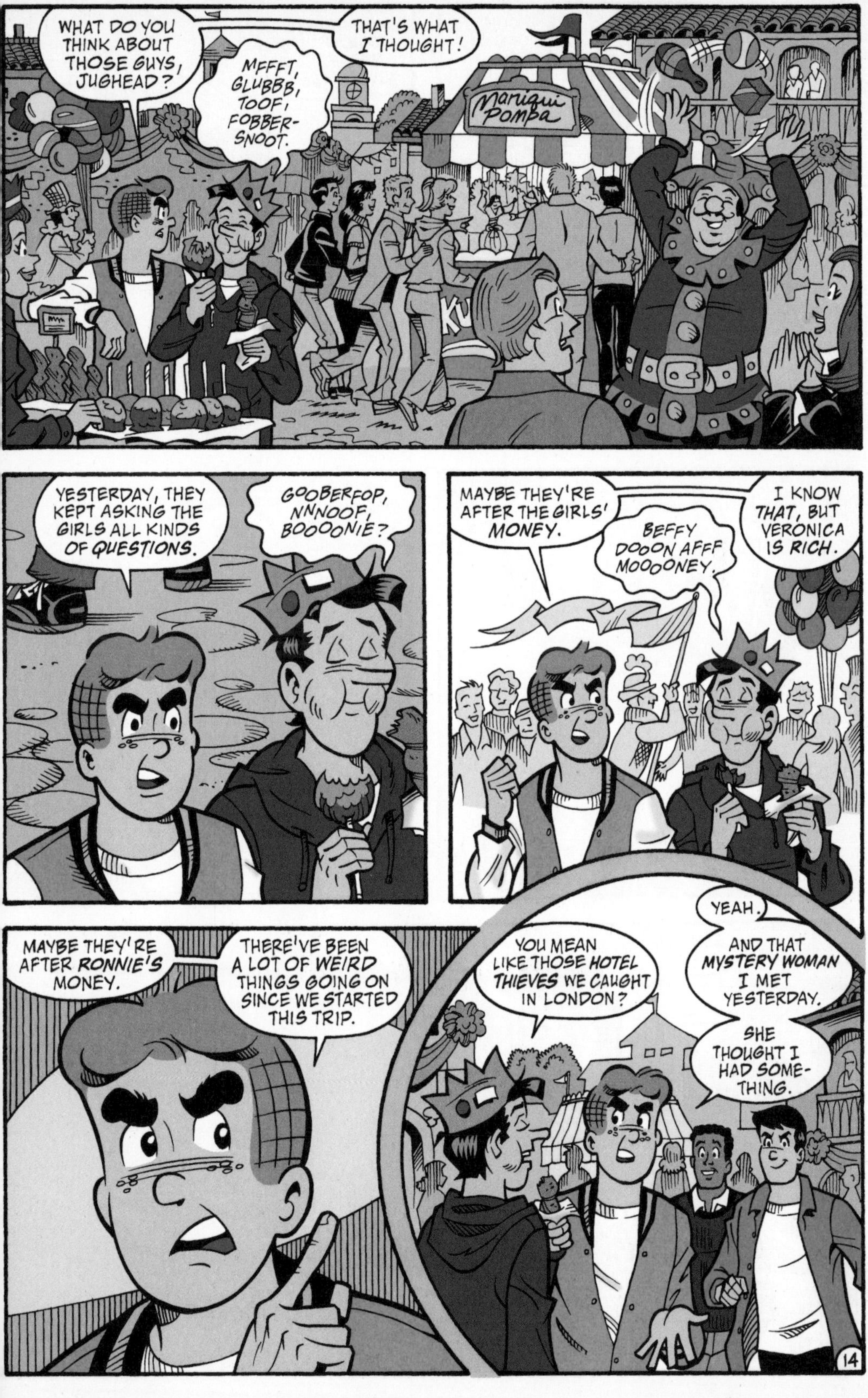

WHAT DO YOU THINK ABOUT THOSE GUYS, JUGHEAD?
MFFFT, GLUBBB, TOOF, FOBBER-SNOOT.
THAT'S WHAT I THOUGHT!
Mariqui Pomba
YESTERDAY, THEY KEPT ASKING THE GIRLS ALL KINDS OF QUESTIONS.
GOOBERFOP, NNNOOF, BOOOONIE?
MAYBE THEY'RE AFTER THE GIRLS' MONEY.
BEFFY DOOON AFFF MOOOONEY.
I KNOW THAT, BUT VERONICA IS RICH.
MAYBE THEY'RE AFTER RONNIE'S MONEY.
THERE'VE BEEN A LOT OF WEIRD THINGS GOING ON SINCE WE STARTED THIS TRIP.
YOU MEAN LIKE THOSE HOTEL THIEVES WE CAUGHT IN LONDON?
YEAH.
AND THAT MYSTERY WOMAN I MET YESTERDAY.
SHE THOUGHT I HAD SOME-THING.

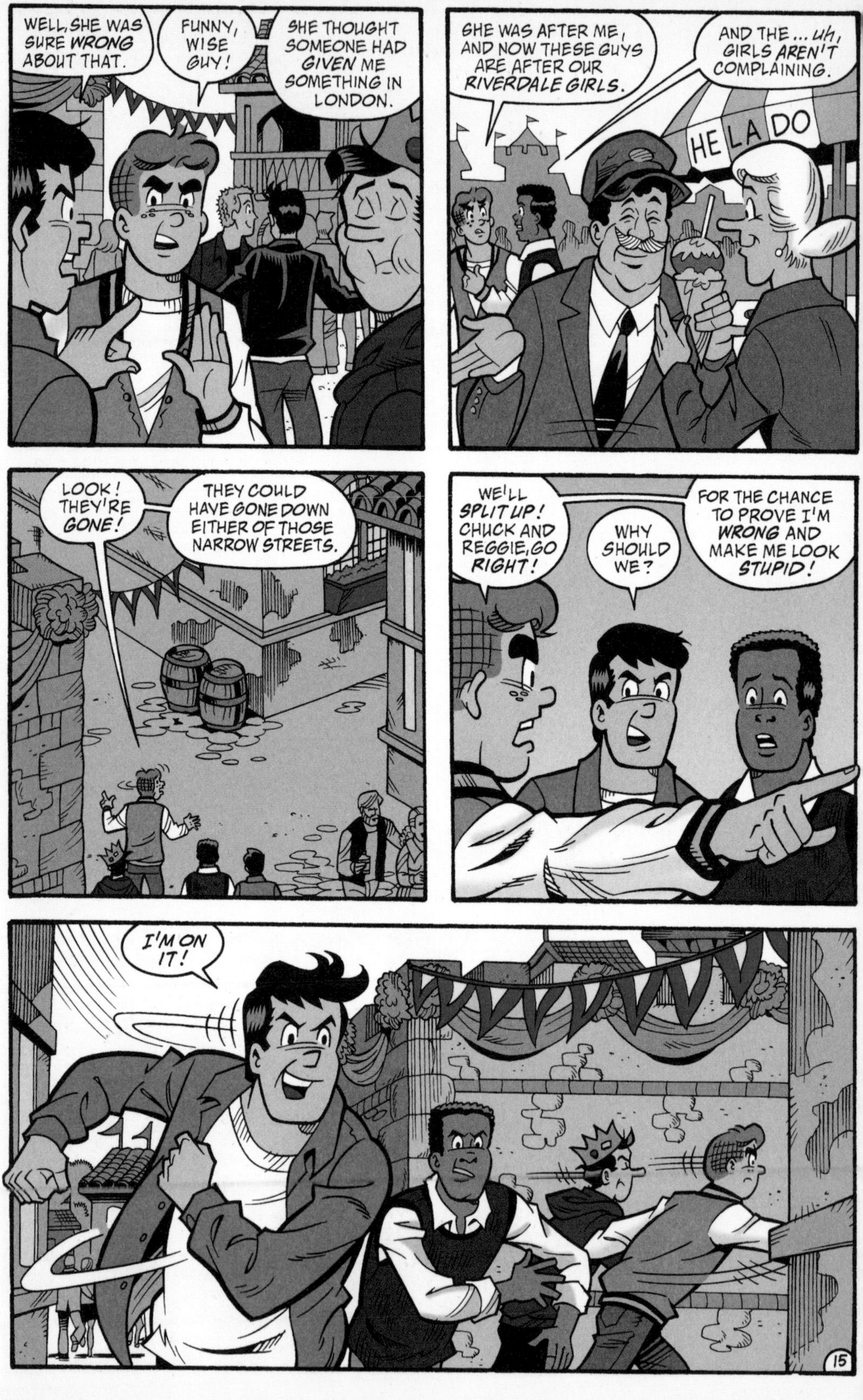

WELL, SHE WAS SURE WRONG ABOUT THAT.
FUNNY, WISE GUY!
SHE THOUGHT SOMEONE HAD GIVEN ME SOMETHING IN LONDON.
SHE WAS AFTER ME, AND NOW THESE GUYS ARE AFTER OUR RIVERDALE GIRLS.
AND THE ... uh, GIRLS AREN'T COMPLAINING.
HELADO
LOOK! THEY'RE GONE!
THEY COULD HAVE GONE DOWN EITHER OF THOSE NARROW STREETS.
WE'LL SPLIT UP! CHUCK AND REGGIE, GO RIGHT!
WHY SHOULD WE?
FOR THE CHANCE TO PROVE I'M WRONG AND MAKE ME LOOK STUPID!
I'M ON IT!

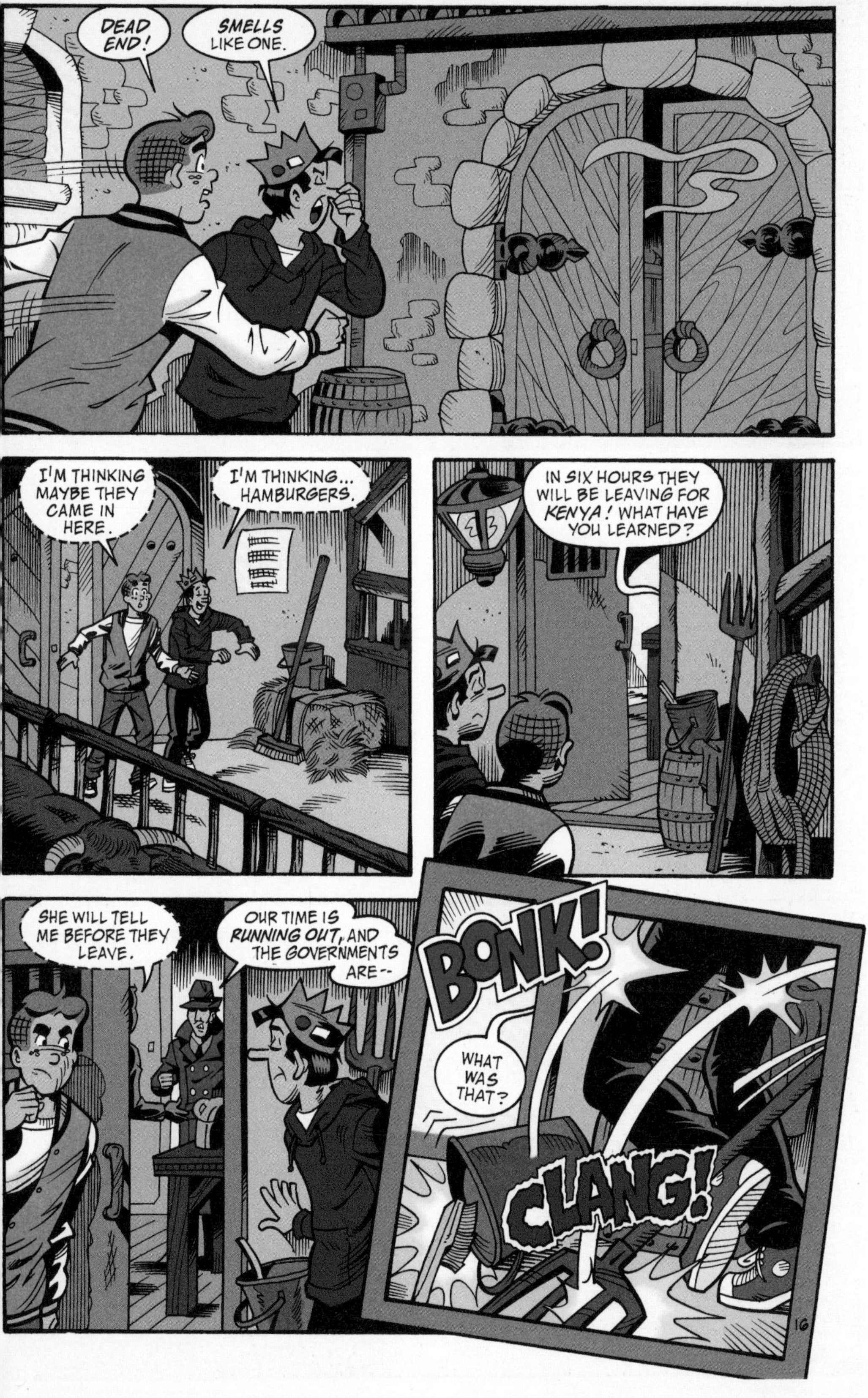
DEAD END!
SMELLS LIKE ONE.
I'M THINKING MAYBE THEY CAME IN HERE.
I'M THINKING... HAMBURGERS.
IN SIX HOURS THEY WILL BE LEAVING FOR KENYA! WHAT HAVE YOU LEARNED?
SHE WILL TELL ME BEFORE THEY LEAVE.
OUR TIME IS RUNNING OUT, AND THE GOVERNMENTS ARE--
BONK!
WHAT WAS THAT?
CLANG!
16

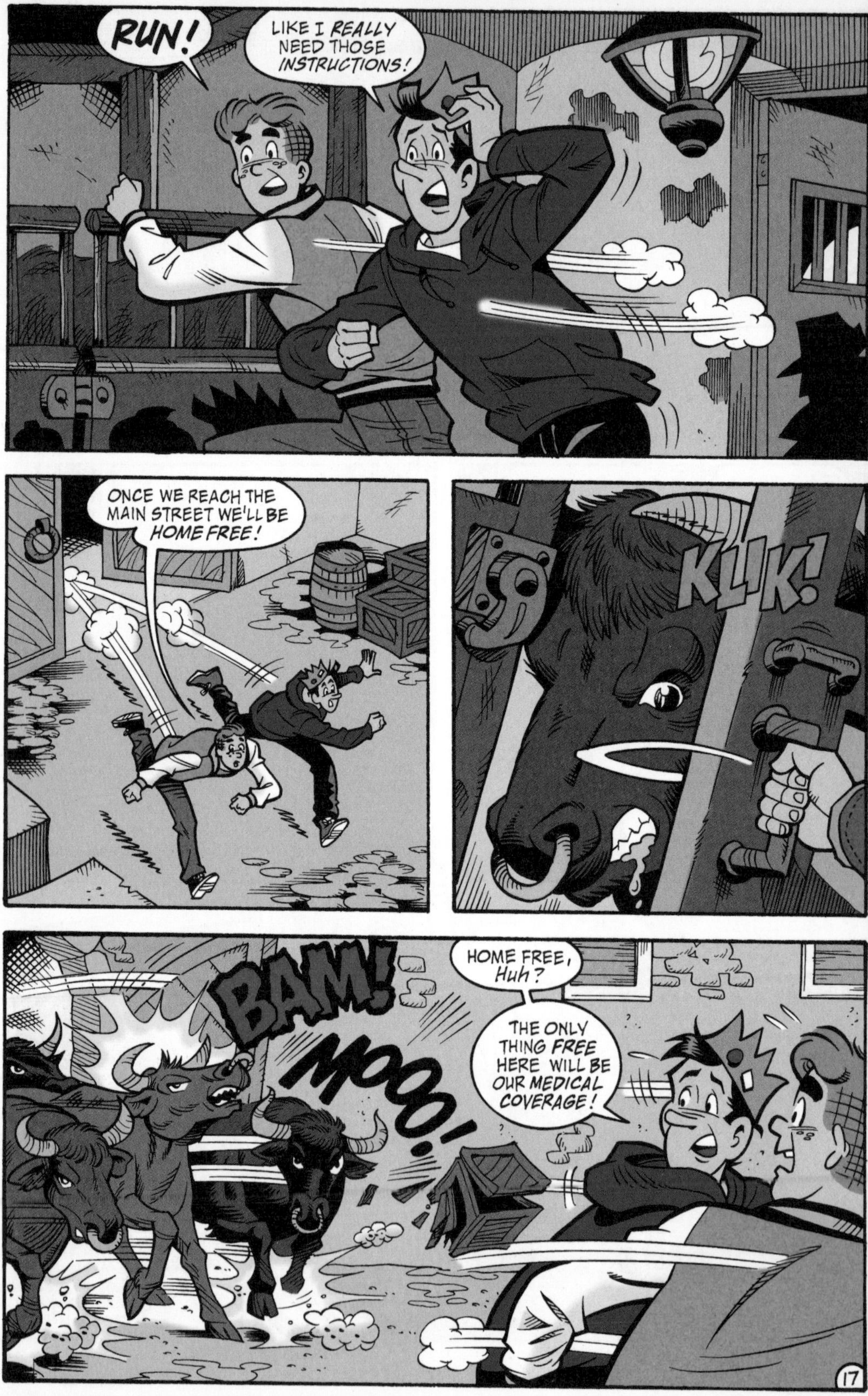
RUN!
LIKE I REALLY NEED THOSE INSTRUCTIONS!
ONCE WE REACH THE MAIN STREET WE'LL BE HOME FREE!
KLIK!
BAM!
MOOO!
HOME FREE, Huh?
THE ONLY THING FREE HERE WILL BE OUR MEDICAL COVERAGE!

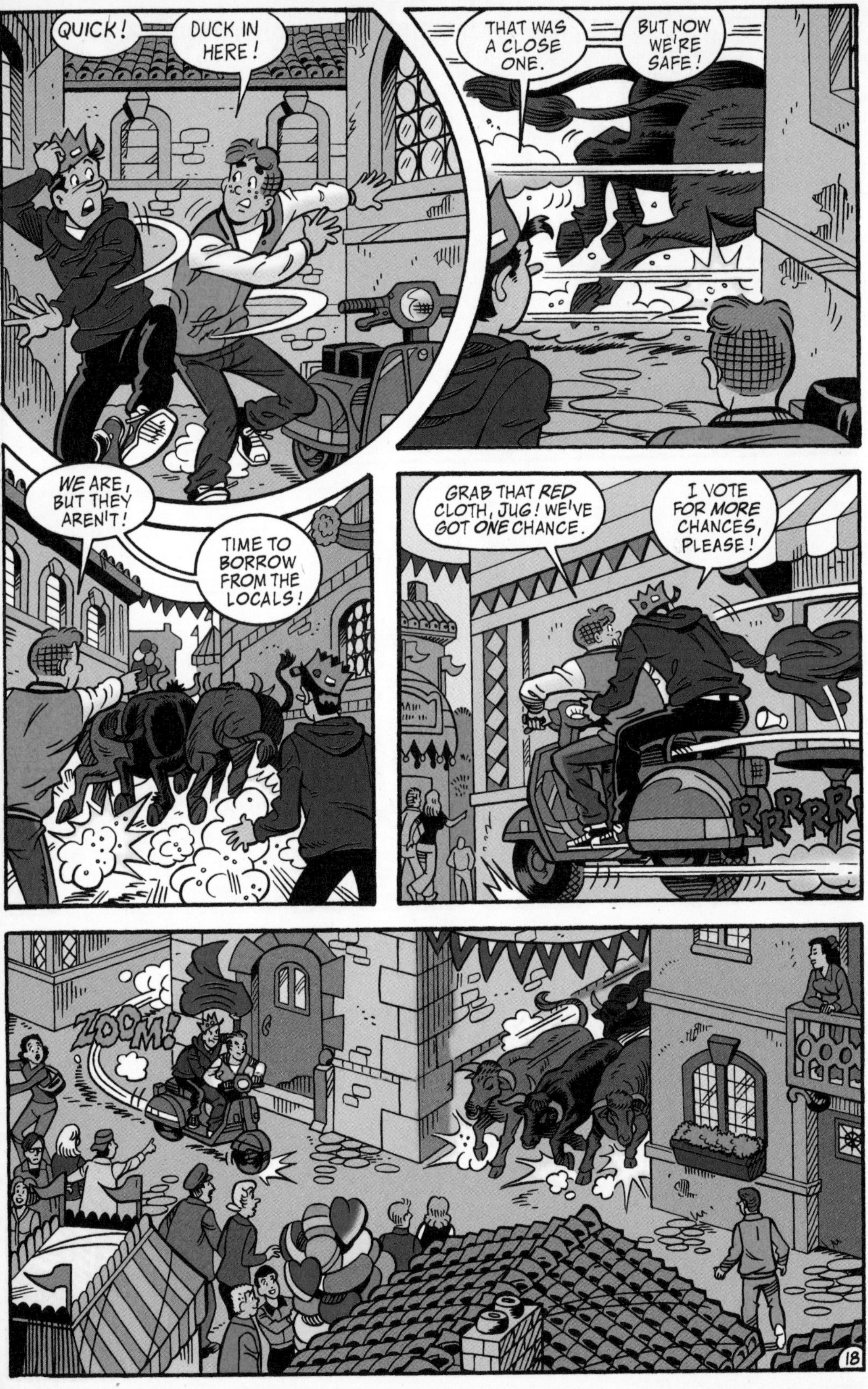

QUICK!
DUCK IN HERE!
THAT WAS A CLOSE ONE.
BUT NOW WE'RE SAFE!
WE ARE, BUT THEY AREN'T!
TIME TO BORROW FROM THE LOCALS!
GRAB THAT RED CLOTH, JUG! WE'VE GOT ONE CHANCE.
I VOTE FOR MORE CHANCES, PLEASE!
RRRRR
ZOOM!

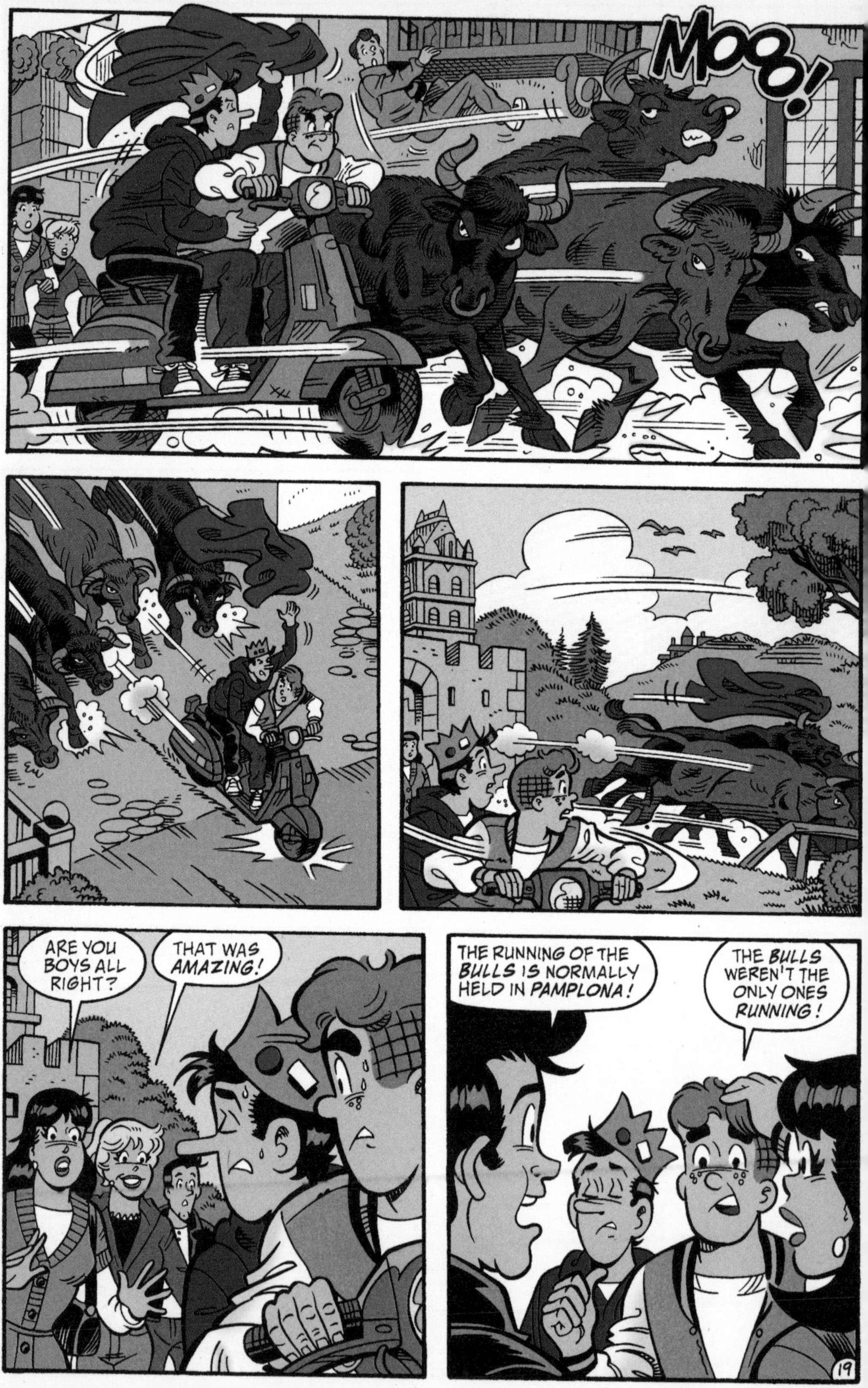
MOO!
ARE YOU BOYS ALL RIGHT?
THAT WAS AMAZING!
THE RUNNING OF THE BULLS IS NORMALLY HELD IN PAMPLONA!
THE BULLS WEREN'T THE ONLY ONES RUNNING!
19

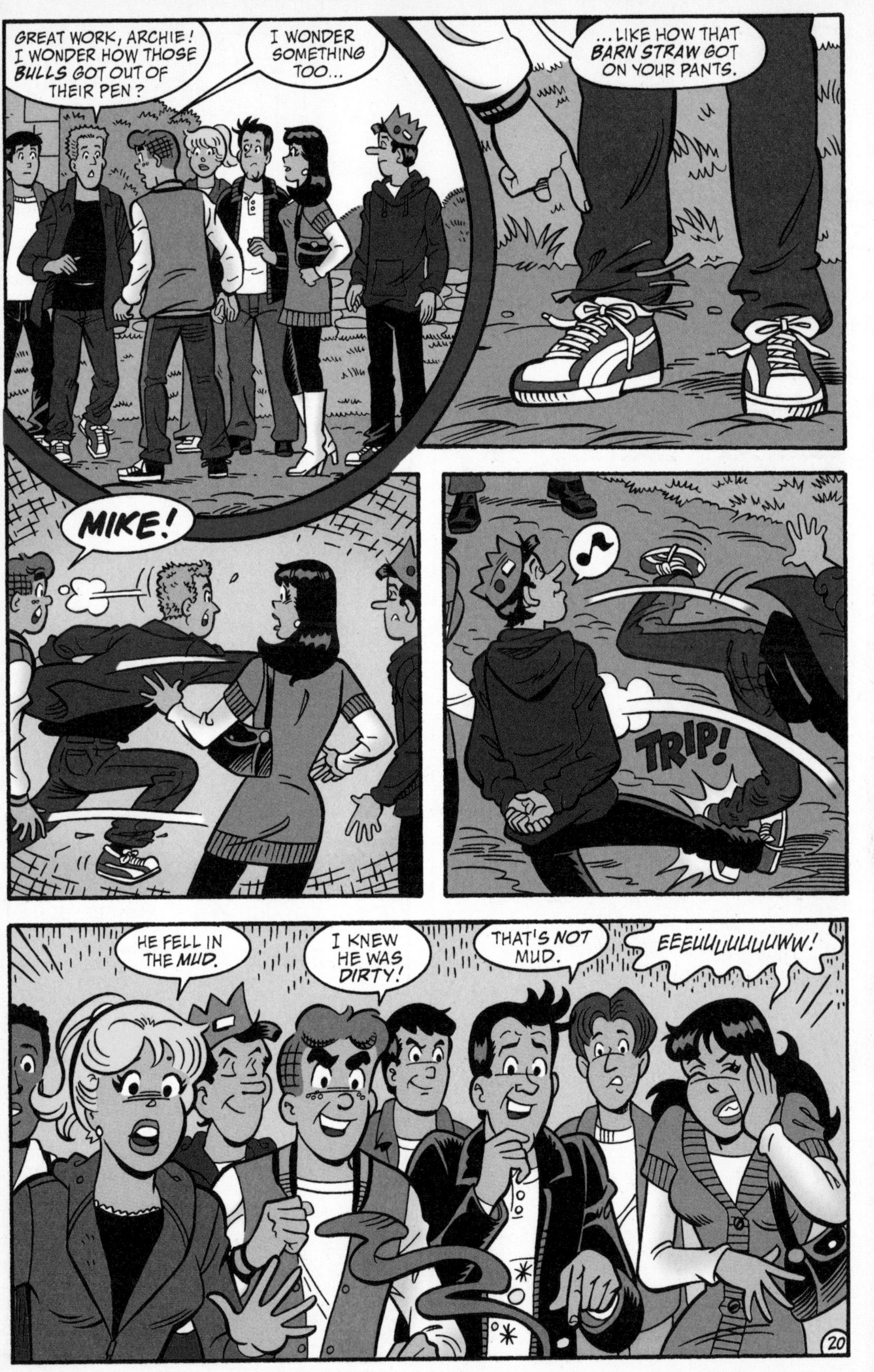
GREAT WORK, ARCHIE! I WONDER HOW THOSE BULLS GOT OUT OF THEIR PEN?
I WONDER SOMETHING TOO...
...LIKE HOW THAT BARN STRAW GOT ON YOUR PANTS.
MIKE!
TRIP!
HE FELL IN THE MUD.
I KNEW HE WAS DIRTY!
THAT'S NOT MUD.
EEEUUUUUUUWW!

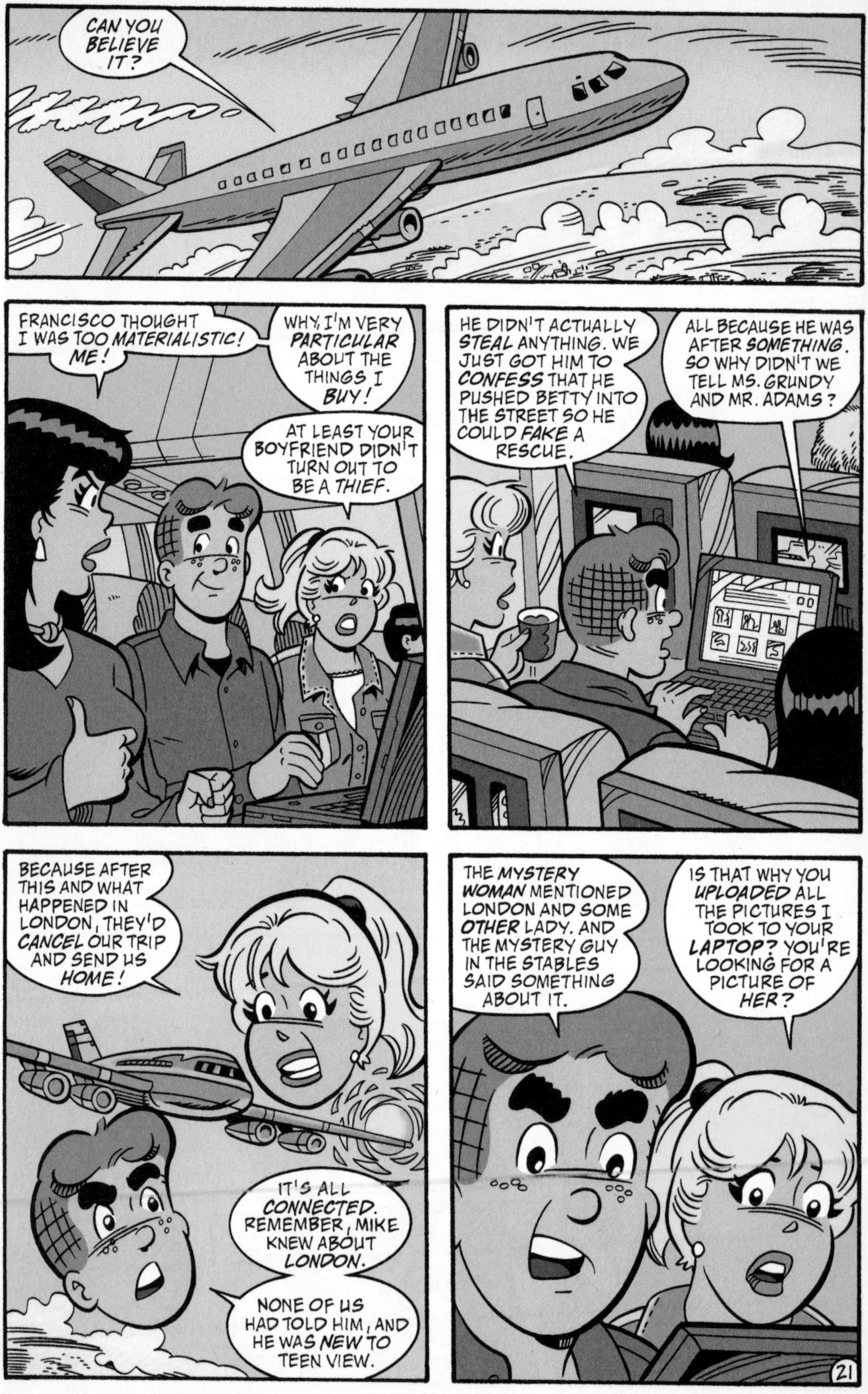
CAN YOU BELIEVE IT?
FRANCISCO THOUGHT I WAS TOO MATERIALISTIC! ME!
WHY, I'M VERY PARTICULAR ABOUT THE THINGS I BUY!
AT LEAST YOUR BOYFRIEND DIDN'T TURN OUT TO BE A THIEF.
HE DIDN'T ACTUALLY STEAL ANYTHING. WE JUST GOT HIM TO CONFESS THAT HE PUSHED BETTY INTO THE STREET SO HE COULD FAKE A RESCUE.
ALL BECAUSE HE WAS AFTER SOMETHING. SO WHY DIDN'T WE TELL MS. GRUNDY AND MR. ADAMS?
BECAUSE AFTER THIS AND WHAT HAPPENED IN LONDON, THEY'D CANCEL OUR TRIP AND SEND US HOME!
IT'S ALL CONNECTED. REMEMBER, MIKE KNEW ABOUT LONDON.
NONE OF US HAD TOLD HIM, AND HE WAS NEW TO TEEN VIEW.
THE MYSTERY WOMAN MENTIONED LONDON AND SOME OTHER LADY. AND THE MYSTERY GUY IN THE STABLES SAID SOMETHING ABOUT IT.
IS THAT WHY YOU UPLOADED ALL THE PICTURES I TOOK TO YOUR LAPTOP? YOU'RE LOOKING FOR A PICTURE OF HER?
21

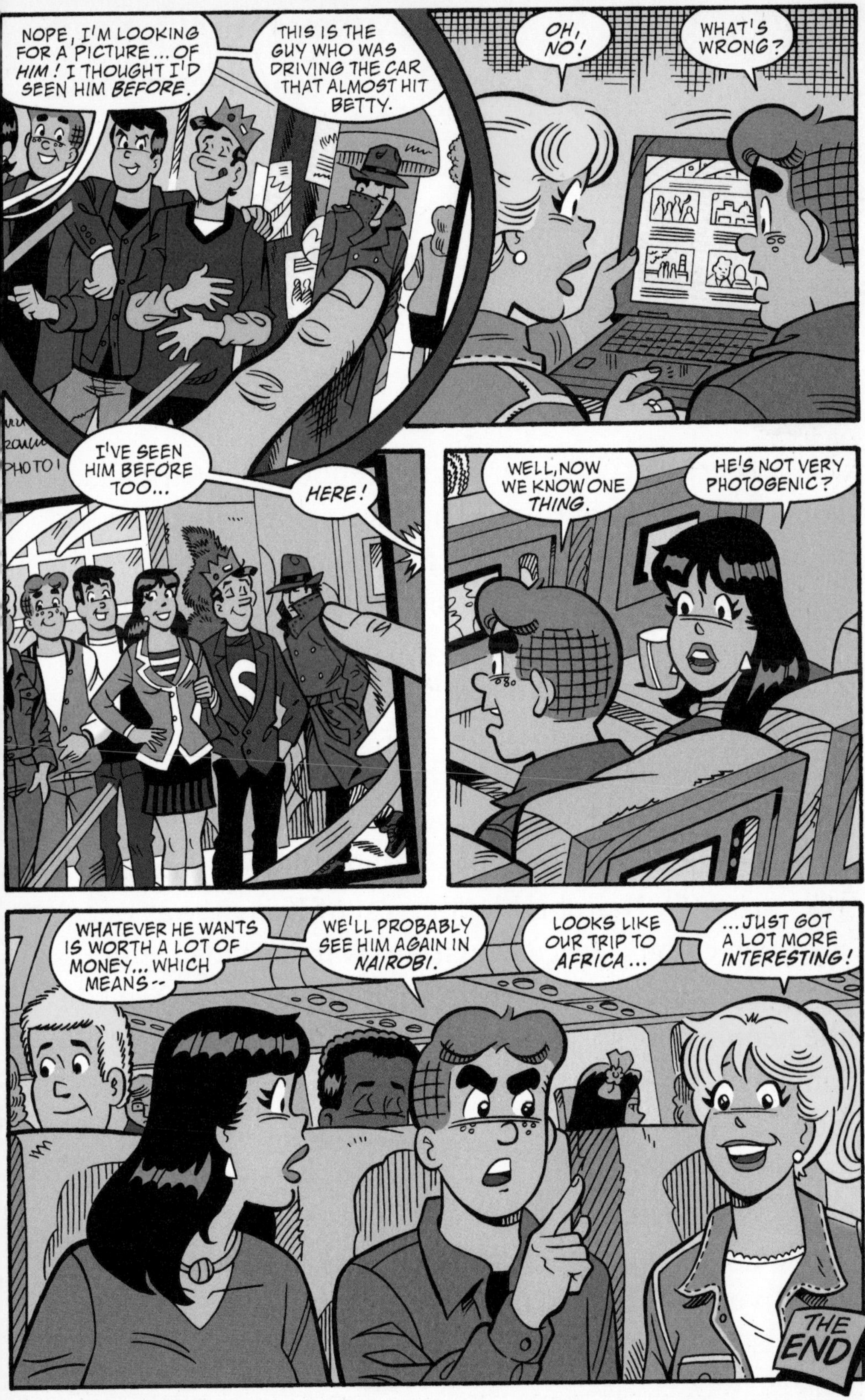
NOPE, I'M LOOKING FOR A PICTURE... OF HIM! I THOUGHT I'D SEEN HIM BEFORE.
THIS IS THE GUY WHO WAS DRIVING THE CAR THAT ALMOST HIT BETTY.
OH, NO!
WHAT'S WRONG?
I'VE SEEN HIM BEFORE TOO...
HERE!
WELL, NOW WE KNOW ONE THING.
HE'S NOT VERY PHOTOGENIC?
WHATEVER HE WANTS IS WORTH A LOT OF MONEY... WHICH MEANS--
WE'LL PROBABLY SEE HIM AGAIN IN NAIROBI.
LOOKS LIKE OUR TRIP TO AFRICA...
...JUST GOT A LOT MORE INTERESTING!
THE END

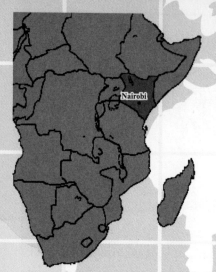
Nairobi

Location: Nairobi, Kenya
Continent: Africa
Population: 3,138,000
Size: 696 square km
Spoken Languages:
Swahili, English

There is a common misconception that Africa is a country. This is not true. Africa is a continent comprised of many countries, each diverse and unique in their own ways. They have some commonalities but feature varying beliefs, cultures and governing rule. One such country is Kenya, and its capital is Nairobi.

Welcome to Nairobi, the capital of Kenya!

Nairobi is a young city, with its history dating back to 1899. Nairobi, like the rest of Kenya, was once a British colony. Since declaring its independence in 1963, Nairobi has been the capital of Kenya. In Nairobi the people may speak English or Swahili, a native Bantu language. Nairobi is known as "The Green City in the Sun."

With their new guide and cultural expert Pios, Archie, Betty, Veronica, Reggie, Jughead and the rest of the Riverdale High teens experience all of the sites and sounds (and tastes!) Nairobi has to offer!

During their journey in Nairobi, the first stop is the Uhuru Monument. "Uhuru" is the Swahili word for "Freedom". The Uhuru Monument was built to celebrate the nation's independence. In addition to the Uhuru Monument, Archie and the Gang visit a ton of other sites including the Nairobi Museum and the Nairobi Zoo.

The Nairobi Museum features a wealth of information and plenty of educational experiences. The artwork, the materials used in the fabrication of outdoor sculptures, the landscaping and the botanic gardens link to the three pillars of Kenya's national heritage: nature, culture and history. Under the nature pillar, there are 5 exhibits: Human Origins, Mammalian Radiation, Ecology of Kenya, Natural Diversity and Geology. Culture has three exhibits: Cycles of Life, Cultural Dynamism and Creativity. History has two exhibits: Kenya Before 1850 and History of Kenya.

The Nairobi Zoo is an especially popular family attraction and contains plenty of exotic animals from all over Africa. Many animals commonly associated with the African savanna are located at the zoo, such as giraffes and lions, as well as crocodiles and countless other species. The zoo is also host to several rare animal species including the Vervet monkey.

Archie®
WORLD TOUR

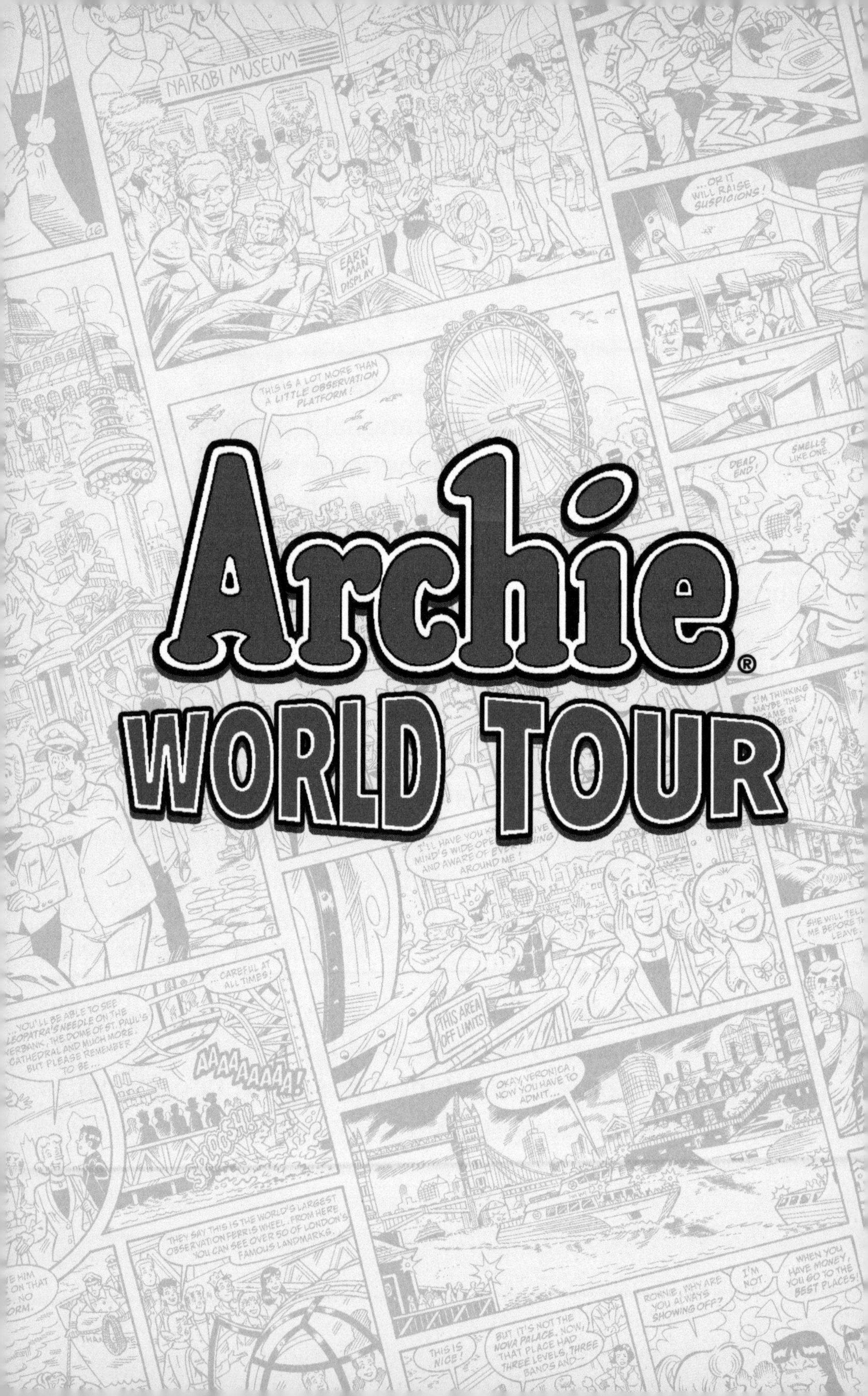

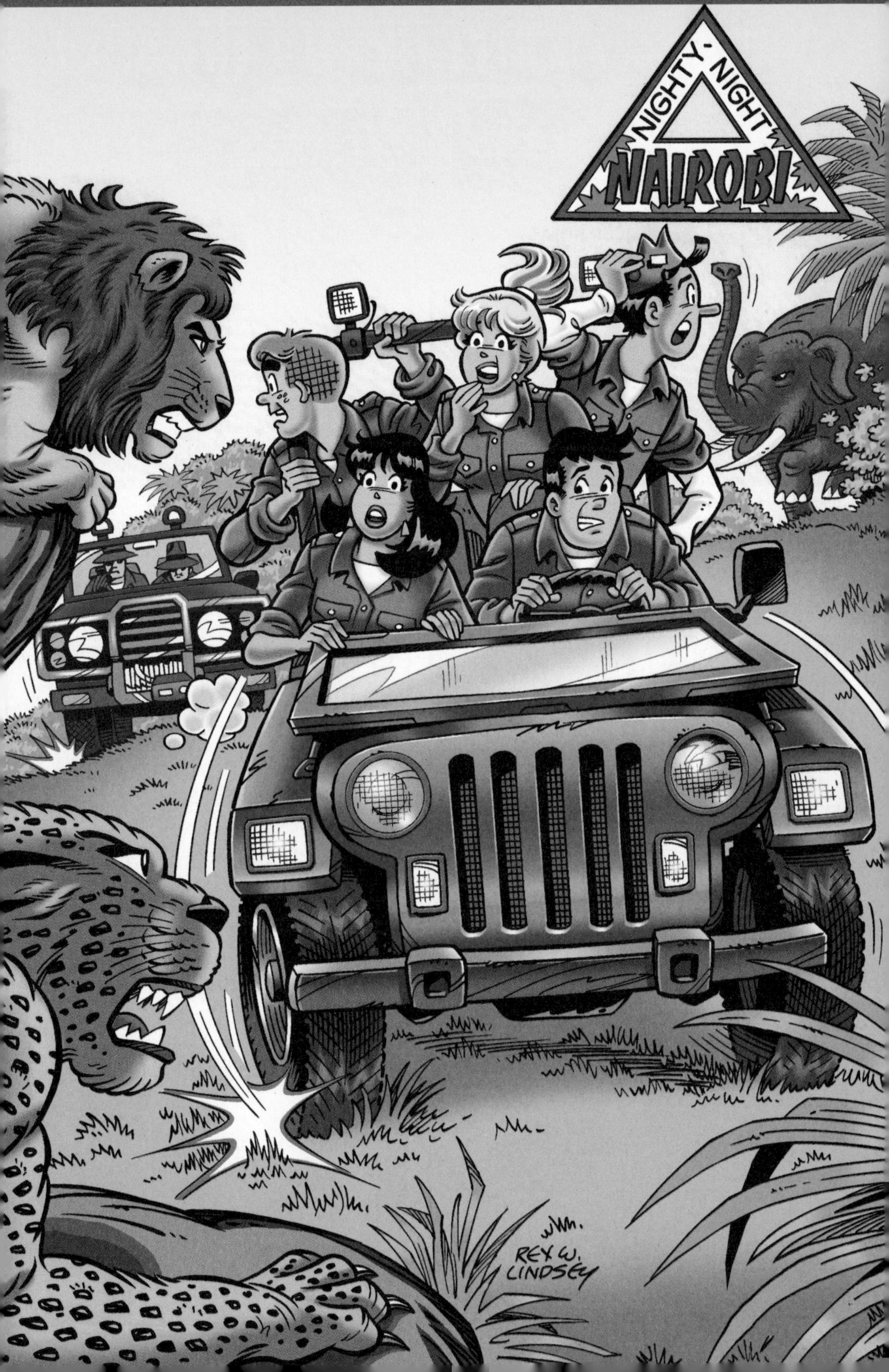
NIGHTY-NIGHT
NAIROBI
REX W. LINDSEY

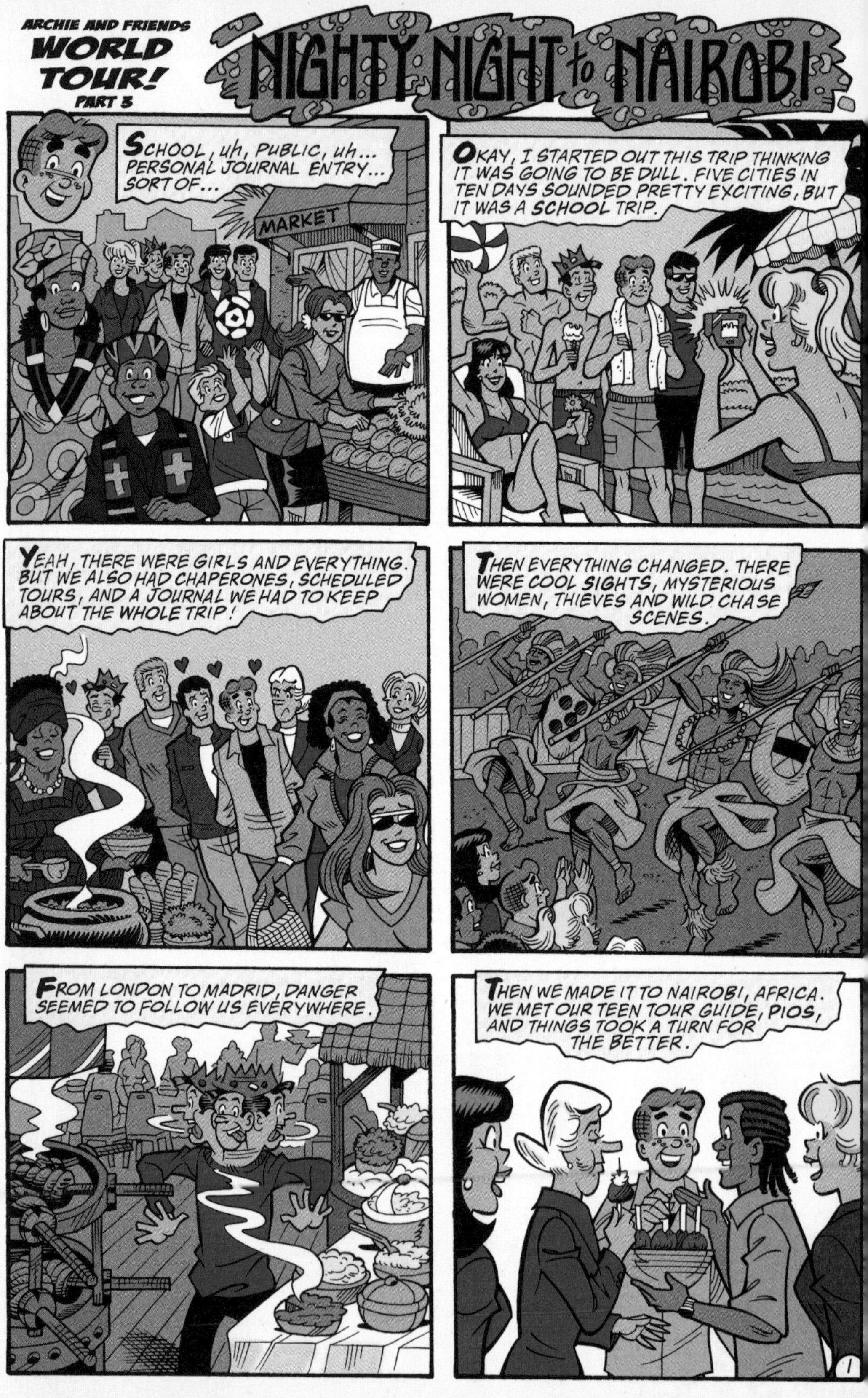
ARCHIE AND FRIENDS
WORLD TOUR!
PART 3
NIGHTY NIGHT to NAIROBI
SCHOOL, uh, PUBLIC, uh... PERSONAL JOURNAL ENTRY... SORT OF...
MARKET
OKAY, I STARTED OUT THIS TRIP THINKING IT WAS GOING TO BE DULL. FIVE CITIES IN TEN DAYS SOUNDED PRETTY EXCITING, BUT IT WAS A SCHOOL TRIP.
YEAH, THERE WERE GIRLS AND EVERYTHING. BUT WE ALSO HAD CHAPERONES, SCHEDULED TOURS, AND A JOURNAL WE HAD TO KEEP ABOUT THE WHOLE TRIP!
THEN EVERYTHING CHANGED. THERE WERE COOL SIGHTS, MYSTERIOUS WOMEN, THIEVES AND WILD CHASE SCENES.
FROM LONDON TO MADRID, DANGER SEEMED TO FOLLOW US EVERYWHERE.
THEN WE MADE IT TO NAIROBI, AFRICA. WE MET OUR TEEN TOUR GUIDE, PIOS, AND THINGS TOOK A TURN FOR THE BETTER.
1

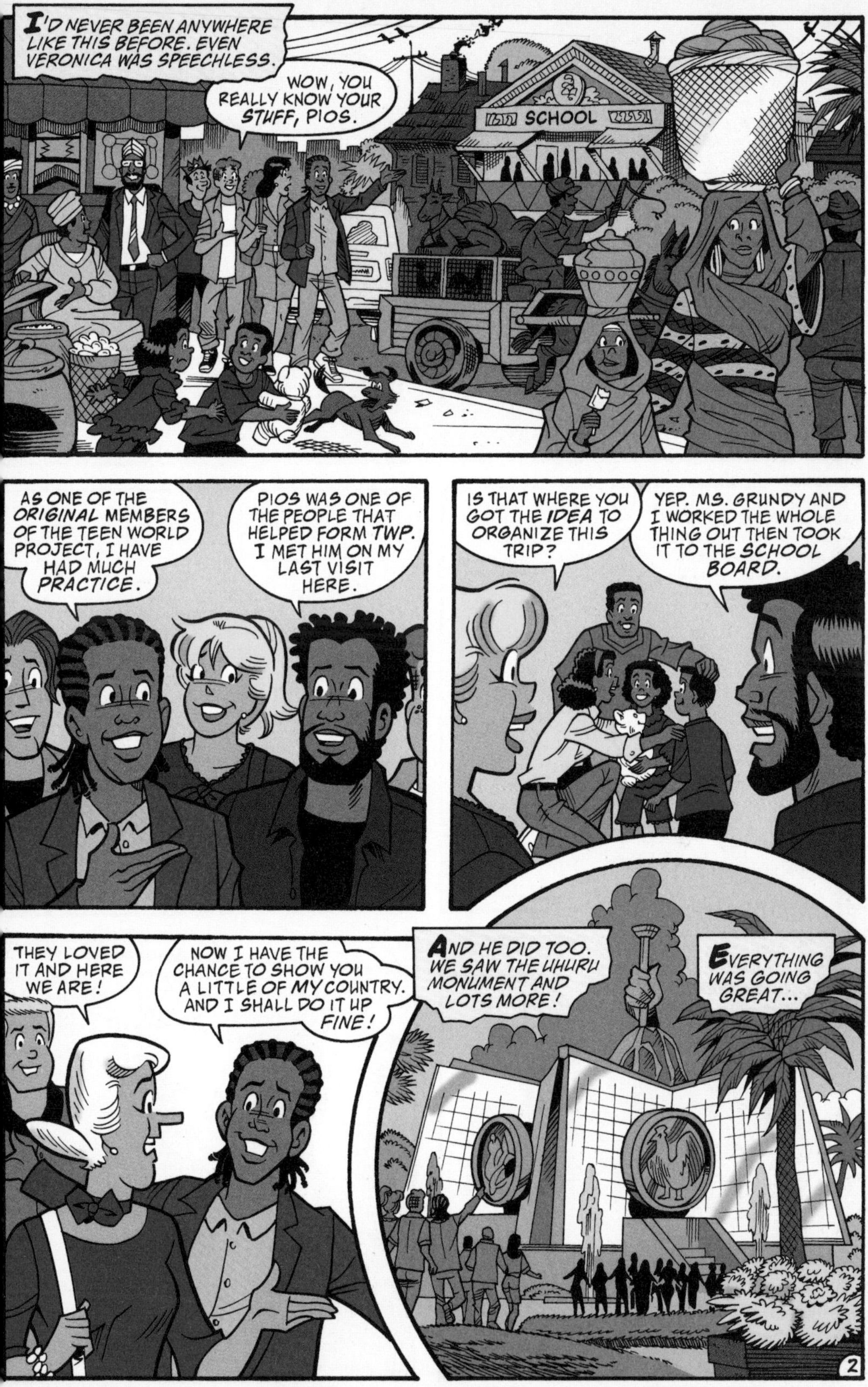
I'D NEVER BEEN ANYWHERE LIKE THIS BEFORE. EVEN VERONICA WAS SPEECHLESS.
WOW, YOU REALLY KNOW YOUR STUFF, PIOS.
SCHOOL
AS ONE OF THE ORIGINAL MEMBERS OF THE TEEN WORLD PROJECT, I HAVE HAD MUCH PRACTICE.
PIOS WAS ONE OF THE PEOPLE THAT HELPED FORM TWP. I MET HIM ON MY LAST VISIT HERE.
IS THAT WHERE YOU GOT THE IDEA TO ORGANIZE THIS TRIP?
YEP. MS. GRUNDY AND I WORKED THE WHOLE THING OUT THEN TOOK IT TO THE SCHOOL BOARD.
THEY LOVED IT AND HERE WE ARE!
NOW I HAVE THE CHANCE TO SHOW YOU A LITTLE OF MY COUNTRY. AND I SHALL DO IT UP FINE!
AND HE DID TOO. WE SAW THE UHURU MONUMENT AND LOTS MORE!
EVERYTHING WAS GOING GREAT...

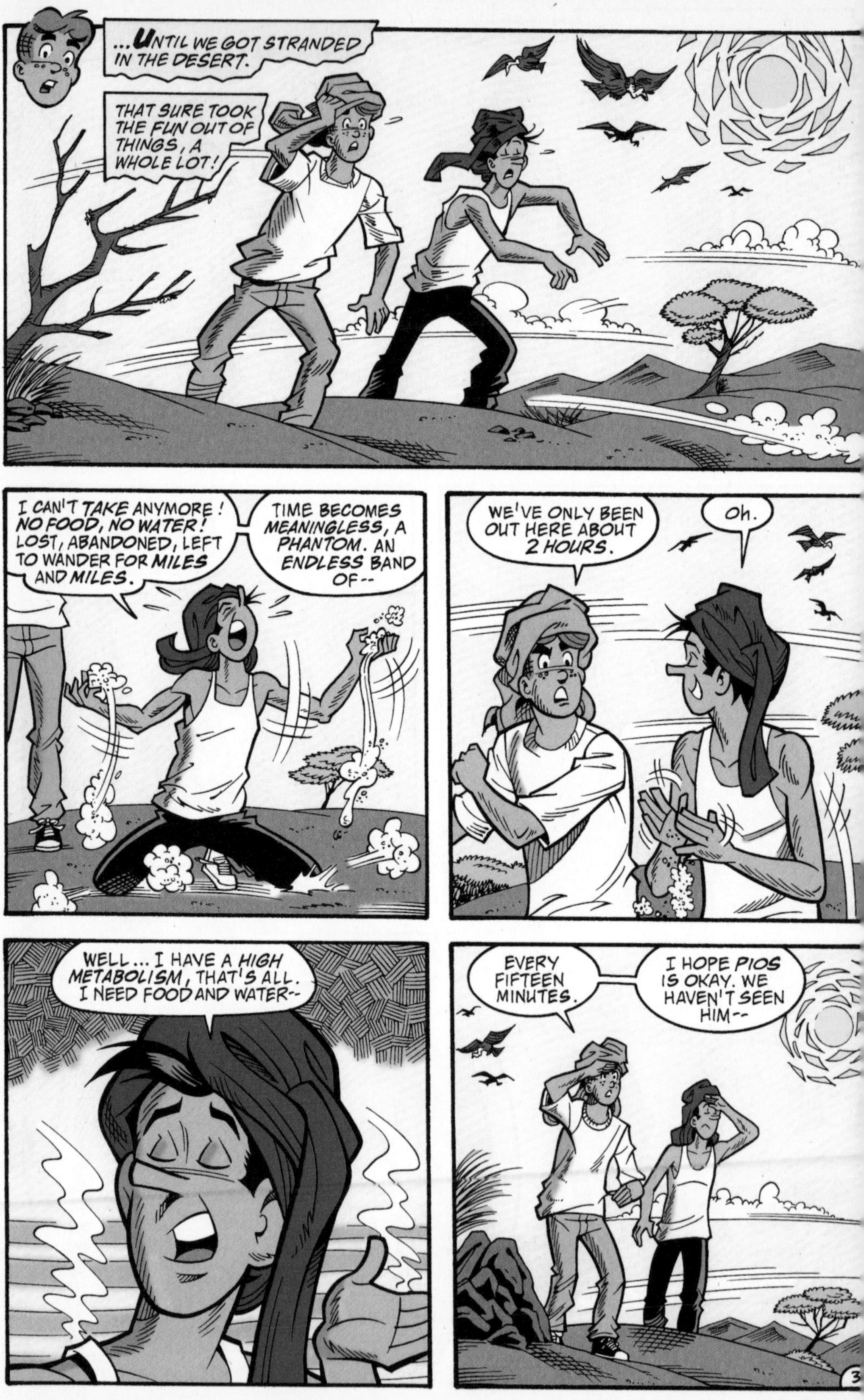
...UNTIL WE GOT STRANDED IN THE DESERT.
THAT SURE TOOK THE FUN OUT OF THINGS, A WHOLE LOT!
I CAN'T TAKE ANYMORE! NO FOOD, NO WATER! LOST, ABANDONED, LEFT TO WANDER FOR MILES AND MILES.
TIME BECOMES MEANINGLESS, A PHANTOM. AN ENDLESS BAND OF--
WE'VE ONLY BEEN OUT HERE ABOUT 2 HOURS.
Oh.
WELL... I HAVE A HIGH METABOLISM, THAT'S ALL. I NEED FOOD AND WATER--
EVERY FIFTEEN MINUTES.
I HOPE PIOS IS OKAY. WE HAVEN'T SEEN HIM--
3

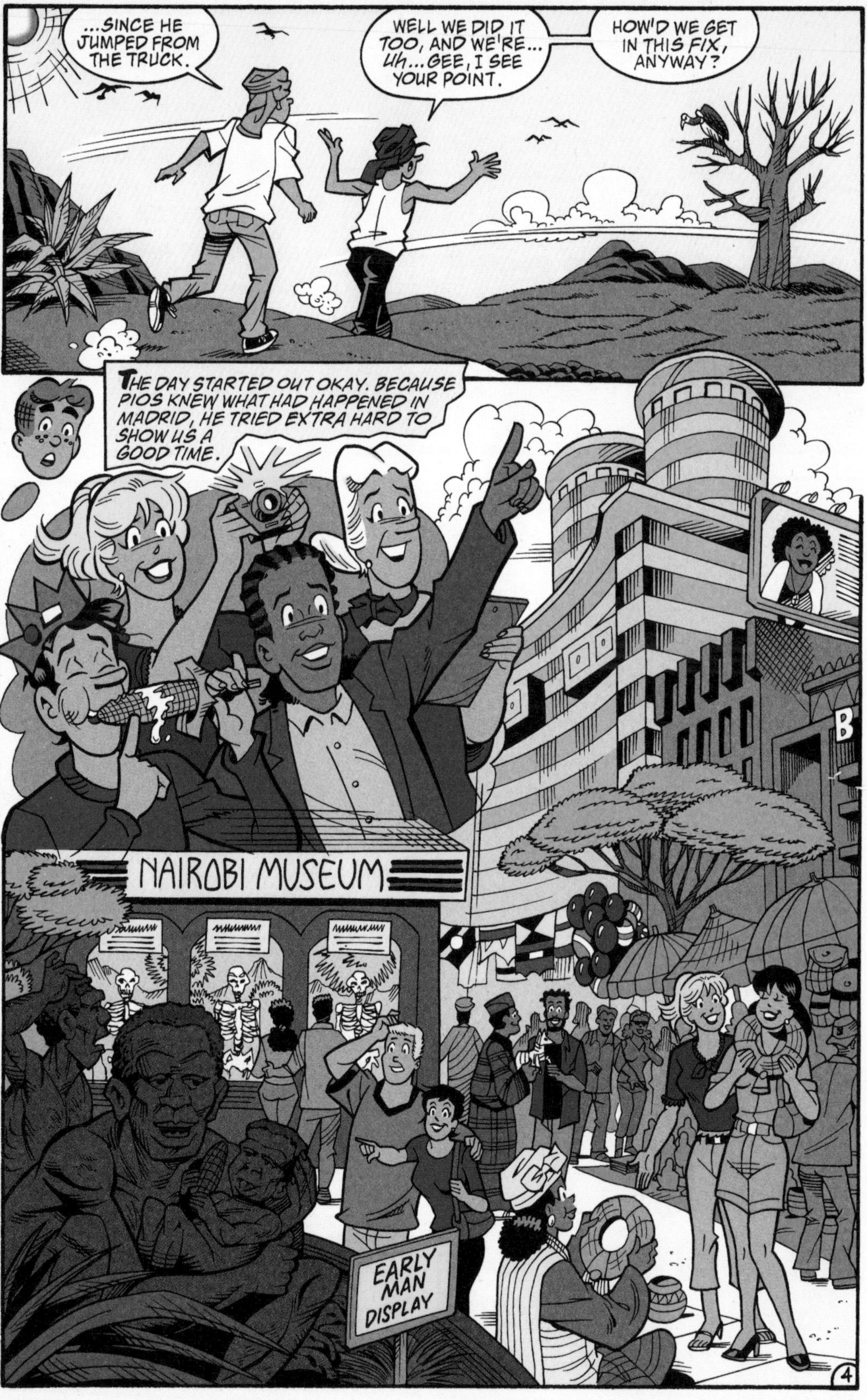

...SINCE HE JUMPED FROM THE TRUCK.
WELL WE DID IT TOO, AND WE'RE... UH... GEE, I SEE YOUR POINT.
HOW'D WE GET IN THIS FIX, ANYWAY?
THE DAY STARTED OUT OKAY. BECAUSE PIOS KNEW WHAT HAD HAPPENED IN MADRID, HE TRIED EXTRA HARD TO SHOW US A GOOD TIME.
NAIROBI MUSEUM
EARLY MAN DISPLAY

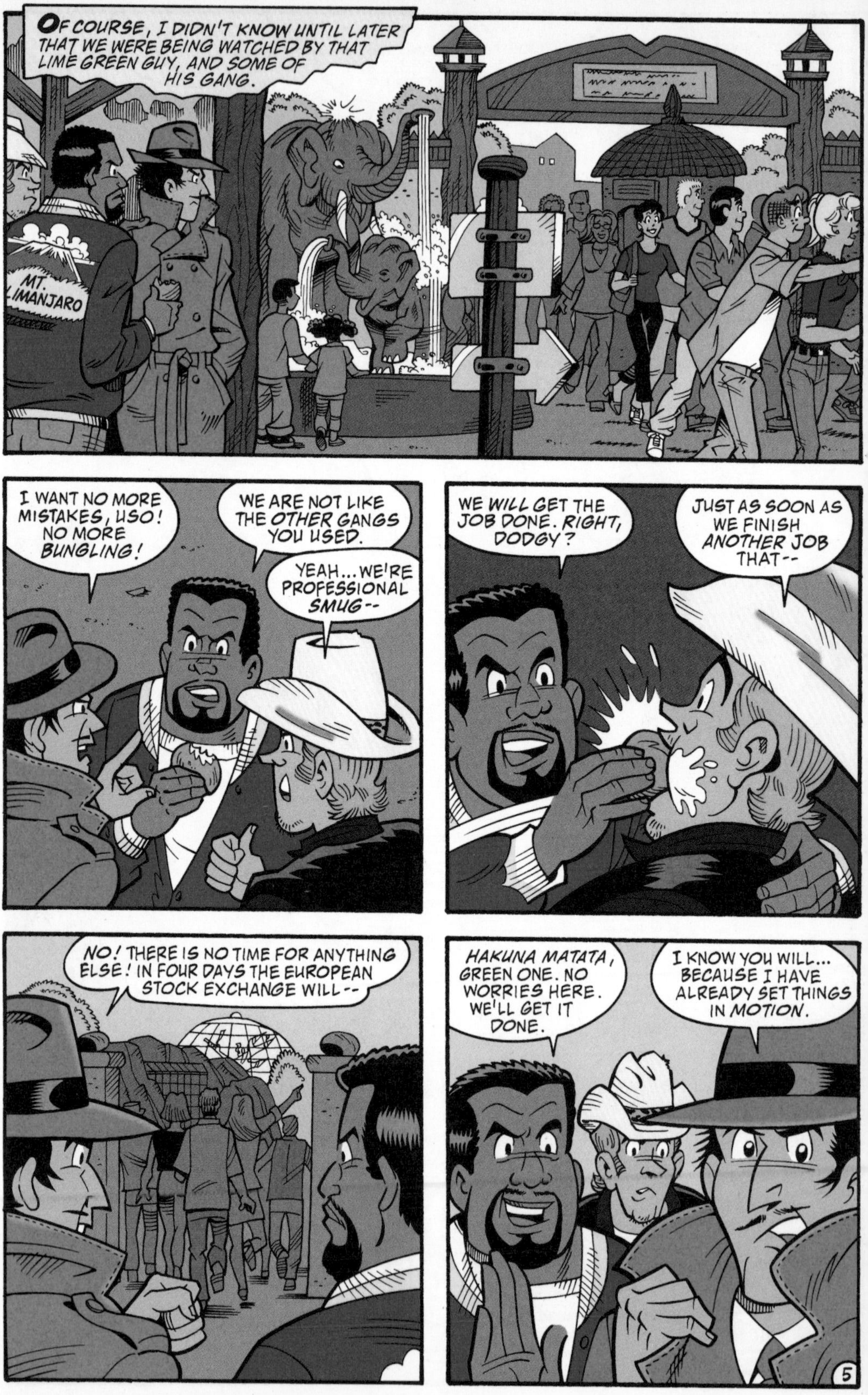
OF COURSE, I DIDN'T KNOW UNTIL LATER THAT WE WERE BEING WATCHED BY THAT LIME GREEN GUY, AND SOME OF HIS GANG.
MT. KILIMANJARO
I WANT NO MORE MISTAKES, USO! NO MORE BUNGLING!
WE ARE NOT LIKE THE OTHER GANGS YOU USED.
YEAH... WE'RE PROFESSIONAL SMUG--
WE WILL GET THE JOB DONE. RIGHT, DODGY?
JUST AS SOON AS WE FINISH ANOTHER JOB THAT--
NO! THERE IS NO TIME FOR ANYTHING ELSE! IN FOUR DAYS THE EUROPEAN STOCK EXCHANGE WILL--
HAKUNA MATATA, GREEN ONE. NO WORRIES HERE. WE'LL GET IT DONE.
I KNOW YOU WILL... BECAUSE I HAVE ALREADY SET THINGS IN MOTION.

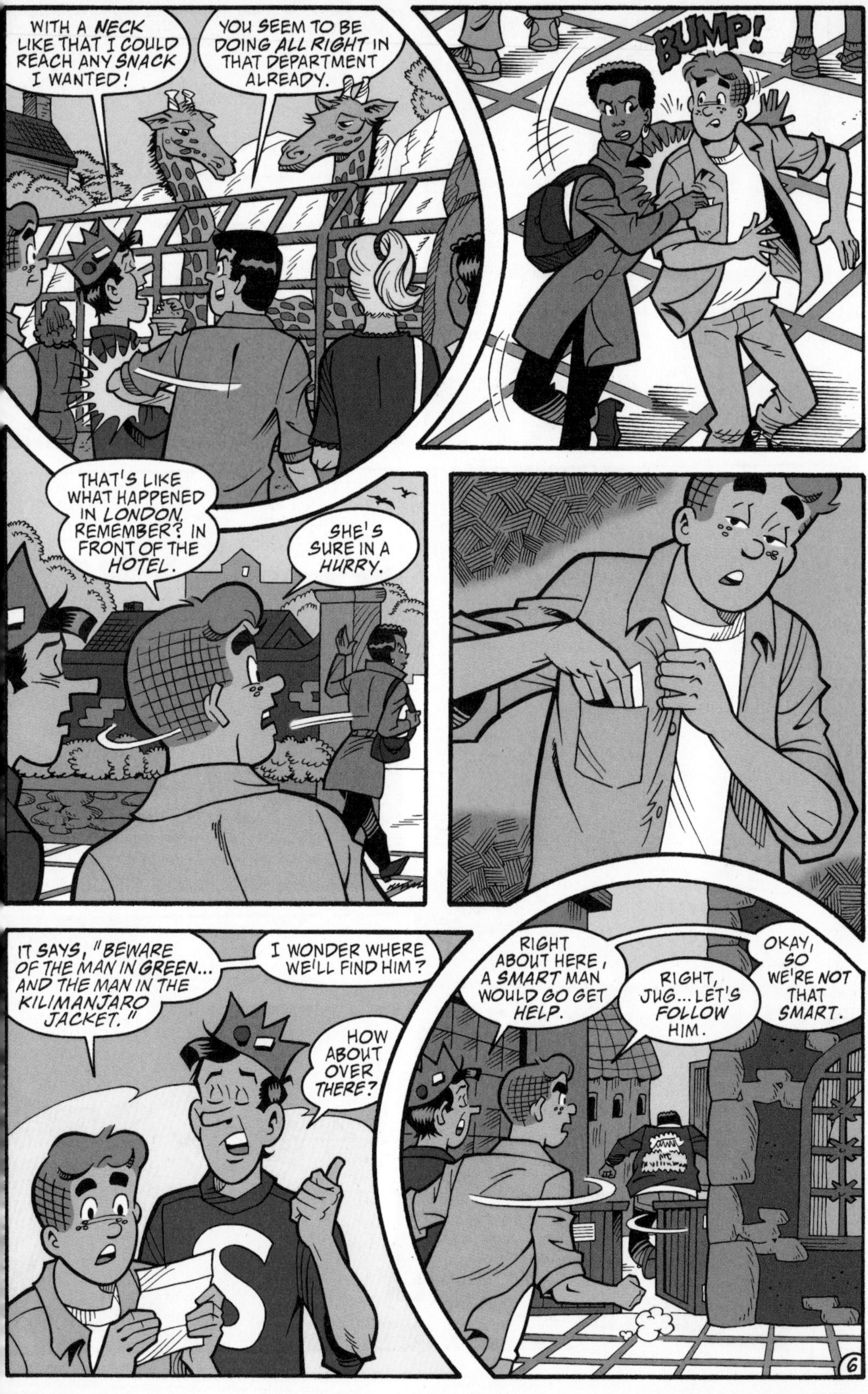
WITH A NECK LIKE THAT I COULD REACH ANY SNACK I WANTED!
YOU SEEM TO BE DOING ALL RIGHT IN THAT DEPARTMENT ALREADY.
BUMP!
THAT'S LIKE WHAT HAPPENED IN LONDON, REMEMBER? IN FRONT OF THE HOTEL.
SHE'S SURE IN A HURRY.
IT SAYS, "BEWARE OF THE MAN IN GREEN... AND THE MAN IN THE KILIMANJARO JACKET."
I WONDER WHERE WE'LL FIND HIM?
HOW ABOUT OVER THERE?
RIGHT ABOUT HERE, A SMART MAN WOULD GO GET HELP.
RIGHT, JUG... LET'S FOLLOW HIM.
OKAY, SO WE'RE NOT THAT SMART.
6

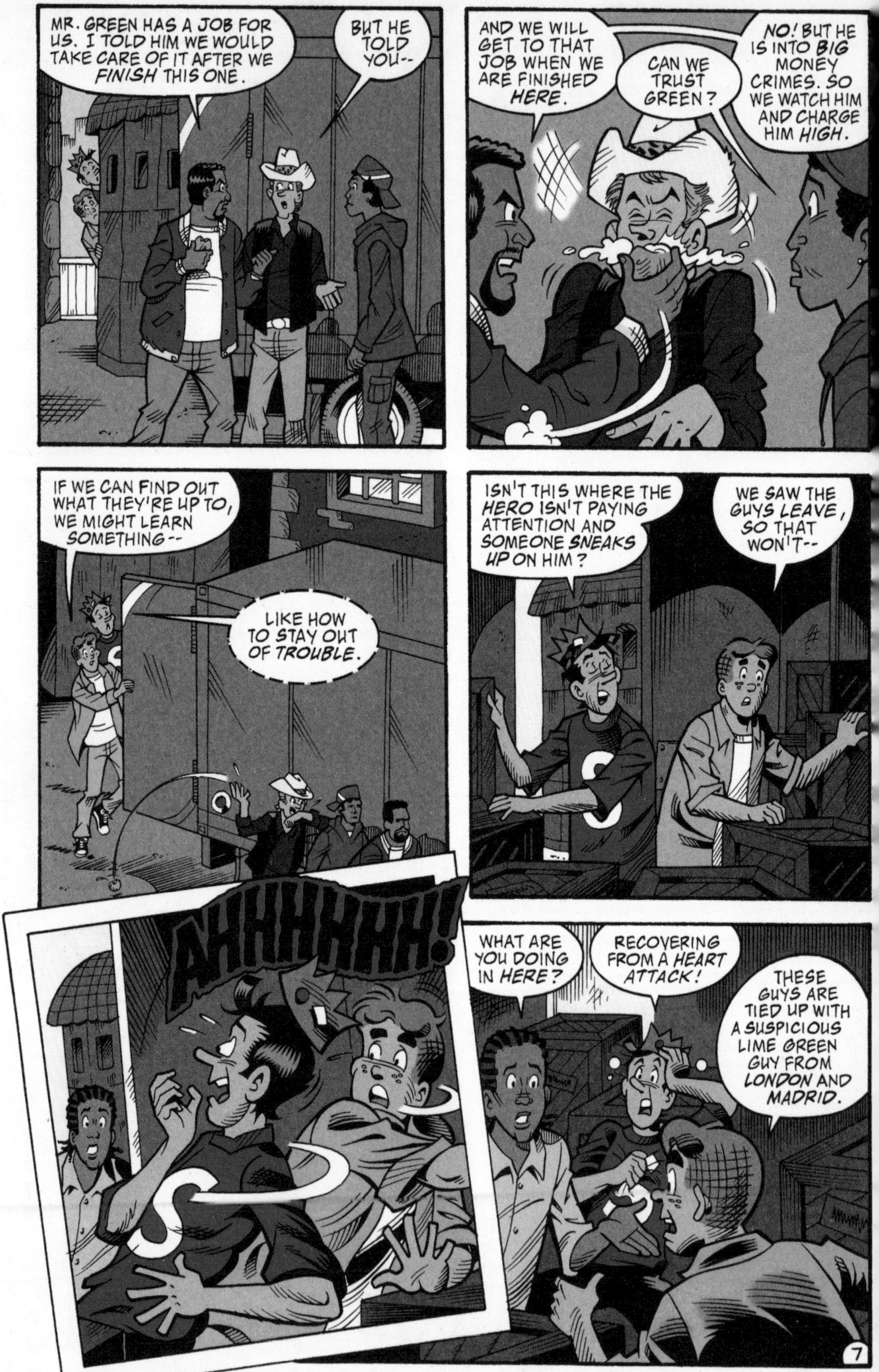
MR. GREEN HAS A JOB FOR US. I TOLD HIM WE WOULD TAKE CARE OF IT AFTER WE FINISH THIS ONE.
BUT HE TOLD YOU--
AND WE WILL GET TO THAT JOB WHEN WE ARE FINISHED HERE.
CAN WE TRUST GREEN?
NO! BUT HE IS INTO BIG MONEY CRIMES. SO WE WATCH HIM AND CHARGE HIM HIGH.
IF WE CAN FIND OUT WHAT THEY'RE UP TO, WE MIGHT LEARN SOMETHING--
LIKE HOW TO STAY OUT OF TROUBLE.
ISN'T THIS WHERE THE HERO ISN'T PAYING ATTENTION AND SOMEONE SNEAKS UP ON HIM?
WE SAW THE GUYS LEAVE, SO THAT WON'T--
AHHHHHHH!
WHAT ARE YOU DOING IN HERE?
RECOVERING FROM A HEART ATTACK!
THESE GUYS ARE TIED UP WITH A SUSPICIOUS LIME GREEN GUY FROM LONDON AND MADRID.

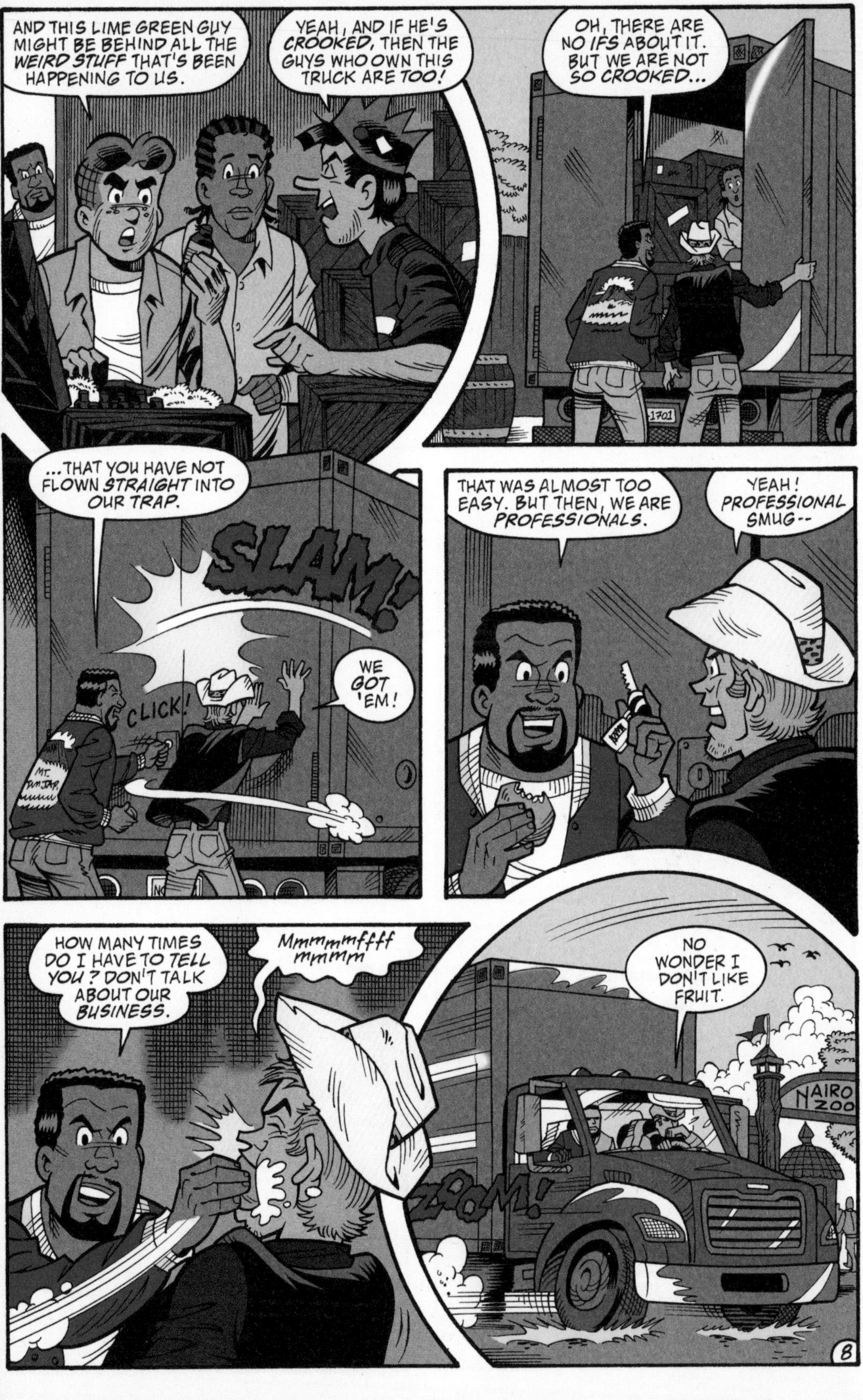
AND THIS LIME GREEN GUY MIGHT BE BEHIND ALL THE WEIRD STUFF THAT'S BEEN HAPPENING TO US.
YEAH, AND IF HE'S CROOKED, THEN THE GUYS WHO OWN THIS TRUCK ARE TOO!
OH, THERE ARE NO IFS ABOUT IT. BUT WE ARE NOT SO CROOKED...
1701
...THAT YOU HAVE NOT FLOWN STRAIGHT INTO OUR TRAP.
SLAM!
CLICK!
WE GOT 'EM!
MT. KILIMANJARO
THAT WAS ALMOST TOO EASY. BUT THEN, WE ARE PROFESSIONALS.
YEAH! PROFESSIONAL SMUG--
HOW MANY TIMES DO I HAVE TO TELL YOU? DON'T TALK ABOUT OUR BUSINESS.
Mmmmmffff mmmm
NO WONDER I DON'T LIKE FRUIT.
ZOOM!
NAIRO ZOO
8

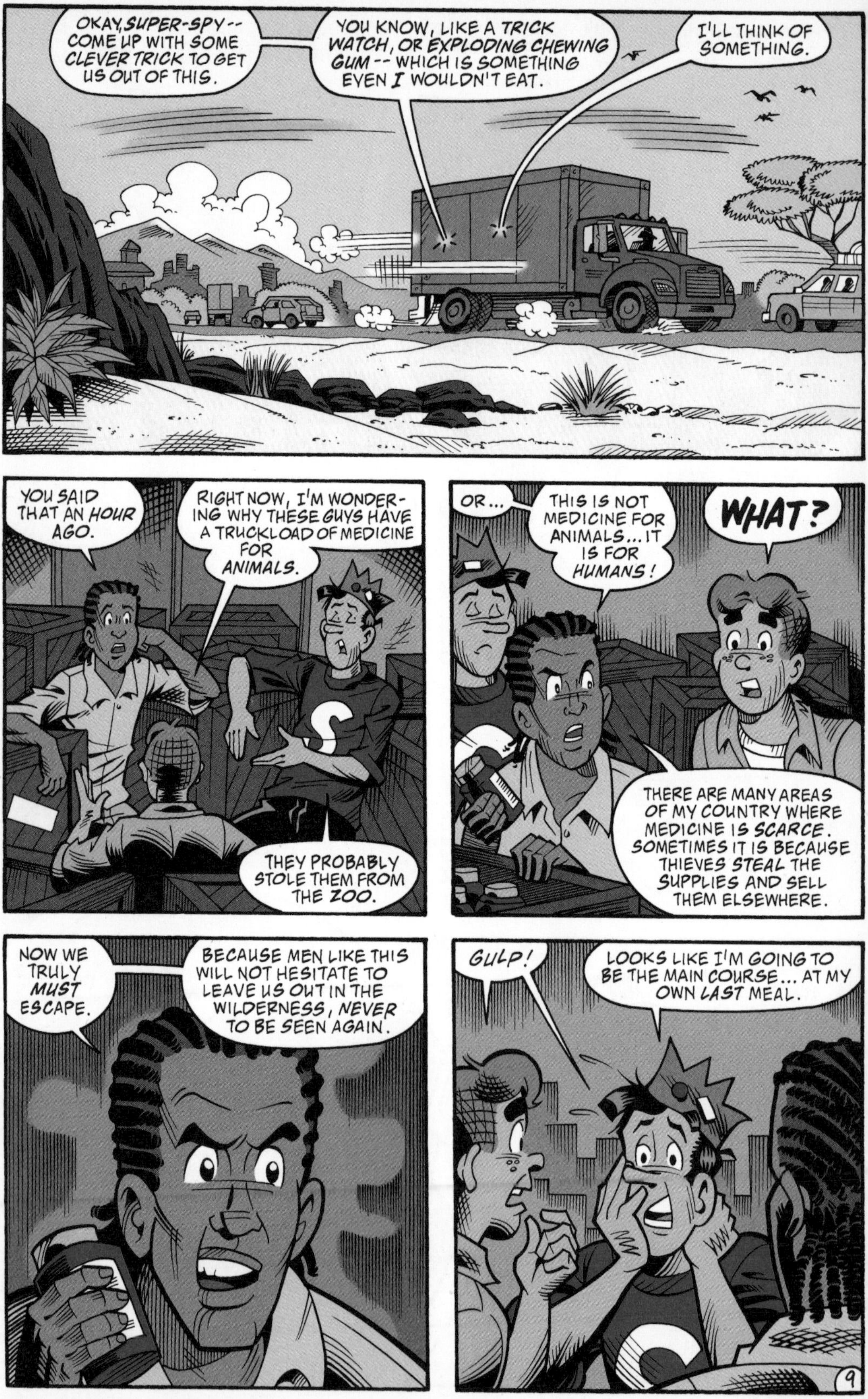
OKAY, SUPER-SPY-- COME UP WITH SOME CLEVER TRICK TO GET US OUT OF THIS.
YOU KNOW, LIKE A TRICK WATCH, OR EXPLODING CHEWING GUM -- WHICH IS SOMETHING EVEN I WOULDN'T EAT.
I'LL THINK OF SOMETHING.
YOU SAID THAT AN HOUR AGO.
RIGHT NOW, I'M WONDERING WHY THESE GUYS HAVE A TRUCKLOAD OF MEDICINE FOR ANIMALS.
THEY PROBABLY STOLE THEM FROM THE ZOO.
OR...
THIS IS NOT MEDICINE FOR ANIMALS... IT IS FOR HUMANS!
WHAT?
THERE ARE MANY AREAS OF MY COUNTRY WHERE MEDICINE IS SCARCE. SOMETIMES IT IS BECAUSE THIEVES STEAL THE SUPPLIES AND SELL THEM ELSEWHERE.
NOW WE TRULY MUST ESCAPE.
BECAUSE MEN LIKE THIS WILL NOT HESITATE TO LEAVE US OUT IN THE WILDERNESS, NEVER TO BE SEEN AGAIN.
GULP!
LOOKS LIKE I'M GOING TO BE THE MAIN COURSE... AT MY OWN LAST MEAL.
9

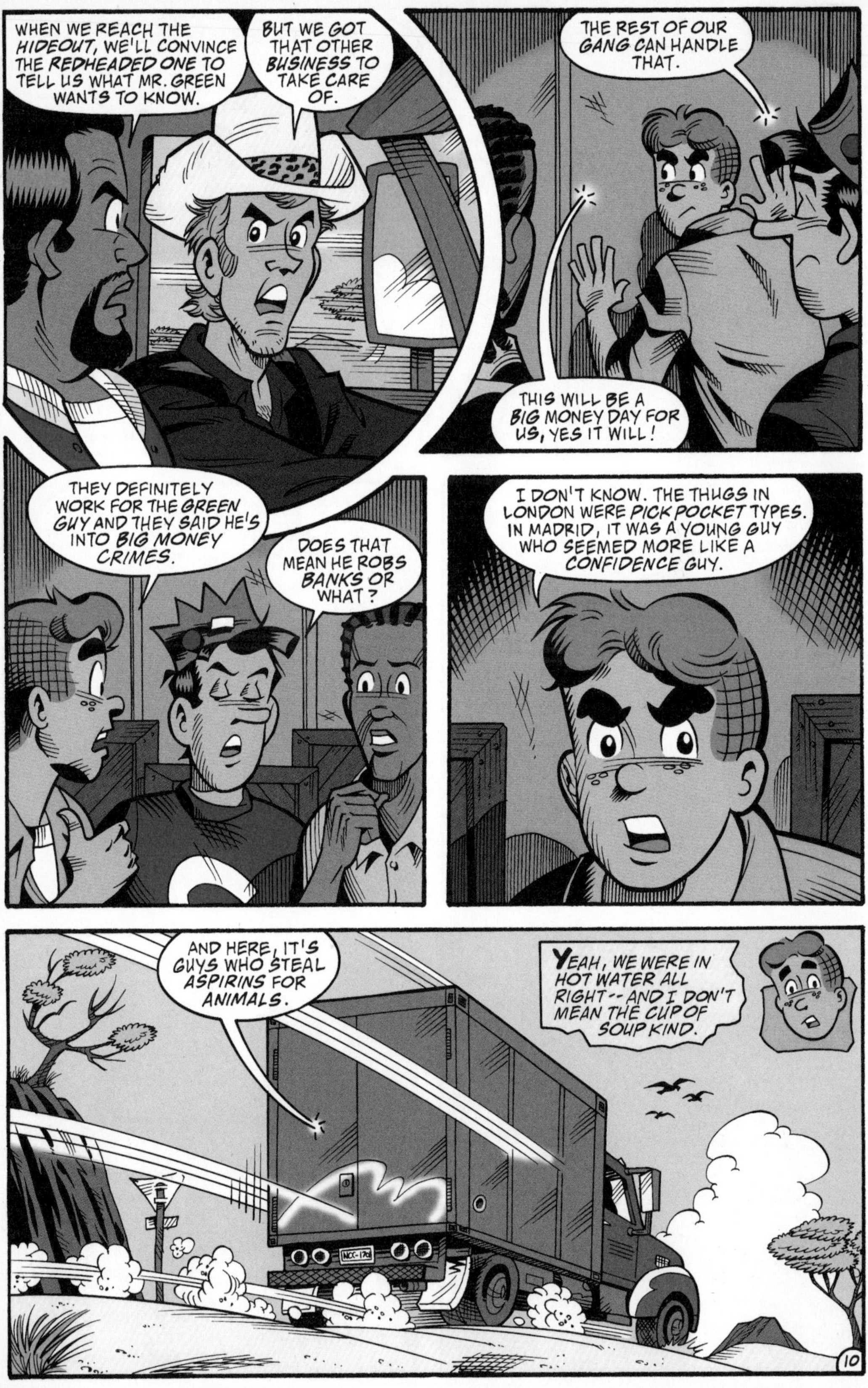
WHEN WE REACH THE HIDEOUT, WE'LL CONVINCE THE REDHEADED ONE TO TELL US WHAT MR. GREEN WANTS TO KNOW.
BUT WE GOT THAT OTHER BUSINESS TO TAKE CARE OF.
THE REST OF OUR GANG CAN HANDLE THAT.
THIS WILL BE A BIG MONEY DAY FOR US, YES IT WILL!
THEY DEFINITELY WORK FOR THE GREEN GUY AND THEY SAID HE'S INTO BIG MONEY CRIMES.
DOES THAT MEAN HE ROBS BANKS OR WHAT?
I DON'T KNOW. THE THUGS IN LONDON WERE PICK POCKET TYPES. IN MADRID, IT WAS A YOUNG GUY WHO SEEMED MORE LIKE A CONFIDENCE GUY.
AND HERE, IT'S GUYS WHO STEAL ASPIRINS FOR ANIMALS.
YEAH, WE WERE IN HOT WATER ALL RIGHT-- AND I DON'T MEAN THE CUP OF SOUP KIND.
10

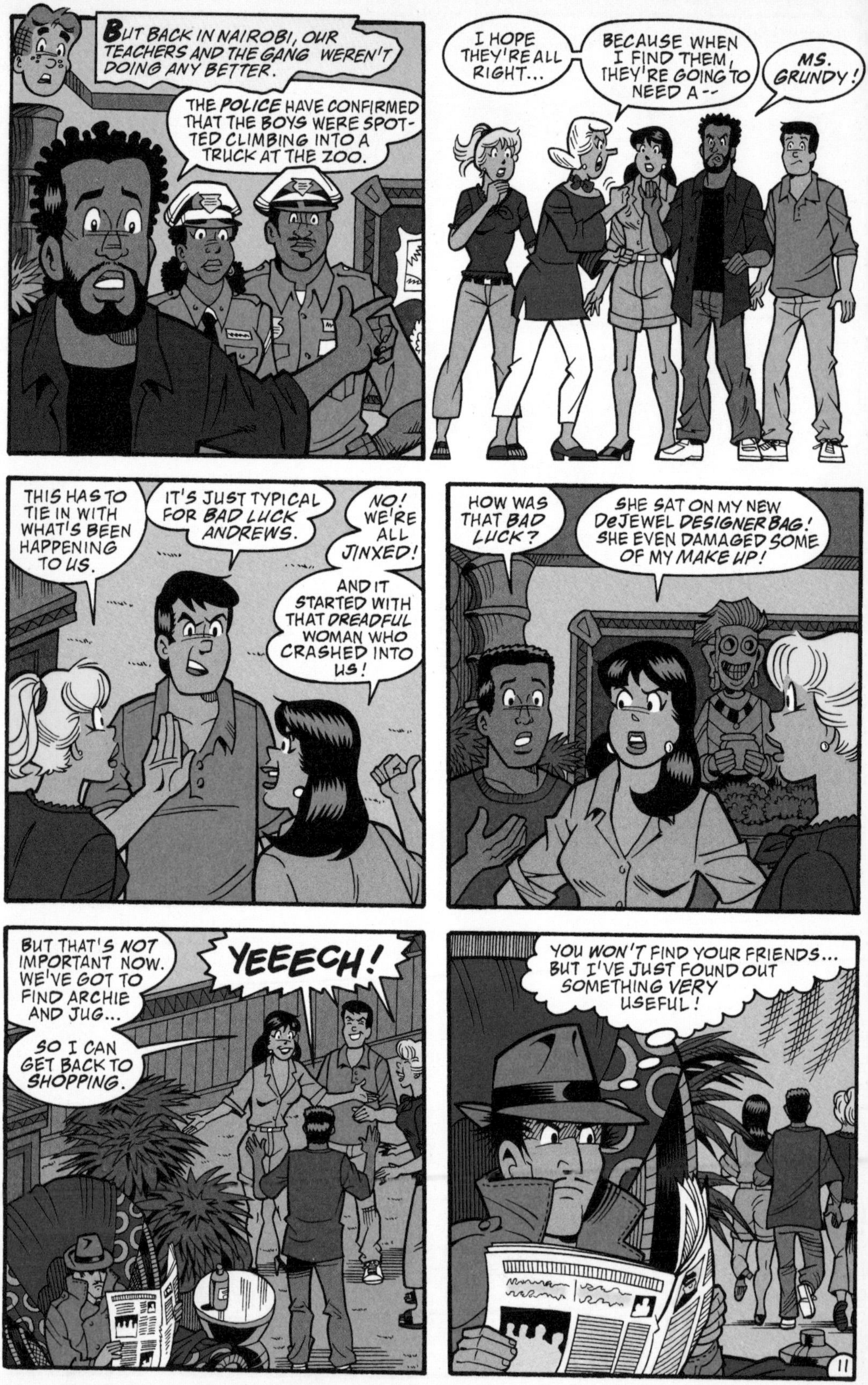
BUT BACK IN NAIROBI, OUR TEACHERS AND THE GANG WEREN'T DOING ANY BETTER.
THE POLICE HAVE CONFIRMED THAT THE BOYS WERE SPOTTED CLIMBING INTO A TRUCK AT THE ZOO.
I HOPE THEY'RE ALL RIGHT...
BECAUSE WHEN I FIND THEM, THEY'RE GOING TO NEED A --
MS. GRUNDY!
THIS HAS TO TIE IN WITH WHAT'S BEEN HAPPENING TO US.
IT'S JUST TYPICAL FOR BAD LUCK ANDREWS.
NO! WE'RE ALL JINXED!
AND IT STARTED WITH THAT DREADFUL WOMAN WHO CRASHED INTO US!
HOW WAS THAT BAD LUCK?
SHE SAT ON MY NEW DeJEWEL DESIGNER BAG! SHE EVEN DAMAGED SOME OF MY MAKE UP!
BUT THAT'S NOT IMPORTANT NOW. WE'VE GOT TO FIND ARCHIE AND JUG...
YEEECH!
SO I CAN GET BACK TO SHOPPING.
YOU WON'T FIND YOUR FRIENDS... BUT I'VE JUST FOUND OUT SOMETHING VERY USEFUL!
11

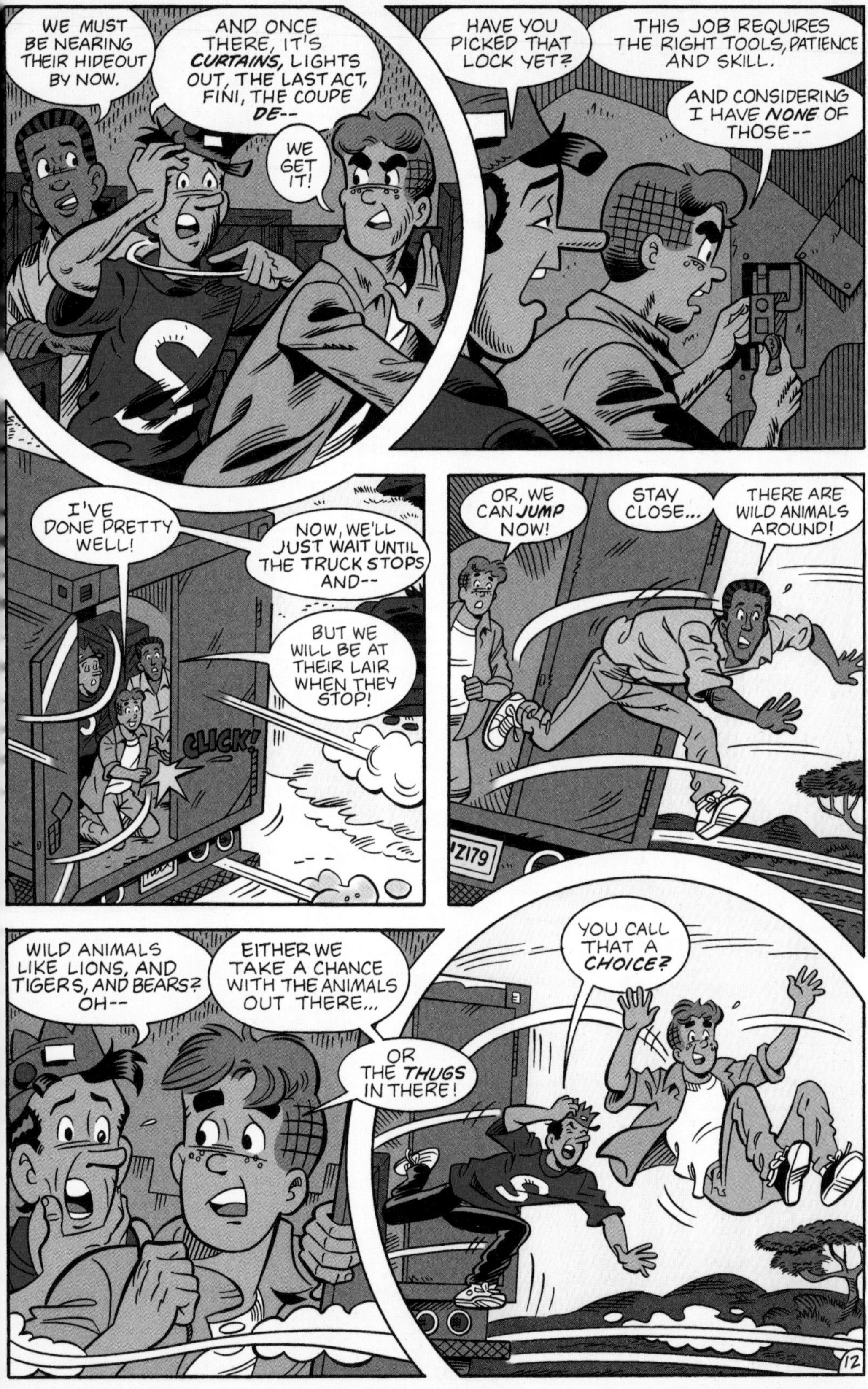
WE MUST BE NEARING THEIR HIDEOUT BY NOW.
AND ONCE THERE, IT'S CURTAINS, LIGHTS OUT, THE LAST ACT, FINI, THE COUPE DE--
WE GET IT!
HAVE YOU PICKED THAT LOCK YET?
THIS JOB REQUIRES THE RIGHT TOOLS, PATIENCE AND SKILL.
AND CONSIDERING I HAVE NONE OF THOSE--
I'VE DONE PRETTY WELL!
NOW, WE'LL JUST WAIT UNTIL THE TRUCK STOPS AND--
BUT WE WILL BE AT THEIR LAIR WHEN THEY STOP!
CLICK!
OR, WE CAN JUMP NOW!
STAY CLOSE...
THERE ARE WILD ANIMALS AROUND!
ZI79
WILD ANIMALS LIKE LIONS, AND TIGERS, AND BEARS? OH--
EITHER WE TAKE A CHANCE WITH THE ANIMALS OUT THERE...
OR THE THUGS IN THERE!
YOU CALL THAT A CHOICE?
12

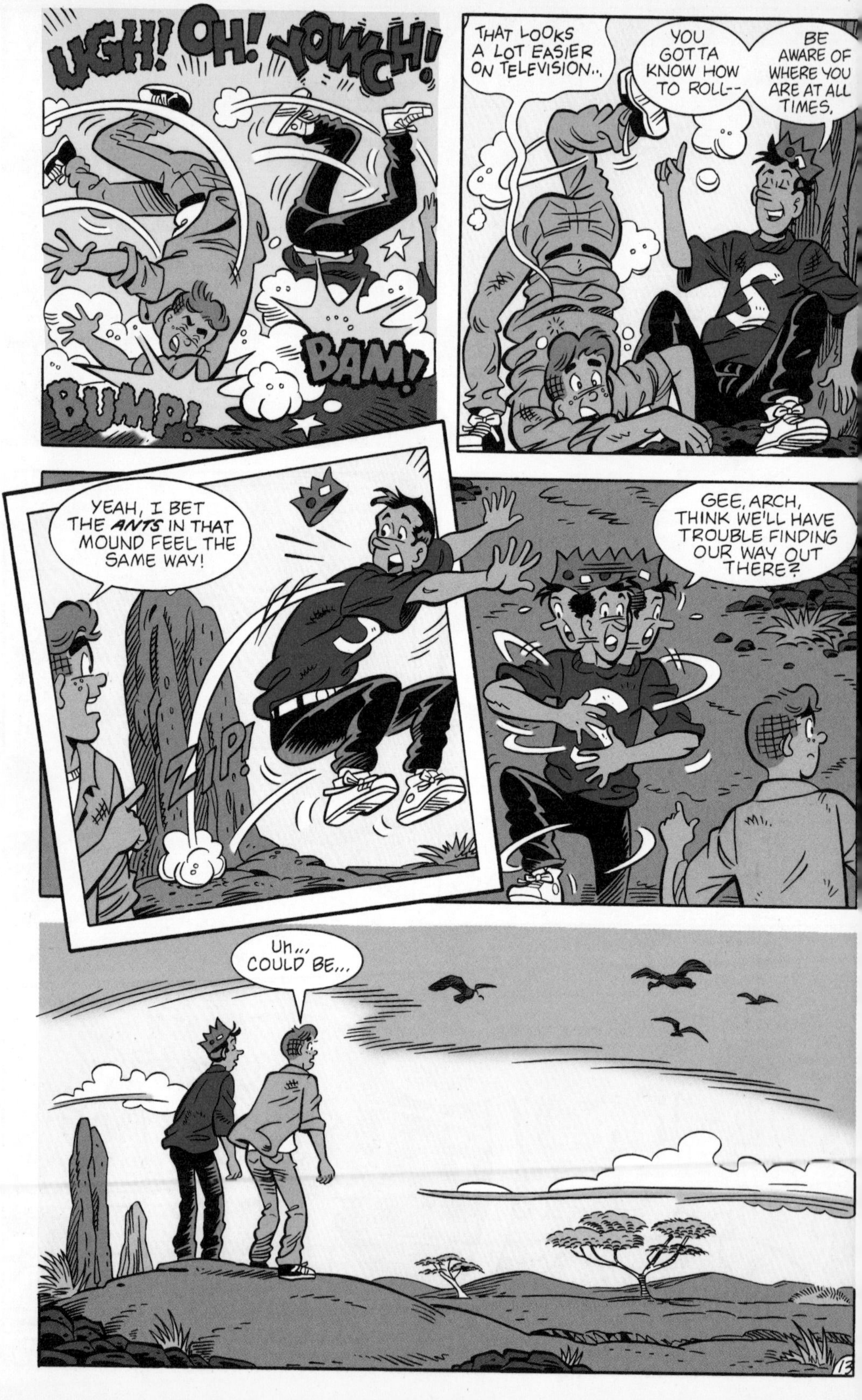
UGH! OH! YOWCH!
BUMP!
BAM!
THAT LOOKS A LOT EASIER ON TELEVISION...
YOU GOTTA KNOW HOW TO ROLL--
BE AWARE OF WHERE YOU ARE AT ALL TIMES.
YEAH, I BET THE ANTS IN THAT MOUND FEEL THE SAME WAY!
ZIP!
GEE, ARCH, THINK WE'LL HAVE TROUBLE FINDING OUR WAY OUT THERE?
Uh... COULD BE...
13

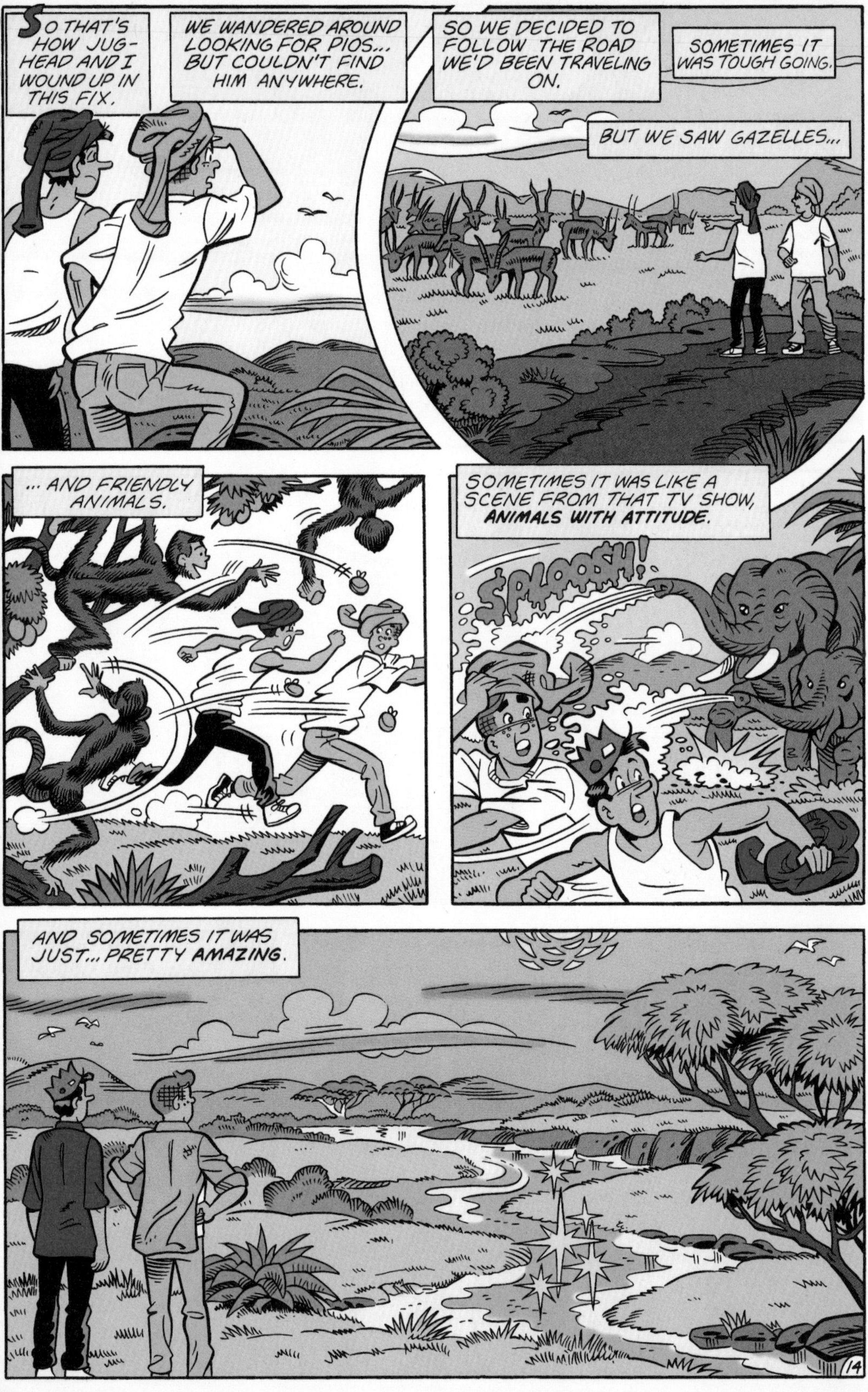
SO THAT'S HOW JUG-HEAD AND I WOUND UP IN THIS FIX.
WE WANDERED AROUND LOOKING FOR PIOS... BUT COULDN'T FIND HIM ANYWHERE.
SO WE DECIDED TO FOLLOW THE ROAD WE'D BEEN TRAVELING ON.
SOMETIMES IT WAS TOUGH GOING.
BUT WE SAW GAZELLES...
... AND FRIENDLY ANIMALS.
SOMETIMES IT WAS LIKE A SCENE FROM THAT TV SHOW, **ANIMALS WITH ATTITUDE**.
SPLOOSH!
AND SOMETIMES IT WAS JUST... PRETTY **AMAZING**.
14

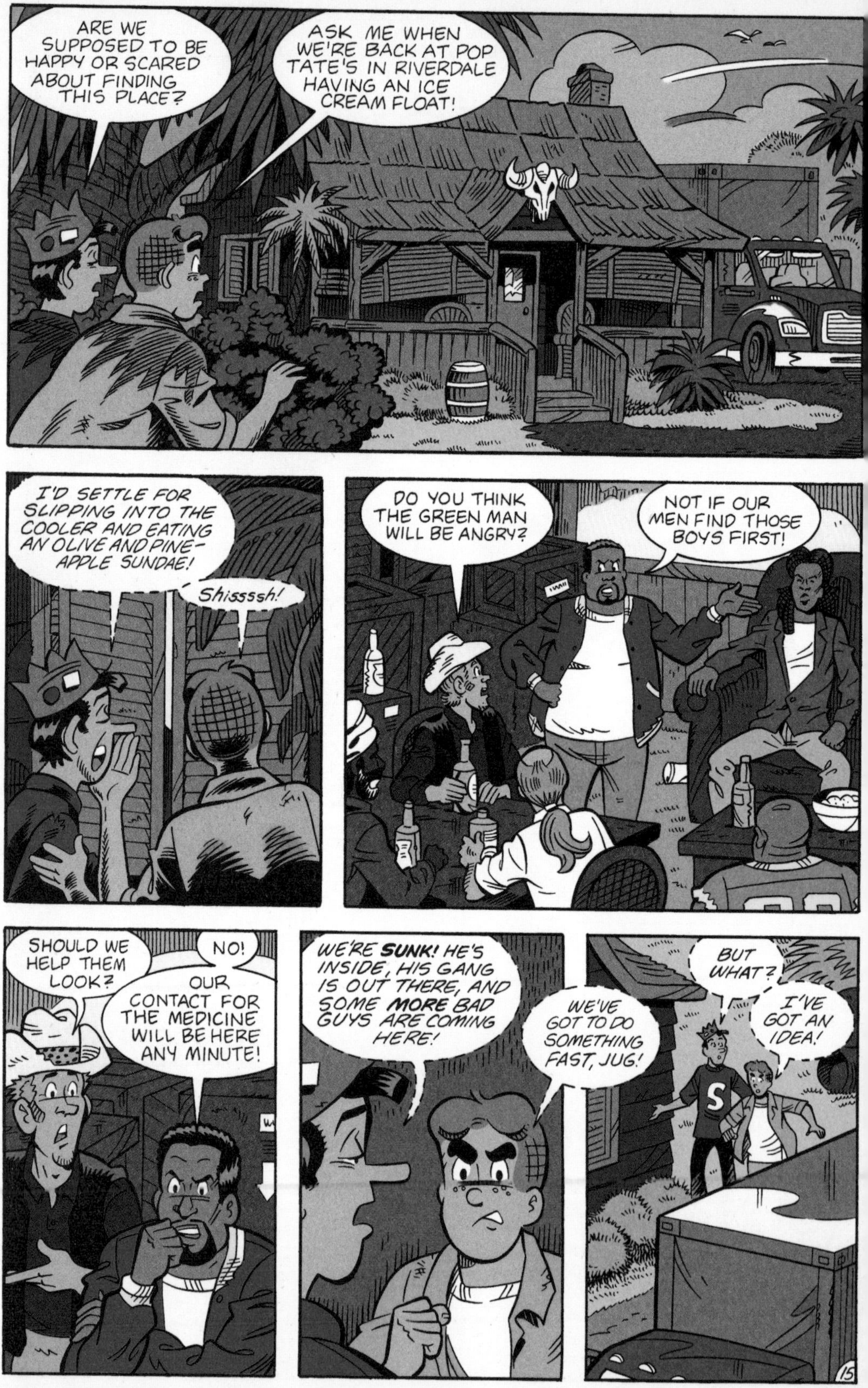
ARE WE SUPPOSED TO BE HAPPY OR SCARED ABOUT FINDING THIS PLACE?
ASK ME WHEN WE'RE BACK AT POP TATE'S IN RIVERDALE HAVING AN ICE CREAM FLOAT!
I'D SETTLE FOR SLIPPING INTO THE COOLER AND EATING AN OLIVE AND PINE-APPLE SUNDAE!
Shissssh!
DO YOU THINK THE GREEN MAN WILL BE ANGRY?
NOT IF OUR MEN FIND THOSE BOYS FIRST!
SHOULD WE HELP THEM LOOK?
NO!
OUR CONTACT FOR THE MEDICINE WILL BE HERE ANY MINUTE!
WE'RE SUNK! HE'S INSIDE, HIS GANG IS OUT THERE, AND SOME MORE BAD GUYS ARE COMING HERE!
WE'VE GOT TO DO SOMETHING FAST, JUG!
BUT WHAT?
I'VE GOT AN IDEA!
15

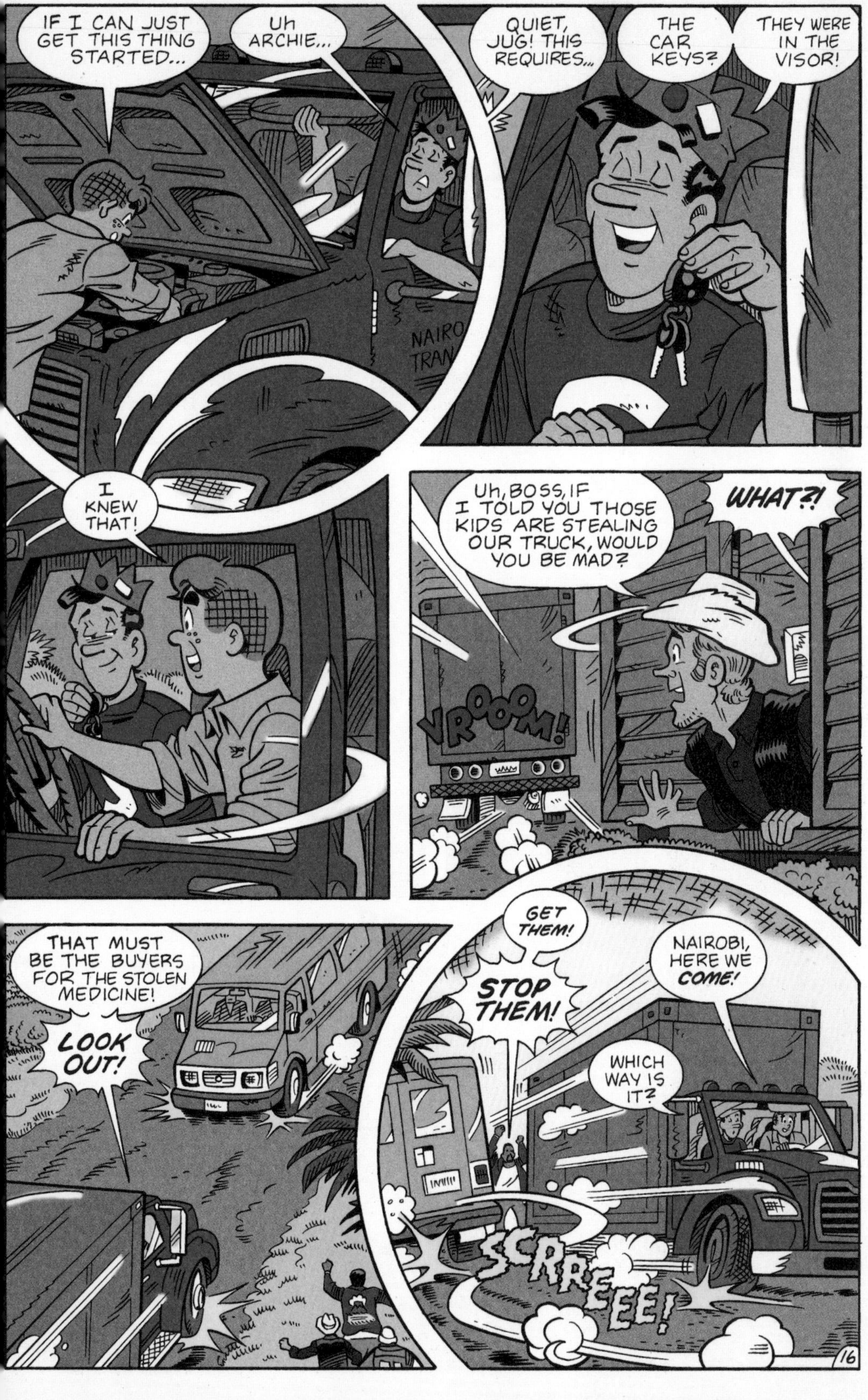
IF I CAN JUST GET THIS THING STARTED...
Uh ARCHIE...
NAIRO TRAN
QUIET, JUG! THIS REQUIRES...
THE CAR KEYS?
THEY WERE IN THE VISOR!
I KNEW THAT!
Uh, BOSS, IF I TOLD YOU THOSE KIDS ARE STEALING OUR TRUCK, WOULD YOU BE MAD?
WHAT?!
VROOOM!
THAT MUST BE THE BUYERS FOR THE STOLEN MEDICINE!
LOOK OUT!
GET THEM!
STOP THEM!
NAIROBI, HERE WE COME!
WHICH WAY IS IT?
SCRREEEE!

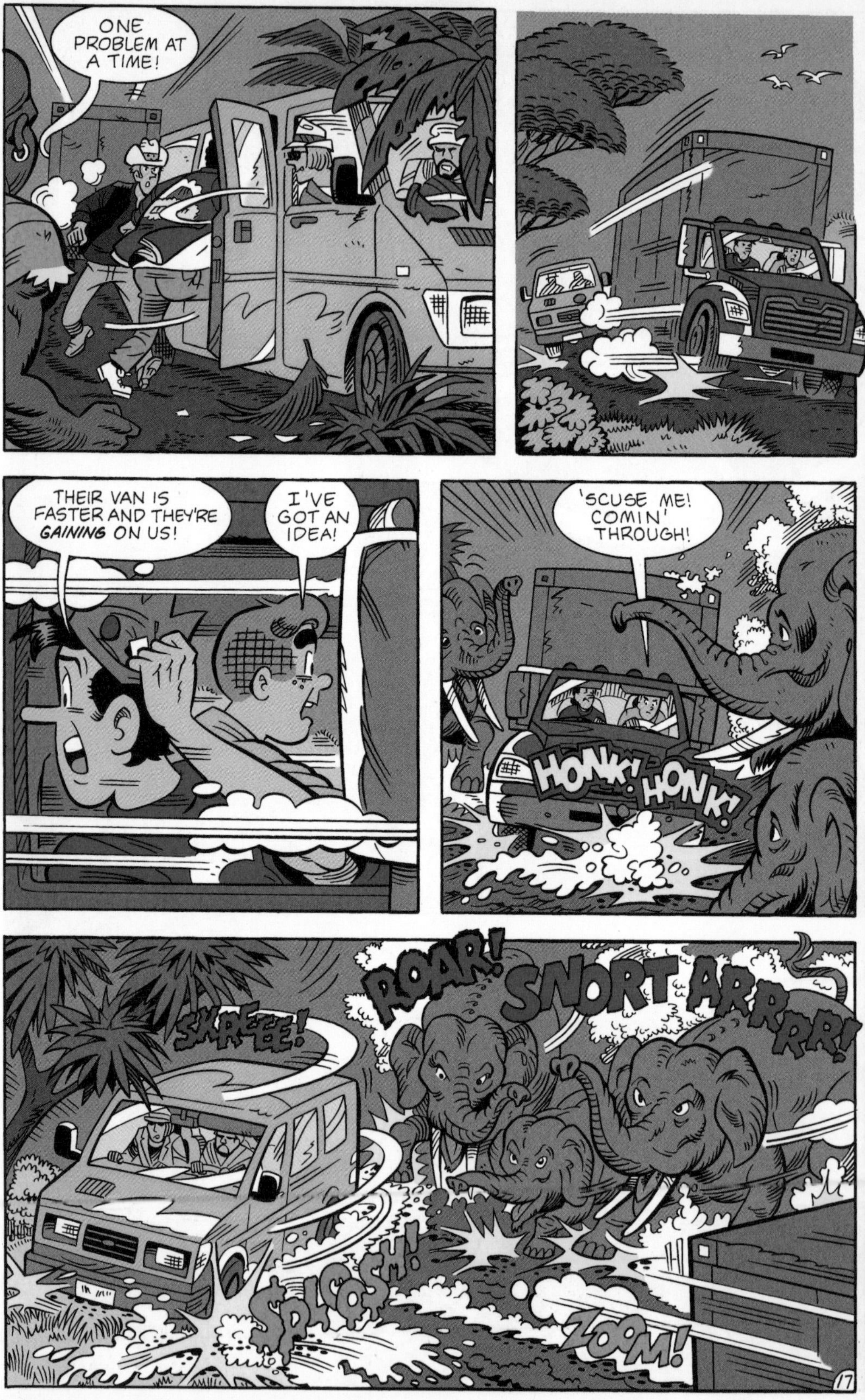
ONE PROBLEM AT A TIME!
THEIR VAN IS FASTER AND THEY'RE GAINING ON US!
I'VE GOT AN IDEA!
'SCUSE ME! COMIN' THROUGH!
HONK! HONK!
ROAR!
SNORT
ARRRRR!
SKREEEE!
SPLOOSH!
ZOOM!

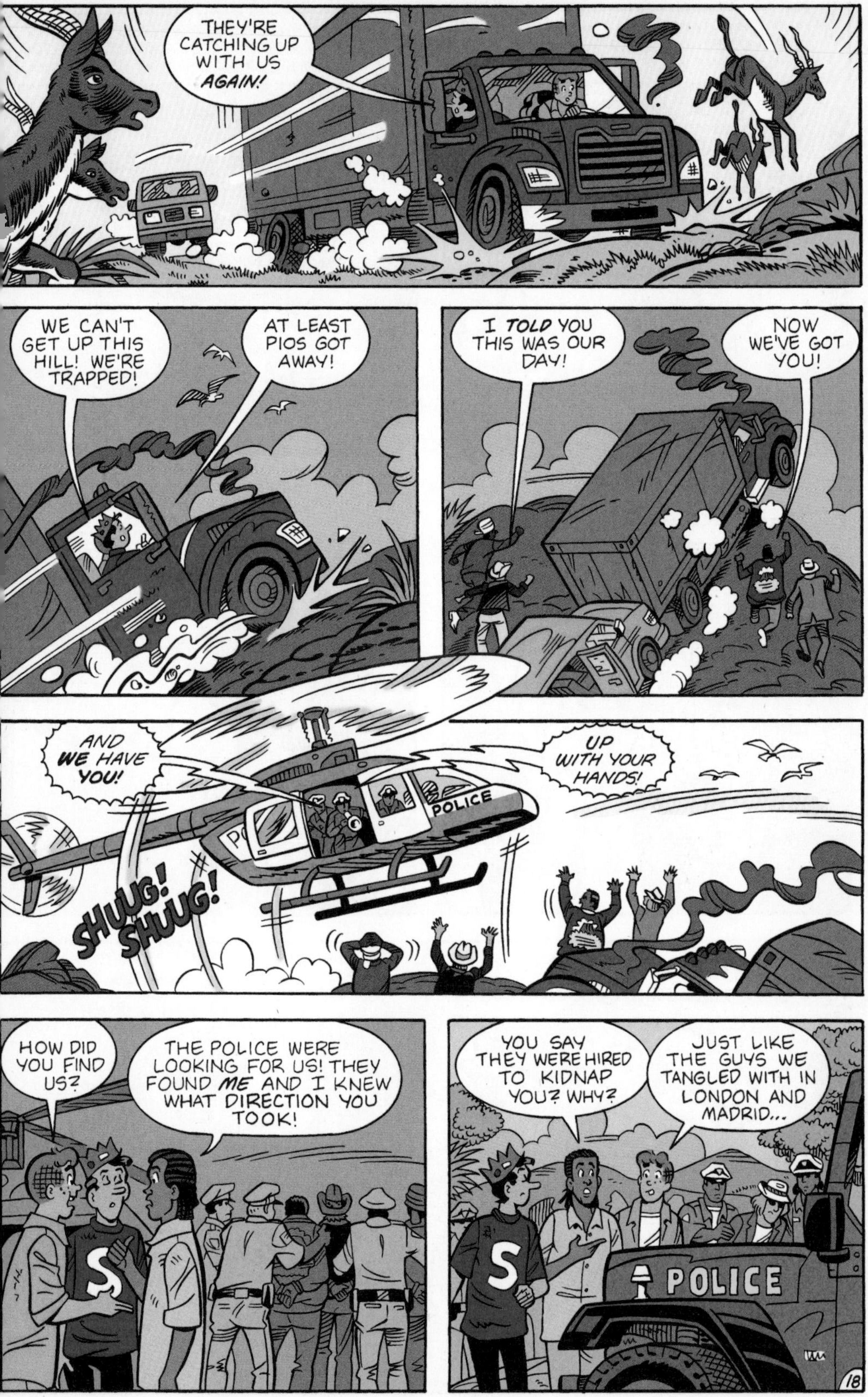
THEY'RE CATCHING UP WITH US AGAIN!
WE CAN'T GET UP THIS HILL! WE'RE TRAPPED!
AT LEAST PIOS GOT AWAY!
I TOLD YOU THIS WAS OUR DAY!
NOW WE'VE GOT YOU!
AND WE HAVE YOU!
UP WITH YOUR HANDS!
POLICE
SHUUG! SHUUG!
HOW DID YOU FIND US?
THE POLICE WERE LOOKING FOR US! THEY FOUND ME AND I KNEW WHAT DIRECTION YOU TOOK!
YOU SAY THEY WERE HIRED TO KIDNAP YOU? WHY?
JUST LIKE THE GUYS WE TANGLED WITH IN LONDON AND MADRID...
POLICE
18

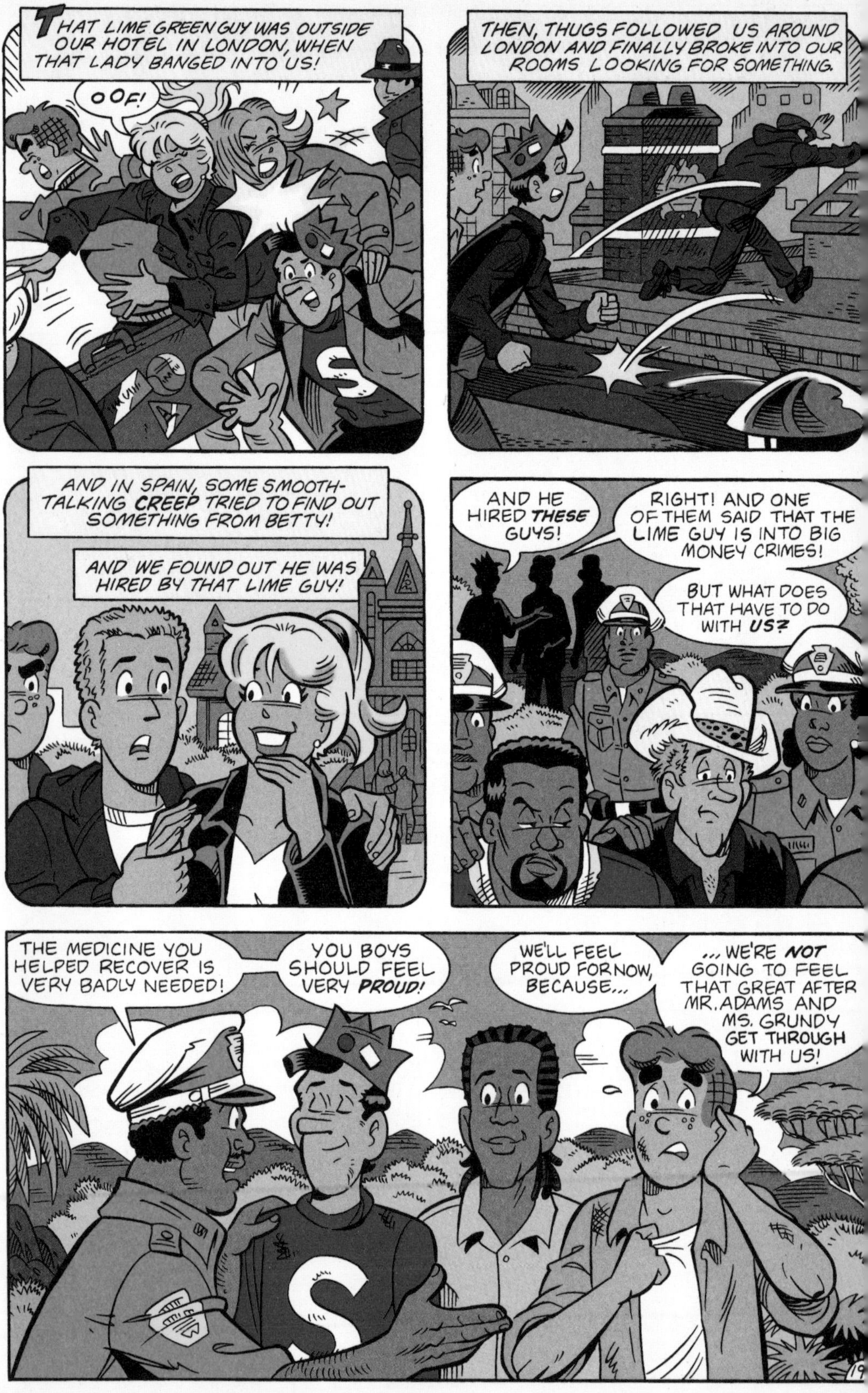
THAT LIME GREEN GUY WAS OUTSIDE OUR HOTEL IN LONDON, WHEN THAT LADY BANGED INTO US!
OOF!
THEN, THUGS FOLLOWED US AROUND LONDON AND FINALLY BROKE INTO OUR ROOMS LOOKING FOR SOMETHING.
AND IN SPAIN, SOME SMOOTH-TALKING CREEP TRIED TO FIND OUT SOMETHING FROM BETTY!
AND WE FOUND OUT HE WAS HIRED BY THAT LIME GUY!
AND HE HIRED THESE GUYS!
RIGHT! AND ONE OF THEM SAID THAT THE LIME GUY IS INTO BIG MONEY CRIMES!
BUT WHAT DOES THAT HAVE TO DO WITH US?
THE MEDICINE YOU HELPED RECOVER IS VERY BADLY NEEDED!
YOU BOYS SHOULD FEEL VERY PROUD!
WE'LL FEEL PROUD FOR NOW, BECAUSE...
...WE'RE NOT GOING TO FEEL THAT GREAT AFTER MR. ADAMS AND MS. GRUNDY GET THROUGH WITH US!

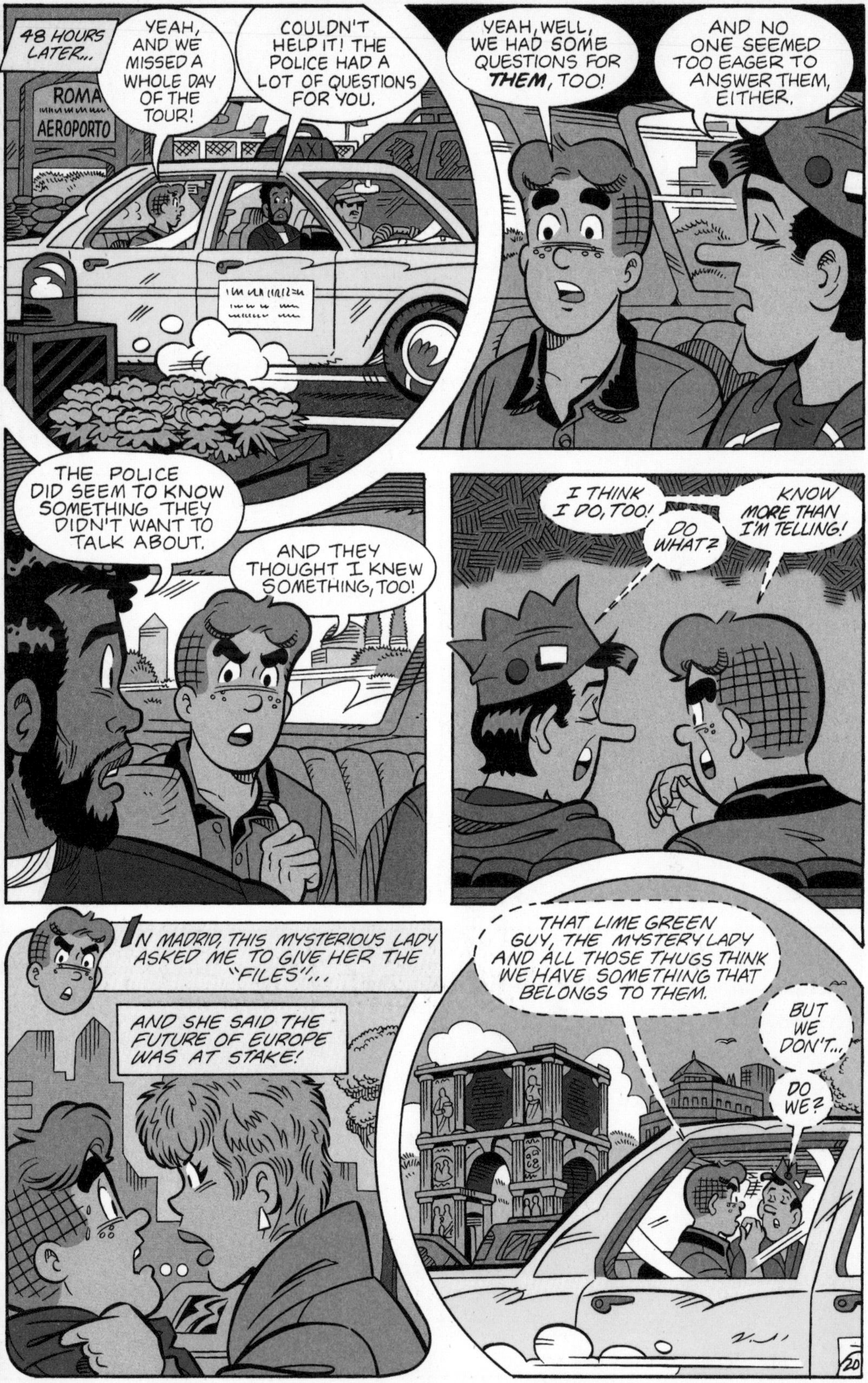
48 HOURS LATER...
ROMA
AEROPORTO
YEAH, AND WE MISSED A WHOLE DAY OF THE TOUR!
COULDN'T HELP IT! THE POLICE HAD A LOT OF QUESTIONS FOR YOU.
TAXI
YEAH, WELL, WE HAD SOME QUESTIONS FOR THEM, TOO!
AND NO ONE SEEMED TOO EAGER TO ANSWER THEM, EITHER.
THE POLICE DID SEEM TO KNOW SOMETHING THEY DIDN'T WANT TO TALK ABOUT.
AND THEY THOUGHT I KNEW SOMETHING, TOO!
I THINK I DO, TOO!
DO WHAT?
KNOW MORE THAN I'M TELLING!
IN MADRID, THIS MYSTERIOUS LADY ASKED ME TO GIVE HER THE "FILES"...
AND SHE SAID THE FUTURE OF EUROPE WAS AT STAKE!
THAT LIME GREEN GUY, THE MYSTERY LADY AND ALL THOSE THUGS THINK WE HAVE SOMETHING THAT BELONGS TO THEM.
BUT WE DON'T...
DO WE?
20

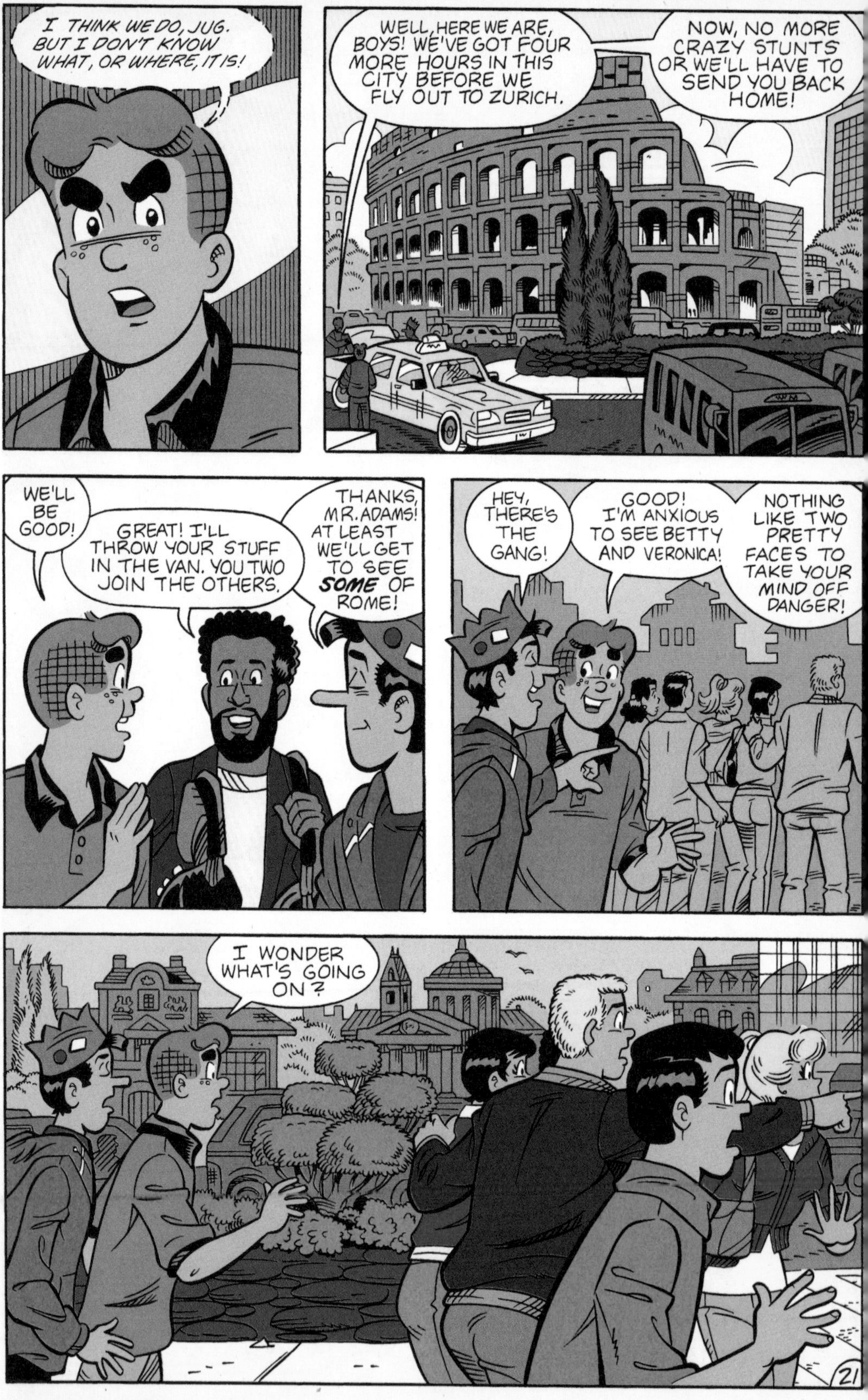
I THINK WE DO, JUG. BUT I DON'T KNOW WHAT, OR WHERE, IT IS!
WELL, HERE WE ARE, BOYS! WE'VE GOT FOUR MORE HOURS IN THIS CITY BEFORE WE FLY OUT TO ZURICH.
NOW, NO MORE CRAZY STUNTS OR WE'LL HAVE TO SEND YOU BACK HOME!
WE'LL BE GOOD!
GREAT! I'LL THROW YOUR STUFF IN THE VAN. YOU TWO JOIN THE OTHERS.
THANKS, MR. ADAMS! AT LEAST WE'LL GET TO SEE SOME OF ROME!
HEY, THERE'S THE GANG!
GOOD! I'M ANXIOUS TO SEE BETTY AND VERONICA!
NOTHING LIKE TWO PRETTY FACES TO TAKE YOUR MIND OFF DANGER!
I WONDER WHAT'S GOING ON?

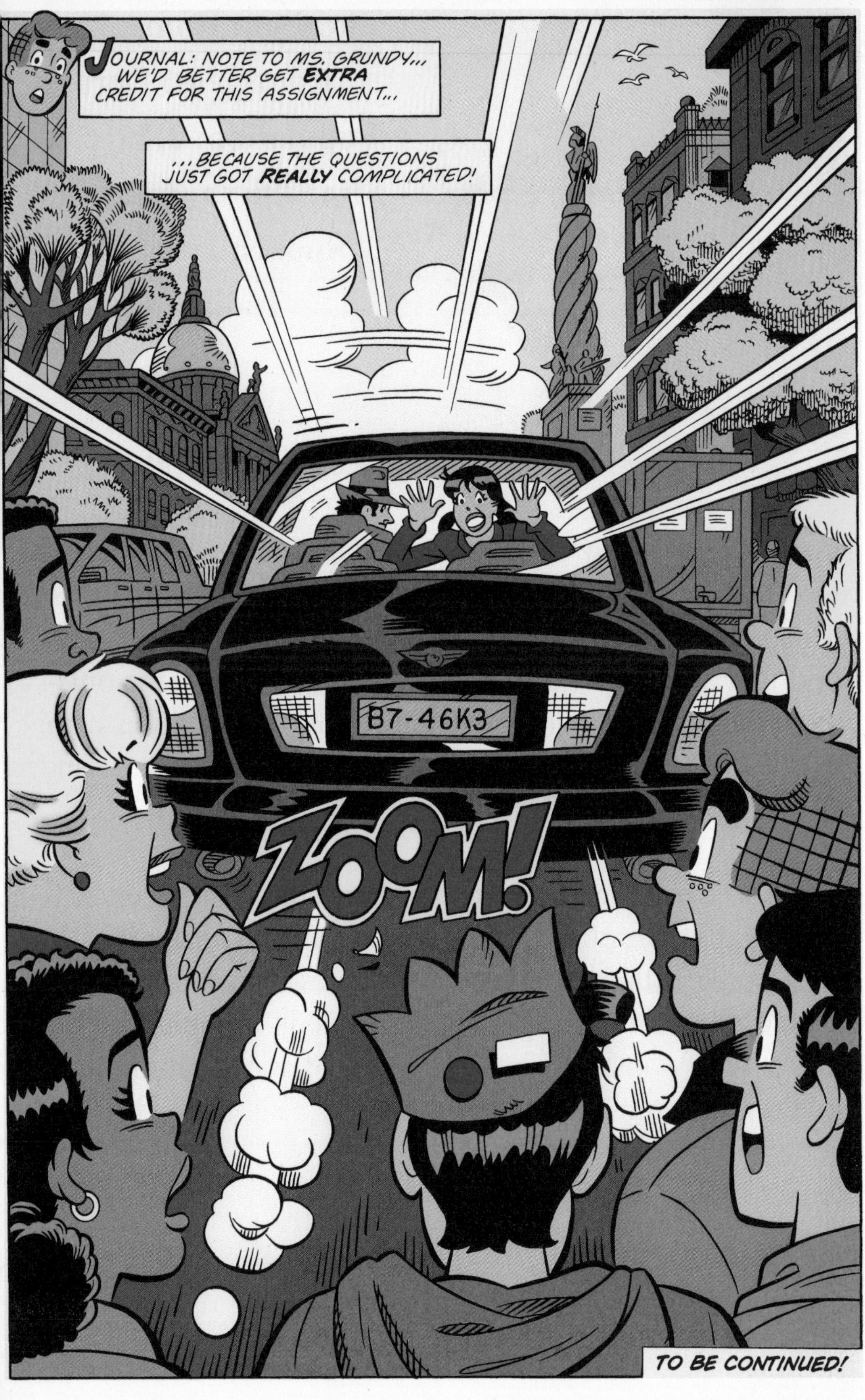
JOURNAL: NOTE TO MS. GRUNDY... WE'D BETTER GET EXTRA CREDIT FOR THIS ASSIGNMENT...
...BECAUSE THE QUESTIONS JUST GOT REALLY COMPLICATED!
B7-46K3
ZOOM!
TO BE CONTINUED!

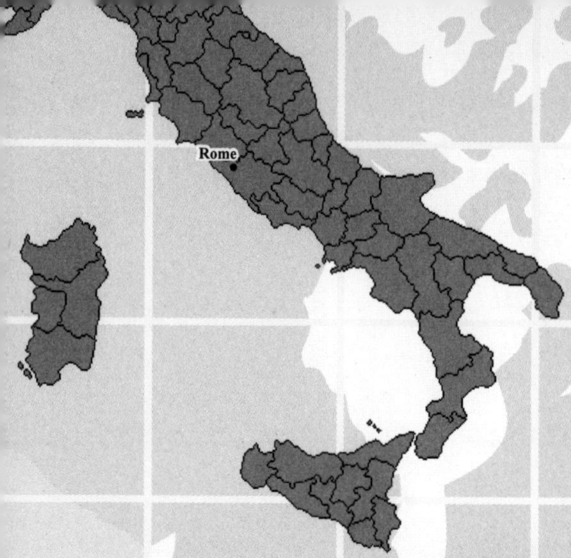
Rome

Location: Rome, Italy
Continent: Europe
Population: 2,761,000
Size: 496 square miles
Spoken Languages: Italian, English

"Benvenuto" to Rome, the capital of Italy!

Rome is one of the oldest cities in the world (over two-and-a-half thousand years old to be exact!) Rome was the capital of the Roman Empire and continues to be a very important city to this day. Did you know Rome is the only city in the world to contain an entire sovereign nation within its walls? It's true! Vatican City is an independent state and exists entirely within Rome.

Rome has always been an important cultural center and was at the forefront of the Renaissance. During this time between the 14th and 17th centuries, new ideas and dialogues spread throughout Europe. Today Rome is a popular city for tourists who want to visit the remains of ancient buildings like the Coliseum and the Pantheon.

Location: Zurich, Switzerland

Continent: Europe

Population: 372,047

Size: 35.48 square miles

Spoken Languages:

German, French,

Italian, Romansh, English

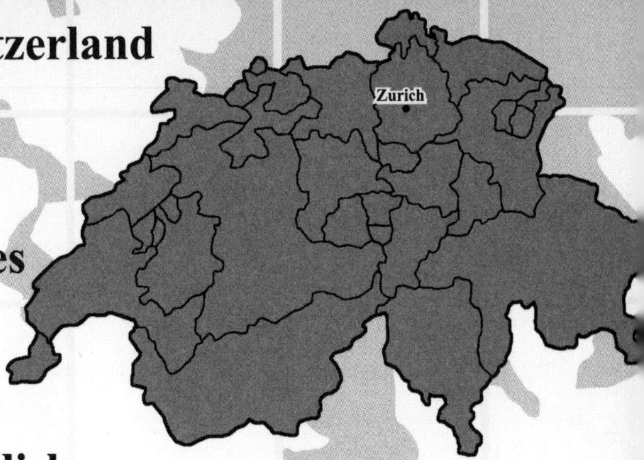
Zurich

Willkommen to Zurich, the capital of Switzerland!

Switzerland lends itself to be one of the most diverse countries in Europe. This is due in part to its borders, which are comprised of five very different countries: Germany to the North, France to the West, Italy to the South and Austria and Liechtenstein to the East. In fact, German, French and Italian are all recognized as official languages in the country.

Switzerland is also one of the wealthiest countries in the world and is noted as one of Europe's most innovative countries. Switzerland is most famous for its neutrality and has not been involved in an international war since 1815.

The history of Zurich dates back to its settling by the Romans in 15 BC. Zurich has had some very famous residents like the composer Richard Wagner, the physicist Albert Einstein, who went to school there, and Irish novelist James Joyce, who is also buried there.

Archie®
WORLD TOUR

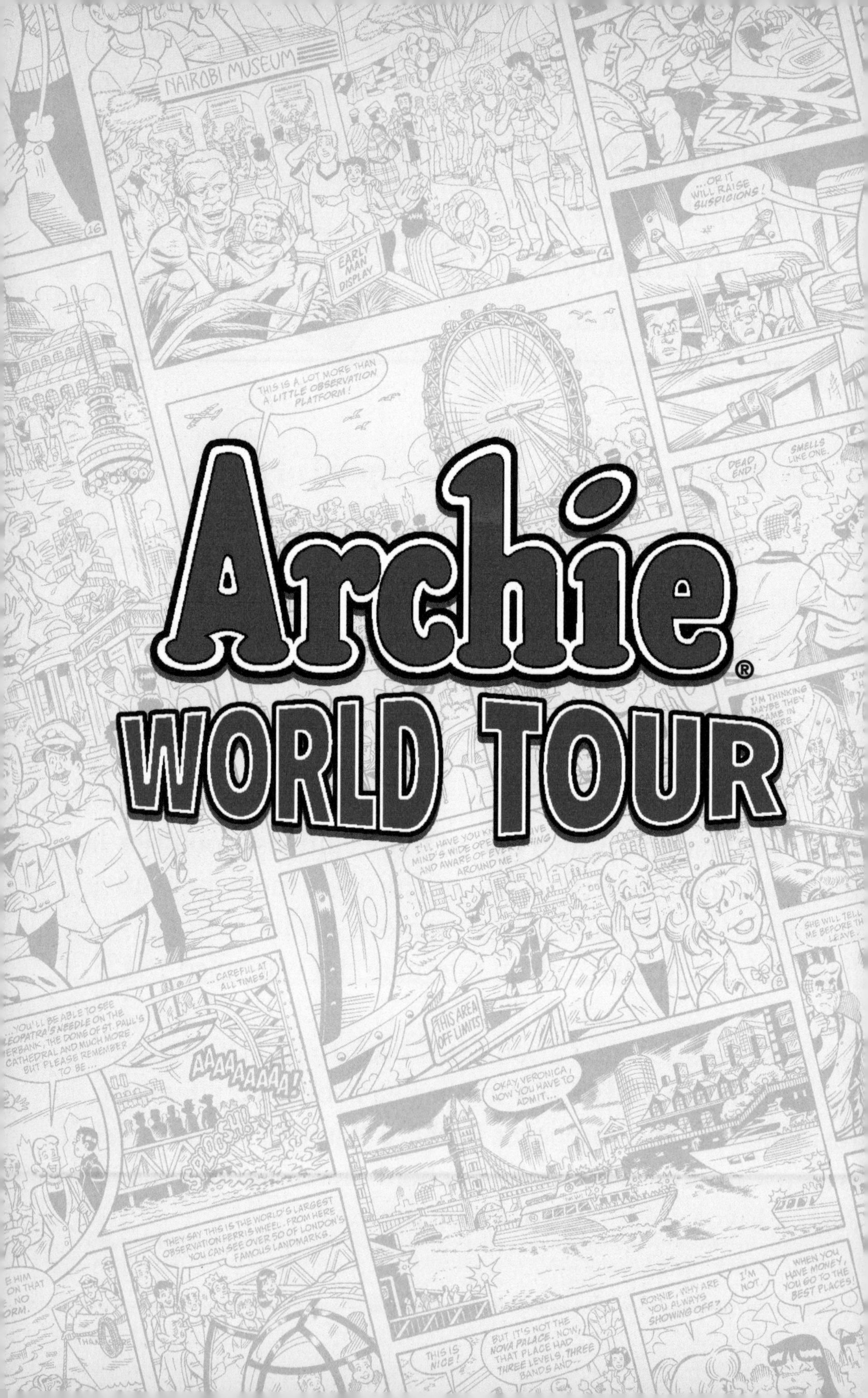

CHAPTER 4: ROME & SWITZERLAND

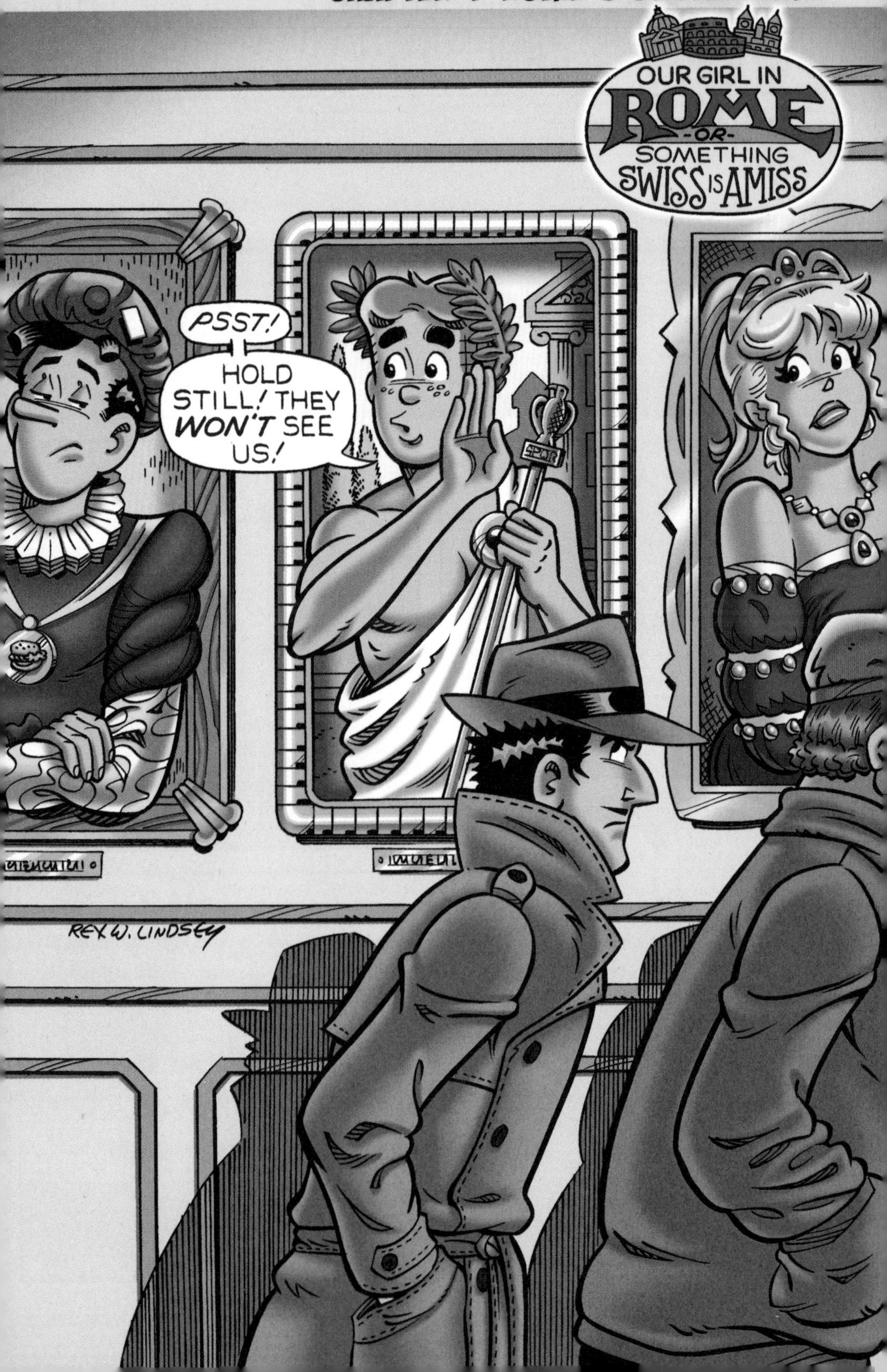
OUR GIRL IN ROME -OR- SOMETHING SWISS IS AMISS
PSST!
HOLD STILL! THEY *WON'T* SEE US!
REX W. LINDSEY

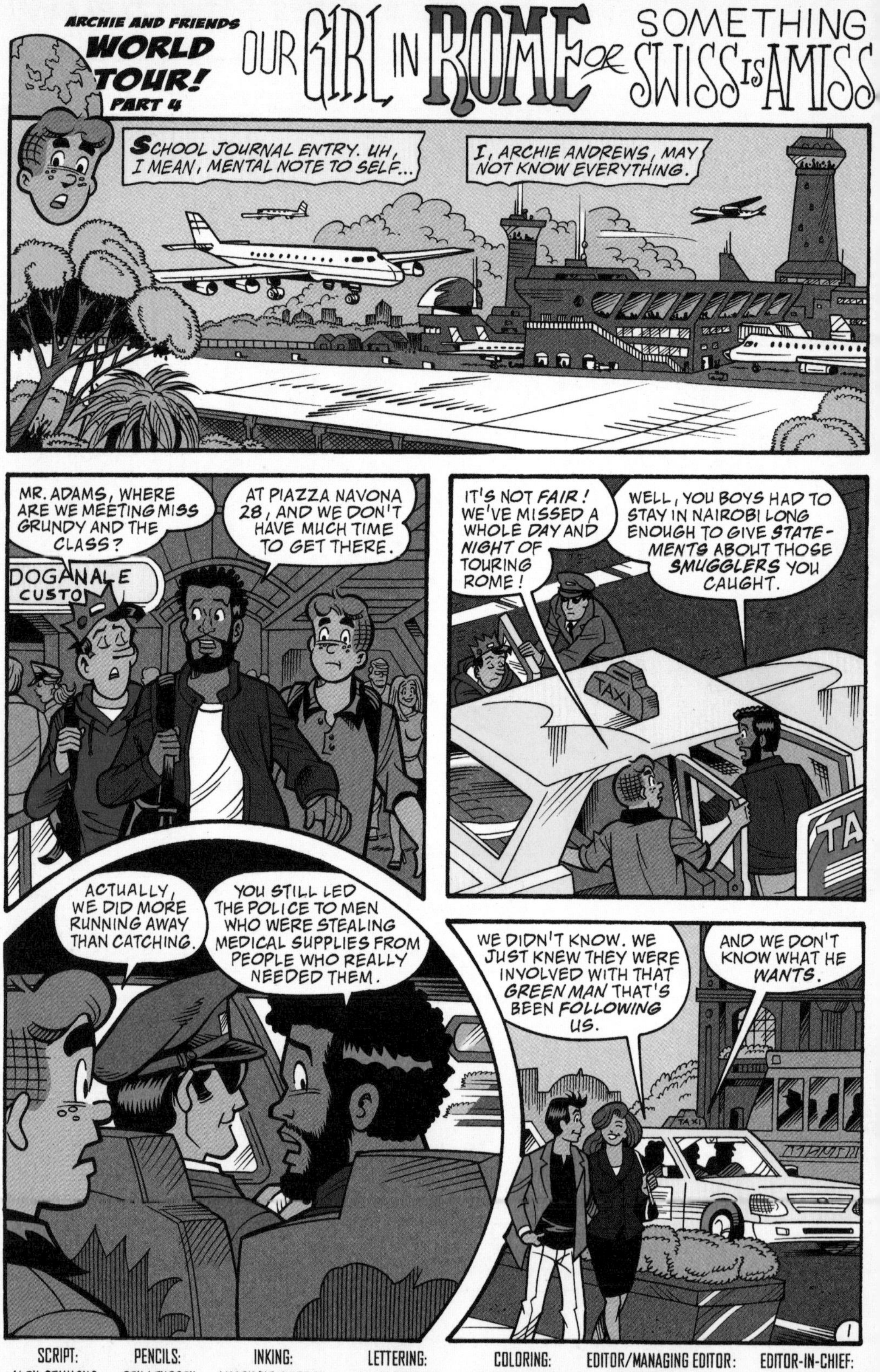
ARCHIE AND FRIENDS WORLD TOUR! PART 4
OUR GIRL IN ROME OR SOMETHING SWISS IS AMISS
SCHOOL JOURNAL ENTRY. UH, I MEAN, MENTAL NOTE TO SELF...
I, ARCHIE ANDREWS, MAY NOT KNOW EVERYTHING.
MR. ADAMS, WHERE ARE WE MEETING MISS GRUNDY AND THE CLASS?
AT PIAZZA NAVONA 28, AND WE DON'T HAVE MUCH TIME TO GET THERE.
DOGANALE
CUSTO
IT'S NOT FAIR! WE'VE MISSED A WHOLE DAY AND NIGHT OF TOURING ROME!
WELL, YOU BOYS HAD TO STAY IN NAIROBI LONG ENOUGH TO GIVE STATEMENTS ABOUT THOSE SMUGGLERS YOU CAUGHT.
TAXI
ACTUALLY, WE DID MORE RUNNING AWAY THAN CATCHING.
YOU STILL LED THE POLICE TO MEN WHO WERE STEALING MEDICAL SUPPLIES FROM PEOPLE WHO REALLY NEEDED THEM.
WE DIDN'T KNOW. WE JUST KNEW THEY WERE INVOLVED WITH THAT GREEN MAN THAT'S BEEN FOLLOWING US.
AND WE DON'T KNOW WHAT HE WANTS.
1

SCRIPT: ALEX SIMMONS PENCILS: REX LINDSEY INKING: AMASH/NICKERSON LETTERING: FELIX/OWSLEY COLORING: GLENN WHITMORE EDITOR/MANAGING EDITOR: MIKE PELLERITO EDITOR-IN-CHIEF: VICTOR GORELICK

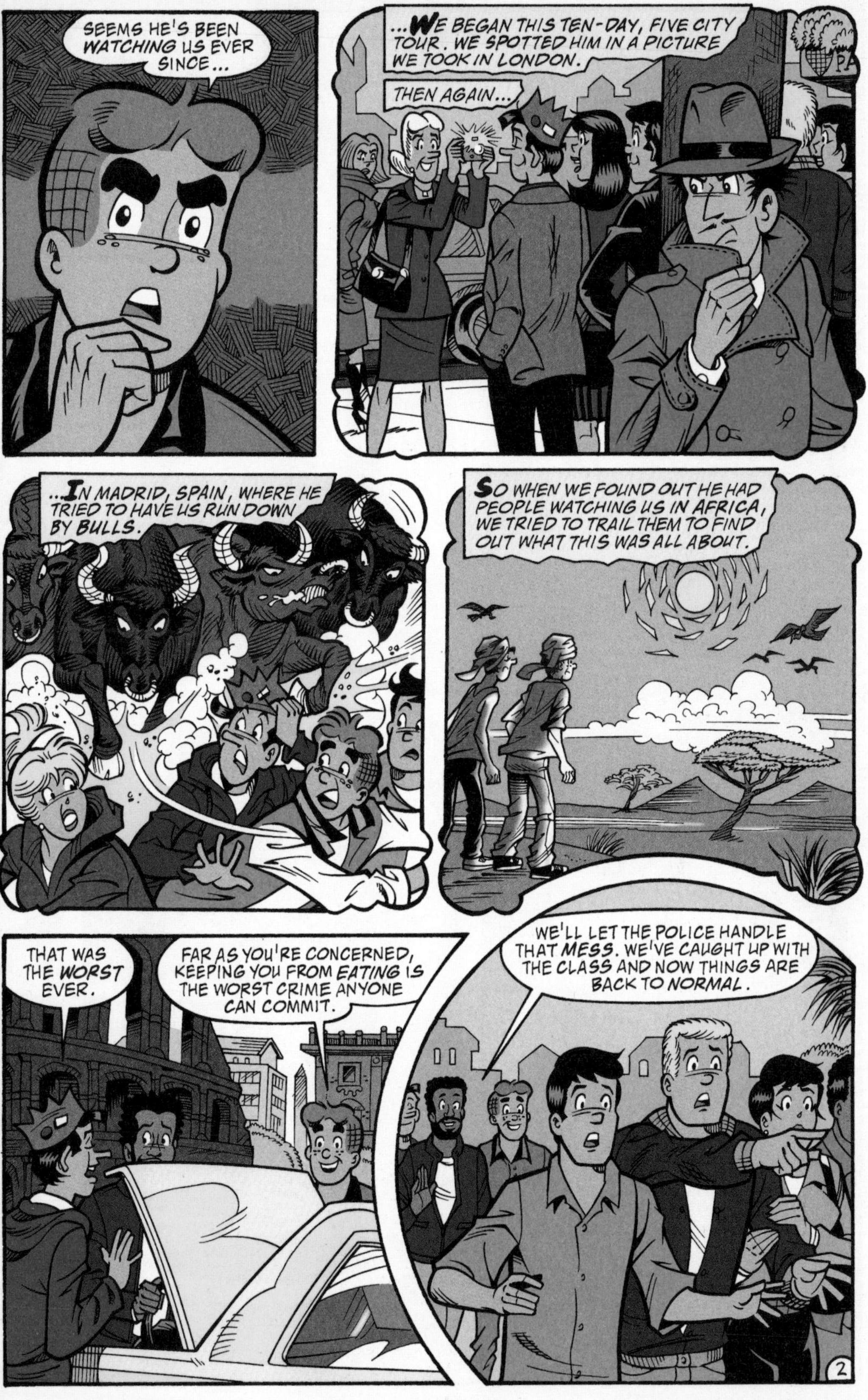
SEEMS HE'S BEEN WATCHING US EVER SINCE...
...WE BEGAN THIS TEN-DAY, FIVE CITY TOUR. WE SPOTTED HIM IN A PICTURE WE TOOK IN LONDON.
THEN AGAIN...
...IN MADRID, SPAIN, WHERE HE TRIED TO HAVE US RUN DOWN BY BULLS.
SO WHEN WE FOUND OUT HE HAD PEOPLE WATCHING US IN AFRICA, WE TRIED TO TRAIL THEM TO FIND OUT WHAT THIS WAS ALL ABOUT.
THAT WAS THE WORST EVER.
FAR AS YOU'RE CONCERNED, KEEPING YOU FROM EATING IS THE WORST CRIME ANYONE CAN COMMIT.
WE'LL LET THE POLICE HANDLE THAT MESS. WE'VE CAUGHT UP WITH THE CLASS AND NOW THINGS ARE BACK TO NORMAL.
2

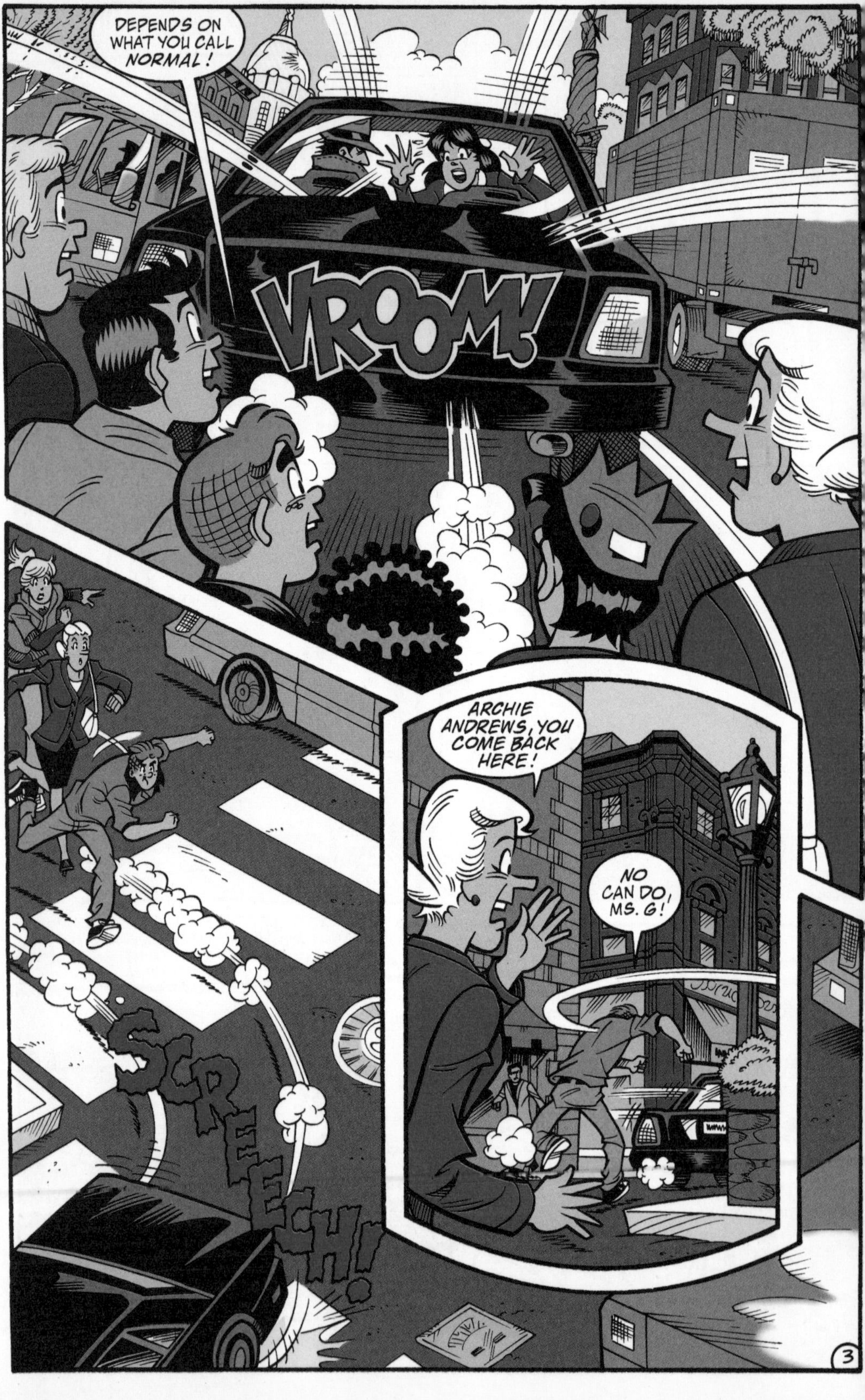
DEPENDS ON WHAT YOU CALL NORMAL!
VROOM!
SCREECH!
ARCHIE ANDREWS, YOU COME BACK HERE!
NO CAN DO, MS. G!

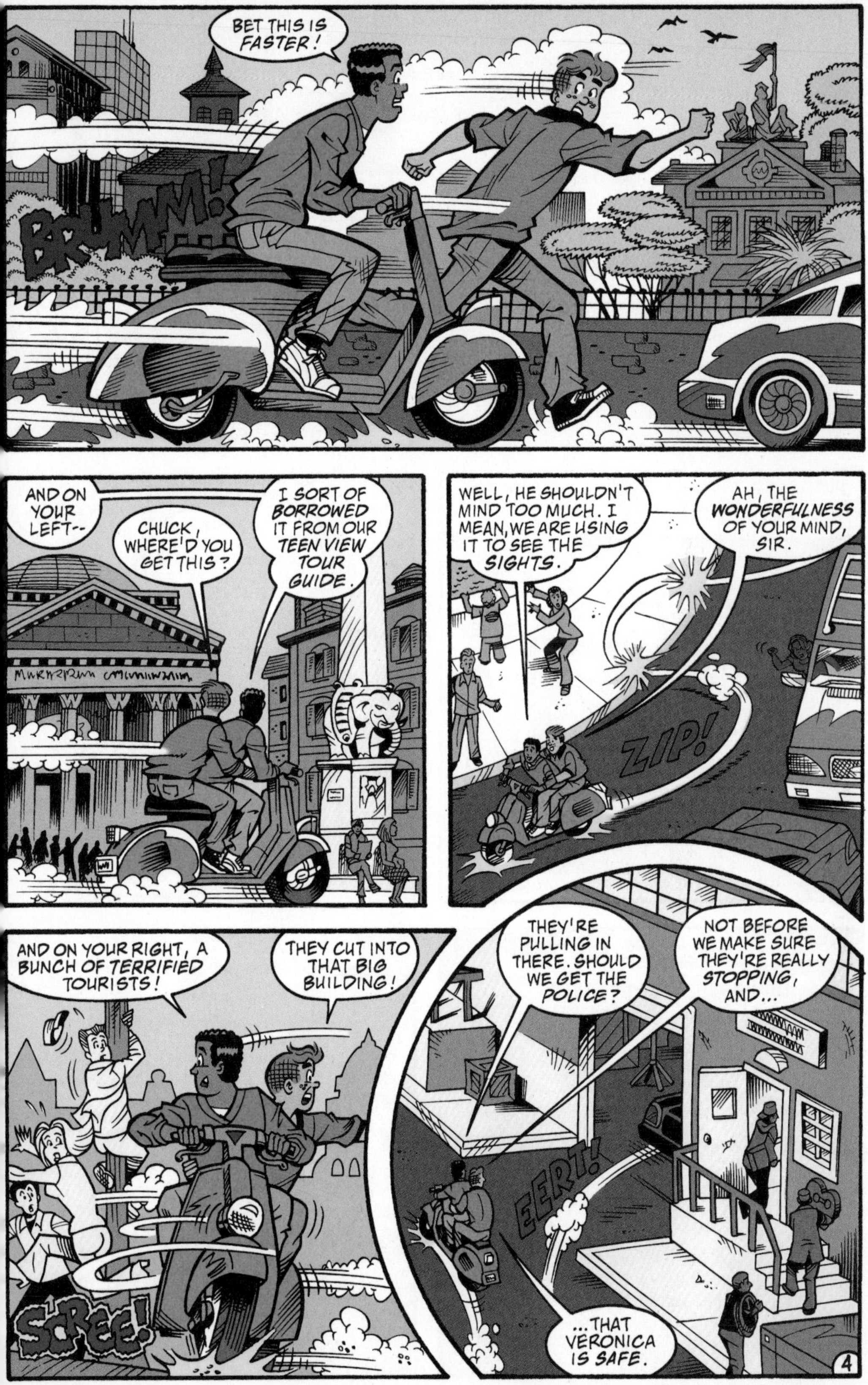

BET THIS IS FASTER!
BRUMM!
AND ON YOUR LEFT--
CHUCK, WHERE'D YOU GET THIS?
I SORT OF BORROWED IT FROM OUR TEEN VIEW TOUR GUIDE.
WELL, HE SHOULDN'T MIND TOO MUCH. I MEAN, WE ARE USING IT TO SEE THE SIGHTS.
AH, THE WONDERFULNESS OF YOUR MIND, SIR.
ZIP!
AND ON YOUR RIGHT, A BUNCH OF TERRIFIED TOURISTS!
THEY CUT INTO THAT BIG BUILDING!
SCREE!
THEY'RE PULLING IN THERE. SHOULD WE GET THE POLICE?
NOT BEFORE WE MAKE SURE THEY'RE REALLY STOPPING, AND...
EERT!
...THAT VERONICA IS SAFE.
4

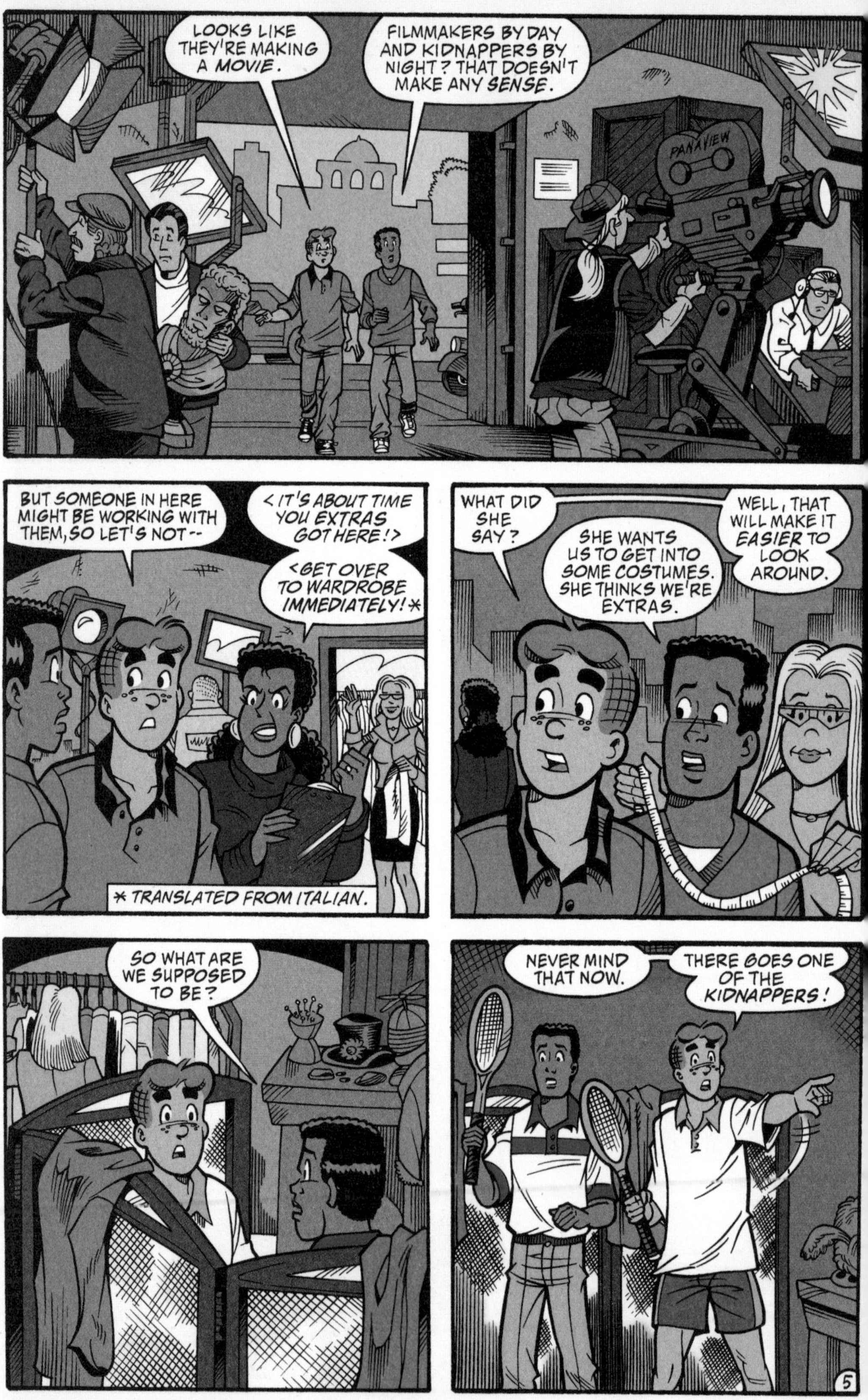

LOOKS LIKE THEY'RE MAKING A MOVIE.
FILMMAKERS BY DAY AND KIDNAPPERS BY NIGHT? THAT DOESN'T MAKE ANY SENSE.
PANAVIEW
BUT SOMEONE IN HERE MIGHT BE WORKING WITH THEM, SO LET'S NOT --
<IT'S ABOUT TIME YOU EXTRAS GOT HERE!>
<GET OVER TO WARDROBE IMMEDIATELY!>*
* TRANSLATED FROM ITALIAN.
WHAT DID SHE SAY?
SHE WANTS US TO GET INTO SOME COSTUMES. SHE THINKS WE'RE EXTRAS.
WELL, THAT WILL MAKE IT EASIER TO LOOK AROUND.
SO WHAT ARE WE SUPPOSED TO BE?
NEVER MIND THAT NOW.
THERE GOES ONE OF THE KIDNAPPERS!

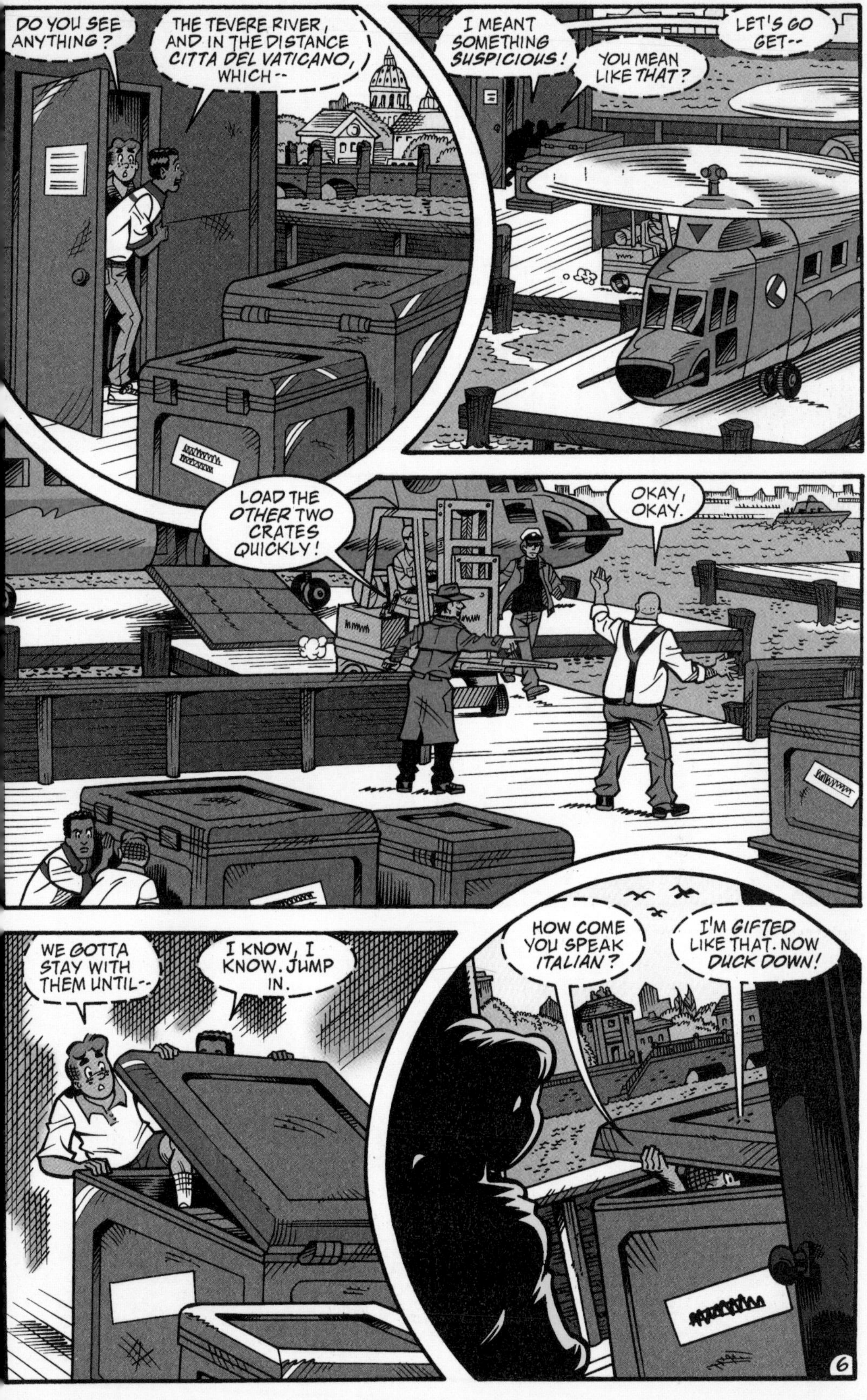

DO YOU SEE ANYTHING?
THE TEVERE RIVER, AND IN THE DISTANCE CITTA DEL VATICANO, WHICH--
I MEANT SOMETHING SUSPICIOUS!
YOU MEAN LIKE THAT?
LET'S GO GET--
LOAD THE OTHER TWO CRATES QUICKLY!
OKAY, OKAY.
WE GOTTA STAY WITH THEM UNTIL--
I KNOW, I KNOW. JUMP IN.
HOW COME YOU SPEAK ITALIAN?
I'M GIFTED LIKE THAT. NOW DUCK DOWN!

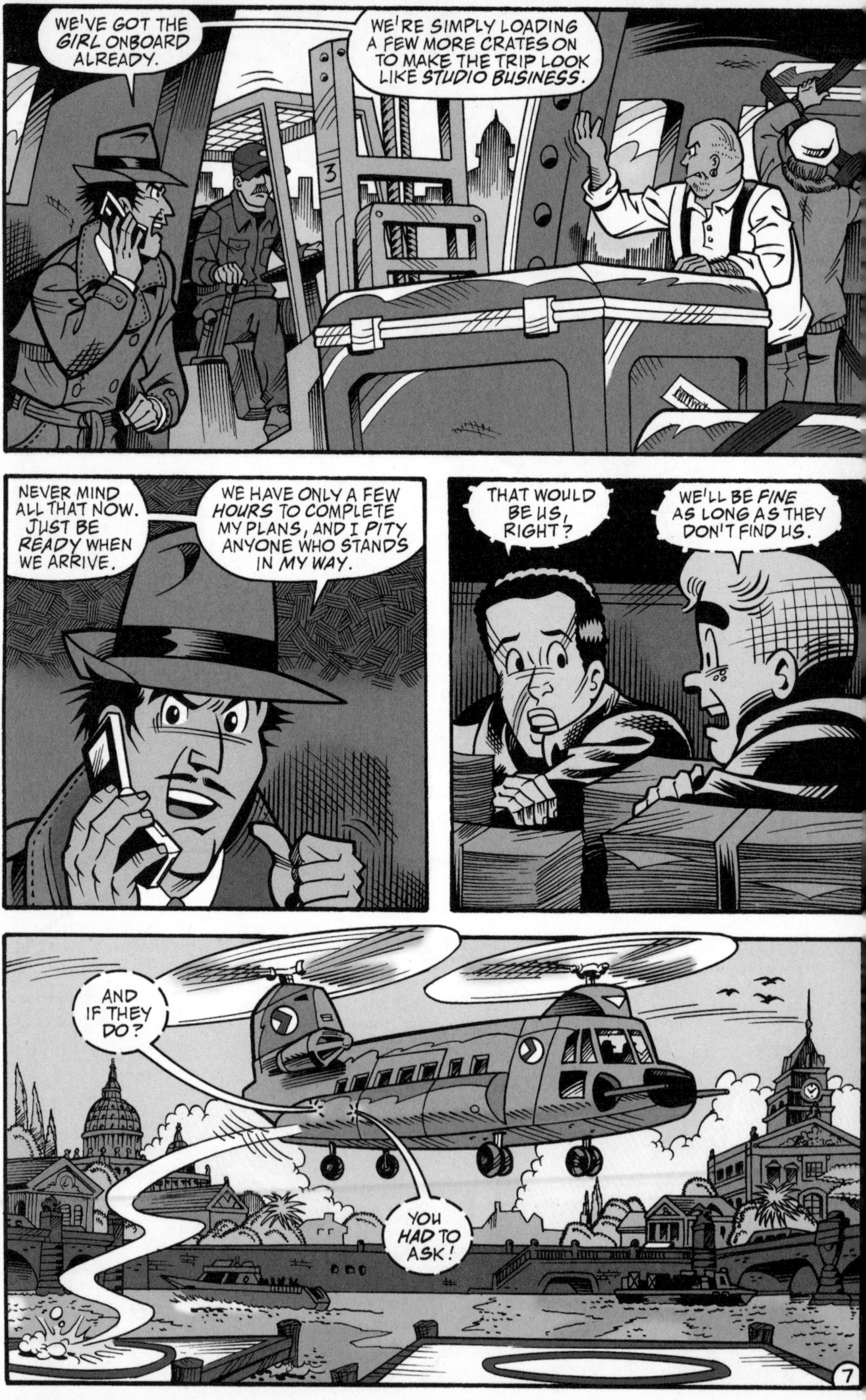

WE'VE GOT THE GIRL ONBOARD ALREADY.
WE'RE SIMPLY LOADING A FEW MORE CRATES ON TO MAKE THE TRIP LOOK LIKE STUDIO BUSINESS.
NEVER MIND ALL THAT NOW. JUST BE READY WHEN WE ARRIVE.
WE HAVE ONLY A FEW HOURS TO COMPLETE MY PLANS, AND I PITY ANYONE WHO STANDS IN MY WAY.
THAT WOULD BE US, RIGHT?
WE'LL BE FINE AS LONG AS THEY DON'T FIND US.
AND IF THEY DO?
YOU HAD TO ASK!

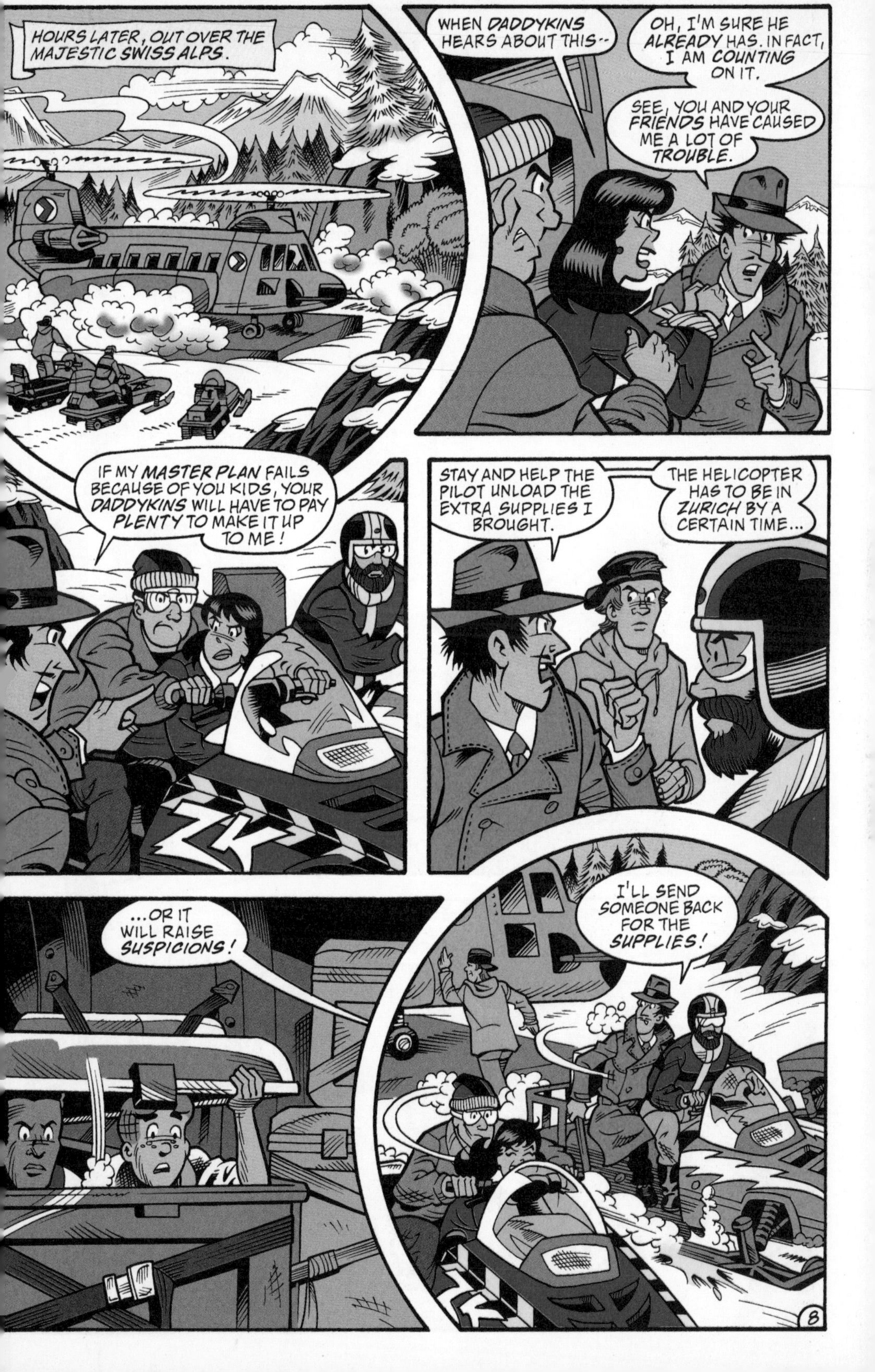
HOURS LATER, OUT OVER THE MAJESTIC SWISS ALPS.
WHEN DADDYKINS HEARS ABOUT THIS--
OH, I'M SURE HE ALREADY HAS. IN FACT, I AM COUNTING ON IT.
SEE, YOU AND YOUR FRIENDS HAVE CAUSED ME A LOT OF TROUBLE.
IF MY MASTER PLAN FAILS BECAUSE OF YOU KIDS, YOUR DADDYKINS WILL HAVE TO PAY PLENTY TO MAKE IT UP TO ME!
STAY AND HELP THE PILOT UNLOAD THE EXTRA SUPPLIES I BROUGHT.
THE HELICOPTER HAS TO BE IN ZURICH BY A CERTAIN TIME...
...OR IT WILL RAISE SUSPICIONS!
I'LL SEND SOMEONE BACK FOR THE SUPPLIES!
ZK
8

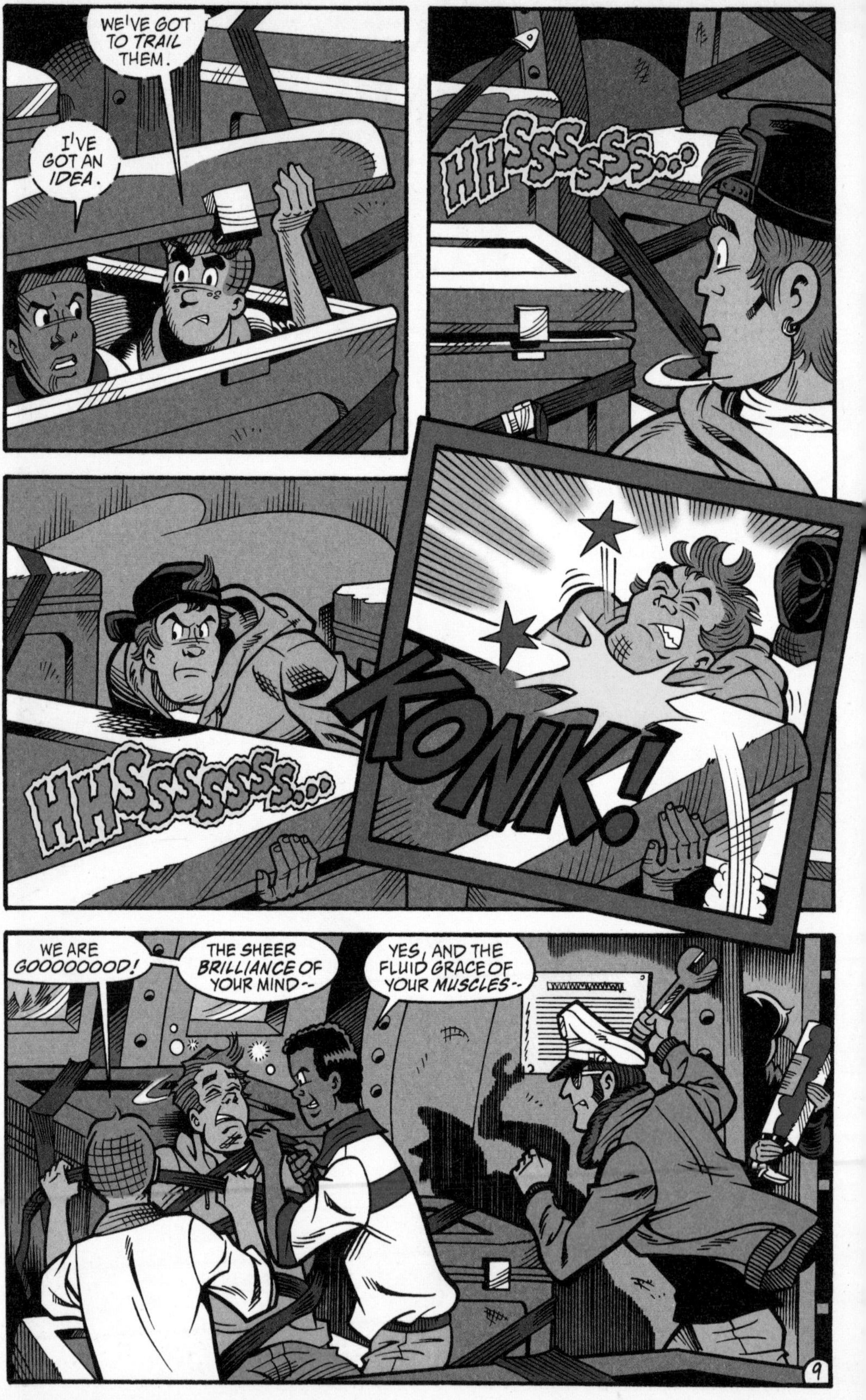
WE'VE GOT TO TRAIL THEM.
I'VE GOT AN IDEA.
HHSSSSSS...
HHSSSSSSS...
KONK!
WE ARE GOOOOOOOD!
THE SHEER BRILLIANCE OF YOUR MIND--
YES, AND THE FLUID GRACE OF YOUR MUSCLES--

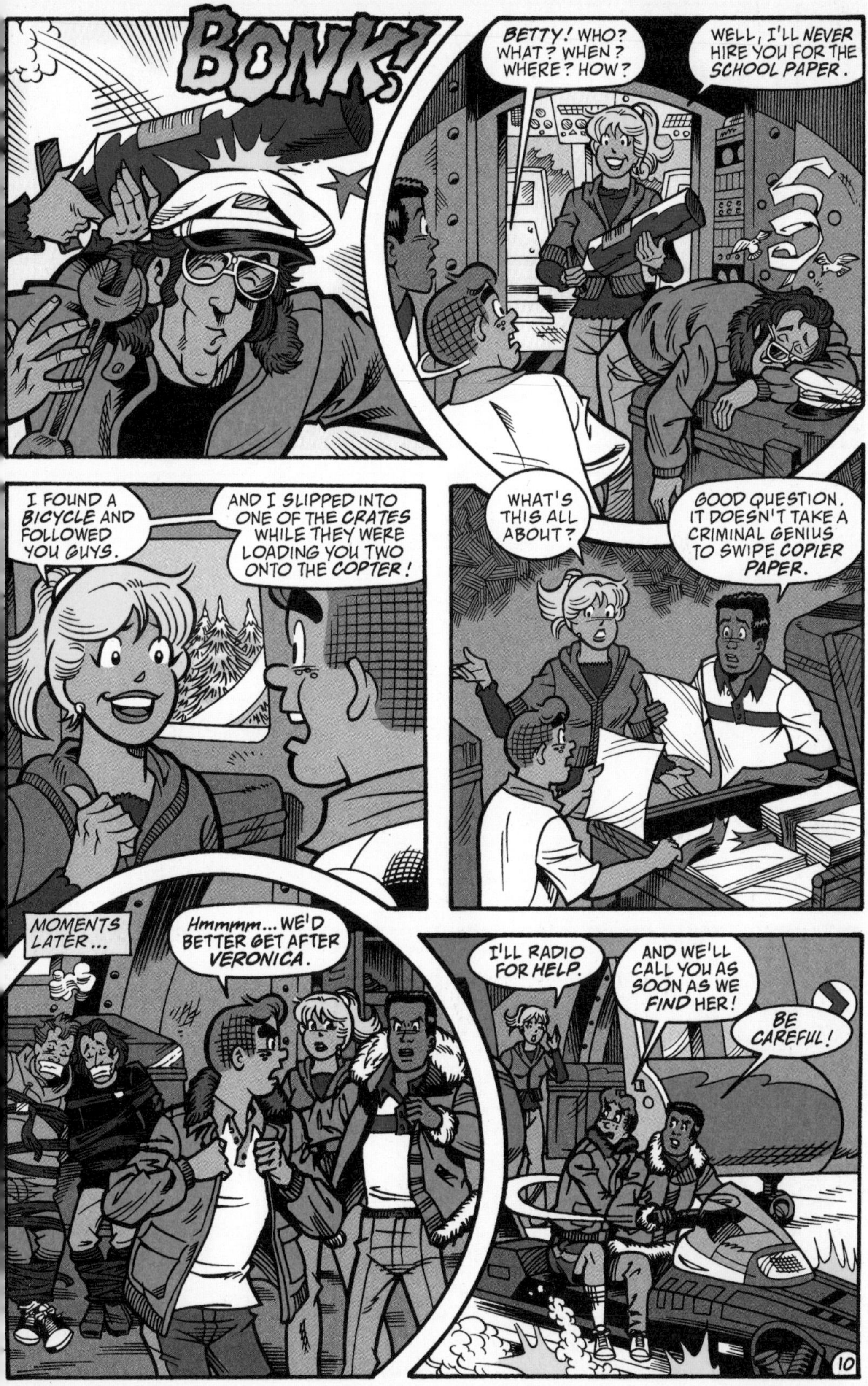
BONK!
BETTY! WHO? WHAT? WHEN? WHERE? HOW?
WELL, I'LL NEVER HIRE YOU FOR THE SCHOOL PAPER.
I FOUND A BICYCLE AND FOLLOWED YOU GUYS.
AND I SLIPPED INTO ONE OF THE CRATES WHILE THEY WERE LOADING YOU TWO ONTO THE COPTER!
WHAT'S THIS ALL ABOUT?
GOOD QUESTION. IT DOESN'T TAKE A CRIMINAL GENIUS TO SWIPE COPIER PAPER.
MOMENTS LATER...
Hmmmm... WE'D BETTER GET AFTER VERONICA.
I'LL RADIO FOR HELP.
AND WE'LL CALL YOU AS SOON AS WE FIND HER!
BE CAREFUL!
10

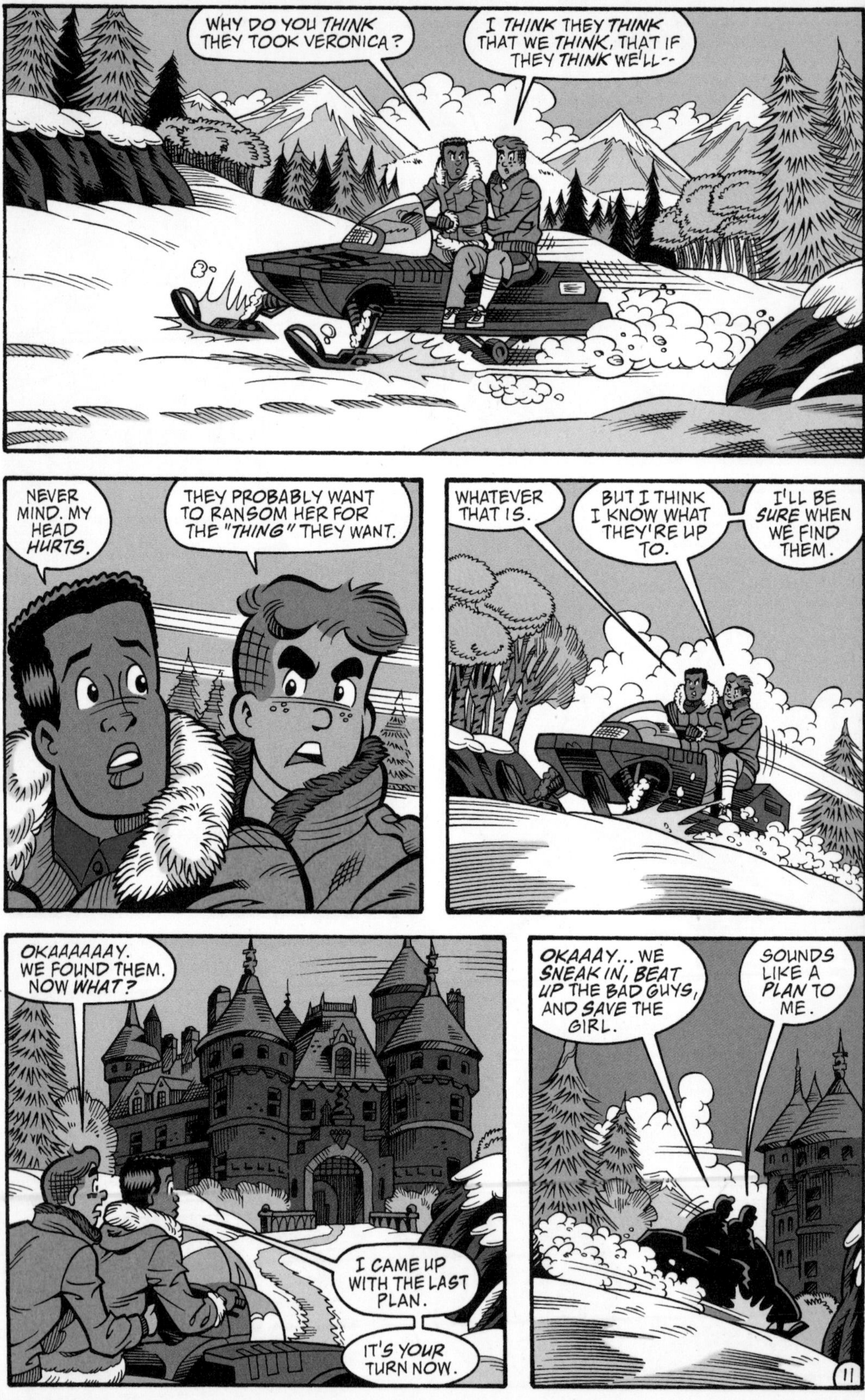
WHY DO YOU THINK THEY TOOK VERONICA?
I THINK THEY THINK THAT WE THINK, THAT IF THEY THINK WE'LL--
NEVER MIND. MY HEAD HURTS.
THEY PROBABLY WANT TO RANSOM HER FOR THE "THING" THEY WANT.
WHATEVER THAT IS.
BUT I THINK I KNOW WHAT THEY'RE UP TO.
I'LL BE SURE WHEN WE FIND THEM.
OKAAAAAAY. WE FOUND THEM. NOW WHAT?
I CAME UP WITH THE LAST PLAN.
IT'S YOUR TURN NOW.
OKAAAY... WE SNEAK IN, BEAT UP THE BAD GUYS, AND SAVE THE GIRL.
SOUNDS LIKE A PLAN TO ME.

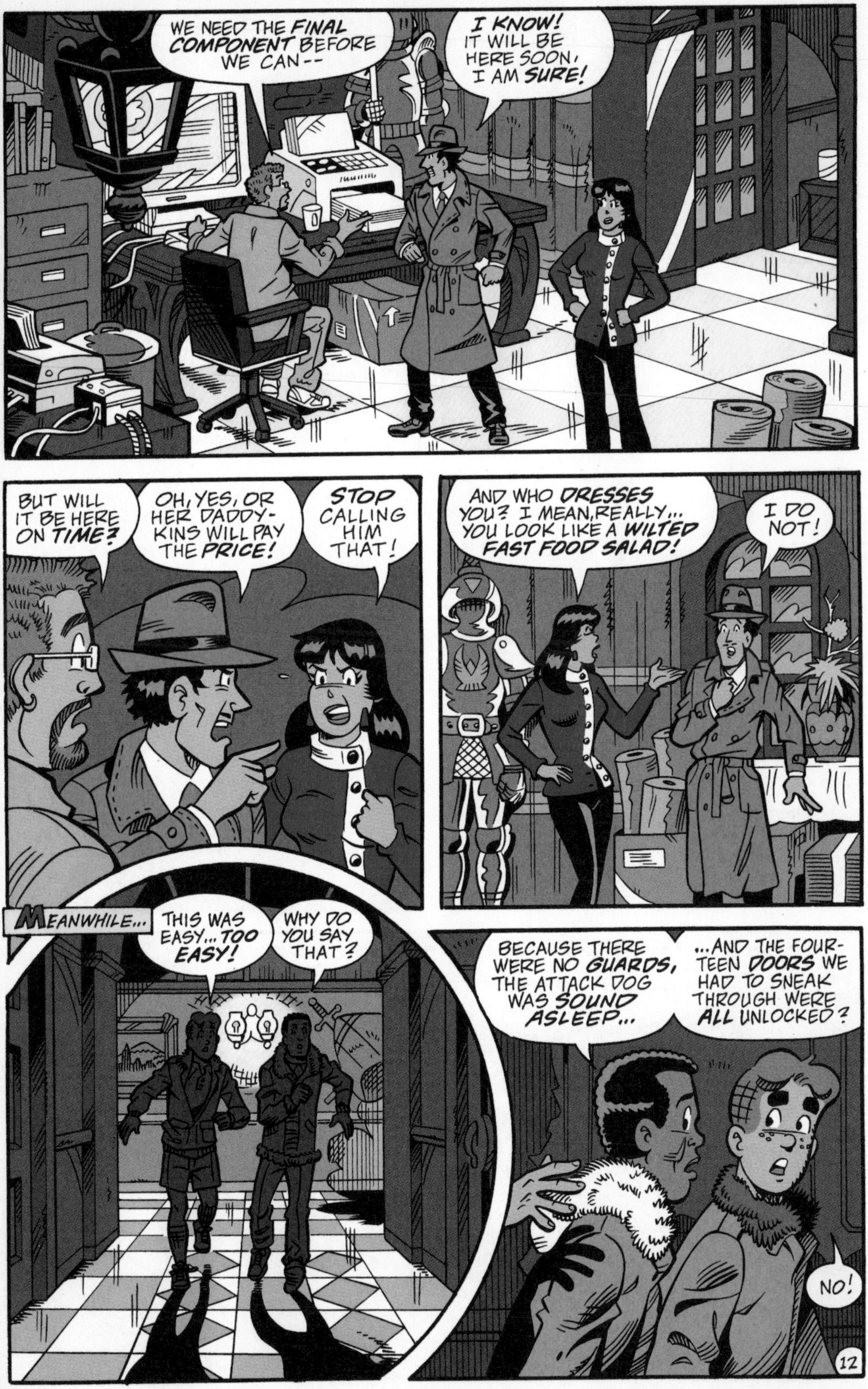
WE NEED THE FINAL COMPONENT BEFORE WE CAN--
I KNOW! IT WILL BE HERE SOON, I AM SURE!
BUT WILL IT BE HERE ON TIME?
OH, YES, OR HER DADDY-KINS WILL PAY THE PRICE!
STOP CALLING HIM THAT!
AND WHO DRESSES YOU? I MEAN, REALLY... YOU LOOK LIKE A WILTED FAST FOOD SALAD!
I DO NOT!
MEANWHILE...
THIS WAS EASY... TOO EASY!
WHY DO YOU SAY THAT?
BECAUSE THERE WERE NO GUARDS, THE ATTACK DOG WAS SOUND ASLEEP...
...AND THE FOUR-TEEN DOORS WE HAD TO SNEAK THROUGH WERE ALL UNLOCKED?
NO!

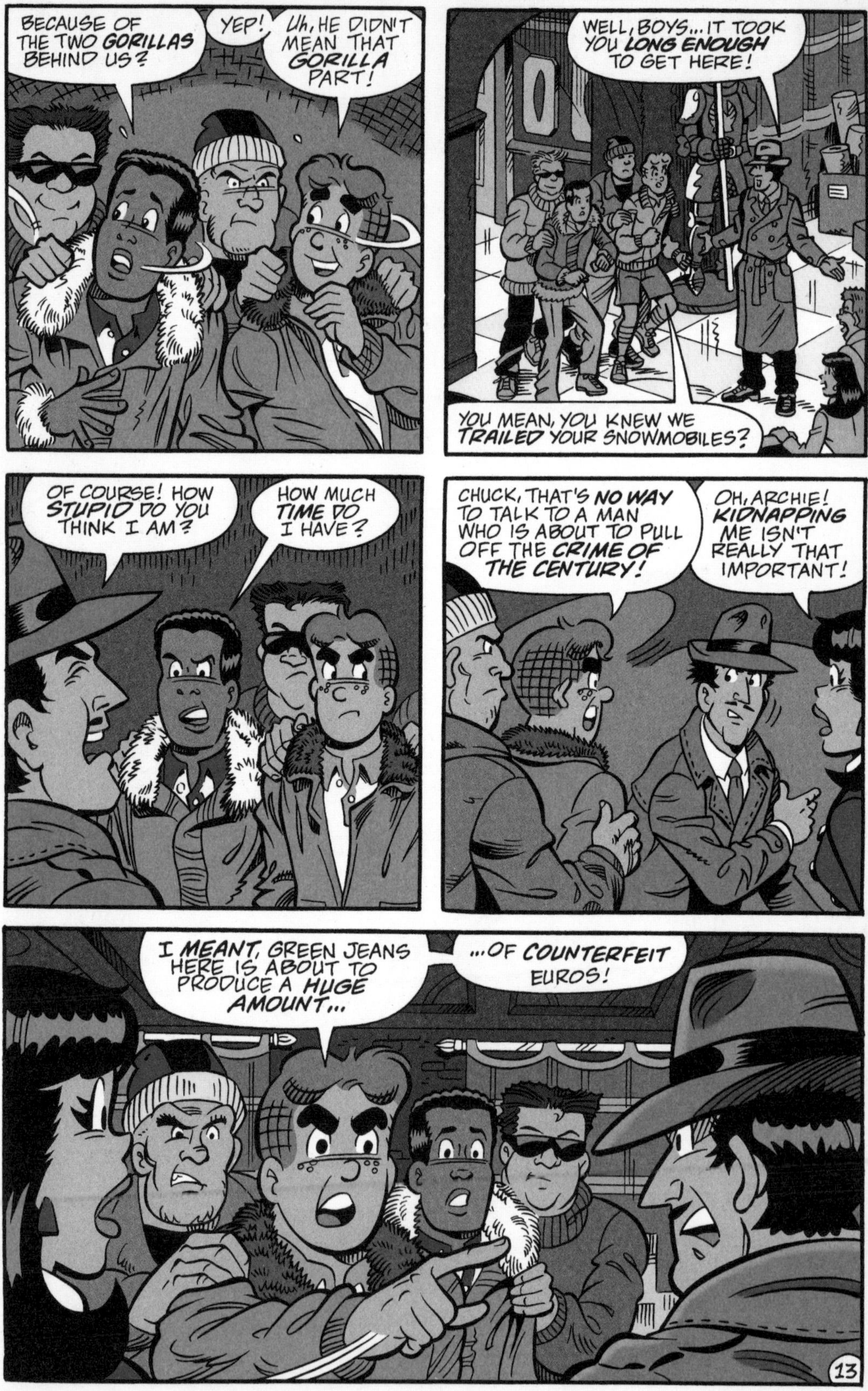
BECAUSE OF THE TWO GORILLAS BEHIND US?
YEP!
Uh, HE DIDN'T MEAN THAT GORILLA PART!
WELL, BOYS... IT TOOK YOU LONG ENOUGH TO GET HERE!
YOU MEAN, YOU KNEW WE TRAILED YOUR SNOWMOBILES?
OF COURSE! HOW STUPID DO YOU THINK I AM?
HOW MUCH TIME DO I HAVE?
CHUCK, THAT'S NO WAY TO TALK TO A MAN WHO IS ABOUT TO PULL OFF THE CRIME OF THE CENTURY!
OH, ARCHIE! KIDNAPPING ME ISN'T REALLY THAT IMPORTANT!
I MEANT, GREEN JEANS HERE IS ABOUT TO PRODUCE A HUGE AMOUNT...
...OF COUNTERFEIT EUROS!
13

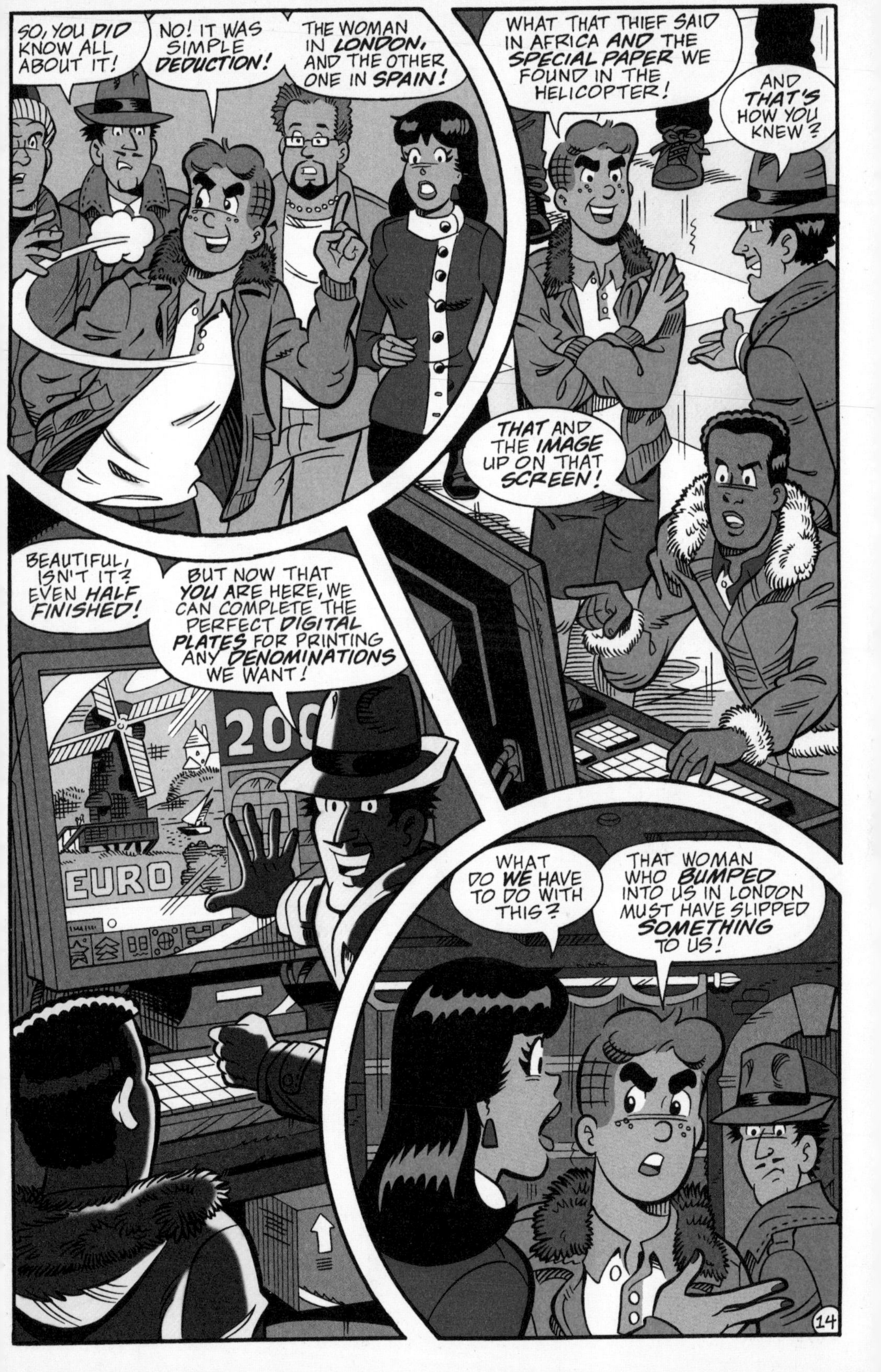
SO, YOU DID KNOW ALL ABOUT IT!
NO! IT WAS SIMPLE DEDUCTION!
THE WOMAN IN LONDON, AND THE OTHER ONE IN SPAIN!
WHAT THAT THIEF SAID IN AFRICA AND THE SPECIAL PAPER WE FOUND IN THE HELICOPTER!
AND THAT'S HOW YOU KNEW?
THAT AND THE IMAGE UP ON THAT SCREEN!
BEAUTIFUL, ISN'T IT? EVEN HALF FINISHED!
BUT NOW THAT YOU ARE HERE, WE CAN COMPLETE THE PERFECT DIGITAL PLATES FOR PRINTING ANY DENOMINATIONS WE WANT!
200
EURO
WHAT DO WE HAVE TO DO WITH THIS?
THAT WOMAN WHO BUMPED INTO US IN LONDON MUST HAVE SLIPPED SOMETHING TO US!

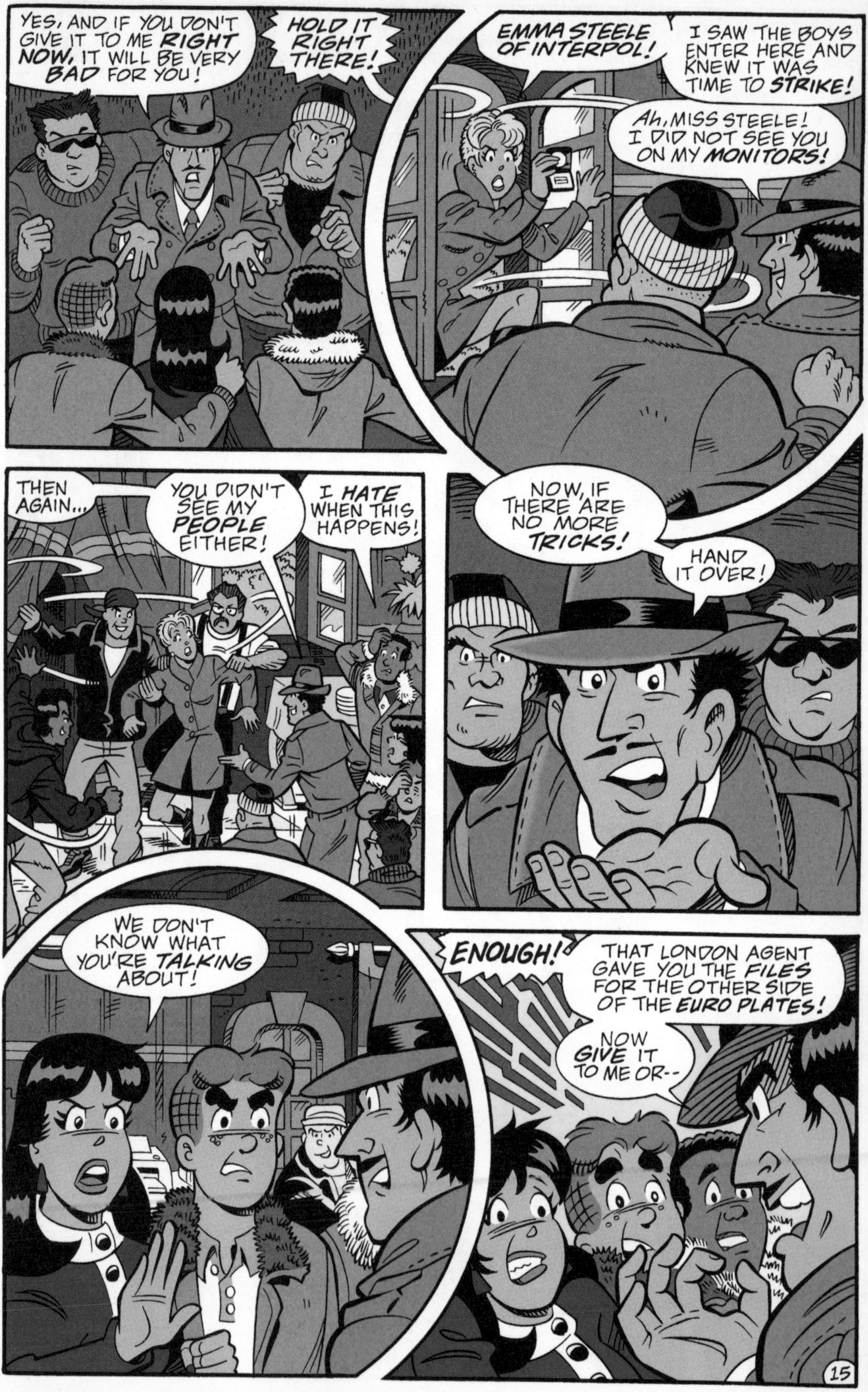
YES, AND IF YOU DON'T GIVE IT TO ME RIGHT NOW, IT WILL BE VERY BAD FOR YOU!
HOLD IT RIGHT THERE!
EMMA STEELE OF INTERPOL!
I SAW THE BOYS ENTER HERE AND KNEW IT WAS TIME TO STRIKE!
Ah, MISS STEELE! I DID NOT SEE YOU ON MY MONITORS!
THEN AGAIN...
YOU DIDN'T SEE MY PEOPLE EITHER!
I HATE WHEN THIS HAPPENS!
NOW, IF THERE ARE NO MORE TRICKS!
HAND IT OVER!
WE DON'T KNOW WHAT YOU'RE TALKING ABOUT!
ENOUGH!
THAT LONDON AGENT GAVE YOU THE FILES FOR THE OTHER SIDE OF THE EURO PLATES!
NOW GIVE IT TO ME OR--

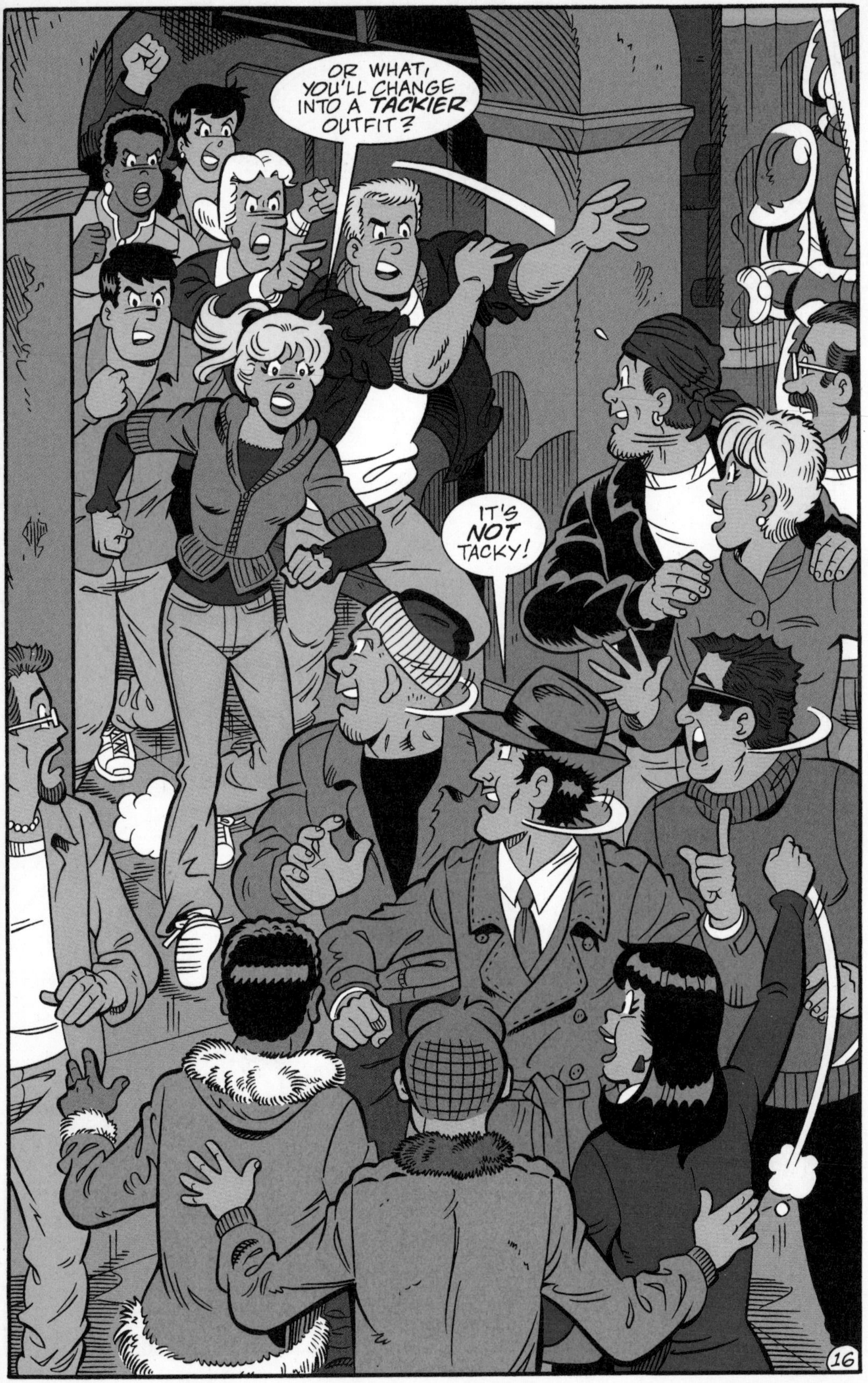
OR WHAT, YOU'LL CHANGE INTO A TACKIER OUTFIT?
IT'S NOT TACKY!

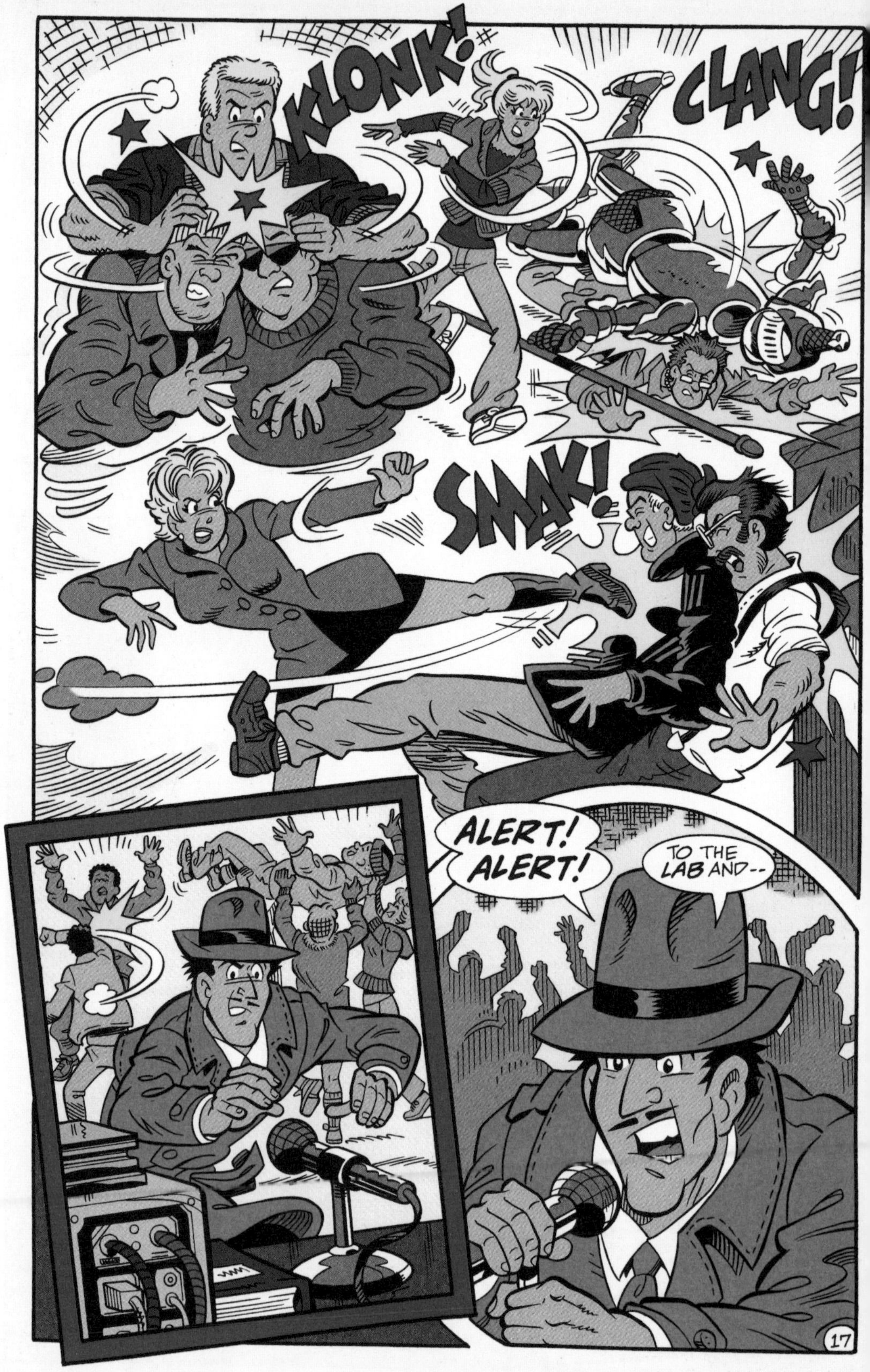
KLONK!
CLANG!
SMAK!
ALERT! ALERT!
TO THE LAB AND--

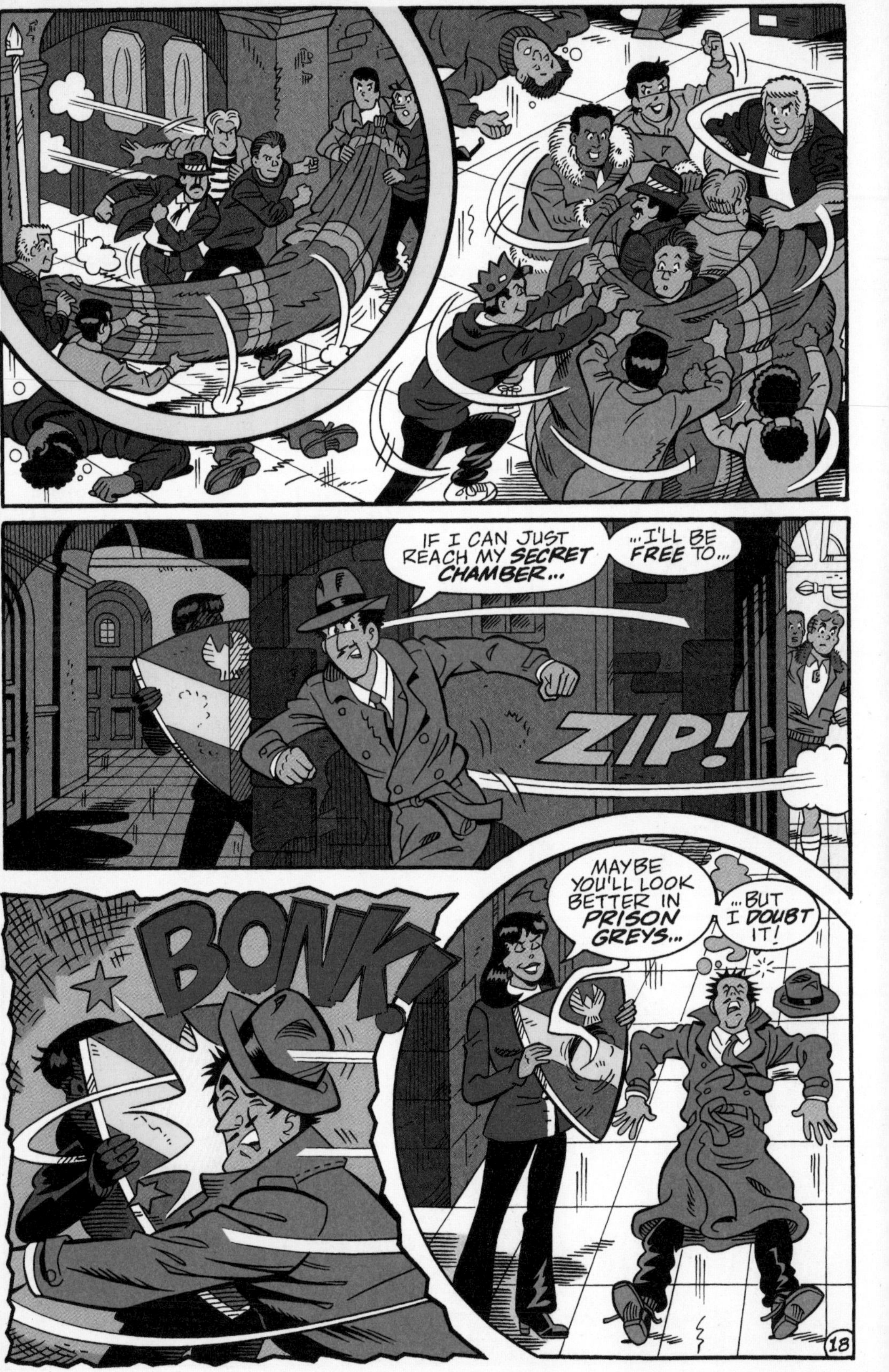
IF I CAN JUST REACH MY SECRET CHAMBER...
...I'LL BE FREE TO...
ZIP!
BONK!
MAYBE YOU'LL LOOK BETTER IN PRISON GREYS...
...BUT I DOUBT IT!
18

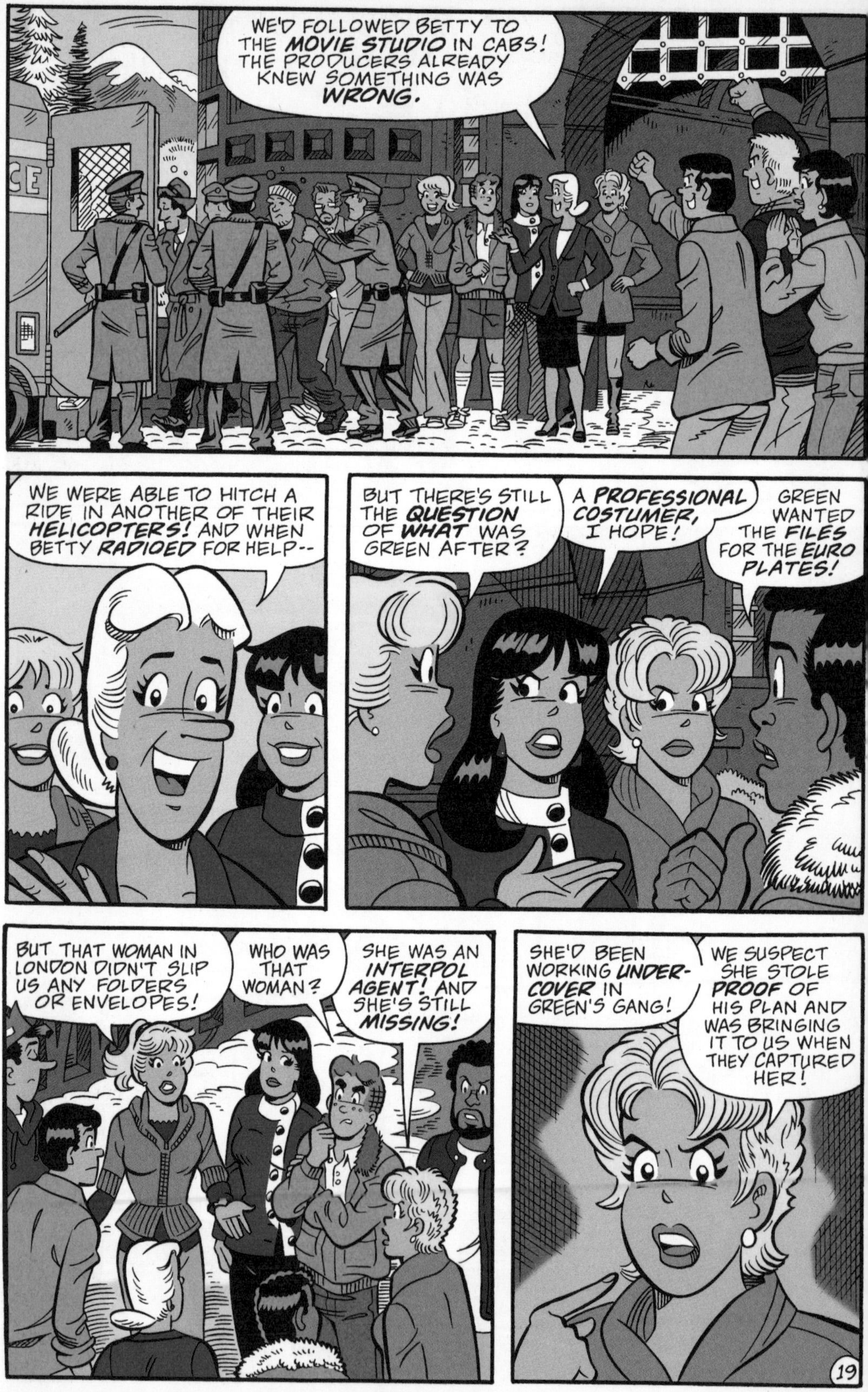
WE'D FOLLOWED BETTY TO THE **MOVIE STUDIO** IN CABS! THE PRODUCERS ALREADY KNEW SOMETHING WAS **WRONG.**
WE WERE ABLE TO HITCH A RIDE IN ANOTHER OF THEIR **HELICOPTERS!** AND WHEN BETTY **RADIOED** FOR HELP--
BUT THERE'S STILL THE **QUESTION** OF **WHAT** WAS GREEN AFTER?
A **PROFESSIONAL COSTUMER,** I HOPE!
GREEN WANTED THE **FILES** FOR THE **EURO PLATES!**
BUT THAT WOMAN IN LONDON DIDN'T SLIP US ANY FOLDERS OR ENVELOPES!
WHO WAS THAT WOMAN?
SHE WAS AN **INTERPOL AGENT!** AND SHE'S STILL **MISSING!**
SHE'D BEEN WORKING **UNDER-COVER** IN GREEN'S GANG!
WE SUSPECT SHE STOLE **PROOF** OF HIS PLAN AND WAS BRINGING IT TO US WHEN THEY CAPTURED HER!

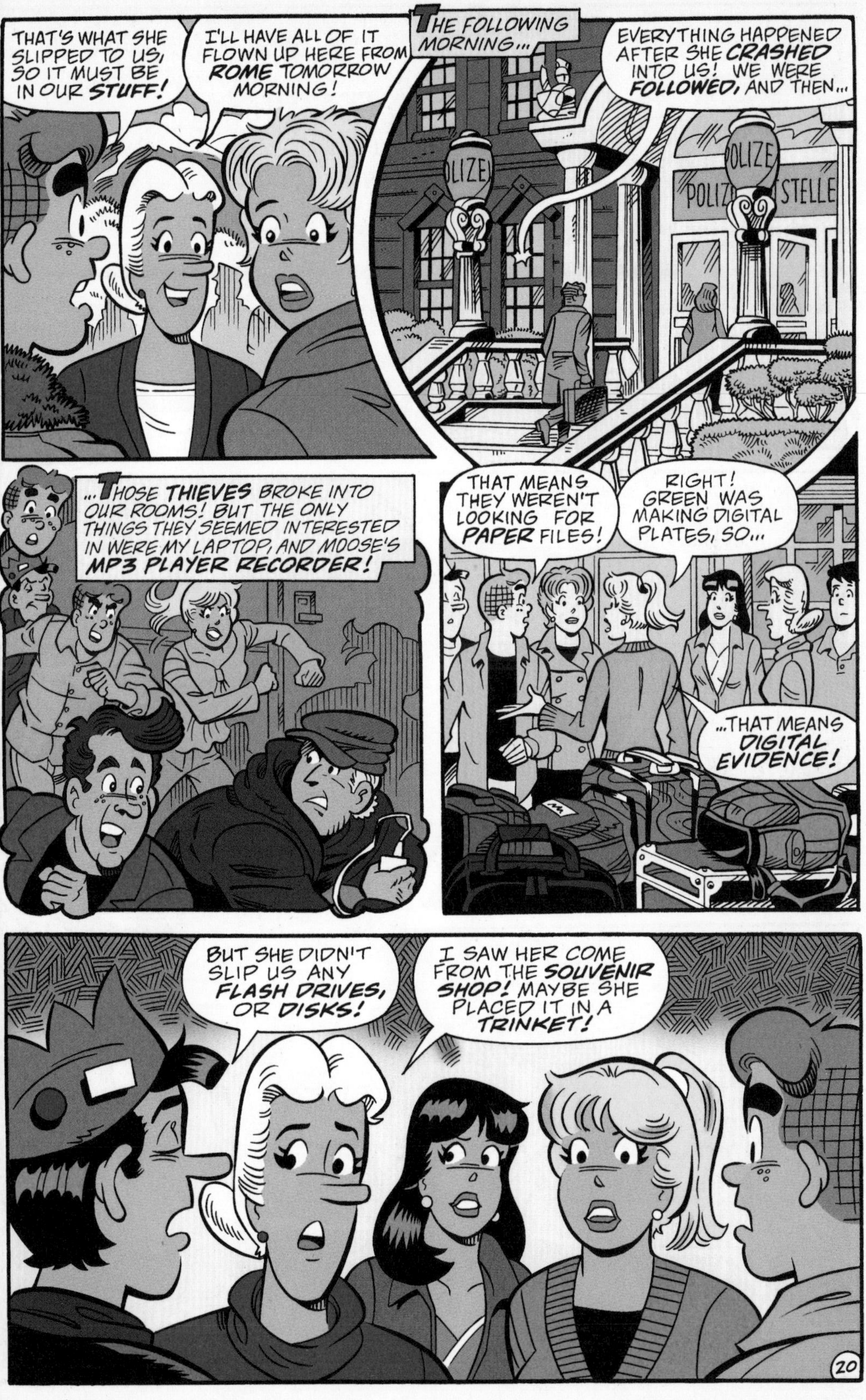
THAT'S WHAT SHE SLIPPED TO US, SO IT MUST BE IN OUR STUFF!
I'LL HAVE ALL OF IT FLOWN UP HERE FROM ROME TOMORROW MORNING!
THE FOLLOWING MORNING...
EVERYTHING HAPPENED AFTER SHE CRASHED INTO US! WE WERE FOLLOWED, AND THEN...
POLIZEI
POLIZEI
POLIZ STELLE
...THOSE THIEVES BROKE INTO OUR ROOMS! BUT THE ONLY THINGS THEY SEEMED INTERESTED IN WERE MY LAPTOP, AND MOOSE'S MP3 PLAYER RECORDER!
THAT MEANS THEY WEREN'T LOOKING FOR PAPER FILES!
RIGHT! GREEN WAS MAKING DIGITAL PLATES, SO...
...THAT MEANS DIGITAL EVIDENCE!
BUT SHE DIDN'T SLIP US ANY FLASH DRIVES, OR DISKS!
I SAW HER COME FROM THE SOUVENIR SHOP! MAYBE SHE PLACED IT IN A TRINKET!

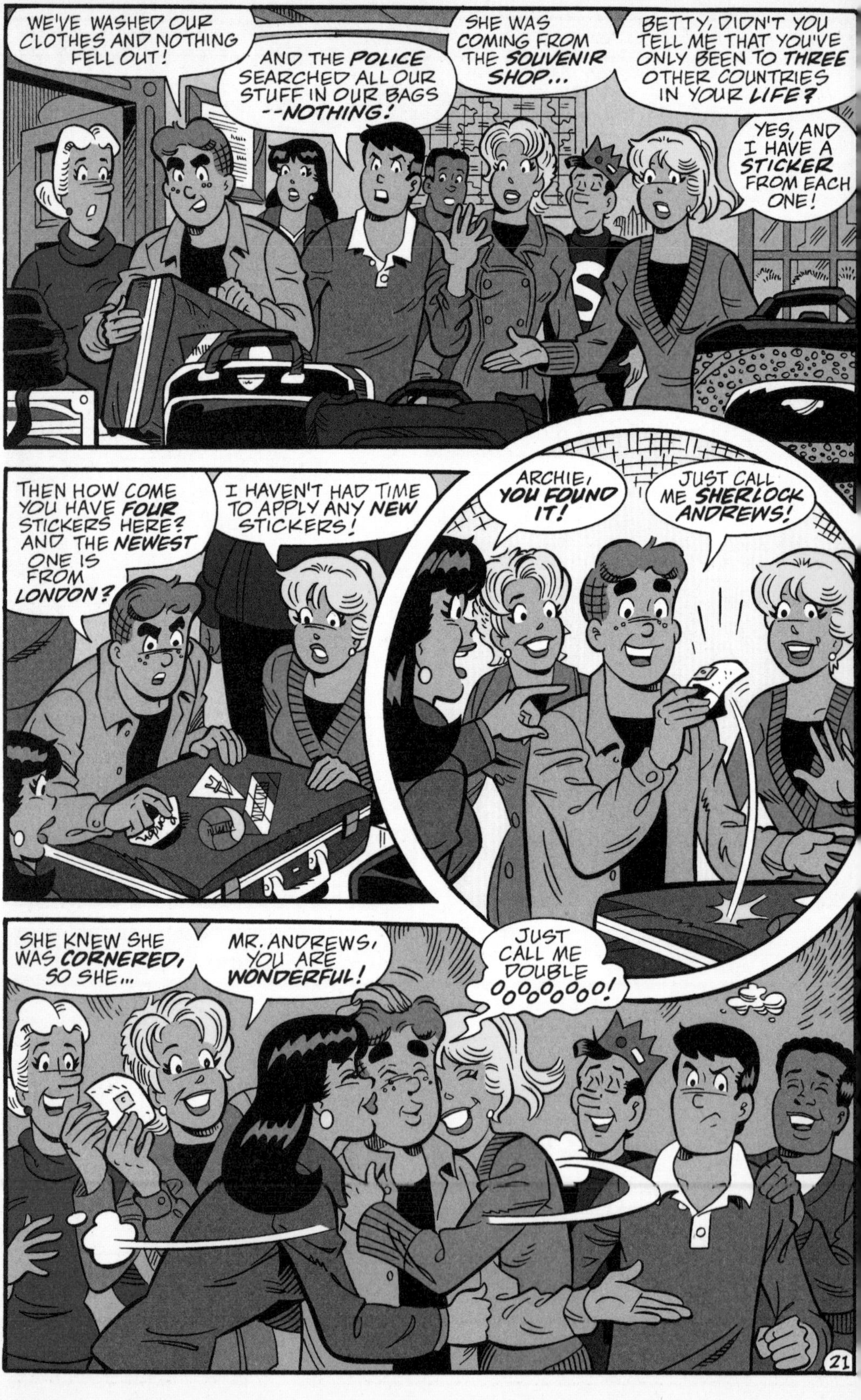
WE'VE WASHED OUR CLOTHES AND NOTHING FELL OUT!
AND THE POLICE SEARCHED ALL OUR STUFF IN OUR BAGS --NOTHING!
SHE WAS COMING FROM THE SOUVENIR SHOP...
BETTY, DIDN'T YOU TELL ME THAT YOU'VE ONLY BEEN TO THREE OTHER COUNTRIES IN YOUR LIFE?
YES, AND I HAVE A STICKER FROM EACH ONE!
THEN HOW COME YOU HAVE FOUR STICKERS HERE? AND THE NEWEST ONE IS FROM LONDON?
I HAVEN'T HAD TIME TO APPLY ANY NEW STICKERS!
ARCHIE, YOU FOUND IT!
JUST CALL ME SHERLOCK ANDREWS!
SHE KNEW SHE WAS CORNERED, SO SHE...
MR. ANDREWS, YOU ARE WONDERFUL!
JUST CALL ME DOUBLE OOOOOOOO!
21

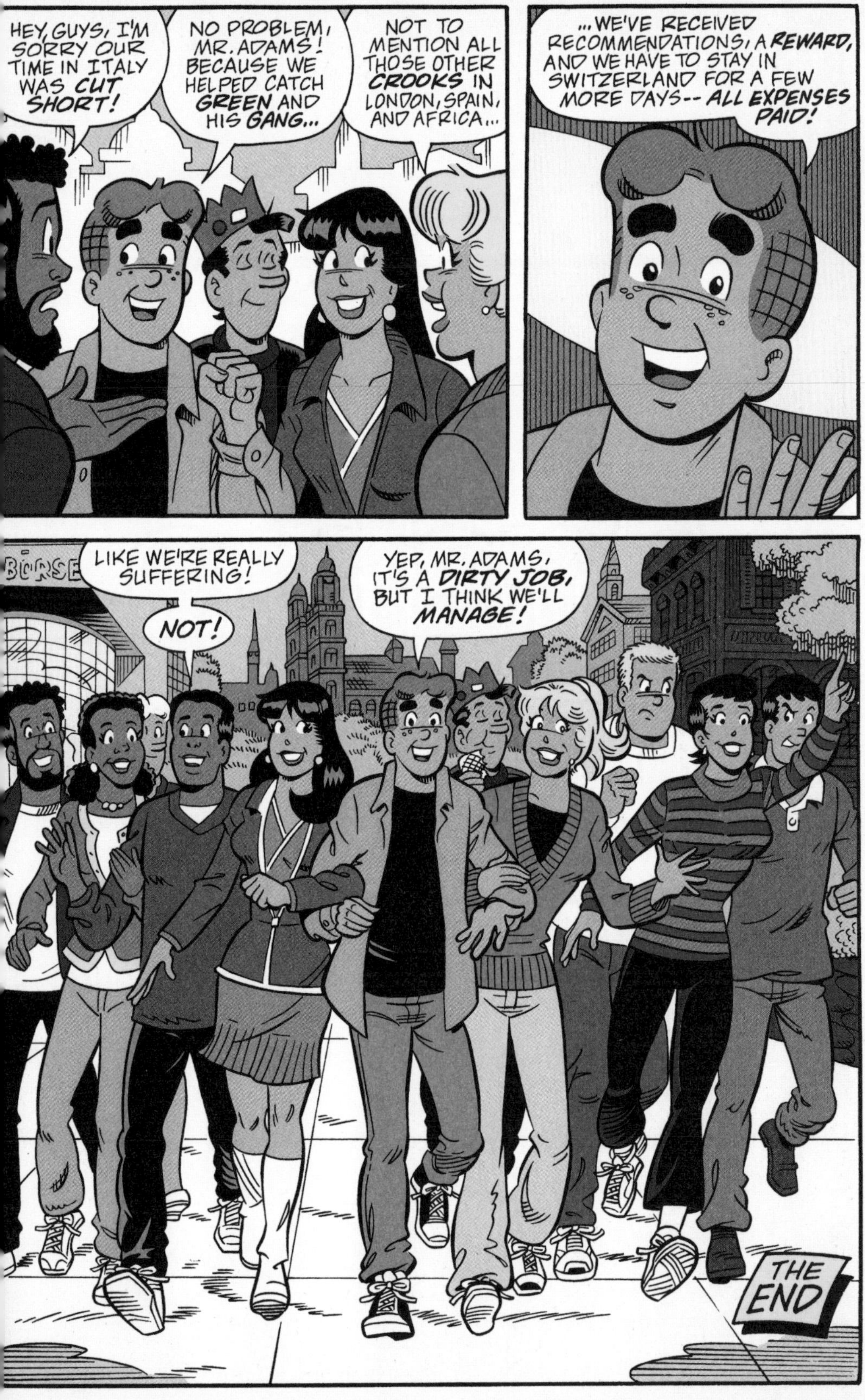
HEY, GUYS, I'M SORRY OUR TIME IN ITALY WAS CUT SHORT!
NO PROBLEM, MR. ADAMS! BECAUSE WE HELPED CATCH GREEN AND HIS GANG...
NOT TO MENTION ALL THOSE OTHER CROOKS IN LONDON, SPAIN, AND AFRICA...
...WE'VE RECEIVED RECOMMENDATIONS, A REWARD, AND WE HAVE TO STAY IN SWITZERLAND FOR A FEW MORE DAYS-- ALL EXPENSES PAID!
BÖRSE
LIKE WE'RE REALLY SUFFERING!
NOT!
YEP, MR. ADAMS, IT'S A DIRTY JOB, BUT I THINK WE'LL MANAGE!
THE END

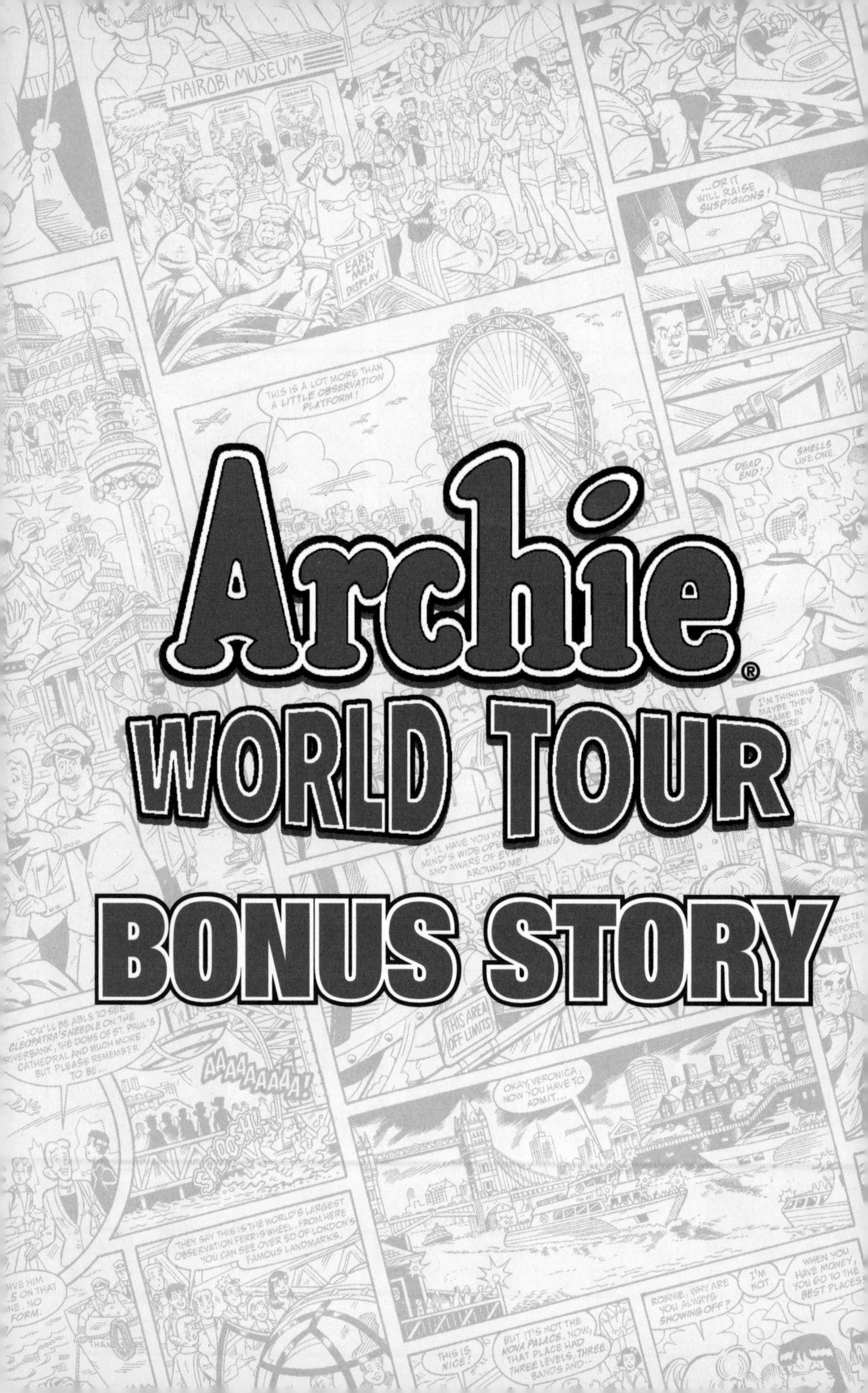

Archie®

WORLD TOUR

BONUS STORY

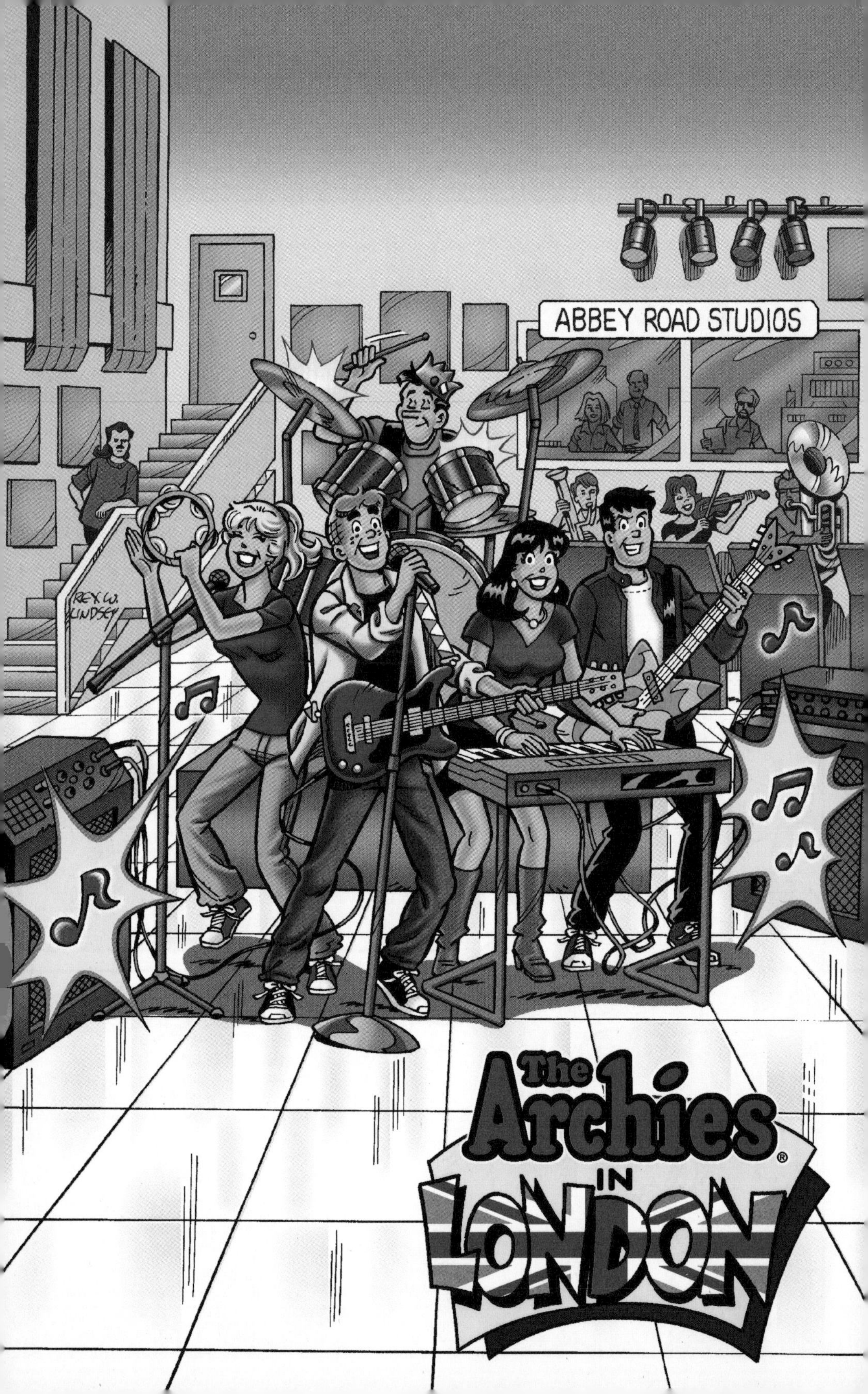
ABBEY ROAD STUDIOS
REX W. LINDSEY
The Archies®
IN
LONDON

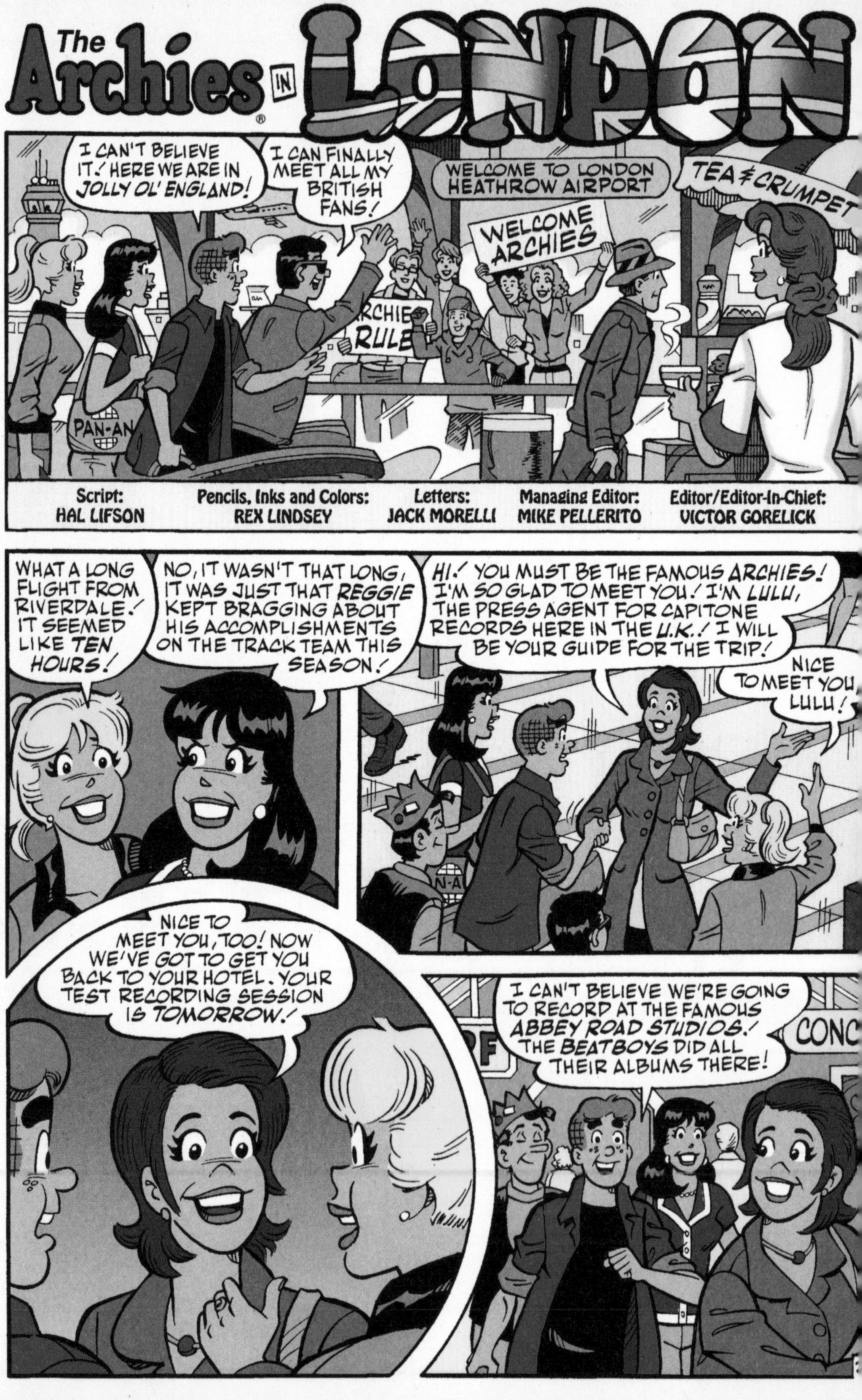
The Archies in LONDON
I CAN'T BELIEVE IT! HERE WE ARE IN JOLLY OL' ENGLAND!
I CAN FINALLY MEET ALL MY BRITISH FANS!
WELCOME TO LONDON HEATHROW AIRPORT
TEA & CRUMPET
WELCOME ARCHIES
ARCHIES RULE
PAN-AM
Script: HAL LIFSON
Pencils, Inks and Colors: REX LINDSEY
Letters: JACK MORELLI
Managing Editor: MIKE PELLERITO
Editor/Editor-In-Chief: VICTOR GORELICK
WHAT A LONG FLIGHT FROM RIVERDALE! IT SEEMED LIKE TEN HOURS!
NO, IT WASN'T THAT LONG, IT WAS JUST THAT REGGIE KEPT BRAGGING ABOUT HIS ACCOMPLISHMENTS ON THE TRACK TEAM THIS SEASON!
HI! YOU MUST BE THE FAMOUS ARCHIES! I'M SO GLAD TO MEET YOU! I'M LULU, THE PRESS AGENT FOR CAPITONE RECORDS HERE IN THE U.K.! I WILL BE YOUR GUIDE FOR THE TRIP!
NICE TO MEET YOU LULU!
NICE TO MEET YOU, TOO! NOW WE'VE GOT TO GET YOU BACK TO YOUR HOTEL. YOUR TEST RECORDING SESSION IS TOMORROW!
I CAN'T BELIEVE WE'RE GOING TO RECORD AT THE FAMOUS ABBEY ROAD STUDIOS! THE BEATBOYS DID ALL THEIR ALBUMS THERE!

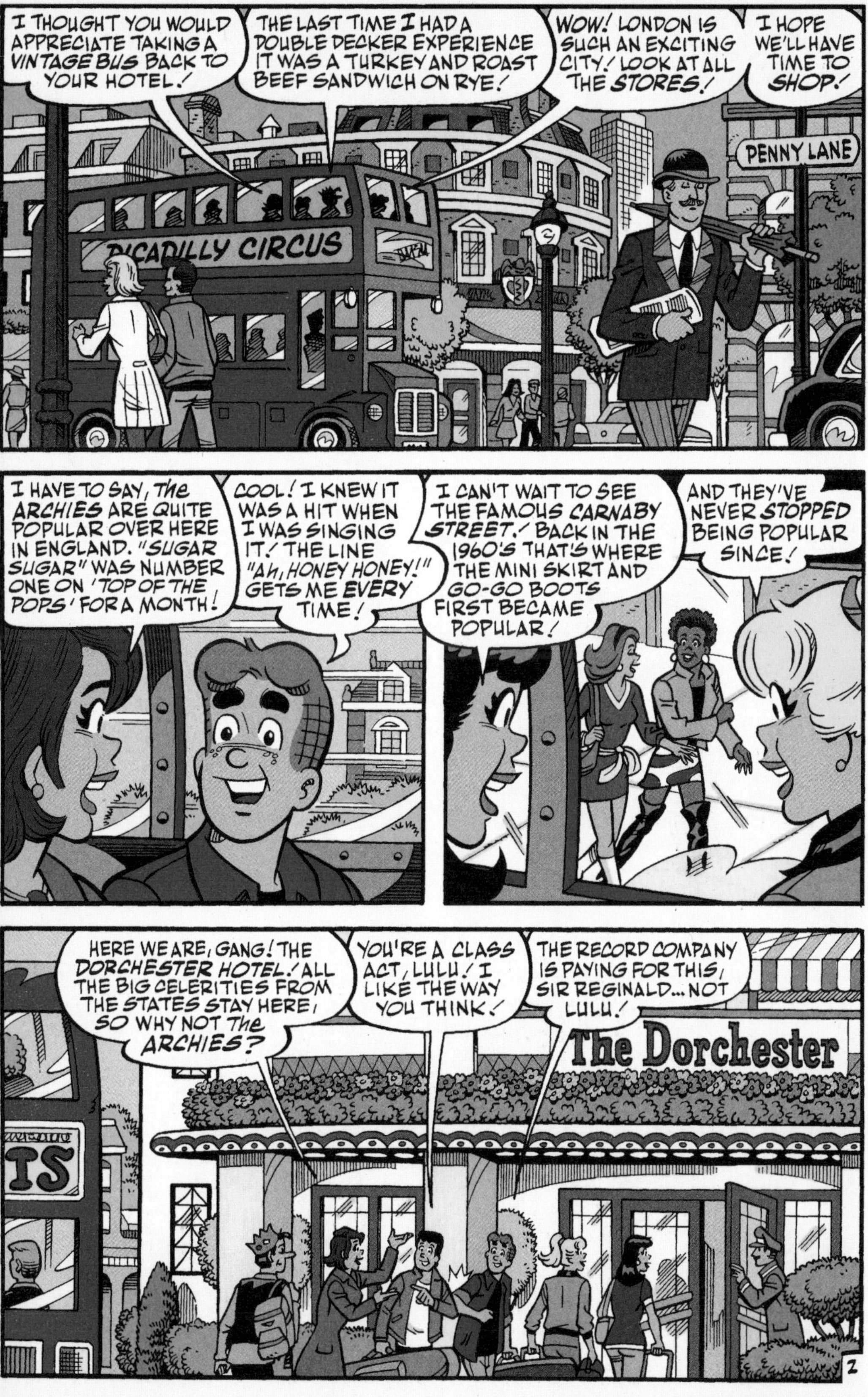
I THOUGHT YOU WOULD APPRECIATE TAKING A VINTAGE BUS BACK TO YOUR HOTEL!
THE LAST TIME I HAD A DOUBLE DECKER EXPERIENCE IT WAS A TURKEY AND ROAST BEEF SANDWICH ON RYE!
WOW! LONDON IS SUCH AN EXCITING CITY! LOOK AT ALL THE STORES!
I HOPE WE'LL HAVE TIME TO SHOP!
PENNY LANE
PICADILLY CIRCUS
I HAVE TO SAY, THE ARCHIES ARE QUITE POPULAR OVER HERE IN ENGLAND. "SUGAR SUGAR" WAS NUMBER ONE ON 'TOP OF THE POPS' FOR A MONTH!
COOL! I KNEW IT WAS A HIT WHEN I WAS SINGING IT! THE LINE "AH, HONEY HONEY!" GETS ME EVERY TIME!
I CAN'T WAIT TO SEE THE FAMOUS CARNABY STREET! BACK IN THE 1960'S THAT'S WHERE THE MINI SKIRT AND GO-GO BOOTS FIRST BECAME POPULAR!
AND THEY'VE NEVER STOPPED BEING POPULAR SINCE!
HERE WE ARE, GANG! THE DORCHESTER HOTEL! ALL THE BIG CELERITIES FROM THE STATES STAY HERE, SO WHY NOT THE ARCHIES?
YOU'RE A CLASS ACT, LULU! I LIKE THE WAY YOU THINK!
THE RECORD COMPANY IS PAYING FOR THIS, SIR REGINALD... NOT LULU!
The Dorchester

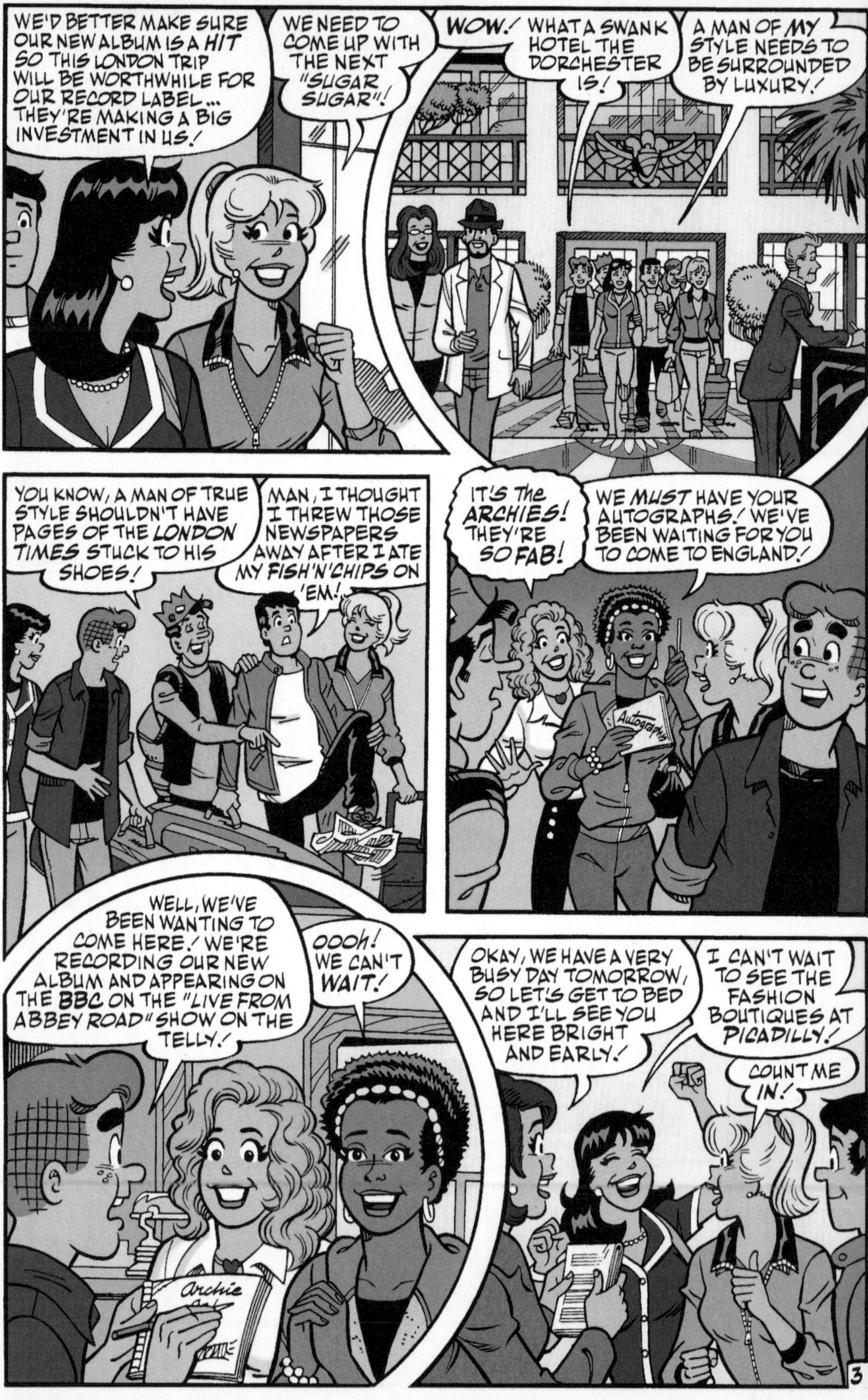
WE'D BETTER MAKE SURE OUR NEW ALBUM IS A HIT SO THIS LONDON TRIP WILL BE WORTHWHILE FOR OUR RECORD LABEL... THEY'RE MAKING A BIG INVESTMENT IN US!
WE NEED TO COME UP WITH THE NEXT "SUGAR SUGAR"!
WOW! WHAT A SWANK HOTEL THE DORCHESTER IS!
A MAN OF MY STYLE NEEDS TO BE SURROUNDED BY LUXURY!
YOU KNOW, A MAN OF TRUE STYLE SHOULDN'T HAVE PAGES OF THE LONDON TIMES STUCK TO HIS SHOES!
MAN, I THOUGHT I THREW THOSE NEWSPAPERS AWAY AFTER I ATE MY FISH'N'CHIPS ON 'EM!
IT'S THE ARCHIES! THEY'RE SO FAB!
WE MUST HAVE YOUR AUTOGRAPHS! WE'VE BEEN WAITING FOR YOU TO COME TO ENGLAND!
Autographs
WELL, WE'VE BEEN WANTING TO COME HERE! WE'RE RECORDING OUR NEW ALBUM AND APPEARING ON THE BBC ON THE "LIVE FROM ABBEY ROAD" SHOW ON THE TELLY!
OOOH! WE CAN'T WAIT!
Archie
OKAY, WE HAVE A VERY BUSY DAY TOMORROW, SO LET'S GET TO BED AND I'LL SEE YOU HERE BRIGHT AND EARLY!
I CAN'T WAIT TO SEE THE FASHION BOUTIQUES AT PICADILLY!
COUNT ME IN!

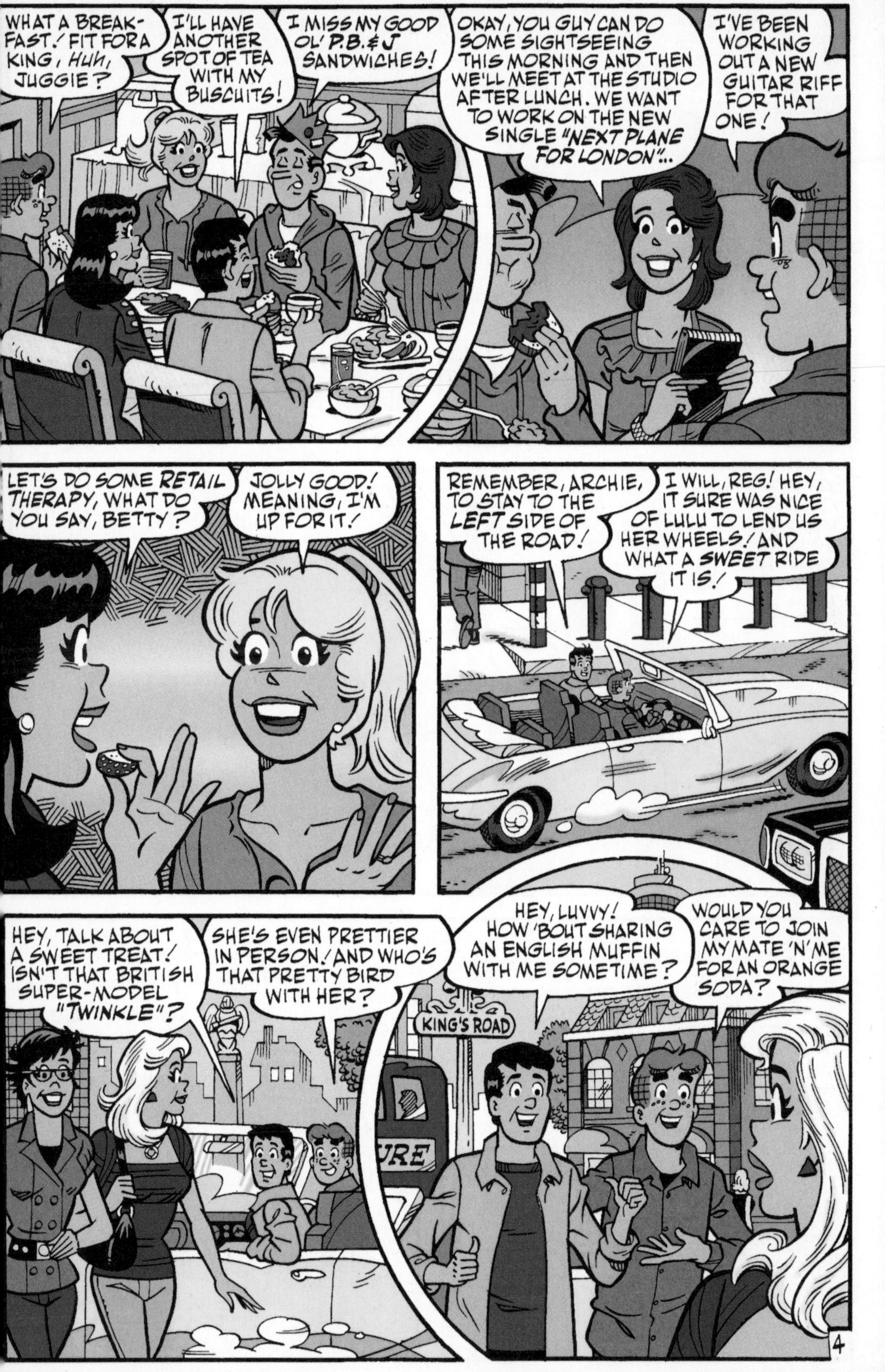
WHAT A BREAK-FAST! FIT FOR A KING, HUH, JUGGIE?
I'LL HAVE ANOTHER SPOT OF TEA WITH MY BUSCUITS!
I MISS MY GOOD OL' P.B. & J SANDWICHES!
OKAY, YOU GUY CAN DO SOME SIGHTSEEING THIS MORNING AND THEN WE'LL MEET AT THE STUDIO AFTER LUNCH. WE WANT TO WORK ON THE NEW SINGLE "NEXT PLANE FOR LONDON"...
I'VE BEEN WORKING OUT A NEW GUITAR RIFF FOR THAT ONE!
LET'S DO SOME RETAIL THERAPY, WHAT DO YOU SAY, BETTY?
JOLLY GOOD! MEANING, I'M UP FOR IT!
REMEMBER, ARCHIE, TO STAY TO THE LEFT SIDE OF THE ROAD!
I WILL, REG! HEY, IT SURE WAS NICE OF LULU TO LEND US HER WHEELS! AND WHAT A SWEET RIDE IT IS!
HEY, TALK ABOUT A SWEET TREAT! ISN'T THAT BRITISH SUPER-MODEL "TWINKLE"?
SHE'S EVEN PRETTIER IN PERSON! AND WHO'S THAT PRETTY BIRD WITH HER?
KING'S ROAD
HEY, LUVVY! HOW 'BOUT SHARING AN ENGLISH MUFFIN WITH ME SOMETIME?
WOULD YOU CARE TO JOIN MY MATE 'N' ME FOR AN ORANGE SODA?
4

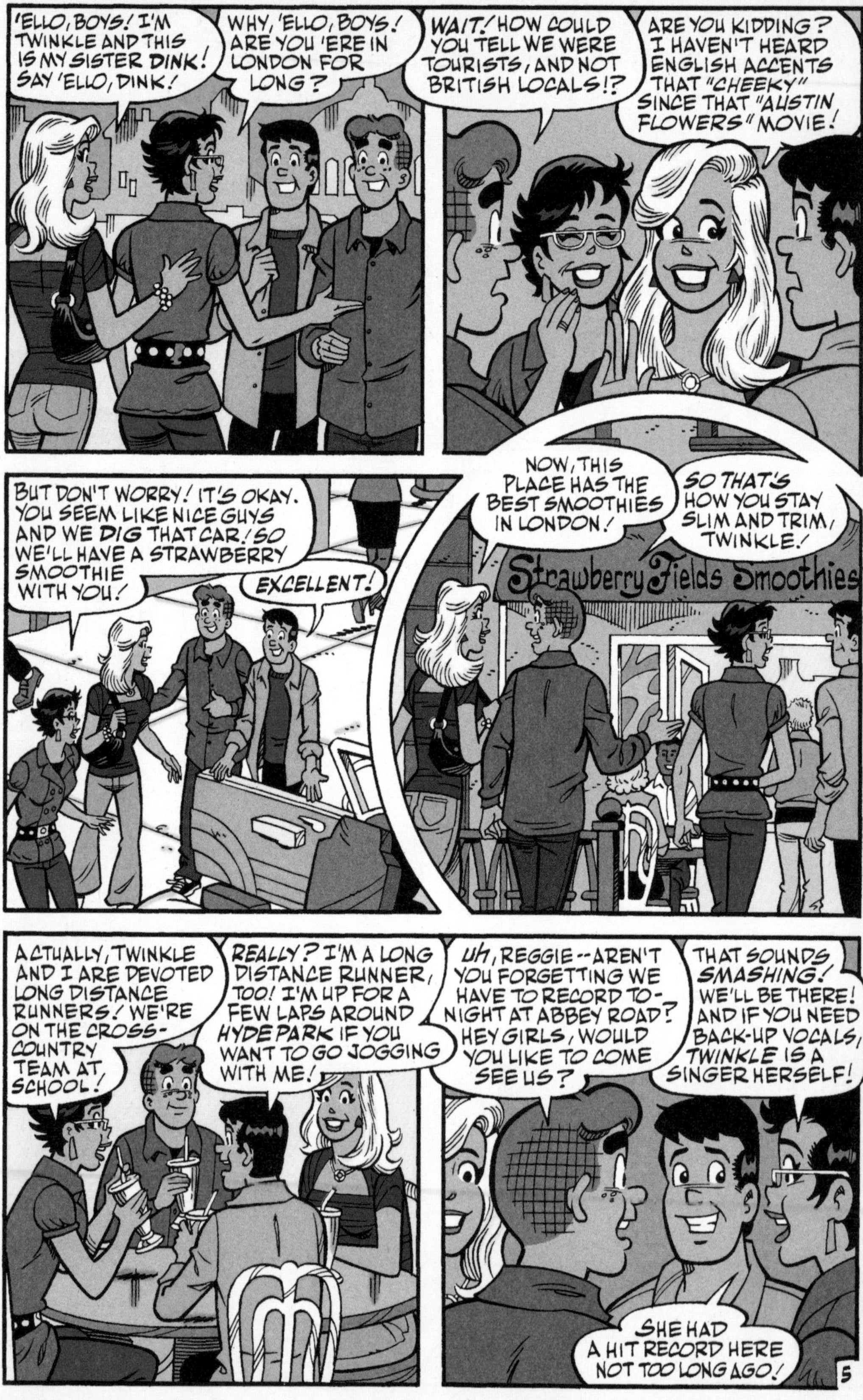
'ELLO, BOYS! I'M TWINKLE AND THIS IS MY SISTER DINK! SAY 'ELLO, DINK!
WHY, 'ELLO, BOYS! ARE YOU 'ERE IN LONDON FOR LONG?
WAIT! HOW COULD YOU TELL WE WERE TOURISTS, AND NOT BRITISH LOCALS!?
ARE YOU KIDDING? I HAVEN'T HEARD ENGLISH ACCENTS THAT "CHEEKY" SINCE THAT "AUSTIN FLOWERS" MOVIE!
BUT DON'T WORRY! IT'S OKAY. YOU SEEM LIKE NICE GUYS AND WE DIG THAT CAR! SO WE'LL HAVE A STRAWBERRY SMOOTHIE WITH YOU!
EXCELLENT!
NOW, THIS PLACE HAS THE BEST SMOOTHIES IN LONDON!
SO THAT'S HOW YOU STAY SLIM AND TRIM, TWINKLE!
Strawberry Fields Smoothies
ACTUALLY, TWINKLE AND I ARE DEVOTED LONG DISTANCE RUNNERS! WE'RE ON THE CROSS-COUNTRY TEAM AT SCHOOL!
REALLY? I'M A LONG DISTANCE RUNNER, TOO! I'M UP FOR A FEW LAPS AROUND HYDE PARK IF YOU WANT TO GO JOGGING WITH ME!
UH, REGGIE -- AREN'T YOU FORGETTING WE HAVE TO RECORD TO-NIGHT AT ABBEY ROAD? HEY GIRLS, WOULD YOU LIKE TO COME SEE US?
THAT SOUNDS SMASHING! WE'LL BE THERE! AND IF YOU NEED BACK-UP VOCALS, TWINKLE IS A SINGER HERSELF!
SHE HAD A HIT RECORD HERE NOT TOO LONG AGO!

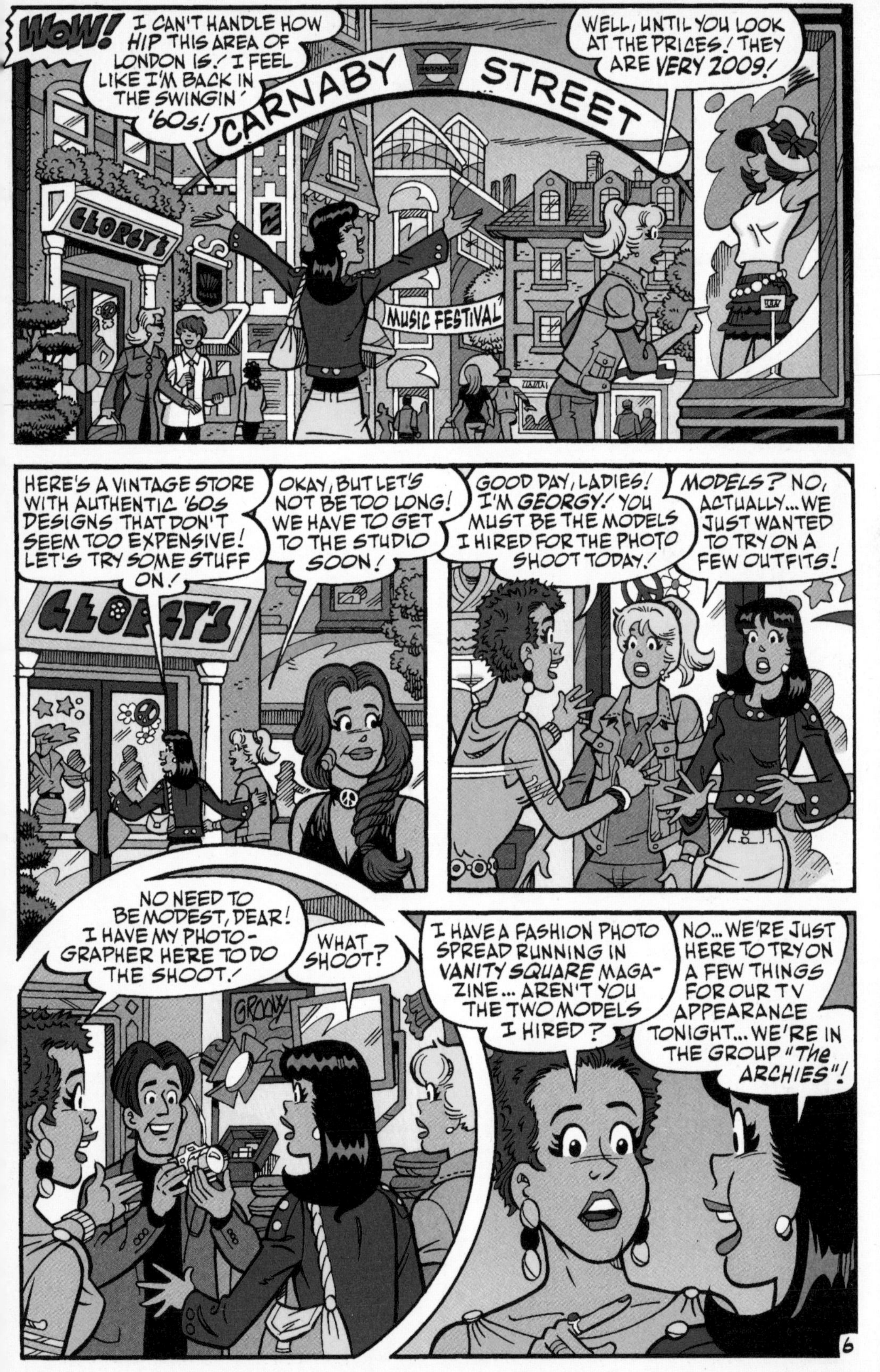
WOW! I CAN'T HANDLE HOW HIP THIS AREA OF LONDON IS! I FEEL LIKE I'M BACK IN THE SWINGIN' '60s!
CARNABY STREET
WELL, UNTIL YOU LOOK AT THE PRICES! THEY ARE VERY 2009!
GEORGY'S
MUSIC FESTIVAL
HERE'S A VINTAGE STORE WITH AUTHENTIC '60s DESIGNS THAT DON'T SEEM TOO EXPENSIVE! LET'S TRY SOME STUFF ON!
OKAY, BUT LET'S NOT BE TOO LONG! WE HAVE TO GET TO THE STUDIO SOON!
GEORGY'S
GOOD DAY, LADIES! I'M GEORGY! YOU MUST BE THE MODELS I HIRED FOR THE PHOTO SHOOT TODAY!
MODELS? NO, ACTUALLY... WE JUST WANTED TO TRY ON A FEW OUTFITS!
NO NEED TO BE MODEST, DEAR! I HAVE MY PHOTO-GRAPHER HERE TO DO THE SHOOT!
WHAT SHOOT?
GROOVY
I HAVE A FASHION PHOTO SPREAD RUNNING IN VANITY SQUARE MAGA-ZINE... AREN'T YOU THE TWO MODELS I HIRED?
NO... WE'RE JUST HERE TO TRY ON A FEW THINGS FOR OUR TV APPEARANCE TONIGHT... WE'RE IN THE GROUP "The ARCHIES"!

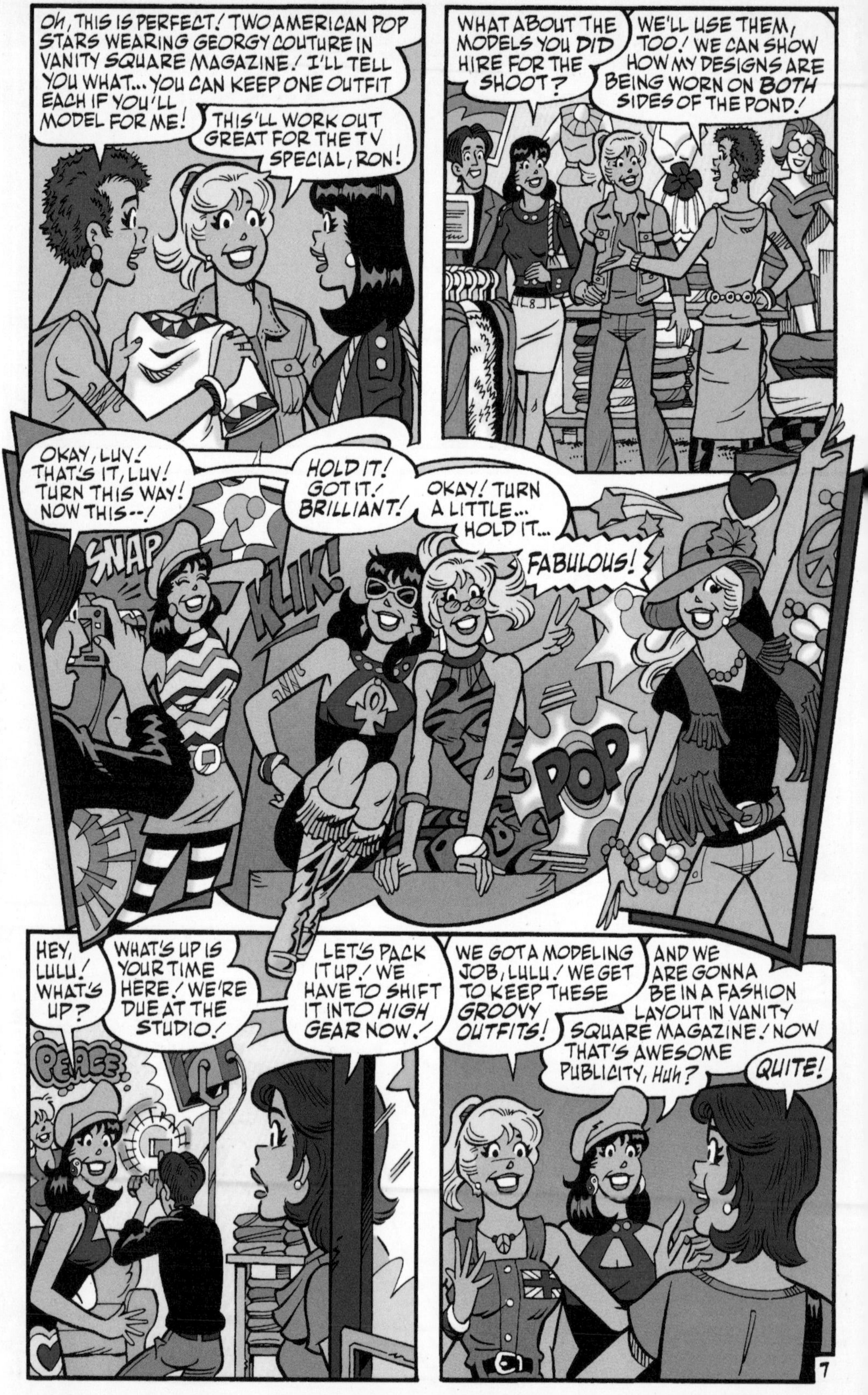

OH, THIS IS PERFECT! TWO AMERICAN POP STARS WEARING GEORGY COUTURE IN VANITY SQUARE MAGAZINE! I'LL TELL YOU WHAT... YOU CAN KEEP ONE OUTFIT EACH IF YOU'LL MODEL FOR ME!
THIS'LL WORK OUT GREAT FOR THE TV SPECIAL, RON!
WHAT ABOUT THE MODELS YOU DID HIRE FOR THE SHOOT?
WE'LL USE THEM, TOO! WE CAN SHOW HOW MY DESIGNS ARE BEING WORN ON BOTH SIDES OF THE POND!
OKAY, LUV! THAT'S IT, LUV! TURN THIS WAY! NOW THIS--!
HOLD IT! GOT IT! BRILLIANT!
OKAY! TURN A LITTLE... HOLD IT...
FABULOUS!
SNAP
KLIK!
POP
HEY, LULU! WHAT'S UP?
WHAT'S UP IS YOUR TIME HERE! WE'RE DUE AT THE STUDIO!
LET'S PACK IT UP! WE HAVE TO SHIFT IT INTO HIGH GEAR NOW.!
PEACE
WE GOT A MODELING JOB, LULU! WE GET TO KEEP THESE GROOVY OUTFITS!
AND WE ARE GONNA BE IN A FASHION LAYOUT IN VANITY SQUARE MAGAZINE! NOW THAT'S AWESOME PUBLICITY, HUH?
QUITE!

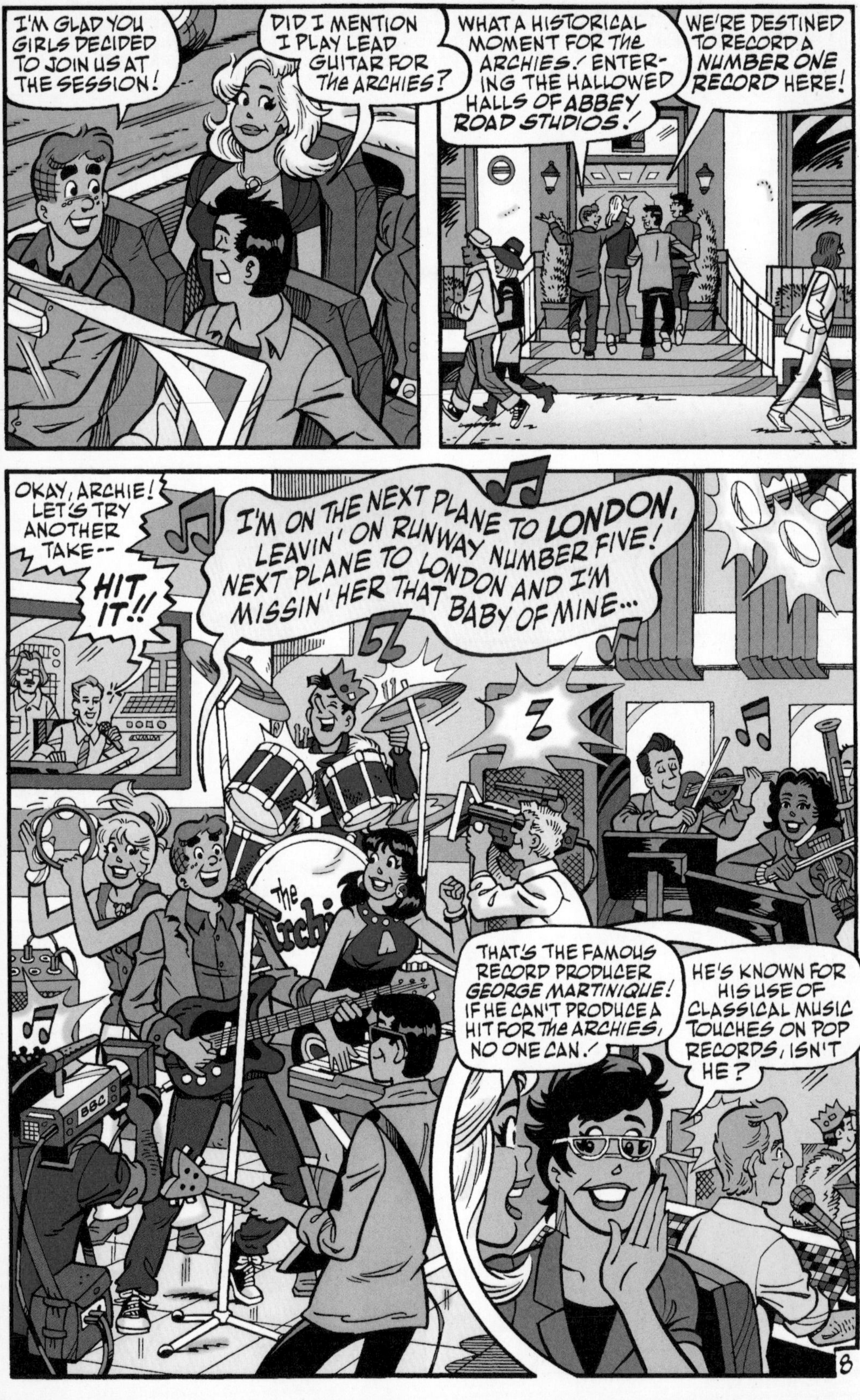
I'M GLAD YOU GIRLS DECIDED TO JOIN US AT THE SESSION!
DID I MENTION I PLAY LEAD GUITAR FOR THE ARCHIES?
WHAT A HISTORICAL MOMENT FOR THE ARCHIES! ENTERING THE HALLOWED HALLS OF ABBEY ROAD STUDIOS!
WE'RE DESTINED TO RECORD A NUMBER ONE RECORD HERE!
OKAY, ARCHIE! LET'S TRY ANOTHER TAKE--
HIT IT!!
I'M ON THE NEXT PLANE TO LONDON, LEAVIN' ON RUNWAY NUMBER FIVE! NEXT PLANE TO LONDON AND I'M MISSIN' HER THAT BABY OF MINE...
THAT'S THE FAMOUS RECORD PRODUCER GEORGE MARTINIQUE! IF HE CAN'T PRODUCE A HIT FOR THE ARCHIES, NO ONE CAN!
HE'S KNOWN FOR HIS USE OF CLASSICAL MUSIC TOUCHES ON POP RECORDS, ISN'T HE?

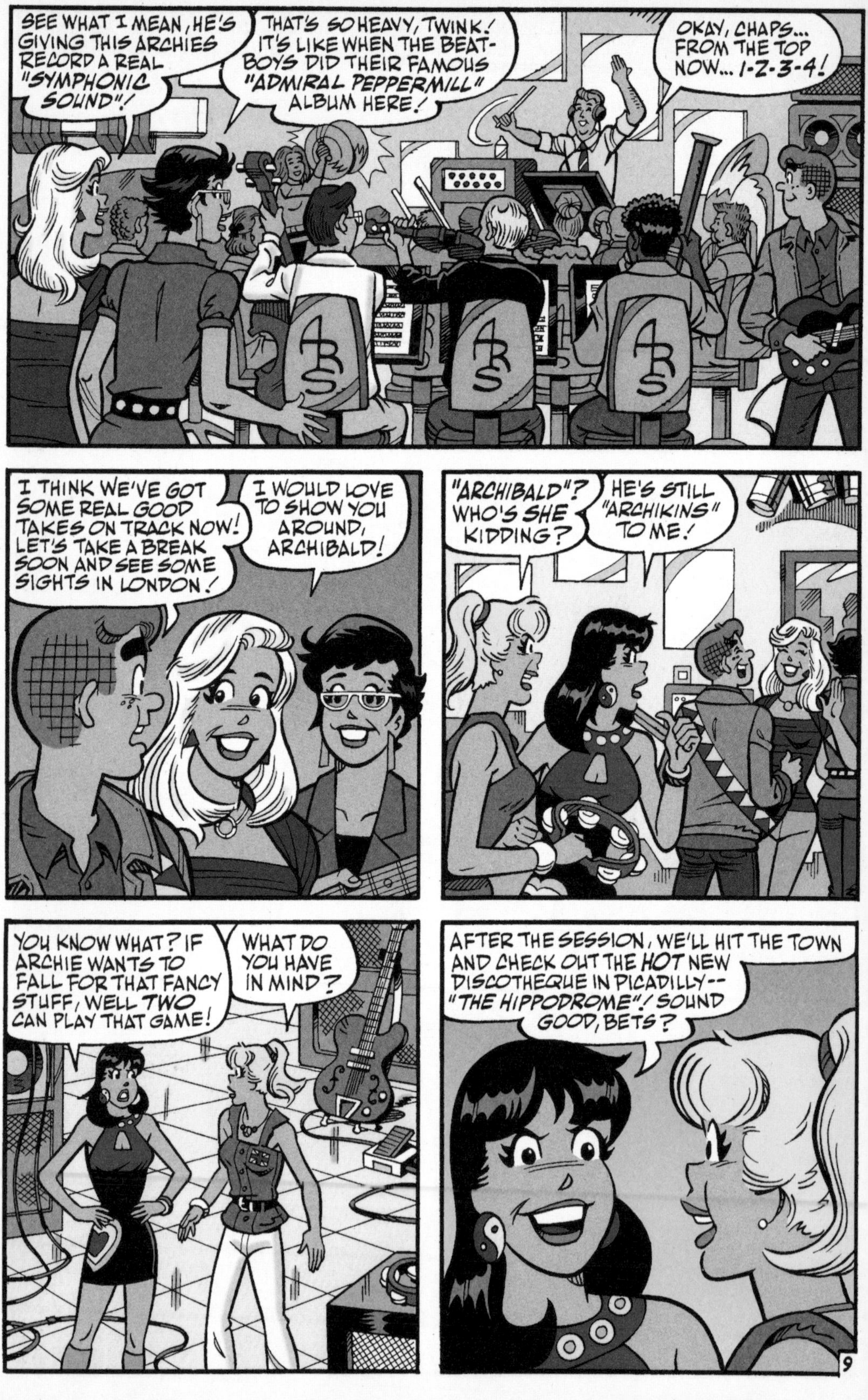
SEE WHAT I MEAN, HE'S GIVING THIS ARCHIES RECORD A REAL "SYMPHONIC SOUND"!
THAT'S SO HEAVY, TWINK! IT'S LIKE WHEN THE BEAT-BOYS DID THEIR FAMOUS "ADMIRAL PEPPERMILL" ALBUM HERE!
OKAY, CHAPS... FROM THE TOP NOW... 1-2-3-4!
I THINK WE'VE GOT SOME REAL GOOD TAKES ON TRACK NOW! LET'S TAKE A BREAK SOON AND SEE SOME SIGHTS IN LONDON!
I WOULD LOVE TO SHOW YOU AROUND, ARCHIBALD!
"ARCHIBALD"? WHO'S SHE KIDDING?
HE'S STILL "ARCHIKINS" TO ME!
YOU KNOW WHAT? IF ARCHIE WANTS TO FALL FOR THAT FANCY STUFF, WELL TWO CAN PLAY THAT GAME!
WHAT DO YOU HAVE IN MIND?
AFTER THE SESSION, WE'LL HIT THE TOWN AND CHECK OUT THE HOT NEW DISCOTHEQUE IN PICADILLY-- "THE HIPPODROME"! SOUND GOOD, BETS?

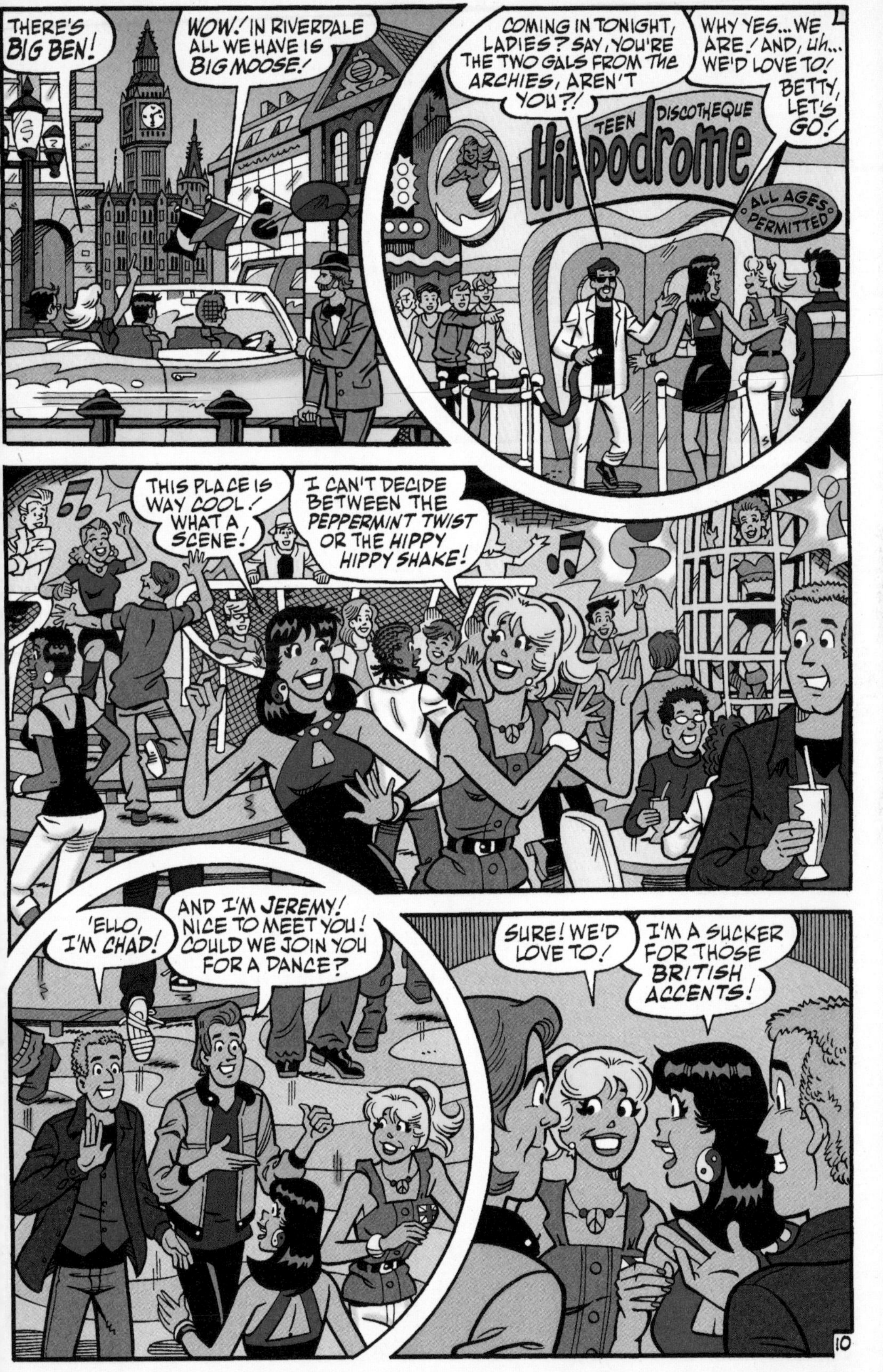
THERE'S BIG BEN!
WOW! IN RIVERDALE ALL WE HAVE IS BIG MOOSE!
COMING IN TONIGHT, LADIES? SAY, YOU'RE THE TWO GALS FROM THE ARCHIES, AREN'T YOU?!
WHY YES... WE ARE! AND, uh... WE'D LOVE TO!
BETTY, LET'S GO!
TEEN DISCOTHEQUE
Hippodrome
ALL AGES PERMITTED
THIS PLACE IS WAY COOL! WHAT A SCENE!
I CAN'T DECIDE BETWEEN THE PEPPERMINT TWIST OR THE HIPPY HIPPY SHAKE!
'ELLO, I'M CHAD!
AND I'M JEREMY! NICE TO MEET YOU! COULD WE JOIN YOU FOR A DANCE?
SURE! WE'D LOVE TO!
I'M A SUCKER FOR THOSE BRITISH ACCENTS!

JUGHEAD! WHERE IS EVERYONE?

ARCHIE AND REGGIE TOOK OFF WITH TWINKLE AND PINK, AND BETTY AND VERONICA WENT DANCING...

AND YOU'RE STILL HERE?

THE DRUMMER IS ALWAYS THE LAST TO LEAVE!

WELL, JUGGIE, I KNOW HOW HARD YOU WORKED AT GETTING THE DRUM FILLS JUST RIGHT! SO LET ME TAKE YOU TO THE BEST AMERICAN STYLE DINER IN LONDON! YOU'LL FEEL LIKE YOU'RE BACK AT POP TATE'S!

THAT SOUNDS GREAT, LULU! I'M STARVING AND HAVEN'T HAD A BURGER SINCE WE GOT HERE!

YOU'VE OUTDONE YOURSELF, LULU! THIS LOOKS AMAZING! I CAN'T THANK YOU ENOUGH! I'M IN CHEESE-BURGER PARADISE!

KOOL KATS DINER   AMERICAN FOOD

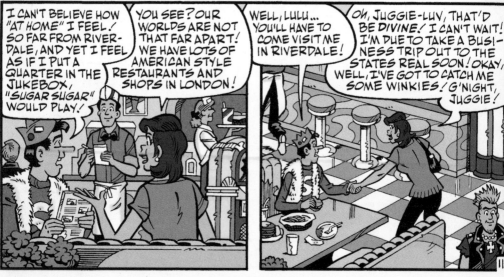

I CAN'T BELIEVE HOW "AT HOME" I FEEL! SO FAR FROM RIVERDALE, AND YET I FEEL AS IF I PUT A QUARTER IN THE JUKEBOX, "SUGAR SUGAR" WOULD PLAY!

YOU SEE? OUR WORLDS ARE NOT THAT FAR APART! WE HAVE LOTS OF AMERICAN STYLE RESTAURANTS AND SHOPS IN LONDON!

WELL, LULU... YOU'LL HAVE TO COME VISIT ME IN RIVERDALE!

OH, JUGGIE-LUV, THAT'D BE DIVINE! I CAN'T WAIT! I'M DUE TO TAKE A BUSI-NESS TRIP OUT TO THE STATES REAL SOON! OKAY, WELL, I'VE GOT TO CATCH ME SOME WINKIES! G'NIGHT, JUGGIE!

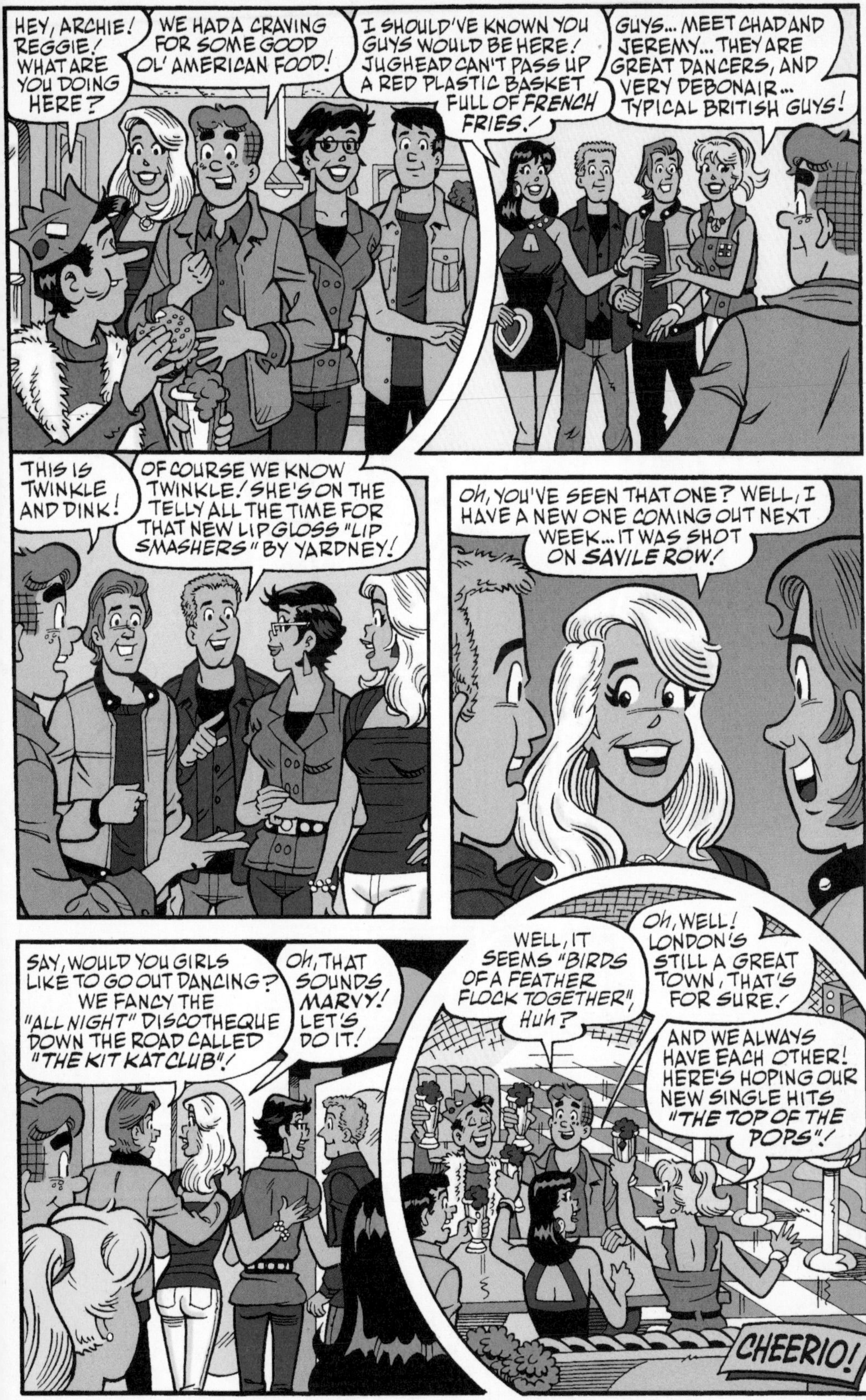
HEY, ARCHIE! REGGIE! WHAT ARE YOU DOING HERE?
WE HAD A CRAVING FOR SOME GOOD OL' AMERICAN FOOD!
I SHOULD'VE KNOWN YOU GUYS WOULD BE HERE! JUGHEAD CAN'T PASS UP A RED PLASTIC BASKET FULL OF FRENCH FRIES!
GUYS... MEET CHAD AND JEREMY... THEY ARE GREAT DANCERS, AND VERY DEBONAIR... TYPICAL BRITISH GUYS!
THIS IS TWINKLE AND DINK!
OF COURSE WE KNOW TWINKLE! SHE'S ON THE TELLY ALL THE TIME FOR THAT NEW LIP GLOSS "LIP SMASHERS" BY YARDNEY!
Oh, YOU'VE SEEN THAT ONE? WELL, I HAVE A NEW ONE COMING OUT NEXT WEEK... IT WAS SHOT ON SAVILE ROW!
SAY, WOULD YOU GIRLS LIKE TO GO OUT DANCING? WE FANCY THE "ALL NIGHT" DISCOTHEQUE DOWN THE ROAD CALLED "THE KIT KAT CLUB"!
Oh, THAT SOUNDS MARVY! LET'S DO IT!
WELL, IT SEEMS "BIRDS OF A FEATHER FLOCK TOGETHER", Huh?
Oh, WELL! LONDON'S STILL A GREAT TOWN, THAT'S FOR SURE!
AND WE ALWAYS HAVE EACH OTHER! HERE'S HOPING OUR NEW SINGLE HITS "THE TOP OF THE POPS"!
CHEERIO!

Archie® WORLD TOUR
BONUS
COVER GALLERY

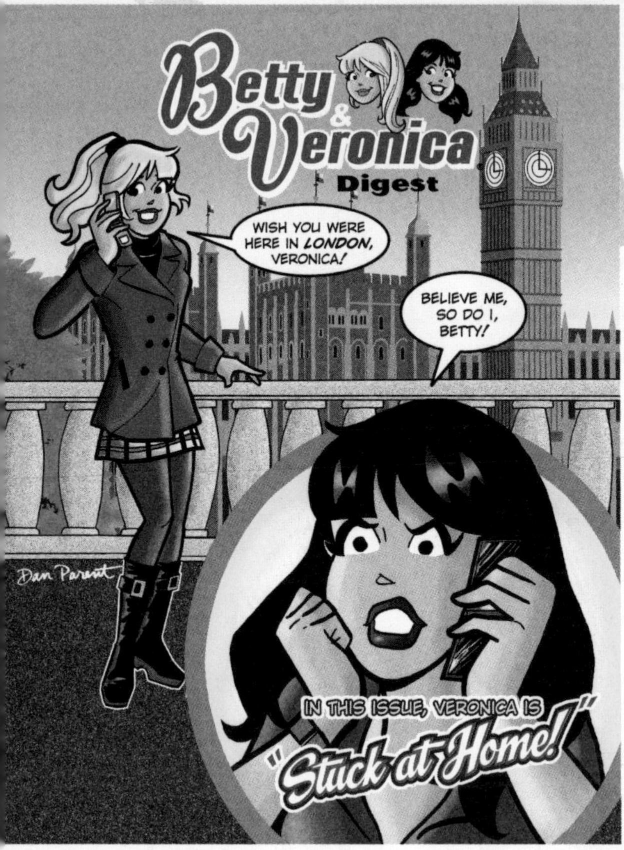
Betty & Veronica Digest
WISH YOU WERE HERE IN LONDON, VERONICA!
BELIEVE ME, SO DO I, BETTY!
Dan Parent
IN THIS ISSUE, VERONICA IS
"Stuck at Home!"

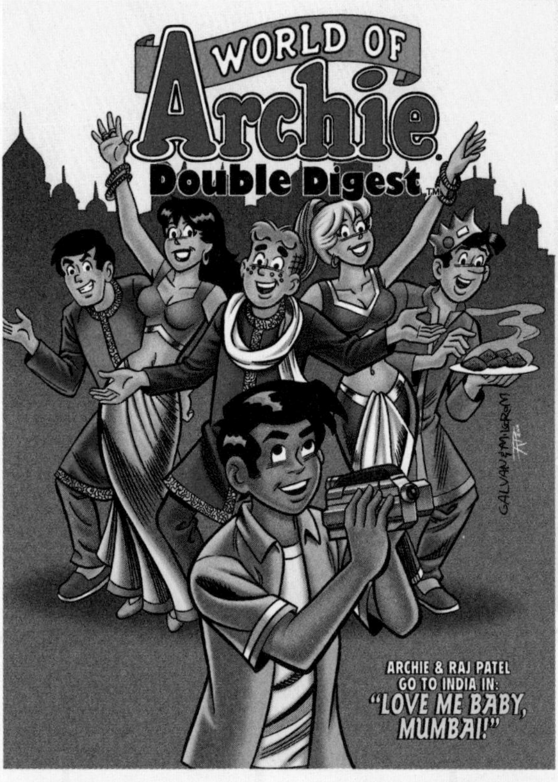
WORLD OF Archie Double Digest
ARCHIE & RAJ PATEL GO TO INDIA IN:
"LOVE ME BABY, MUMBAI!"

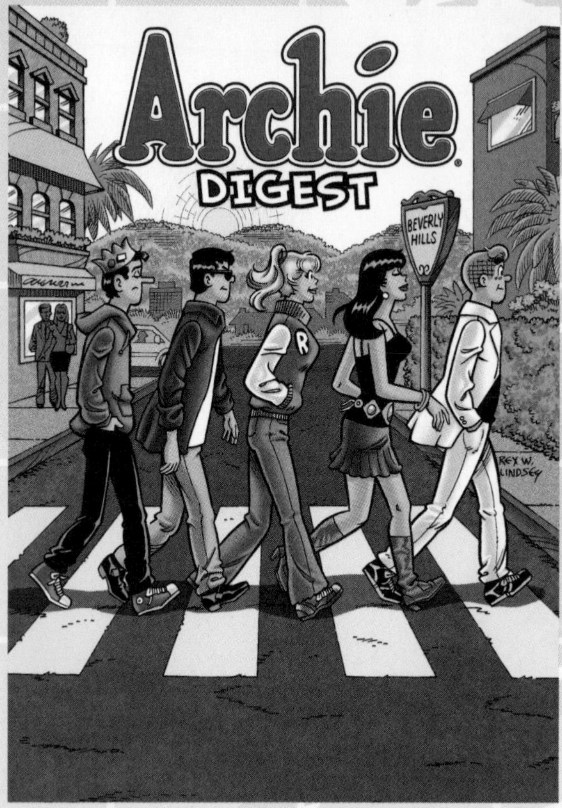
Archie
DIGEST
BEVERLY HILLS
REX W. LINDSEY

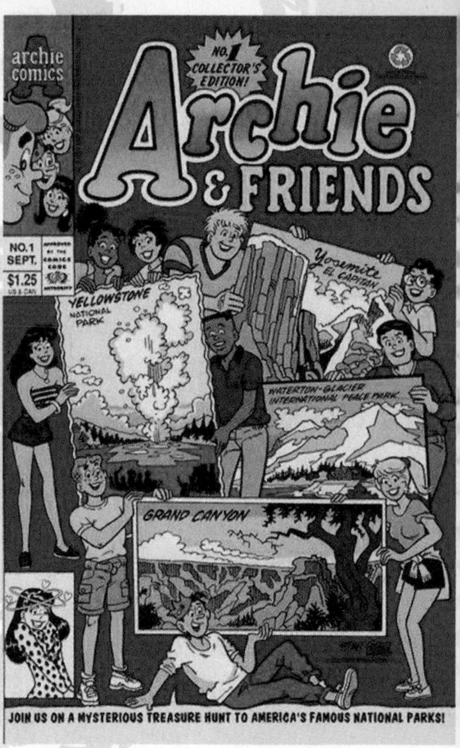
archie comics
NO.1 COLLECTOR'S EDITION!
Archie & FRIENDS
NO.1 SEPT.
$1.25
YELLOWSTONE NATIONAL PARK
Yosemite EL CAPITAN
WATERTON-GLACIER INTERNATIONAL PEACE PARK
GRAND CANYON
JOIN US ON A MYSTERIOUS TREASURE HUNT TO AMERICA'S FAMOUS NATIONAL PARKS!

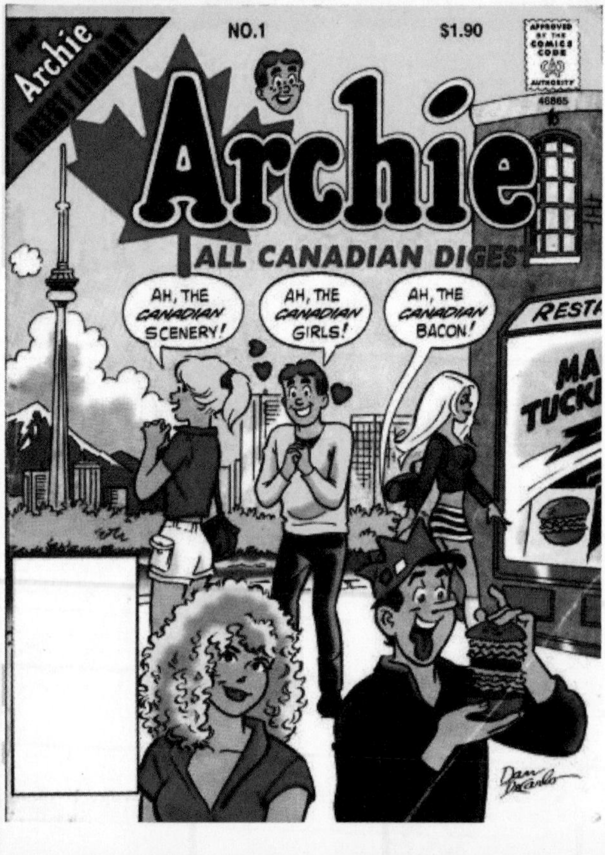
Archie
NO.1
$1.90
Archie
ALL CANADIAN DIGES
AH, THE CANADIAN SCENERY!
AH, THE CANADIAN GIRLS!
AH, THE CANADIAN BACON!
RESTA

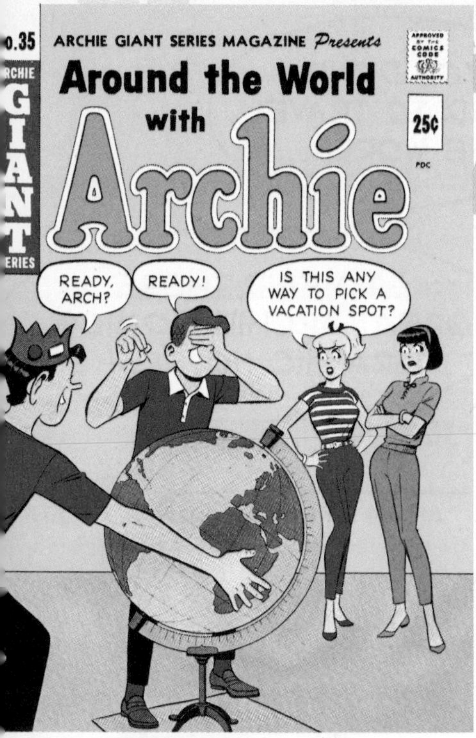
NO.35
ARCHIE GIANT SERIES MAGAZINE Presents
Around the World with Archie
ARCHIE GIANT SERIES
APPROVED BY THE COMICS CODE AUTHORITY
25¢
PDC
READY, ARCH?
READY!
IS THIS ANY WAY TO PICK A VACATION SPOT?

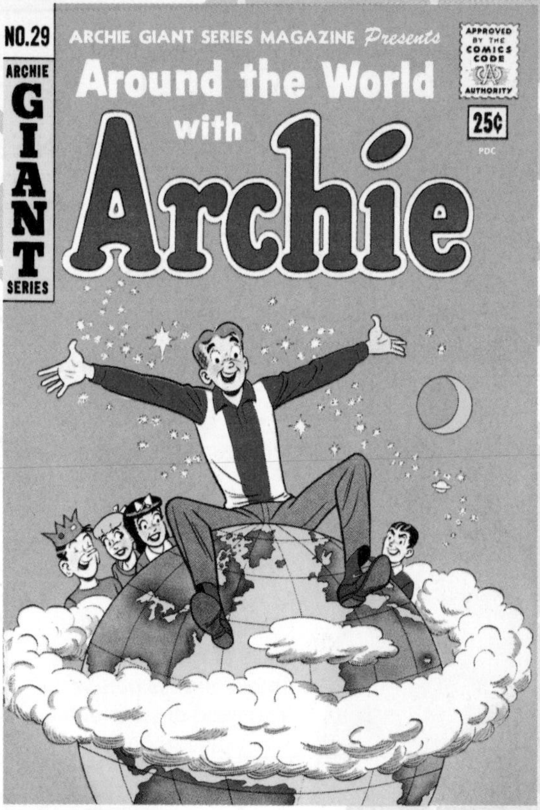
NO.29
ARCHIE GIANT SERIES MAGAZINE Presents
Around the World with Archie
ARCHIE GIANT SERIES
APPROVED BY THE COMICS CODE AUTHORITY
25¢
PDC

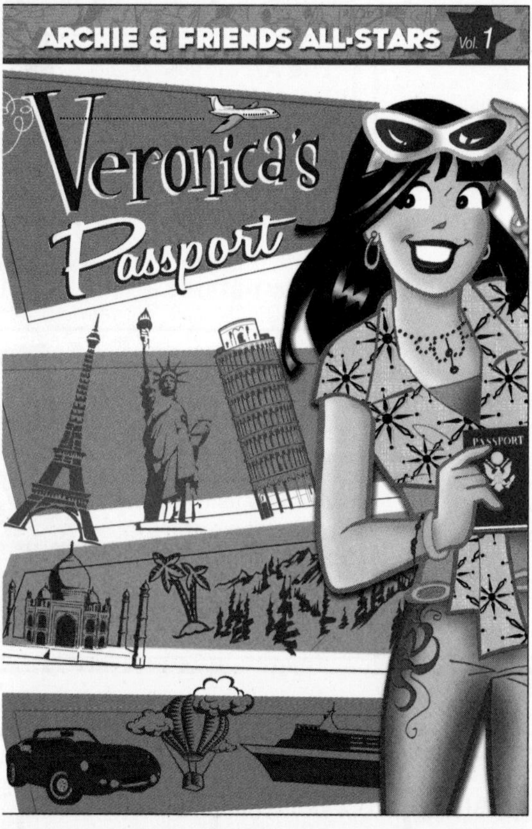
ARCHIE & FRIENDS ALL-STARS Vol. 1
Veronica's Passport
PASSPORT

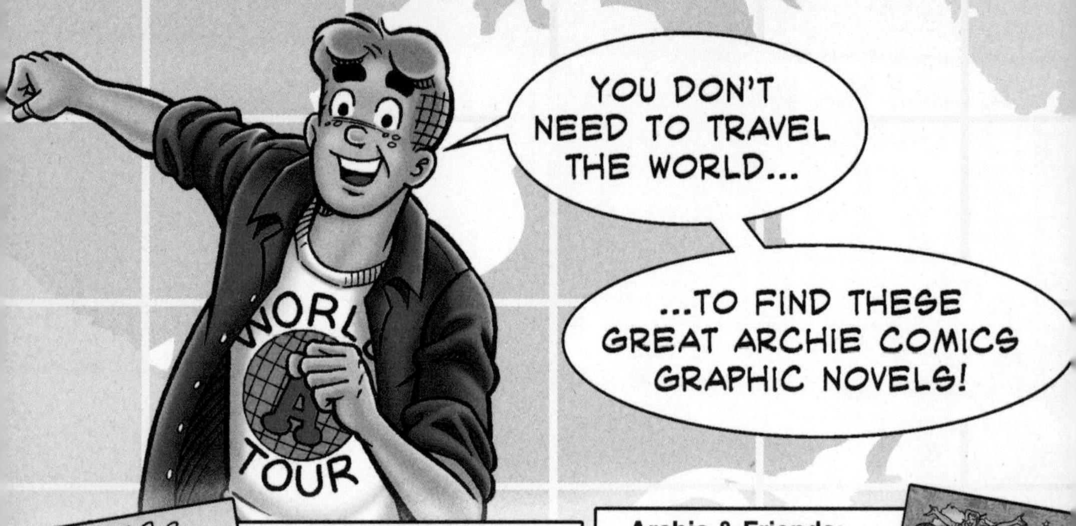
YOU DON'T NEED TO TRAVEL THE WORLD...
...TO FIND THESE GREAT ARCHIE COMICS GRAPHIC NOVELS!
WORLD TOUR

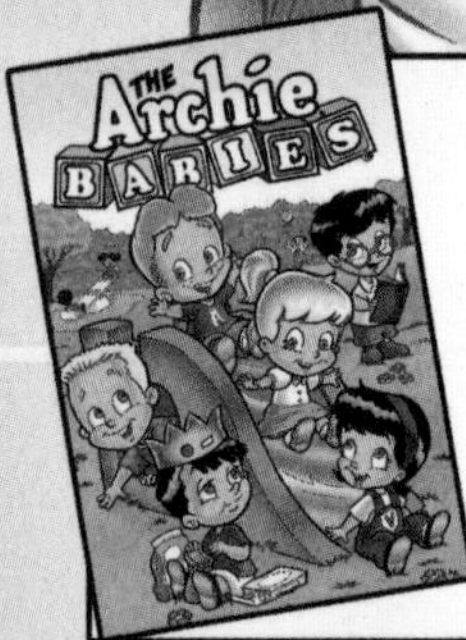
The Archie BABIES

The Archie Babies

Before they ruled the halls of Riverdale High, Archie and his pals were kings and queens of the playground!

ISBN: 978-1-879794-72-6

Archie & Friends: Night at the Comic Shop

Classic comic characters leave their four-color worlds to wreak havoc on Riverdale!

ISBN: 978-1-879794-69-6

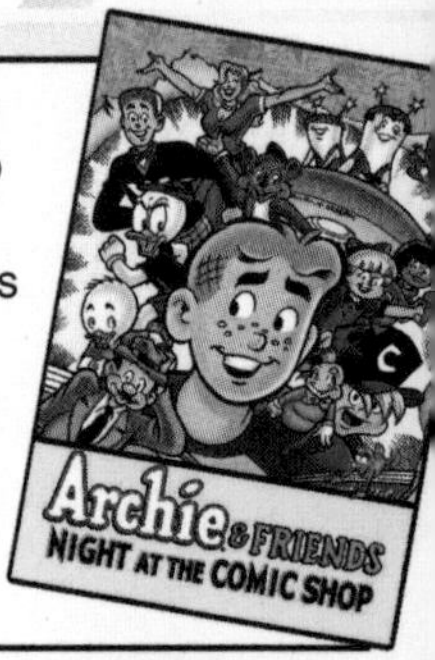
Archie & FRIENDS
NIGHT AT THE COMIC SHOP

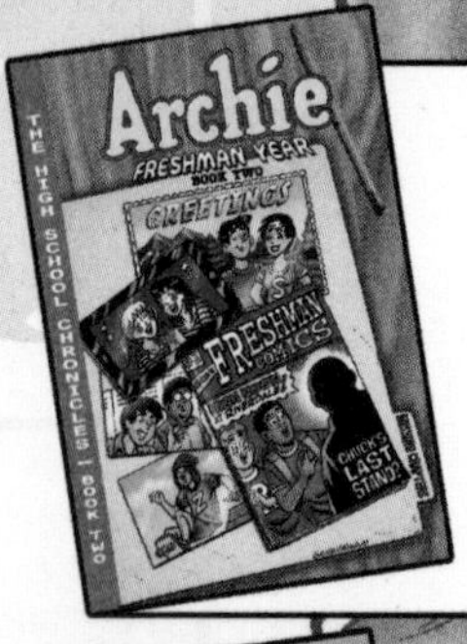
Archie
FRESHMAN YEAR

Archie: Freshman Year Book 2

The coolest freshmen at Riverdale High are back for an all-new semester of hilarity!

ISBN: 978-1-879794-71-9

The Archies & Josie and the Pussycats

Two of the hottest bands get together to make some sweet music!

ISBN: 978-1-879794-61-0

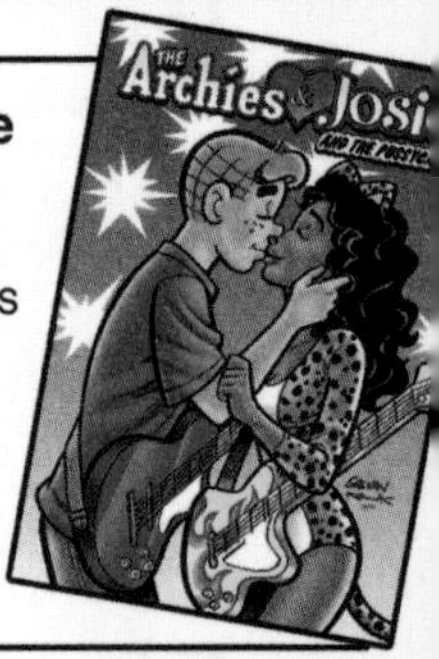

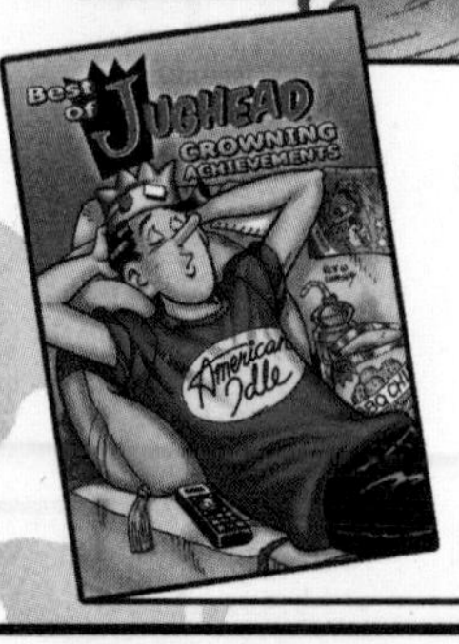
Best of JUGHEAD
CROWNING ACHIEVEMENTS

Best of Jughead: Crowning Achievements

Get ready for a buffet of comedy with everyone's favorite foodie, Jughead! Bon Appetite!

ISBN: 978-1-879794-67-2

Archie: The Man from R.I.V.E.R.D.A.L.E.

Archie suits up for adventure as he takes on some of the world's most diabolical ne'er-do-wells!

ISBN: 978-1-879794-68-9

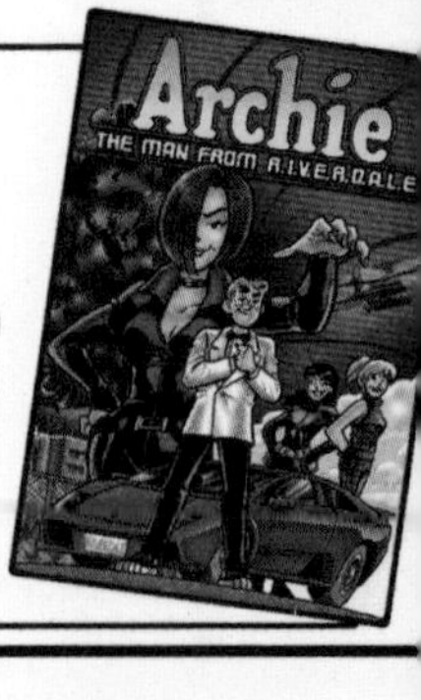
Archie
THE MAN FROM R.I.V.E.R.D.A.L.E.

Archie COMICS

LOOK FOR THESE AND OTHER GRAPHIC NOVELS AT COMIC SHOPS AND BOOKSTORES EVERYWHERE!

ALSO AVAILABLE ONLINE AT ARCHIECOMICS.COM

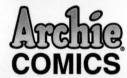